AND AT MY BACK I ALWAYS HEAR

Other Books by Scott Nicolay:

Ana Kai Tangata
after
Noctuidae

PRAISE FOR SCOTT NICOLAY'S

AND AT MY BACK I ALWAYS HEAR

"The captivating stories in Nicolay's surreal collection teleported me into multi-dimensional characters and settings that felt familiar, but unraveled in the shadows. Each mesmerizing tale slipped me over the edge, into the unknown where the monster wasn't what/who I expected. I couldn't look away."

—Linda D. Addison, award-winning author and
Science Fiction Poetry Association Grand Master

"Scott Nicolay's welcome second collection, *And at My Back I Always Hear*, shows that he has not lost a step. On the contrary: he's better than ever. These novellas are sleek, angry, and bloodthirsty. They are also wonderfully, creepily weird. A true delight, from beginning to end."

—Nathan Ballingrud, author of *Wounds*

"Scott Nicolay is one of the master practitioners of the modern Weird Tale. Whether set on the Jersey Shore or in an unexplored cave, his fiction is imbued with eerie energy. Full of strange monsters and dark magic, these stories are always rooted in character and a strong sense of place. His work belongs alongside Ballingrud and VanderMeer."

—Craig Laurance Gidney, author of *A Spectral Hue*

AND AT MY BACK I ALWAYS HEAR

SCOTT NICOLAY

WORD HORDE

PETALUMA, CA

First Edition

ISBN: 978-1-956252-02-6

A Word Horde Book
http://www.WordHorde.com

TABLE OF CONTENTS

To Jacqueline Rosler Salisbury (1941-2016)
and
Joseph S. Pulver Sr. (1955-2020)

You always believed in me.
I will always remember you.

"I heard all things in the heaven and in the earth. I heard many things in hell."

—E.A. Poe, "The Telltale Heart"

"Darkly I gaze into the days ahead."

—Claude McKay, "America"

INTRODUCTION

GEMMA FILES

We talk a lot about what writing horror is "good for," and when I say "we" I mean not just insiders but outsiders to this very debatable genre of ours. Good for letting off steam; good for playing out our fears in controllable ways; good for highlighting the underside lurking beneath a light, bright, perpetually "happy," virtue-signalling world. Very recently—and given I'm writing this in 2022, I think you all know what I'm talking about—there's been a certain amount of recognition given to the thesis that in times of turmoil, threat and disturbance, horror provides confirmation that the illusion of universal safety was only ever that. So maybe we shouldn't spend so much time berating ourselves for our inability to simply buck up, keep calm and carry on in the face of immediate existential dread.

Another thing horror's always been good for, however, is for routinely skewing perspective away from the default towards the non-. As a genre founded by women, from stories of "raw-head and bloody bones" told by grandmothers over Christmas and Lady Cynthia Asquith's ghost story collections to the world-rocking narrative depth charge of Mary Shelley's

1

Frankenstein, its true roots have forever lain less in normativity than in derangement, in prising up the rock of received wisdom to watch what squirms out from beneath. Throughout cultural history, it's been consistently typified as abnormal, sick, Weird and queer, obsessed with things supposedly better left unexplored, unstated...and you know what? So it should be. So it should always be.

This is the liminal space where Scott Nicolay—archaeologist and teacher, meticulous translator of "Belgian Poe" Jean Ray (*Whiskey Tales*, *Cruise of Shadows: Haunted Stories of Land and Sea*, *The Great Nocturnal*, and *Circles of Dread*, Wakefield Press), both rabid fan and hard-working perpetrator of the dark fantastic Weird Renaissance in all its many shades—has chosen to live, the supposedly polluted, salt-sown soil he's chosen to till. And these, the stories you're about to read, are his latest fruits.

In many ways, Nicolay's work might best be glimpsed through the same lens provided by the demon-inhabited Viewmaster screen of his 2015 World Fantasy Best Short Story Award-winning tale "Do You Like To Look At Monsters?": As a series of tiny slices of cosmic horror, strained through localized, almost documentary, fragments of contemporary hell. A dusty parade of the lost and the lonely, the ruined, the ruinous.

His perspective is always outsider-identified, entirely concerned with characters who refuse to settle, both literally and figuratively; his protagonists often hover on a knife's edge, caught in some sadly inescapable moment of realization. They've failed and been failed, left discarded amongst the wreckage of systemic inequity. And now that they have nothing left to cling to, their inner eye pops open, suddenly able to see the darkness lurking inherent in every crevice, the emptiness revolving inside every atom.

In Nicolay's work, I believe, we see the sort of horror we need going forward, particularly as we face a fresh yet ever-darkening millennium: Forewarned and fore-armed, conscious, conscience-guided. Stories in which we can sense the author deconstructing his own comfort zone, widening himself to fit not the world we hope for but the one we now live in, no matter how much it might sting to do so. A world whose limits have become suddenly un-guessable.

Enjoy, or don't. It works equally well either way, really.

That's what horror's for.

2

...and the red light was my mind.
—Robert Johnson

TENEBRIONIDAE

COAUTHORED WITH JESSE JAMES DOUTHIT-NICOLAY

Dumont wriggled his shoulders shoved from his feet and twisted at the hips to inch himself further into the back of the foxhole. Not so cold yet and it was hell for comfortable but he wanted room to bend his legs so he could keep as much of himself away from the gritty metal floor as possible. You weren't careful in a cold train car, metal would suck the heat out of you like *nuthin*. Without a sleeping bag best he only touched bare metal at his shoulders boots and butt.

Missy lifted her head from his chest to wedge a wet nose against his chin and neck, lick up at his cheek. Dumont wrapped his left arm around her and winced. He hadn't peeked yet to see how deep the cut ran. He was gonna have to look soon. Last he could see, the dirty bandanna he tied round it was soaked a darker red all across the top. Not enough light to check it now anyway.

Least he managed to score a good ridable from NOLA on a grainer porch. Damn lucky but that didn't change how fucked his situation was overall. He thought about his pack. Fucking Shadow Riders had it, together with his sleeping bag and most of the rest of his shit. Who knew what they were doing to it? Trashing it all, dividing it up…most likely putting some bullshit black magic curse on it. And his last pint of whiskey was in there too. With time to grab one thing only he went for his guitar, the scratched-up acoustic Susie True-Bright gave him at Eufaula Lake two Novembers back. He was probably going to regret that choice. With neither whiskey nor water left, he knew he was going to regret it *soon*. He craned forward to check he at least hadn't lost the guitar, right now riding by the bottom of the grainer's ladder since it wouldn't fit with him in the hole. The bottom edge of the case cut a thin arc from what light the moon still dribbled down. The case seemed steady, moving only in time with the slow swaying rhythms of the train.

He let the back of his head rest against the crook of his arm and tuned in to the trainsong, hoping it would lull him to sleep.

Only five things could steady him, still the deep waters of his chaos. Whiskey. Missy. Playin'. Fuckin'. And the sound train wheels made over steel rails. *Rat ta tat tat rat ta tat tat.* Best lullaby ever. Better than any his foster parents ever sang him, that was fersure…

Fersure.

He couldn't catch the rhythm tonight though, ride it into sleep. Not yet. Too much rage and anger ran still through his veins, the gin in a cocktail spiked with confusion and fear.

That was *some* fucked up shit there at the squat, Shadow Riders comin' in like they did… Yeah sure, Bald Jonny Ben warned him 'bout them way back when, first time he came through NOLA, but that time Dumont only nodded, passing the stories off as fairy tales in his mind. Occultist train riders? Seriously? Only they *were* real and they were *very* serious. So was their black magic. 'Course Tigger tried to tell him the same but he tuned her out too. Now he could tell his own story about them if he wanted. If he ever got the chance…

What he'd seen at the squat twisted in his brain like a wind-whipped plastic bag snagged on a barbed wire fence. He'd been chilling there waiting for Tigger. They were s'posed to meet up, hitch out of NOLA, take their love on the road. Maybe not love exactly, but close enough. She was good for him and she said *he* made her feel safe.

First though she was gonna try to get this money some ex owed her while he went to busk in the Quarter. Only he drank a little whiskey to get his nerve up then a little more and a little more after that and ended not leaving the squat.

Tigger said meet her 'round 7:00 but she never showed. Best he could estimate she was already an hour late. Still, everything was copacetic till right before the Shadow Riders appeared.

He had a seat up against one wall, a flipped over five-gallon plastic bucket, bright orange once, writing under all the scuffs and scratches said it came from Home Depot long time ago. Missy lay on his right, tongue out and panting softly, his battered pack, packed and ready, propped against the wall on his left. He was thinking about breaking out the guitar, maybe tuning it or working on a song. Then things twisted up, got all strange.

The smell hit him first, a bitter edge coming on beneath the general mist of wet plaster, rust and mildew and his own unwashed body. Missy must've caught it before him 'cause she sat up and growled, her growl becoming a whine before it choked off in silent tension. Right as his nose registered it too a thin ripple rode over every horizontal line, kinked level architecture downward a moment before pulsing on and out the corners. Shit might make sense if he were shrooming but he only had whiskey in him, and he knew that drink's distortions full well as a sea captain knows the waves and the sky or whatever. He sat up and was still watching for a repeat when the graffiti went wrong.

That came instant, a spasm. The lines of spraypainted scrawl across all four walls, the artful head high plaques of balloon letters, the smallest penciled scribbles…it all became ugly, rough, illegible. All at once every letter was an affront in both texture and intent though he could no longer read a one. There'd been names before, profanity and hobo hieroglyphs, some with tiny train tracks and an X for the crossing to show they were riders. Scraps of lyrics and fragmented rants—*If you stay here your a fuckin oogle*—shit like that, the ubiquitous anarchy symbol… All gone. Incomprehensible ciphers swirled out at him now.

The whole room pulsed next and…altered, made no architectural sense. Missy barked and twitched her tail against the bucket and Dumont placed a hand on her back. He felt dizzy and fought the urge to puke. The doorway spun around him several times—round and round and round she goes, and where she stops—Ratch and Worm and Marlo stood. The two sidekicks drifted into place behind Marlo right away, assuming generic bully positions so fast Dumont was tempted to laugh. But Marlo had his K-Bar out beside his thigh and the other two each wore their general bulk as a weapon so no way was it time for wisecracks or laughter. The room no longer spun, only rocked a bit side to side in a seasick way as if whatever whirlwind torqued it had settled in overhead for now.

—*Lookit the schwag bitch*, Marlo sneered at him, spoke the words as a slow smoldering threat. His voice oscillated in tempo as if the distance between them were stretching and receding. Dumont felt another twinge of nausea and struggled to suppress it. Ratch and Worm sneered in their special fleshy ways but said nothing. Missy pressed closer against his thigh, hindquarters stiff with tension as she barked in bursts. He stroked her head to calm her.

—Are you *sad* because your girl ain't here? Well you can go ahead an' cry now 'cause she ain't comin'. Little Miss *Tigger*. Turns out she don't bounce too well.

Dumont didn't much care to hear what he was hearing but he knew Marlo was s'posed to be big on head games. Didn't mean any of it counted for a damn thing. If it did then he failed her just like he failed Hector, the kid younger than him at the foster home, what they'd done to him.

He could stand—he was taller than all but Worm—only that would likely take things physical quick, and they were three on one. Maybe they only came to threaten him, scare him into leaving town. They could threaten away. He'd been ready to leave anyway, only *with* Tigger. But what had they done to Tigger?

She told him about the Shadow Riders almost at the start, how she hooked up with Marlo till someone tipped her off he only wanted her for some kind of sacrifice. How she found it out Dumont didn't know but the whole story confused him anyway. Tigger was holding some big pieces back, he could tell that easy. Made it all hard to follow but main thing was he could see she was scared. Way shit scared. Now she was missing maybe worse and the Shadow Riders were all up in his face.

He never dealt with Marlo or his crew himself before, only saw them from a distance and Tigger would whisper *that's them* or sometimes their names. There were others, Crunch and Skurd, Arkansas Jason and Jimmy Whip, more whose names he could not recall. But Marlo was supposed to be their king or ruler or some shit like that, Ratch and Worm his left hand and right.

TENEBRIONIDAE

—*Du*-mont. That girl took something from me, Du-mont. Something she shouldn'a took. Did she give it to *you*, *Du*-mont? I think she did. Hey, we understand how these things can happen. It's *na-chur-al*. Why don't you just let us take a look in your pack Du-mont? We'll take what's ours and leave you with your mutt. No harm no foul, whadda you say?

Ratch stepped hands out toward Dumont's pack. Although he seemed to move in slow motion Dumont didn't try to block him, but he teetered sideways away from the Rider, his bucket seat tilting almost toppling.

Marlo started to say something like *That's it*— and nod before he saw how Dumont slid himself several inches along the wall, bent to grab the bucket handle, then pushed up the wall all the way and with his sea legs at least half back beneath him swung the bottom of the bucket at Worm. Ratch was closest but Worm was the tallest so Dumont went for him first. The bucket with its half dozen rough crusted inches of concrete at the bottom took Worm full on the side of the head and he. Went. Down.

Missy lunged for Ratch and her teeth sank into his left calf above his boot so he cursed and stumbled back a step. Marlo jerked to his right, brought the K-Bar full up just as Dumont yanked back hard on the bucket only to feel the wire handle tear free from plastic. The battered orange cylinder tumbled away into the shadows and slammed loud against a wall somewhere off in the dark. Everyone looked surprised. Everyone except Worm, who lay staring at the dirt floor. Staring at it real close, like point blank close. Staring at his blood pouring on the dirt.

Dumont yelled to Missy and grabbed the guitar case, booked it for the exit. He felt a tug on his arm as if someone grabbed him and he yanked hard to get free. He heard Ratch pound after him several steps till Marlo shouted —Leave him, asshole! Get the pack! The pack!

Missy hit the doorless doorway ahead of him and staggered as she went. As he trucked through he felt himself swing up sideways on an incline a second, the whole room pitched over the major part of ninety degrees. His applicable senses all told him brace for the fall but he did not fall. Missy yelped ahead so he knew she felt the same still they both pressed on and came level again in three more steps. His stomach prepared to purge but he fought it down one last time, staggered forward anyway. Not now. Not here.

Marlo called from behind —Run, sad punk! We'll see you again. Run run

run and we'll all have some fun. Later on down the line.

Dumont ran. At least half a dozen blocks, Missy skittering always several feet ahead before Dumont felt the warm wetness on the fingers of his left hand and held it up to see first the blood dripping off them, then the red-streaked facing crescents of pink white muscle revealed in the deep slash across his forearm. He was leaving a trail but he didn't stop to bandage himself till he reached the yard.

***

He was pissed he left his pack. *Pissed to leave the squat.* Pissed most of all he had to leave without Tigger. Sick over Tigger and whether she was okay. Tigger mighta helped him keep it together but even that hope was gone now.

He actually liked that squat. Better than the Pink House, which most everyone said was haunted by ghosts of all the junkies who ODed there. His squat was a derelicted grain and feed store in the 8th Ward, right up close to the decommissioned levy that carried freights along the border strip between the 8th and 9th. The hobos hippies train kids and gutterpunks who came and went there called the location Ward 8 and 3/4. The drunker Dumont got the better he liked the joke. He wasn't stupid. He read those books when he was a kid. Some of them anyway, the ones he could find at the school library because his foster parents never bought them. Those books were Satan's work. If wizard books were Satan's work then what were the things they did to their foster children? Dumont had his own ideas about Satan's work in this world.

The squat itself they called Viking House for the inked and bearded white boys who came and went there in this mostly Black and Latin town. Dumont himself bore the nickname *The Norse* for his dirty blond and tangled beard.

He found family at the Viking House. Better and truer than his birth family. Better fersure than his fosters and their own two sons. Folks came and went but they were mostly *real* people, *good* people. His people. Fucking Shadow Riders made him leave too soon. Made him leave without Tigger. Tigger, mellow and quiet in spite of her name. How she held so tight to him not only when they fucked, and how she cried softly with him in her but laughed when she came. The eye of his own private hurricane. Tigger with him this shit would not be so bad. But Tigger was gone for now. Only how gone? Was Marlo for real or talking shit?

The farther he rode this freight, the less likely she'd ever find him, or he her. Her pale blue eyes. Her streaky blonde bowl cut, overgrown and combed crossways above her face. Her super old school Navajo rug poncho they used for a fuck blanket. The accustomed tang of her unwashed bod, and the way it blended with his own aromas.

In time he'd reach another yard. Once there he could aim for a freight headed back to NOLA. Back to Tigger. Yeah, and back to the Shadow Riders. Maybe. If they were even still there. If Tigger was…

Or he could strike out alone for…what did those old time writers call it? *Terro incognito? The Territories?* He didn't much like to ride further east or north than NOLA. His winter home for three years running. He had only a vague sense of this freight's next destination. Mississippi somewhere maybe. Or Alabama. He felt the train was headed either north or east. Maybe northeast. When it came to a yard he'd get off, try to find where he was, maybe ask the crew if they seemed cool. Good as lost for now with only vague ideas where to go next. If Marlo and his crew were coming behind him, it might be best to switch up, hitch to the next city, get away from the freight lines a while.

***

Dumont and Missy both slept in fits. He shielded her short fur from the cold metal but it bit him where it could. His ass caught it worst, gone all numb. Legs barely responding, hard to bend. Too low to stand in the foxhole so he flexed his painful frozen legs inside, kicked numbly at the scoured wall.

The brakes screeched and he realized the train was slowing. Soon it shunted onto another track. He could tell they weren't coming into a freight yard yet. He'd see other trains if they were in a yard. The only shapes he saw in the night were trees. The junker he was riding was just siding out to let a faster train pass.

He couldn't see the sky much but where he could it was taking on pink. As he watched the voices came.

So faint at first he pegged the sounds as his imagination. Then he thought *bulls*, but bulls didn't ride the trains. Mostly lazy they patrolled their yards from trucks or golf carts, checked inside cars at stations only.

Not till the volume of the voices rose did he recognize Marlo. Coming from somewhere above. Ahead or behind he could not tell, but close. No words came clear but Dumont knew. He *knew*. And somehow *they* knew. *They knew he was on this train.* They hopped out too and now they were hunting him. Coming over the tops of the cars like some idiots in a western movie. One of the craziest things you could do in real life whether the train was rolling or not.

The guitar. They'd spot it from above. Fersure. The case was too big to squeeze into the hole with him. Aw fuck. But maybe not the guitar.

He set Missy on her feet and flopped on his front. His legs remained unresponsive. Wriggling half out the hole he tugged the case close and popped the snaps. And got another surprise. Atop the soundboard was a kind of book. A grubby thing bound with crooked staples, big crude letter C backward on the cover in Sharpie. He knew it at once: a *Crew Change*. The hobo bible to hop outs. What Marlo must be hunting. When had Tigger stashed it in his case? And why? Fuck. Was that what this was all about? But a *Crew Change* was not all that hard to get. Not *easy*—he never had one himself before—but not something you followed someone over the tops of cars for. Not something you killed over…

The freight they sided out for came on now, an almost endless intermodal stacked double deep with shipping containers. Dumont tugged the book in with him, hefted the guitar by the neck and with its body pushed the case over the edge. Any sound it made was lost in the clamor of the passing train. Fucking Shadow Riders. First his pack and now his case, all his favorite stickers on it best of all the Hank III.

After forever the IM was past and his train lurched forward a few feet forcing Dumont to grip the rim of the foxhole. As they moved he heard the case crunch under the wheels of the next car back and right away Marlo called out. Dumont hoped the sound would draw them away. He hoped Marlo and his crew fell off, broke their fucking necks. Not likely he'd be so lucky though. Another halting advance and they pulled back onto the main track, picked up speed. He withdrew into the grainer's next interior compartment, wiggled the guitar in after him. Missy hopped through and sidestepped a bit before she huddled with him as far from sight as they could get.

He was trapped now if they found him, no weapon in this confined space. Fists and feet, what he was best with anyhow. Missy would bite, though if he hadn't lost her leash he would hold her back. No room to swing his smiley. Forget the guitar he couldn't swing it in here either. He waited, listening for the sounds of their feet or Marlo's voice above, or worse on the platform outside. Meanwhile he curled the *Crew Change* into a slit tube, slid it up his right sleeve then redid the buttons at his wrist. This might prove useful, if not for its content then as armor up his sleeve. It might save that arm from getting cut like the other. Like the padding folks wore to train guard dogs.

In his hidey hole he stayed on alert despite the sleep he needed. But the voices did not return. No voices, no footsteps above. Had they given up? Found their own car to wait out the ride? Too much to hope they'd jumped or fallen off. Most likely they'd be waiting to grab him when the train stopped and he got off.

Missy also kept alert, body tensed, ears up, but she didn't bark or growl. He massaged the tips of her ears to calm her and whispered —Smart girl, yes you're a smart girl—then smiled and nodded as he waved a finger before her face. She licked his hand once then paused and began to bathe it.

She curled against him next almost the same as when he met her, hiding in a shed in El Paso with another gutterpunk named Clutch, waiting for a hop out on a freight to Houston. Clutch stepped out to take a leak and came back ten minutes later tugging Missy by the scruff, his hand streaked with blood. —Look what I found. Bitch bit me too! He dropped her and she trotted right up to Dumont, curled in his lap. The three of them hopped out right after that but Clutch parted ways at the next yard. Missy stayed with Dumont. He got her cleaned up, groomed and dewormed. Whenever they got to a field or park they played for an hour or more, her puppy energy inexhaustible.

Missy slept now, head tucked within Dumont's secondhand army jacket. Slowly a dim pink glow began to ooze through the opening of the foxhole. The train blew its whistle more often which meant it was coming to a town or city with roads and crossings. Somewhere ahead it'd stop. They couldn't stay on long then—they needed to get off quick but not get caught. Run like hell was not an option—no matter how he shifted his legs stayed half numb from the cold. He'd be stumbling when he hit the ground. But he couldn't stay. If the Shadow Riders didn't find him the bulls probably would.

He jostled Missy gently to wake her and she raised her head, rolled to one side and stood as he began wriggling back to the outer compartment. He had to be ready when the train stopped. His legs remained a mix of numb and pain. Not good. He stretched and flexed them best he could. It didn't do much.

Outside the portal was near full light now though the sky he saw was filmed with haze and white. Beyond the tall grass he saw ranks of pine interspersed with random spreading magnolias. A highway paced them on one flank a bit, though traffic was scant. Dumont guessed westbound. The train began to slow, tempo of the trainsong diminishing. Before long they slowed to a crawl as stilled trains slipped around them right and left. A yard. Soon their train would stop and he and Missy would need to make their move. Hop out on another freight or hoof it to the highway and hitch a ride from there. No matter what, they needed to *move*. Bulls and Shadow Riders would be checking the cars.

He scrambled out stiff legged and caught Missy in his arms, almost tripping before he set her on the ground. No one else in sight, but the voices came again, close, only from behind the train. He rolled under an old coaler on the next track, Missy dodging ahead then looking back. Circulation was returning in his lower half, and quick as he could he cut across two more parked freights. Let the Riders check the train he rode in on first. One more train traversed and they reached the edge of the yard. A dismal section of town extended before them.

Whatever the station, Hattiesburg or Meridian or who knew where, the stop came near the obligatory industrial park. Factories, warehouses, a few wholesale operations. Yet Dumont saw no activity. Was it Sunday? He'd lost track of days. Or had the shit economy stifled enterprise here? No matter. He'd have to hoof it through this part of town till he came out on a residential or commercial zone. Then he could make his way to an intersection and hitch to the next big town or city, find a hop out on a line the Riders hadn't infested. Mobile seemed like a good destination. Someplace he and Missy could maybe sleep on the beach.

He figured ten blocks at most till he came out in a more congenial neighborhood but he had to hurry 'cause he had to take a dump now. He needed a convenience store or a library, someplace with an open restroom but where they wouldn't call the cops.

He made his best guess as to where the long buildings gave way and struck crosswise toward what he thought might be north. Missy's nails clicked on the pavement behind him. He needed to clip her, that was overdue. But not right now. Not today.

Something struck him funny about the factories and warehouses in this district. They were the usual colors, gray and brown, white and blue. But their paint seemed more washed out faded than those he'd seen elsewhere. And the signs…the letters on some swam in his vision, impossible to read. Did he have a concussion? But he hadn't taken a hit on the head. Could blood loss cause this all alone?

The few he could read made little sense. *Tortoise Stapling. Kabinet el Sand. Plumb Coriolism. Carpenter Carpenter…* The address numbers on the buildings were lost on him altogether. Each time he tried to focus on a sign either it or his vision shifted to one side so he found himself staring at blank wall.

He saw no workers. Few cars in the lots, and none on the roads. No traffic at all. No trees, no grass. Just pavement, asphalt roads and concrete walks, flat threads of tar patching networks of cracks. Sky overcast gray. No wind. No birds. No sound. Some of these buildings shoulda hummed. Buzzed. But nuthin. Obvious Missy disliked the whole area. She stuck close to Dumont, sniffing the ground, her ears down and tense.

The humped cracked sidewalk led him past one building with glass front doors hanging open. All he could make out of its name was *AZOTY*. There seemed to be more letters but the rest defied his vision, their rusted outlines blurred and swimming. Missy stopped, lifted her leg in that halfhearted girl dog way she sometimes did and let loose on something. Possibly a fire hydrant, possibly a tree stump. Whichever, it was painted white. Or gray. He knew he had to let it out soon too.

Dumont peered inside the open doors and saw no receptionist's desk, only a wide empty room. Further down the opposite wall he saw the windowless cabin of a probable restroom. One, two steps inside yet still no workers. To his left the manufacturing floor stretched to an uncertain horizon, bare but for a few shrouded hulks in the middle distance, tarp-covered machinery of unknown function. No one was visible. No activity. Why not? He scuttled all the way in, made his way to what he thought was the men's room. Both the lettering and the icon were uncertain to his eyes, but the simplified woman in a dress on the opposite door showed clear so he knew he had the men's by process of elimination…

He wanted to get in and out quick so he whistled Missy along in case any workers arrived. The things she'd seen for lack of space…

Inside all was normal, even clean. Until he opened the only stall and looked in the commode. Though no foul splatter marked its rim or lid a burnt orange haze hung still within, at its center a denser clot, sunk and obscured. The murk was the hue of blood diffused in water, the clot some unseen discarded hunk of flesh or gland. Dumont had his zipper half down when something splashed and the water in the toilet rippled as if whatever was hidden beneath the cloud of blood within got restless of a sudden. Oh *fuck* this! Dumont staggered out of the restroom in reverse yanking up his zipper as he went, and Missy followed close, growling but not barking yet. He'd shit in an alley if he had to, if he could find a safe one. Wouldn't be the first time. He'd taken shits in all kinds of crazy places and was not picky but shitting on whatever was in that toilet was not in the plan. He would have to hold it, clench his bowels till the next opportunity.

The long floor remained empty. Still no workers. He shuffled toward the front doors, Missy hugging his thigh. She knew something was off with the place same as he did. Strange thing though, she wasn't sniffing. There were always smells.

Outside things were even stranger now. Not only the signs but the buildings themselves seemed ill defined, their shapes distorted, lines gone off plumb, sides and facades fuzzed and blurred as if through TV interference. The lump Missy pissed on before, hydrant or stump, nothing but a fizzing gray puddle now. As he and Missy passed it the mass oozed flat viscous tendrils toward them, impossibilities they had to dodge. Dumont cursed softly as they hurried along their path back to the yard.

Missy meanwhile whimpered and hugged his leg, sleek flank pressing against his calf. The structures around them lost definition and stretched like taffy, flattened in the air. Had he really lost enough blood to cause these distortions? Or had Marlo dipped his K-Bar in some hallucinogenic poison only kicking in now. Not like shrooms or acid or even K. Real ugly stuff. But Missy wasn't cut and she was seeing something wrong too, same as back at the squat. She bit Ratch though—could his blood have dosed her?

TENEBRIONIDAE

He backtracked best he could. Back to the yard to try for another hop out. This town was major fucked up. He hoped the yard wasn't fading into static too. He hoped they could make it back before it did. He hoped he wasn't dying or going insane.

Even the sidewalk felt wrong beneath his feet, giving softly as if cut from tough rubber. The clicks of Missy's nails were muffled. Around him the buildings shifted into forms he could no longer pick out yet he pressed on in the direction he thought took him back.

What was left of his luck held and the yard reappeared, if not quite where he remembered. The trains were still trains though veiled in a vague gray shimmer. Then another break came his way. One of the freights had begun to roll, slow.

The last half dozen cars were all coalers, no good for riders unless already filled. They'd cover your clothes and flesh with black dust, make you cough and burn your eyes, but worst of all was if they got filled while you were inside. Then you got crushed and buried. Behind the coalers though was another engine facing back. Empty engines were excellent rides. This one was a blue and yellow CSX, what they called the *Dark Future* paint scheme. What coked up corporate dickhead came up with a name like that?

Bald Jonny Ben taught him early on the basic rule for hopping freights on the fly. If you could count the nuts on a turning hub, you were good. He could.

He cut across the yard, paced the engine's inching crawl. First he raised the guitar and slid it onto the unit's outer catwalk. He hefted Missy up the first stair next, cut left arm protesting, and she scrabbled up the rest on her own. With his right he pulled himself up the rail to the little walkway and yanked on the door, yellow with a bold blue C dead center. It was like cracking the hatch on a ship. He watched Missy perk up as the warmth of the heated cab wafted out. She slipped around him to get inside where she turned and looked back, wagging her tail and waiting for him to join her. He swept up the guitar by its neck and ducked in after her.

Inside the engine were leather seats. A little fridge. And a *restroom*, oh thank you Jesus!

He took care of the most important business first then shut the door so Missy wouldn't try to drink from the squat chemical toilet. They still needed water though. Both of them.

15

He tried the miniature metal fountain but nuthin. Out of order no doubt. He checked the fridge, Missy peering in hopefully beside him, but they found no food, only five pint water bottles. He took two out and closed the door. Missy stared up at him in expectation. With his left forearm he pressed one bottle against his side while he used both hands to unscrew the lid from the other. Missy wagged tail and tongue together. —You want some water, don't you girl? Problem was the dinged up little aluminum bowl he carried for her was lost like so much else with his pack.

Fuck it. He tipped the water bottle slowly above her nose. She craned her neck and lapped at the water as it dribbled down. Over half dripped onto the floor. He tilted the bottle up again and after an expectant moment Missy bent to lick the water from the floor. He hated for her to have to do it this way, but better than the toilet. Three rounds of this left the bottle drained and the floor almost dry. He drew the second bottle from beneath his arm and drank.

Dumont knew to take it slow. He'd eaten nothing for over a day and now he felt the chill water settle in his empty stomach. It hurt at first, a dull cramping ache in the depths of his abdomen. He spasmed, bent over, pressed his right forearm into his guts, but didn't puke. The pain faded in increments and once it was mostly gone he sank back into the righthand engineer's seat, cradled the half empty bottle at his crotch. Sleep took him quick though it did not hold him well.

He rose and fell from the depths of his rest on and off for hours, Missy curled and sleeping at his feet. Dreams visited him, vivid and important, but he remembered none on the waking side. Outside the windows the day grew dim again in time as a divided forest receded in his sight.

He went to the fridge and got another water bottle for Missy, poured it out as before and drank the fourth himself. Stuffed the fifth and final in a pocket of his jacket. He knew he could no longer put off inspecting his cut—but what was he gonna do for it anyway? He had nothing to sew it up with and only their last pint of water to clean it. Maybe he could drain it if he had to at least.

Slowly he unwrapped the blood-crusted bandanna he wore around it. He expected the cloth to stick, to cling, to pull painfully at his flesh, but it came off easy. The wound beneath was like nothing he'd seen, not the expected narrow cañon of maroon surrounding a canal of pus, but a charcoal swath of desiccated black.

TENEBRIONIDAE

Puffs of dust rose from the cut and he whiffed the same bitter undercurrent he caught at the squat, initial herald of the Riders' approach. Probably he needed this slice seen to and soon…which meant he was gonna have to tough it out. The idea of doctors was a joke in his world. Nuthin else for it now so he wrapped the bandanna back around. It didn't hurt all that bad anymore. Kind of numb around the cut, the numbness maybe spreading, but he was gonna be all right. He'd find some iodine, figure something out.

Dumont settled again into the engineer's chair. If all he did today on this ride was snooze, his time would be well spent. He wished for some whiskey…but if he wished in one hand and shit in the other he knew which would fill up first. His foster father used to say that, and who ever gave Dumont more shit than him? Damn those Shadow Riders, takin' his fuckin' whiskey…farther this train carried him away from them the more he liked it. He slipped back into sleep until…

Missy tugged his right hand with her teeth, her grip nowhere near so soft as their normal play. He cursed then saw how she sought to drag him toward the short stair back down to the hatch. And saw now what she must've heard. Someone turning the door handle. Could it be one of the Riders? No way they could've tracked him here, not this time. Probably bulls. But the train was moving, far from any yard. Bulls stayed each in their own yard, checked the trains there. So couldn't be bulls then. Couldn't be good, whoever it was.

Whoever wanted to open the door was doing it with painstaking slowness, which meant they knew he was in there. Probably saw him through the windows, asleep in the chair. Dumont tried to rise but his arms had gone to tingling jelly, effect of poor circulation and his position in the seat. He leapt to shaky feet, wobbling, unsteady, flapping his arms to get the blood back in them fast. The door latch opened with a muffled click. Without further thought he dove down the stairs toward the door itself right as it began to ease open, leading with his left shoulder. He stumbled on the steps but traded equilibrium for momentum, slammed the part open door hard and into whoever was outside. He felt first metal crack against skull then connect with padded flesh as the door flung the other back onto the railing and Dumont tumbled out on top.

Dumont shoved himself away from the hulking figure on the catwalk. He saw black leather a pale blocky head and gray fuzz for hair. Ratch. And he recognized the jagged C on the shoulder of Ratch's jacket as *the same sign on the Crew Change what the fuck?* Ratch caught the cold steel rail with his right hand to keep from going over. Dumont drove forward kicked the Rider hard in the crotch with booted foot while he was still off balance then struck twice again quickly at Ratch's hand on the rail. The Shadow Rider gasped a muffled —*Fuck* and sought to pull back but he had nowhere to go. Dumont kept a loose grip on the flapping hatch door with his numb left hand as he kicked Ratch in the shoulder the ribs the side of his head. Dumont knew he had only this moment's advantage and had to press it, his leg pumping at the knee aiming and striking in vicious reflex. He could no way let Ratch draw in, grapple with him, drag him down on the catwalk or back into the cab. The guy was a fuckin' tank. His only hope was to finish it here, now. Most of all if Marlo or any others were coming. He had no chance if he had to take on more than one. Adrenalin powered his attack.

Ratch's right hand was blood and pulp, shreds of muscle showing and even bone at a couple knuckles but he still found strength enough to throw his left into Dumont's own crotch and drive him back against the cab though the shot missed hitting his balls dead on and took him more on the upper right thigh. Dumont gasped and spun but kept his grip on the door even as it swung to on his fingers and gouged them. Crotch and cut arm shooting pain, he drove two more quick kicks at Ratch's wrist before the other fumbled for the rail with his free left. Bone cracked and Ratch's bloody ruined right grip slipped and he tumbled backward from the platform, flopping left to keep from falling off and thrusting himself instead half over the righthand stairs. Dumont rained kicks against his feet and crotch and thighs, anything to propel him further...and *off this fucking train.*

Ratch struggled to rise but this only cost him further traction and dragged him down. He bumped flailing over the stairs, skull grinding a second in the right of way gravel before he slipped off the ramp altogether, whipped away quick in the outside wind. He didn't cry out or scream and the train-song covered any thump he might've made as he struck.

Oh fuck oh shitfuck had he just killed a man? Dumont fought near as often as he ate—sometimes more—but he never sought to kill, only to defend himself, a friend or a dog, only to protect, only to survive. True he might've done for Worm already but he had no way to be sure so he wasn't going to count that one. Not just yet at least. Dumont leaned panting on the rail, wounds and bruised scrotum still screaming with dull aching pain, and looked into the night along the route they left behind. He saw Ratch's crumpled form beside the tracks receding at twenty plus miles an hour… then rising. First the Rider was on his feet again then he was running down the tracks after them in ever-lengthening strides, right arm flopping loose at his side. Coming closer.

   With no time and still too pumped to reflect on this latest madness Dumont glanced around the platform for something to throw and so missed the moment a vast blot of blackness shuffled out of the night on the left, a thing impossible in size, larger than an elephant though smaller than a house, stumpy limbs visible only as hints. It bent over the running Rider and dipped, engulfing him to the waist and hefting him up. Ratch's legs kicked half a minute then the top part of whatever…clenched. Or something. Ratch's lower half tumbled back to the tracks in a dark spray. Dumont turned away. He'd seen enough. This time Ratch was dead. No question. Those legs would not be running after him all on their own.

He stared and the mass astride the tracks cocked the hump he took for its top as if to watch him but it did not pursue, halting there instead above Ratch's bottom half, disappearing back into the dark in the wake of the train. Missy barked from between his ankles but he shushed her, herded her back inside the hatch door and relatched it.

Inside Dumont pressed his hands to the chill trembling walls for balance, stability, tried to process what he'd seen. Shit had gone from crazy to what he couldn't even say. And yet he'd taken out two of the Riders, if Worm was truly down for the count and he included Ratch in his tally. He had a little help on that one. Somehow he got the jump on each of those guys though. They were as big or bigger than him and experienced brawlers both. But they hadn't shown it and he had. They'd been slow. Could be Marlo doped them with something to guarantee obedience, but Dumont never heard of any such drug. And what about Marlo? Was he somewhere on this train too? How often did he rely on his flunkies? Or could it be he and Ratch split up to hunt for Dumont on separate trains? Or did he send Ratch ahead alone because he himself was a coward? He had that coward stink, big talk but bigger buddies. Could be Marlo had his whole cult or crew with him now, scouring the train for Dumont from front to back and Ratch was only the first to arrive. Two more Shadow Riders might show up next.

Maybe three or four or five, Marlo with them. Dumont could make his way back up the train but he was probably gonna run right into them like that. Getting Missy over the tops of cars wasn't likely either, and he wasn't going anywhere without her. He could hide with her in the engine's restroom but he knew Marlo would look there and he and Missy would be trapped. In the end he slumped back in the leather seat, determined to stay more alert for the next attack or the end of the line, whichever came first. He slid into sleep again almost at once.

***

When he woke a gray fingered light reached in for him through the windows and his balls still ached. The train was slowing though. Fersure.

Missy remained on guard at his feet, lying on her side but head still up, her vigilance more consistent than his. Must be she'd been like that all along. He slid down, crouched beside her, scratched behind her ears. Oh you're a smart girl, yes you are. You done good. *Way good.* She saved his life already once this ride. Both their lives. He stroked her sleek black fur and she rolled on her back, offered her belly, legs quivering with unrestrained joy while he scratched her. He knew they could go on like this forever but it was time to hop off so he stopped. She arched to lick his hand and he leaned over, hugged her once quick tight. She licked his cheek, his ear. His intended laugh emerged as a grunt and he released her after a final squeeze.

He felt their pace slow further, the trainsong tempo extending in an exhausted drawl. They were moving slower now than when they hopped on. —Time to go, he whispered in Missy's ear. She seemed to understand, rolled to her feet, watched him expectantly.

He led her down the steps to the hatch, opened it slowly this time and peeked around. No more Shadow Riders, no Marlo, no bulls, no one at all. No monstrous globs of night behind them either. He supposed some Riders might be out of sight on the roof, approaching like spiders or ants, but he and Missy would have to risk it.

They worked their way down the stairs, Missy turning her nose up at streaks of Ratch's blood on the steel. She leapt from the still moving engine then paced the train till he stepped off behind her toting the caseless guitar with a hand around its neck.

TENEBRIONIDAE

***

They'd got off before the yard this time, though they could see it ahead. He had no clue where they were. To their left the backs of shops butted up all but on the railroad's right of way. Retail stores, not the sort of industrial stuff they'd waded into before. At least now he could hitch out of a proper town, shake whatever scent Marlo and his crew somehow followed on the freights. Might be he'd head up north where he was supposed to have family. Real family, blood family. He knew he had cousins he never met somewhere. Jersey, he was pretty sure. Yeah. Jersey fersure.

He called to Missy and they set off toward the shops, crossing several empty tracks and crawling under a chain link fence before reaching the back street. He wished he could clip a leash on her but that was lost with his pack. He'd keep his eye out for a scrap of rope that might do the trick. She still wore her collar at least.

From there they took an intersecting side and a short block later came out on what had to be Main. The sidewalks remained empty of pedestrian traffic this early in the day and the only cars were parked, but it seemed otherwise solid and real, not like the industrial park in Meridian or wherever. He could read the signs on the stores even, across the street a Rexall Drugs beside an antique shop, display window crowded with old clothes and ottomans and a faded red Radio Flyer sled. A grubby dive bar that hadn't opened yet two doors down. Everything closed but otherwise normal.

He took off with Missy in a direction he thought perpendicular to the now obscured yard, hoping to spot the red and blue shield of an interstate on-ramp or at least a local highway or truck route. They passed more restaurants and stores and bars, everything closed. Even this early something ought to be open, a lunch counter serving breakfast maybe, not like he had the cash, or that they wouldn't throw him out 'cause he was dirty and he smelled.

At least the stores were normal and he could read the signs. This wasn't another mindfuck trap like the last stop. Just an uptight southern town where they rolled up the sidewalks at night and put them back out late in the morning and…he spotted *them* ahead, four or five all scrunched up together near the next corner, a bunch of gutterpunks same as him.

Okay…if they were cool they would help him, tell him where to find food, water, where to catch a ride. Maybe share some whiskey. Best to come up slow though, be all nonthreatening, most of all not look like he planned to stay any while. Talking up his search for a ride out ought to help that.

Closer in he saw four dudes and a girl, backs to him all, mix of leather jackets with Carhartt overalls, hoodies, flannels, camo. All with their heads down and angled away from him.

About ten feet out he stopped and called to them —Wassup dudes? No response. He came forward a few more steps, spoke again —Hey, no hassles you know. All I'm lookin' for is the best place to hitch a ride on to F.L.A., maybe some water and some dumpster pizza. Then I'm outta here, fersure. Can you be cool with that?

None of them turned but at last the girl began to speak, a blunt susurrus Dumont could not understand. The first phrase he could pick out came across as —Along alas alack a leak…

Followed by the boy in leather…

—Tracks leak to the dark star call for a bite of blood bad bitter or better.

Had leather boy said leak or *lead*? No way to tell. And the girl—what the fuck, were these kids talking French? Could be they were Cajun, but all the way out here? Wherever here was…'Bama, Georgia maybe…

—Hey guys, we're just looking for a good spot to hitch out from, head north maybe, you know?

He paused so they could respond. They said nothing but one began to turn, a boy with ragged dreads wearing filthy Carhartts over a torn green Army jacket.

The boy had no face. Beneath his dreads and a bare inch of greasy forehead the front of his head was a round dark hole. Other than the teeth that lined it Dumont saw nothing inside. The blank aperture contracted slightly in an irregular quivering rhythm, pulsing to narrow its diameter just barely then expanding again, all as if with some unseen breath.

The faceless boy began to chitter and hiss. The other four turned and Dumont saw the same impossible lamprey faces gaping each in dark lopsided holes rimmed with rough and irregular teeth, each with its singular rhythm of expansion and contraction, each hissing or even screeching at him now in its own particular pitch. Some spoke in broken words others simply chittered or moaned and one cried —*Dumont Dumont Dumont*…but he couldn't tell which.

He staggered back feeling Missy dodging and feinting around his calves. She didn't bark though. She really was one smart girl. She knew when to sound the alarm and when not to push it. Was he hallucinating? If Marlo's blade dosed him there should be other effects…there was that last town of course—that and the thing that bit Ratch clean through.

He saw the worst then. The five faceless punks were not just scrunched together—they had only one body below the waist, cloaked beneath folds of filthy cloth. Their heads all twisted toward him now, necks extending to impossible lengths and writhing like flower stalks in the wind, like baby birds begging for puked up food from their mom. They chittered or chanted nonsense except for the one repeating his name.

He backed away two more steps as the whole distorted distended mass began to advance his way, crawling heavily over the concrete sidewalk same way as a slug—a slug the size of a rhinoceros. He turned and ran, Missy pacing ahead but glancing back every few feet. The punk glob came on only at a slow and plodding pace and he soon opened up a lead, the better part of a block. He turned the corner and…there they were ahead. Crawling toward him again from the end of the block. Same overlapping clothes, same many-headed configuration reaching toward him like an enormous hand.

Dumont turned back, saw them still there advancing as if in a mirror. He ran with Missy back to Main…and there they were as well, crossing toward him from in front of the Rexall. He found a side street leading away from Main and it was empty. He and Missy hustled down it and came out close to the yard. No one blocked their path, no mass of toothed blind heads, no Riders, no bulls.

In the yard itself he found an open corrugated aluminum shed and crouched beside a stack of rusted parts. Missy paced before him and he stroked her back each time as she passed. Dogs were a big part of this life but he never saw any of the Shadow Riders with one. Another reason to give them space, keep away. Never trust anyone who rode the rails without a dog.

A sketchy rain began falling, fat scattered drops plink plopping over the rippled roof and puffing small tired question marks of dust from the ground outside. Dumont thought about plucking out a song on the guitar, practicing one of his originals, but he had to remain vigilant, couldn't risk it. Bulls,

Riders, those freaky gape mouthed kid things…all might be hunting him. Best not to call their attention down. Seemed like they were safe here for now at least.

He dozed in fits. At some point the rain stopped. A bit later he woke. The rain began again. It didn't last this time, ten minutes tops. As it faded he heard train wheels beginning to roll.

Gripping his guitar he made his way into the yard, Missy close behind. Rounding three trains he found a fourth pulling out, a row of rust hued boxcars passing close. He eyed one of only two still open and as it came close he trotted to pace it, shoved the guitar across its floor, lifted Missy inside, then followed along till he could clamber up to join her, his cut arm almost altogether numb.

Boxcars. The classic hobo ride still good after all these years. Dumont rested on his back several minutes as the train picked up speed. But he could not ignore the door for long. Another of Jonny Ben's basics was when riding in a boxcar always wedge the door open with a spike in its track. If the door slid shut on a slope somewhere it might be months before anybody opened it again and found the withered mummy of your corpse.

Problem was the rusty spike he carried for just this purpose was in the pack he lost. He had nothing but the book and the guitar and neither seemed right for the job. The floor of the boxcar around him was all bare, but in the shadowed rear he saw a dark mound of lumps and sticks. Might be something there he could use. If not, he had major problems.

He rolled onto his right side, rose and shuffled toward the neglected heap. He had to hold his lighter down close but he saw quick it wasn't sticks.

The mound of rags and bones rose two feet high, all dismal black and tarry. A scatter of broken skulls made it clear at least the majority were human. He saw a dogskull too and something else he couldn't identify, a skull with five eyeholes, incomprehensible in shape and over three feet long.

Repressing his first impulse to retreat yet again, he scraped out a dehydrated thought and nodded, bent to tug loose a knob-ended long bone from the general mass. A black tarry nastiness coated it all over and it stuck a couple seconds in the rags of the pile before it came free.

Prize in his hand he bopped for the side of the train, set the bone at an angle between wall and floor then stomped it hard with booted heel, once, twice. On the second shot it shattered along a long jagged angle though the two pieces hung together. Dumont took the broken bone in hand and slammed it against the boxcar's wall till one half fell free. He soccer kicked the fragment out the door and jammed the piece he held point end first into the track, stamping his heel down on the joint end once, twice, three times so it was good and set.

That done he stepped to the side opposite the door, dipping to retrieve his guitar, and slid down against the wall where he could stare out the open door. He hadn't even reached the floor before it hit him just how beat he was, how whipped and weak and worst of all dehydrated. Hungry too but he could handle that. At least for now. All the crazy shit he'd seen, monsters, slug punks, whole fake towns…was it all just poison or dehydration? Could any of this craziness be real?

Missy walked over and laid her head in his lap. Poor girl. She had to be as bad off as he. Her food had all been lost with his pack. He dug the remaining bottle of water from his pants and dribbled it into her mouth in fits till it was gone, saving only the final sip for himself.

Outside a wooded landscape rolled on by. Engines and even grainer foxholes might be more comfortable, but an open boxcar really was the way to ride. Dumont felt connected to the old time 'bos of the depression in a boxcar, back when riding freights was almost respectable. He loved the scenery he could see like this. Trains were a different world. They moved through night and day, they were neither here nor there, they traveled forgotten parts of the country. Once crossing Georgia he swore he saw a Civil War battle out the door of a boxcar just like the one he rode now, the blue and the gray, bloodied bodies, cannons firing and the low fog of smoke from ordnance everywhere just overhead.

The wall of trees on this route stretched on for miles, something he never saw riding out from Albuquerque and El Paso, where empty spaces came in a thousand shapes, sometimes trucks or trailers or dim toiling figures in the distance but little else to mark. Here the trees approached dense and sudden just outside the right of way, interrupted only as the train passed nameless towns where the backs of buildings displayed elaborate graffiti as they faced the tracks. Slowly wisps of smoke threaded in, outliers of some forest fire or perhaps simply fog.

The scenery revived memories from when he counted his age in single digits, how he'd take his temporary escape from his foster brothers into the undeveloped country west of their rundown neighborhood on the seedy south Cerrillos side of Santa Fe. He would run out and into the pink-brown sand and scattered sage till the houses behind were the dimmest strip then crouch behind bushes or in a shallow arroyo, sometimes bruised and bleeding still, crying and poking in the sand with a branch. He never drew anything, but he watched the large dark beetles that came and went, occupied on cryptic errands known only to themselves. No matter how far he followed them he never saw them eat or sneak down any holes. They just walked and walked—unless he got too close and they hiked up their butts, extruded bits of foul orange tube. If you tried to pick them up and they rubbed that nasty odor onto you it took several days to wash it off.

He had his own idea about where to go next. He was still heading east, he was pretty sure of that much, and would have to hit the coast or Florida soon. If Missy and he could make their way to Tampa they could catch a juice train. Word was Tropicana ran *three* juice trains a day, one to Jersey, one to Ohio, and one all the way to L.A. Fastest things on rails, right of way all the way and forcing even the fastest freights to side out. He'd never ridden one and he heard from Jonny Ben they were hard as hell to hop, with Missy most of all, but if they could, any of the three would carry them far beyond the Riders' reach. Despite whatever fam he might have in Jersey, Cali seemed the best bet, a straight shot back across the country in only two days and far far away from Marlo and his crew. Dumont was sure he could shake the Shadow Riders then.

A thick fog ruled beyond the doors. He stepped closer to the opening so he could inspect it. The mist looked close enough he could run his fingers through it if he only leaned out but he felt somehow that would be unhealthy. Instead he withdrew, positioned himself half behind the boxcar's door as if it could shield him. Light flashed at intervals inside the smoky curtain, red and pink and without visible source. With each pulse something like veins lit within the vapor, red branching networks glimpsed for a moment and lingering briefly as afterimages, seeming to follow the direction of their travel. Down below the tie ends blurred by, the gravel bed beneath them an uncertain blur. The train swept on through this medium for hours, the better part of a day perhaps. Dumont strode across the car, far away from the tarry tangle of bones and clothes, curled up best he could and slept. Twice he awoke and each time still saw the same weird fog outside. He wondered if it was just him or the engineers saw it too. What they made of it if they did. He wondered if this train even had engineers anymore…

He unbuttoned his sleeve and slipped out the *Crew Change* figuring to see what it said about the juice trains and the Tampa yard, at least get some guidance from this thing that caused him so much grief and cost maybe three lives already. Only when he opened it the lines seesawed left and right and the size of the type itself shrank and swelled in his tired and crusty eyes. He tossed it down beside him in disgust and saw Missy shy away from it. Fuck it. He got on fine without a *Crew Change* all this time. He didn't need one now.

He lifted the guitar instead, propped it on his thigh, drew the last pick from his pocket—at least he hadn't lost that—began to strum out some chords. The thing was way out of tune—carrying it by the neck hadn't helped no doubt. He powered through the song anyway. One of his own. No title 'cause he hated titles. Titles were labels and he had enough of labels already. No chorus either. Fuckin' knowitalls always asked him where was the chorus, where was the bridge, and he'd say why do I need a chorus if I'm all alone, why do I need a bridge if I ain't goin' nowhere?

Freight trains and whiskey is all that I need
Cause I'm far away from my home
Whiskey keep me warm train roll me along
I'm all alone right now
Spare some fuckin' change right now
Cause I'm hoppin' on and I ain't comin' back
I'm hellbound for the devil's plains
I'm just a loner who's gone insane
I just watch those wheels spin as I'm carried to my grave
I live for the moment I live for today
Salvation is a thousand miles away
Knowin' me I'm not gonna stop
I just keep on rollin' on
Freight trains and whiskey is all that I need

He wrote that a year or so back after finding this bullshit Christian tract called *The Hellbound Train* in another boxcar he rode. He did not miss out though on how the lyrics suddenly became more true. He understood irony and it seemed to be gunning for him most of the time.

Missy perked up as he played. He could never decide whether she liked his playing, but she always listened at least.

—You like that girl? He half expected her to nod but her head held still. —Anyway, I'm not really alone so long as I got you. He shrugged. —It's just a song.

Dumont set the guitar beside him. He knew before he looked up Marlo was in the doorway. He hung there, same way a spider hangs from a strand of web. Except Dumont couldn't see any web, no rope, no wire, no line.

—Listen to the schwag bitch.

Dumont didn't reply, didn't move. He calculated distances, angles, steps and times. He peered beyond Marlo, alert for the appearance of other Shadow Riders.

—*You* were just s'posed to be meat, you and your little girlfriend, just another delivery. Now you've got *their* attention. They've gone back to watch you. Forward and back. You're starting to grow on them. They want to meet you. I say fuck that, you're not growing on *me*, and I still call my own shots on this side.

Marlo slid all the way to the floor, took two steps toward Dumont. The Rider had his K-Bar out again, obscure symbols etched into the blade of the old military knife.

Missy growled. Marlo advanced. Missy barked.

Marlo paused. —You should get your bitch on a leash, *bitch*. They want her too you know. But I say no. You know that's not happening either. I'll take care of her when I'm done with you.

Dumont hissed —No, Missy. He didn't want her running at Marlo, getting cut. He was gonna handle this himself. Dumont did not rise however, hardly moved. Marlo took three more steps and scoped the *Crew Change* on the floor at last.

—Fuckin' bitch I knew you had it all along. Well, time—

Though his angle sucked Dumont arched up and swung the guitar hard as he could, took Marlo just below the left knee. The soundbody crunched and crumpled as the Rider went to his knees. Dumont got full on his feet then, striking down at Marlo with the shattered body first then just the neck when the rest fell loose. *This machine kills fascists.* Right? Missy barked and lunged but held from attack. Marlo scrambled back on buttocks, hands and feet, crabwalking away from this onslaught of wrecked lacquered wood, the guitar itself dying by crunches and groans till even the flat-pegged head dropped from Dumont's hand.

Almost to the door, Marlo rose and shook himself free of shattered fragments, smiled at Dumont, brought the K-Bar to the level of his hip, advanced.

Hands empty, Dumont still held his ground, Missy barking but keeping back of his knees. —All this for a *Crew Change*, Marlo? Can't be that hard to get another…

Marlo paused a second and laughed —Bitch, you think that's a *Crew Change*? Ha!

Dumont bent to lift the rough bound book in his left, fixed his gaze on Marlo's face, targeting the raw red scar that crept up his chest and neck to twist along beside his nose.

—Giving it back is not enough now Du-mont. You and that mutt are gonna—

Dumont flung the book toward the door to Marlo's left, flat like a frisbee, hard as he could. The Rider batted at it with one hand and managed to knock it back to the floor. Dumont rushed forward tugging the tail of the faded blue bandanna that hung from the chest pocket of his weathered jacket, dragging free his smiley, a plated steel padlock tied at the end of the cloth. As Marlo groped on the floor for the book Dumont swung the smiley at the back of his head.

The makeshift weapon's impact felt oddly blunted, dragging across the Rider's skull instead of rebounding with a crack. Marlo spun and shrieked at Dumont, his mouth grown impossibly wide though not round like the slug punks in the town behind them. Instead his whole face split along the scar that ran from his neck to create an irregular quavering gash.

Fixed on that mouth Dumont failed to block the K-Bar when Marlo brought it up and slid it into his guts. Despite the instant waves of pain he struck Marlo's knife wrist with the smiley and heard bone crack like the Rider's skull had not. Marlo lost his grip on the knife though his mouth had grown gigantic now, big as the bell of a tuba. He leaned toward Dumont as if to engulf him as Dumont himself collapsed to his knees.

Marlo's mouth spread like smoke, filling over half of the doorway now and expanding. Dumont felt his hand on the book, dropped the Smiley and yelled —Marlo, here goes your fuckin' book! and lobbed it low off the train. It struck the veiny mist beyond and hung there, shot away with their passage. Marlo spun the meaty bloom of his face to follow it and overbalanced as the book zipped from sight. Dumont flopped back, cocked both feet from the knees and slammed them straight against the pockets of Marlo's Levi's even as he gasped at the pain from the blade embedded below his ribs.

Marlo seemed to vault from the boxcar almost on his own and struck the oppressive soup outside, embedding himself instantly like an insect in amber and shooting away in their wake. Dumont was certain he saw his adversary begin to dissolve before their passage removed him entirely from sight.

Dumont collapsed on his back before the boxcar's open door and laughed. It hurt to laugh but he could not keep it in. —Fucker, he called softly after the vanished Rider. —Fuck you, you fuckin oogle. You're fucking done now.

He made no attempt to rise. Meanwhile outside he witnessed a genuine surprise. The fog began to thin in patches, whole stretches next, and where it did thin he saw the scenery of the south once more. Green again, a vast unbroken curtain of high dark pines. Georgia somewhere most likely. For the barest intervals at first then several seconds at a time.

The old world showed through only to a point though. As Dumont lay panting, Missy licking his face, the intervals of normal began to diminish again.

He knew it was the worst thing to do in his case but he tugged the knife free and flung it aside. Black dust puffed from the wound, followed by slow-pumping gouts of thickened blood, the anticipated crimson streaked with swirling interwoven threads of pitch.

His good arm began to grow numb.

Dumont drew Missy to him, wrapped both arms awkwardly round her. He rolled on his left side, slid toward the door, limbs he could barely feel loose around her sleek black fur.

He timed it, waiting for the world he was leaving behind to flash beyond the open door again. Missy wriggled in his grip, suspecting his plan, not wanting to leave him. The train was moving slower now, not much more than ten to fifteen miles per hour. Trees reappeared. A sky of blue and white. He saw genuine birds, dark streaks and flapping eyebrows, probably crows. Standing water even, a pond or small lake. He tried to lean over far as he could, drop Missy not throw her, but he was weak from blood loss and dehydration and who knew what else so in the end she simply slipped to the gravel from his unsteady hands. She rolled, resilient as ever and back on her feet in a flash, running after him barking, chasing this strange damned train but dropping fast behind. She was a survivor though. His hopes all hung on that. He had time to gasp —I love you girl, and then the red veined haze returned and he knew he'd be alone on the other side. Fuck it. Let this place cope with his chaos. Fersure the other world never could.

...it's easy enough to think of most of us as deep-sea fishes of a kind.
—Charles Fort

NOCTUIDAE

The river flowed right over the road in places but they crossed it barely slowing. A trickle only a few inches deep right now, Sue-Min knew it meant the folks who lived in this canyon were stuck here during floods, maybe months at a time.

They probably didn't mind.

If you lived of your own free will in this canyon, you had to be happy in this canyon. You probably weren't that interested in human company, at least not from outside. You probably had supplies laid in to last a while. And a generator.

She could see the appeal. Deep in and well down Forest Road 281, the Blue River Canyon opened eventually into a narrow valley, widest on the west side of the river, such as it was. There the view stretched to near green hills rising right to green mountains, behind these a higher rolling row of purple mountains—*majesties!*—her backbrain sung the full phrase on its own, fragment from her earliest encounters with English—and beyond and above these a line of blue-gray peaks higher still in the haze, the sort of range one might mistake for clouds in the twilight, if the twilight were the sort in which one might also mistake clouds for mountains.

33

Sue-Min let her head slump back against the weathered seatback's cracked black leather, willing to let the scenery settle her edginess. It really was a damn fine day, despite her half hangover and shitty mood. As much of the sky as she could see overhead was unbroken turquoise. Maybe their day, their hike, would go okay despite it all.

So far, nothing had gone the way they planned on this damn trip. First Pete's date cancelled and left them three instead of four. Sue-Min tried to hint to Ron her discomfort with this configuration but he remained oblivious. What could she do? If Ron went, she was going too.

Then the ranchers.

What their topo map failed to show them was how 281, the only road down the Blue River, led straight onto a private ranch, ended there in fact, wide open cattle gate but handpainted *NO TRESPASSING* signs nailed to the grooved and massive cottonwood trunk beside it. Red paint. Their intended trailhead into Forest Service land and the Middle Blue lay somewhere beyond this private holding.

Though Pete never slowed as he passed the signs, Sue-Min saw them clearly on her side despite the overhanging foliage and shade. She drew in breath to call attention to the warnings, then exhaled. Pete must know what he was doing. Perhaps he met with the landowners in advance, squared things away. She hadn't paid much attention when he and Ron were planning—as a rule, she avoided Pete as much as possible—though she had to admit she was curious to meet his date for this backpacking trip, wanted to see what kind of girl would agree to a remote overnight hike with such a creeper. Only she wouldn't meet the mystery date, not this time. Easy to see why she cancelled—if she ever existed in the first place.

Pete drove on past a squat weathered ranch house, torn pink gingham curtains hanging askew in the windows, fabric likely once red now paled from long sun. They passed low tilting water tanks and clumps of rusted farm machinery hedged in by bleached tufts of high dead brush. Scattered grazing cattle. A mile or so beyond the gate and signs the road petered out, their rough rutted route concluding in a diminished riverbed choked with weeds and cobbles. To their left extended a turnout of sorts, dirt banked in berms ahead of room for several vehicles, marks of steel tread and claws still visible on the soil. Someone had an earth mover, although she hadn't seen it while passing the ranch. Pete braked the truck just shy of the furthest berm and they all three climbed out to stretch and gear up.

Not two minutes and a pair of 4 wheel ATVs buzzed up behind their truck. Right before Sue-Min heard them approach she'd been eyeing some bushes where she thought she could squat in privacy. Too late.

The riders were weather-beaten white men, both in Resistol hats, cotton shirts tucked tight into Wranglers. One was stocky and graying, the other lanky and leathered though likely less than thirty. The rancher and his son or hired hand. She guessed the latter based on their lack of physical resemblance. Both rode with shotguns on their ATVs in plastic scabbards like tubes for rural newspaper delivery, and as they slid from their seats both drew those weapons. Drew, but did not raise or level them. The two men let their guns hang at six, seven o'clock. The level of threat was implicit but limited, deferred.

She caught the hand's eyes flicking on and off her, up and down, that blend of lust and slow rage she knew too well from elsewhere. Smoldering anger over her apparent foreignness, at the shape of her eyes, at her presence in their stronghold. For once she was glad of the Glock that Ron kept in his pack, preferred not to think how Pete probably packed one too. Pete was the kind of guy saw unpermitted concealed carry as a point of pride, a civic duty.

Ron found Sue-Min's hand with his, held it, squeezed. Pete strode ahead to wade in, asking, —Hey guys, have we got a prob—? but Ron called him back, took the lead. He released Sue-Min's hand, strolled out to the pair and spoke. The wind struck up in the leaves overhead so she and Pete heard little more than the general rhythm of the conversation, its ebb and flow. They watched the mismatched sides commence a session of headshaking, hand pointing, the odd nod here and there. At least the two men never brought their guns to bear. That would've meant *time to go*…unless it meant *too late to go*. How close did things come to going that far south? She wasn't sure she wanted to know. Pete sidled toward Sue-Min but she stepped away, determined not to bond.

She had confidence in Ron. She'd watched him work his magic with surly ranchers before on caving trips in the GypKap. Gotten them access to sites no one had seen in a generation or more. His first ten years raised just outside Carrizozo had left him with some social skills in southern New Mexico, the rural version of street smarts. Pete probably would've got them shot.

Several minutes into the conversation the younger rancher pointed back the way they'd come then over the ridge to his right, their left. After final nods and even a lifeless half smile by the senior rancher, a flat expression that never reached his eyes, all parties retreated to their vehicles. The men sheathed their shotguns but did not depart.

Ron returned to where his girlfriend and best friend stood waiting. — Here's how they say it is. Blossom Creek Canyon is over that ridge, and Blossom Creek leads back to the major Blue drainage, only on Forest Service land. *Clear* Forest Service land, not checkerboard, so we can go as far as we like from there. But first we've got to drive back and park *outside* their gate. They don't mind us hiking in so long as we park outside their land and stay on the east bank of the Blue after we cross. They don't want us parking on their ranch or driving through it. We've got to go round.

Pete questioned the arrangement at once —Whatta they got out here they don't want us to see?

—*They* say they're protecting *us*. *They say* a couple of their bulls are prone to ramming unfamiliar vehicles, might do some real damage to your ride with their horns. Or to us. So these ranchers are looking out for us. *So they say*. Us or your truck, whichever. Both. And for their own liability no doubt. Lots of these folks living out the middle of nowhere worry some hunter or hiker or random lost a-hole is going to come on their land, get hurt and sue them into oblivion. And it does happen. Something like that can break an independent rancher.

This was not their original plan. Their map showed the passable road extending through and somewhat past this parcel. Their goal always was to follow the road till it fizzled, park and hike down the valley beyond all roads and habitation, as far as they got till nightfall, camp one night and double back in the morning. But they'd run late. Too much talk and too many Coronas at the lone saloon in Snowflake then sleeping in till nearly noon and not reaching the road's steep descent into the Blue River's canyon till close to 2:00. The scenery was every bit as spectacular as Pete promised, those rolling blue-green peaks in the west offset by higher rugged blue and purple ranges, the whole of it cut by narrow side canyons left and right. Still, by the time they reached even their failed trailhead it was nearly 4:00. They all three knew dark would drop down early in this deep north-south valley despite the season. No way now they'd make it far before night fell upon them, sudden, deep and dense…

The rancher and his man watched wordless as Pete backed his truck onto the road, followed them to the weedy turnout outside the gate across the road from the sign, kept on watching as the trio locked the truck and strapped on their packs. Geared up, they crossed the scrubby strip before the Blue itself, little more than a damp gravel bed here. Once they were over it the hired hand called after them —That's it. Keep on straight up that ridge. Canyon's t'th'other side. You can't miss it you keep goin' straight.

Pete and Ron waved thanks but Sue-Min did not turn back, had no wish to see these men ever again. Once across the diminished Blue they continued up the wide flat ramp of the ridge, convincing themselves they'd caught an actual trail as they picked their way between stunted oaks and twisted pines. As the trees were sparse and their ascent kept them close to the western edge of the ridge, they could look back for some time and still see the two men squatting sidesaddle on their little vehicles, though they soon fell to no more than off-white blurs beside the smudge of Pete's old Dodge. Sue-Min missed the moment the ranchers disappeared entire from sight. Their ascent angled, the trees grew too dense, the vehicles and men shrank too small to see from her height. The trio had left behind every contemporary human trace.

The ridge widened while they were unaware so once they reached a level where it grew mostly flat they realized they could no longer scan its full span side to side. The pines were taller here, the low oaks tight in clumps. Postage stamp meadows separated random rock outcrops and jagged bits of ridge. They'd ascended into a patchwork and come sans compass or GPS. Their original plan had been to follow the river, and how could they get lost then? But they'd lost the river, at least for now. Pete thought the canyon must be to their left, as best any of them could remember left. Ron thought they should head back down or at least to the right to relocate the Blue River edge of the ridge. Pete prevailed before either asked Sue-Min's opinion and they all three began meandering toward a hypothetical directionless port, expecting their way always to open onto a new canyon but coming only into more motley oak and pine after each distinctive bit they traversed, Sue-Min damping her emotions down just short of panic. Ron and Pete? If they were worried, she couldn't tell. They all three tramped along, the guys offering random inanities —*At least the weather's good.* —*I think we're getting close…* But mostly in silence.

They'd just come onto a stretch of bare rock strewn with stones when Sue-Min concluded she should call for a retreat, but before she could speak up Pete called out —Look at this! It's some kind of pattern!

His words still in her ears, she saw it too, gray cobbles around softball size set in wandering arcs and arabesques on the granite ground. Several closed cells remained intact though the arms of their neighbors disintegrated at inconsistent lengths. Ron shook his head. —Somebody built this—but who?

Pete's reply struck Sue-Min as ridiculous, asinine —Maybe it was the rancher's kids.

Ron swept three stones over soccer style with the side of his foot, bent to inspect them. —No lichen on their undersides, only above. They've been here a long, long time.

Pete's next reply seemed even more out of whack than his first —Maybe it was a Pueblo.

Sue-Min wanted so bad to get up in his face and yell *These aren't walls! Where's the rest of the stone then? If this is a dissipated site where is the rest of the stone?* Yes, Ancestral Puebloans, Mimbres, or some backwoods branch of the Mogollon, had inhabited this canyon, though not right here, not like this. Walter Hough had marked and mapped sites up and down the Blue back before World War I, and Steve Swanson had revisited the area almost a hundred years later. She knew as much, had met Swanson more than once, could share that information, but she had no desire to engage the creeper, let alone antagonize him. Nor to drag things out here. She had his number and was maintaining the wall of chill. *Measured, measured. Weighed.* She spoke to him as little as she could, kept interaction at the barest minimum.

Pete must've read something in her gaze though, fixed his own eyes on her expectantly and tilted his head an inch to the left, and after long enough she'd said nothing, gave the least of shrugs, staring at her still. For once Ron came to her aid.

—Hey, look, there's a gap ahead. He pointed beyond their present patch of patterned mystery stones, between the scrub oaks and scraggly pines. Sue-Min and Pete aligned their eyes to his extended finger's course, saw through the dregs of forest to what seemed an empty span. At least a place with no visible trees, little scrub, no upthrust rocks… A shadowed background. Either a seriously major meadow ahead, or Blossom Creek Canyon. *Some* damn canyon anyway…

Noctuidae

If it *was* Blossom Creek Canyon then by dropping into it and following its route they should come around and out again onto the Blue—south of the ranch and the ends of all roads, bypass the former altogether.

They funneled together through the gap, Ron taking the lead and never turning back. Once past the pines and onto a stretch of scattered scrub and grass they saw the gash in the earth from some way off. The canyon. *A canyon* at least. Pete shot forward toward that abyss and almost at once fell hard on his forearms with a rough pained grunt, his foot hooked on some snag invisible in the high grass. He swore without imagination as Ron shuffled up, paying extra attention to his own footing beneath the desiccated thin blades. Pete pushed awkwardly to hands and knees and waved Ron off, palms out —I'm okay, I'm okay…

Sue-Min saw smears of blood on both his palms.

Ron offered a similar gesture in response, though with palms angled down and presumably unbloodied. —Okay, okay, just checkin' bro.

Pete turned and staggered into the treeless span. Ron followed after a backward look and a shrug toward Sue-Min. She hitched her pack back up and followed.

A few minutes later they clumped together to a halt at the edge of a canyon. *Blossom Creek Canyon* they hoped. If the ranchers spoke true, this route would take them back to the main trunk of the Blue and its trackless and uninhabited middle stretch. Pete and Ron high-fived without a glance at Sue-Min who stood just a step behind.

Pete sauntered to the edge and the others followed, Sue-Min squeezing between Ron on her left and the branches of a thick twisted fir on her right. Dirt-cliffed at the top here, some eighty meters deep and at least that wide a span. Away to their left the canyon boxed off, but not so far ahead it jogged to the right and out of sight. Looked like the east wall rose there and some stone began to show through the slopes of soil. The bottom was a cleft too tight to see.

Descending the dirt wall before them held zero appeal. They saw no paths, no ramps, no natural stairs in the crumbling unstable face, no hand or footholds. Just pink grainy soil, scattered bleached protruding stones, random precarious cacti. Attempting any route down here without rope seemed likely suicide. Even on rope the descent would be sketchy. But a rock face would be different if one were ahead.

Onward then.

Now they at least had a feature to follow. So they followed. They were not lost. *Probably* not anyway. Probably not *yet* anyway. Sue-Min's incipient panic faded some. Pete took the lead again and they picked their way along the ridge, working around standing trees and fallen snags, retreating from the indented edges of scalloped collapse.

The sun where they could see it hovered just above the western slate range in the haze. They held no discussion on the subject, but she knew they all understood they'd have to make plans for night soon. They wouldn't be going much further than this, not today.

They came to the canyon's bend, rounded it. Ahead two changes leapt out at once. From here on, the walls on both sides were stone, steep scoured pink tuff ribbed with dubious holds. In addition their ridge dropped away, grew lower, just as the opposite wall ascended.

They quickened their pace, worked their way down to a less elevated section of the west wall, an almost level grassy area studded with the dark forms of juniper and pines. Across the narrow canyon almost close enough to throw a stone, the east wall—or was it south now?—rose near three hundred meters overhead. The steep stone face was more of the same, scoured and striated and pink, pyroclastic tuff of some sort, ash deposited in strata over how many millennia from what volcano or volcanoes, super or just giant, then cut through by slow eons of flash flood and flow…

That was when they saw the cave. Sue-Min was certain she spotted it first, but she only stared in silence so it was Ron who got to point it out and proclaim its presence. Maybe two thirds of the way up the wall and a hundred meters down canyon, a black horizontal oval in the rugged salmon scarp. Ahead of her Pete and Ron conferred close, heads bent together, low excited tones.

—Let's make for that cave. *Ron.*

—Yeah bro, we can camp there. We're gonna need to camp for the night soon anyway. *Pete.*

No shit Sherlock. She knew that already. They *all* knew that already. Probably no bear or mountain lion in there, high as it was. And it was August, not hibernation season yet. So steep though. Her stomach fluttered contemplating the climb, *but fuck it. She* was in better shape than either of the guys.

First they needed to cross. Ron stared from the edge, left-right, down, said —I think we can descend here, hike up to the cave from below, choose the best ascent there.

—Sounds good to me, bro. Lead on. *Pete.*

Ron looked back at Sue-Min a second, said —Whadda you think, baby? Looks good?

Only he turned before she could answer, dropped to his knees and slid his legs over the edge. Pete followed soon as Ron was all below. He looked up at her once his head had descended, said —Come on in, the water's fine!

What an asshole. Why did creepers always tell such suckass jokes? She let him climb down at least two full body lengths before she commenced her own descent.

The slope on this side was moderate, the handholds regular and reliable. Soon she reached Pete and Ron at the bottom, or almost at the bottom, wedged between walls only a few feet apart and tapering beneath to a terminal V too tight for traverse, both braced in position with arms and legs splayed out, an awkward pair of mothmen. She wished she'd worn her gloves for this shit. She saw Pete had his on now.

The stagnant murk in the crease beneath their feet could only be Blossom Creek. What they saw of the stream was little more than a foot wide and all but dry, its pitiful arrested trickle of water a black coffee hue. *Oily* black coffee. Only hard rain or snowmelt would make it flow again. Broken branches choked the creekbed's acute angle. She considered how much further each flash flood would propel the jumble of jagged wood, how long some of it lingered in this isolate groove...

They had to chimney along from there, splayed legs and outstretched arms holding them over the creekbed's crevice. It was a familiar caver's maneuver, and they progressed in this peculiar style as if awkward angels.

Below them bleached branches clogged the trench, broken ends awaiting only one missed step to punch through cloth and flesh and draw blood, or just the next flash flood to move them along. She looked upstream at what she could see of the sky. Distant rain would send a torrent toward them even when the sky overhead was blue. No cumulus clouds, no rain. At least not so far as she could see.

They made their clumsy way along, hand foot foot hand. Where the cave mouth had to be close to overhead Sue-Min saw forms below like broken rib bones protruding from the opaque water. *Human* ribs. Three curved gray somethings arching up from the coffee hued creek amidst more vegetal forms. And there—wasn't that cracked rod a barely submerged long bone? Once more she took a breath to speak out, but froze.

No way those could be human bones. No way would she give Pete a chance to mock her, think he was bonding that way. Or worse, to offer sympathy if Ron mocked her. Just funky sticks, bones of livestock or mountain goats at most, move along, move along, nothing to see here...

Neither of the guys noticed. They pressed ahead until they estimated the cave was right above. The left slope seemed steeper now, nearly vertical. Sue-Min contemplated climbing it wearing her frame pack, how to balance. Yet the alternative was to leave the pack down here, with all her gear, likely to slip into the foul stagnant cola below no matter how tightly wedged. No way to open it here either, take out just those items she might need—and no way to tote that stuff up without a pack if she did. Going up would be all or nothing.

Ron went first, gripping the corroded ridges of tuff, faded khaki pack bobbing on his back as he rose. Pete followed straight off. Sue-Min was ready to go second after Ron, but got no chance. It hadn't taken long for that to become the pattern...Ron...Pete...her...repeat.

Her turn came. The rock was not so friable as it appeared, and the thin horizontal ridges cut by ancient floods and flows offered hand and footholds more stable than expected. The slope, though not as extreme as she anticipated, was still steep, and she steeled herself to flatten against it if she slid to avoid tumbling backward and losing all stability. Pressed face forward she might yet regain her grip in a slide. Somehow they all three made it without mishap, crawled and scrambled over a rough rock lip and into the cave. Sue-Min let herself collapse back panting on the pebbly dusty cave floor with her pack pushed up for an uncouth pillow. Both her hands were sore and torn in several places, and she could feel the palm of her left wet with blood. Ron reclined in a position much like hers, but Pete still stood, though he trembled. She thought already of their inevitable return, whether experience would render it easier on the descent or the change in direction might make it worse. She'd at least dig her gloves out of her pack for that.

Once she got back up and looked around she found the cave was not deep, only a rockshelter really, its rear walls extending nowhere full into dark zone, barely deep enough for permanent twilight at best. The ceiling rose in half a dozen low scalloped domes whose curves extended out to the walls, giving the shelter's interior the look of a dirty compressed cathedral. Its floor area altogether amounted to little more than a good-sized theater stage, especially if all the curtains were drawn.

While the guys unpacked and set up camp she strolled about the hole. Beneath the rear north side dome she found the excised wings of dozens of Catocala moths, strewn in a tight spread little more than one meter round. Hindwings only, some up, some down, like powder-scaly tarots, their insides striped in red and black, outsides black and white. She'd seen this sort of thing once before, in a famous shrine cave near Capitan, New Mexico. The wing scatter marked a spot where bats fed. Or perhaps the work of a single energetic bat.

But no bats hung overhead here. And why only the bright-striped hind-wings, evolved to startle birds in flight? Where the drab forewings?

She found the probable culprits over in the final south side alcove, a loose cluster of at least two dozen Townsend's big-eared bats, their little charcoal bunny ears poking down within reach, so cuddly she wanted to pet them. But, rabies. It was always a maybe. Not just from a bite—the aerosol of their saliva could spread it alone. No ungloved non-expert should make even in-direct contact.

Sue-Min noted the shifting feel of the floor beneath her feet, a sense of gravel grinding. She looked closer at the layer of tiny cobbles covering much of the cave. *River* cobbles. Dusty pebbles two, three, four centimeters around. Rounded, roughly. From the river. Someone hauled them up here a handful at a time. The Mimbres or other Mogollon who worshipped in this place? Why? She knew of prehistoric Southwest cave shrines strewn with sandals in the hundreds, sometimes a thousand or more...others stuffed with inordinate numbers of broken bows and arrows, painted prayer sticks, cane cigarettes... These rounded but dusty river cobbles though? Could this rocky carpet be the remnant of some rain ritual, some offering to ancestors in the watery under-world of night, the rain-bringers who returned as the clouds themselves, came back as the very raindrops...?

Ron called her to where he was making camp. Sue-Min opened her own pack and drew out what she'd need for the night. She forgot to pack a sleeping pad so Ron placed his own under her bag despite the perfunctory protest she made. That settled, they zipped their bags together, creating a single quilted envelope. She smiled at Ron across this square…then saw what Pete was doing, what he held…

Pete hadn't yet spread his bag out at all…instead he moved methodically through the cave, a flattened wand coated in gray plastic extending from his hand.

Sue-Min turned on Ron. —No way. You brought me here with a *looter?* Did you not know about this? Tell me you didn't know he was gonna do this. Tell me honestly.

—Aw baby, I didn't think it mattered. He's only looking for Spanish gold, not the stuff you study. Studied. It's a total long shot anyway. Still, Coronado *did* come up the Blue, you know. And they do say he stashed some gold in a cave here somewhere.

—Coronado came here *looking* for gold! He didn't *bring* any!

—Sure he did. He had to pay his men with it. Makes sense he would cache some for the return trip, when he would need it the most.

—You know looters are like my natural enemy, right? Archaeologists hate looters worse than we hate…Nazis.

—Well, you're not really an archaeologist, are you? I mean, not anymore, not since they kicked you out.

He looked up at her, seemed to catch the blank stare that paved over her rage and turned away…then dared an amendment —And Pete's *not* a looter. He's not looking for *Indian* artifacts. He's only looking for *Spanish* gold…or maybe Spanish armor.

Sue-Min's voice came clipped as she answered, precise as a laser —Pothunters, treasure seekers, metal detectorists…they're all the same. They trash sites, remove artifacts from their context, erase their provenience, leave them with no connection to their origin, and ruin any data. They destroy our national heritage.

Ron was down on one knee, unpacking items she mostly thought unnecessary—why had he brought four bags of *unpopped* popcorn? He did not look up. Pete meanwhile continued crisscrossing the cave floor, electronic wand angled down around 45 degrees. He swept it in short arcs to either side and ahead, ignoring Sue-Min and Ron.

—You *know* how I hate these guys, and *now* you drag me out in the middle of nowhere with one? I'm telling you, if he really finds anything I'm shutting him down the second he moves to break the ground!

She had no idea how she'd do any such shutting down unless perhaps Ron backed her up, but thin as Pete's chances were of finding Spanish gold, things would probably never come to that.

Pete doubled back. Apparently he'd struck out so far. Beelined toward their bedroll till Ron requested he hold.

—Whasamatter, Bro?

—Can you maybe leave off with that thing till morning? Any gold here isn't going anywhere before then. Night's coming down and we should all crash soon, get an earlier start than we did today, you know?

Pete shot back a puzzled look and shrugged. He flicked a switch on the detector and let the hand that held it drop to his side, turned and stepped back to his pack to begin spreading his own bedroll.

The cave held no wood except a few dusty twigs, so they built no fire. Instead they chatted across the gap between the sleeping bag islands where they sat, passing Ron's half empty flask back and forth as they spoke. Their prospects for tomorrow, their luck in finding the cave, the strange pattern of the rocks they'd passed. Then Ron changed the topic altogether —When you get down to it those ranchers were decent guys, you know? Real all-Americans, really. I mean, what could be more American than cattle ranchers living down a canyon in Arizona?

Sue-Min hung her head, said nothing, which was fast becoming her routine when Ron was wrong, so she was surprised when Pete replied —Dude, those ranchers were fucking *assholes*. Their story about the bulls was…bullshit, and you know it. And don't tell me you didn't see how that one guy was checking out your girlfriend.

Sue-Min was shocked she agreed with Pete for once, but still she held her tongue.

—Duuude… Ron's answer was forced and artificial, hands palms up on his knees in a phony Buddha pose. —Dude. You're just projecting. They're all right.

—Ha! Canyon dwelling inbred weirdoes…we'll all be lucky if they're not burying your truck somewhere with their backhoe right this minute.

Ron shook his head. —Chill, man. We'll be fine.

That was it for the conversation, and as the Jack Daniel's in the flask was already exhausted, they tugged off their hiking boots, crawled into their sleeping bags, and slipped into sleep, one by one.

***

Sue-Min woke to a mass crushing her midsection and a beefy hand clamped hard over her mouth. The cave was dark but the reek of sweat and Polo over the low aroma of rock dust told her at once it was Pete. Who the hell else slathers cologne on for a backpacking hike? She sought to struggle but her legs were trapped in the sleeping bag and Pete knelt on her arms so all she could do was thump her knees bluntly against his back through the padding of the bag. She torqued her neck, tried to scan to the sides, but the burly builder increased his pressure and pinned her head in place. *What the fuck was going on? Where was Ron? How could Pete have gotten on top of her with Ron sleeping right next to her?*

That was *if* Ron was still right next to her…

She couldn't see Ron, but she couldn't see much. Though the cave was shallow its roof was so low no moonlight entered far. *Where the fuck was Ron?* She squeezed out a short set of stifled squeals, hoping to get Ron's attention or at least wake him up if he could somehow stay asleep while his best friend raped his girlfriend. *'Cause she knew right off that's what this was.* Any woman would know. Pete gave her that creeper vibe from the start. She hadn't worried much because Ron was always with her when Pete was around. But where was Ron now? The first flashes of heart-pounding panic faded and a wintry calm filled her frame in its place. She *was* going to survive. Not only *survive*. She was going to stop this, stop Pete. Even if she had to hurt him. Even if she had to *kill* him. In that moment her mind became icy clear. She would *not* be a victim. Nothing else mattered.

She tried to bite Pete's hand but his grip on her jaw covered her chin and was too firm for her to open her mouth. She struggled again to scream but her whimpers dwindled in the back of her throat. Pete shook the shadowed silhouette of his head. His movements seemed at once both frantic and subdued. Something suddenly didn't add up. Was Pete himself frightened of something? His face was no more than a blur but she felt certain now he was scared. *Terrified.* Of what—*of Ron?* Where *was* Ron? *Where. Was. Ron?*

Pete was linebacker big, outweighed Ron pretty well and her maybe double. She was no weakling but he was strong and he had the advantage of surprise. She needed a weapon. What? Her Leatherman was zipped out of reach in her pack. A loose rock might be good but the cave floor offered only a mix of dust and the little river cobbles. A few scattered sticks. If she could find a sharp stick she might stab him in the eye. Worked for Ulysses, right? But his knees pinned her arms at the elbows, her hands already growing numb. Still, if he really wanted at her he would have to get up and peel her bag back at some point. She had to be ready to make her move when that happened. She couldn't expect a second chance.

Sue-Min gasped in another breath and Pete pressed her down so hard she could feel individual stones through her sleeping bag and pad and the dense cover of dust beneath. He held his left index finger to his lips to shush her. Then he pointed into the night outside the cave mouth and rolled her head that direction with a shift of his heavy sweaty paw.

She had no clue what he wanted her to see. Outside was just more dark. Then it clicked. Part of the outside was *too* dark. *Far* too dark. She remembered stars when she fell asleep beside Ron, the sky above the opposite ridge thick with them. Now the sky without was a pool of ink. No stars, no moon, no silvered clouds. Nothing.

Pete pointed once more into the night. She understood he was giving instructions, asking a question. Asking if she saw…*what*? He rolled her head beneath his hand again, pointing out along the angles at the corners of the cave mouth. Left, right, and thin strips of stars there to either side. Pale moonglow on the canyon's facing ridge beneath. Between, *nothing*. Then she knew this nothing was what he wanted her to see. Something blocked the stars from sight in a broad rising swath straight ahead. Not clouds. Something closer. Some impossible bulk rising from the canyon outside to blot the sky and stars.

Pete held her gaze to the side one more time and pressed his own face forward. She tried to shrink back, expecting he sought to force his mouth on hers, but he only offered the down nod again as he stared at her, his coarse porous face mere inches from her own. He whispered —Promise you won't scream if I take my hand away. If *you* scream, we're *both* dead.

She stared up at him and willed her eyes into Tesla death rays. No luck.

—Listen to me *Sue*. This is life or death. That thing outside, I think it already got Ron. Killed him, ate him, I don't know.

She felt a deep chill emptiness rush through her chest, ice water flooding her guts. Ron. Dead. She already knew it—had known it somehow from the moment she woke. Now she was alone with Pete…with Pete and whatever was outside. Which was worse?

She struggled to scream again—from grief, from fear, from simple rage—but Pete kept his hand squeezed tight across her mouth. She gasped rapid breaths through his fingers as best she could.

—I want to let you go but you *got* to be quiet. *Promise me.*

Again she beamed back her most concentrated hate. She *never* wanted him on this trip. *Oh, we'll make it a double date* Ron told her. Except Pete's alleged date was a no show, surprise, surprise. If the woman was ever even real. Oh god, was Ron really dead? Then she thought of the vast shadow obscuring the night outside. Oh what the fuck? She managed a stillborn miserable nod beneath his hand. Anything to get him off her. Who would she scream to anyway?

Pete stared down at her, his face suspended so close to her own. She felt certain if they could see each other clearly he would see her hatred and she would see his doubt. She had doubts of her own though. Legit ones. She distinctly felt the rigid root of his cock pressed against her where his crotch splayed over her pelvis, and she remembered from a cultural anthro class how guys were *not* supposed to get hard if they were genuinely scared. Their course text had shown carvings, erect angry effigies from around the world. Ithyphallic. An erection in the face of threat was alleged to demonstrate courage. If Pete wasn't really afraid what else wasn't true? *And what really happened to Ron?*

Still, best to play along at this stage. Getting loose would allow her to call for help, *run* for help, find a weapon, maybe even find Ron. Pinned down this way she had no options, no chance. Nothing.

Again she offered what constrained nod she could, and this time Pete first eased the pressure of his hand then lifted it a few inches above her face. He did not rise off her though and kept close watch on her mouth.

Sue-Min gulped air and turned to the right causing Pete to drop his hand not quite but almost back to her mouth. No Ron in sight. The cave was small, Ron's half empty pack still beside her. Ron was not. Ron was no-where, nowhere she could see. Outside still the enormous shape of shade, a monstrous blotch of darkness blotting out the night and stars. Inside Pete still straddled her, his gaze fixated on her mouth, knees pinning her arms above the elbows, gag hand prepared to clamp down at once if she screamed or yelled, made any sound. He leaned in close and she twisted her head to one side to avoid the unwelcome kiss she still anticipated.

Yet he only whispered in her ear. His voice crackled with what she took for genuine panic. She heard it clear now. *He* was barely keeping it together himself. Which likely made him more of a threat.

—Listen to me. If you want to live through this night you *got* to listen to me. Here's what I can tell you. Ron got up. To pee I suppose. I remember that. I half woke as he passed. I looked over at you and you were still asleep. Next thing I know Ron was *gone*. Just. *Gone*. I got up to check on him and when I came to the edge I saw what was out there. I stayed quiet, backed up slow, *real slow*. I'm sorry I sat on you but I was afraid you would scream and call it down on us if I woke you and showed you without measures. There's more to all this but I can't just explain. You've got to see for yourself.

Whoa. All this freaking out over what—a shadow? Was this all a setup? Still, hard-on or no, big burly Pete was visibly upset and she'd never seen him even ruffled before. But was he truly scared? She couldn't deny *something* was bugging him. Plain old-fashioned guilt maybe? What if *he* had done something to Ron. She didn't see how the shadow could be rigged though, and she never pegged Pete for much of an actor, despite his occasional tendency to quote from *Hamlet*. Seriously, what *was* that thing outside? And *where. Was. Ron?*

Pete sank to all fours beside her. She wriggled away fast and as far as the now oversized tandem bag allowed, which was not far. He watched her but let her go.

—Okay. You need to follow me now. Keep low, be as quiet as you can, not a sound. Just trust me—you'll understand when you see. And he swung his incurved arm like a swimmer, like a scythe.

Pete began crawling toward the cave mouth, but Sue-Min's thighs shook so bad she couldn't keep his pace, even after she got free of the sleeping bags. A couple meters on he crooked his neck, looked back at her behind him, barely out from the bag, made mute jerking motions with his chin for her to follow, another inward sweep of his arm. Could he see how she trembled?

She feared to set a precedent by taking his directions in any way, but she knew she needed to see it for herself, whatever *it* was. She steadied her legs some with deep breaths and effort and went on, shuffling over the dusty cobbles in her stocking feet silent as she could.

A few meters from the edge Pete pulled back, chinwagged again for her to go on alone. And again her situation devolved to an undesirable choice. As she crawled past Pete she mouthed —*My choice to go on. MY choice, understand?* He only stared back blank as she came to the edge where —*Oh holy fucking shit!*

The dark shapeless form outside rose high above them to where a sort of huge translucent fan crowned it. Some forty meters up or more. Long, broad, veiny...*petals*...caught the scant moonlight, glinting purple red green white blue back to red in oily inconsistency, marking passage en route through other hues unknown from any crayon box. The colors bore the elusive character of iridescent insects, shimmering back and forth from bright indefinable luminescence to matte absence with a hidden and indefinable rhythm. She gaped at the display, altogether strange yet almost beautiful.

The immense pitch bulk or trunk behind the array seemed immune to the moonlight, showing only as an enormous hole in the night. Despite its limited brightness Sue-Min somehow sensed a lack of life in the mass, an overall deadness as if it were a virus or remnant, a thing that lacked any animating spark.

The deathly petalled spread hung overhead like the centerlight pop of a single stillborn firework, one lone frozen moment from a forgotten Fourth of July. Behind it the unlit trunk rose above and hung below till blocked either way by the cave mouth such that she could not decide the direction of its source, whether it was child of the riven Earth beneath or progeny of the very sky it concealed from view.

Was this great dark thing in the canyon some kind of massive night blooming cactus? Or was she witnessing the manifestation of a gigantic nocturnal beast, perhaps a Godzilla-sized star-nosed mole? Either way where had it been in the light? How could such an enormity simply *appear*?

A muted crunch came from behind. She swung to see Pete on his feet beneath the bat roost, waving his hands in an apparent attempt to roust the bats and shoo them out. She heard him whisper —Why aren't you outside? It's night! *Get out!* Get, get! *Go!*

And after all why were the bats still inside this night? That didn't seem right. She pressed herself to the pebbles as they flew overhead, none coming near her. Outside the attenuated moonlight caught the bats as they scattered. They seemed disoriented, flittering in twisted zigzags as if ill till one struck a blade of the object's glimmering fan! She thought she saw the membrane twitch or ripple to intercept the bat, which stuck and hung there and as she watched began to dissipate, the veins glowing brighter around it. She could see the bat's essence streaming in toward the spread's hidden center through the network of sinuous vessels. Their luminosity increased a moment then diminished and the bat was gone.

Pete stood beside her. She almost gasped but her fear was internal enough for its force to seal her mouth. He moved fast and soundless for a guy his size, even traveling over this gravel. A finger first over his mouth then pointing back into the shallow recess of their meager shelter. He turned, crawled, and she followed.

Opposite where the bats had hung, all the way against the east wall, they were just out of sight of the entrance itself. Pete scrunched down in the farthest spot and Sue-Min did the same, keeping a full two meters space between them to her left though thus forced to leave herself the barest hair in view of the mouth.

Pete turned to her, whispered —The bats…did it get any? I wanted you to see.

—Yes. I saw one get stuck and melt. Poor thing.

—I watched the same thing happen to an owl while I was looking for Ron. *Fuck!*

Ron's unwitnessed yet presumably parallel dissolution filled the silence between them.

He didn't open his eyes as he half turned toward her to speak… Cocky Pete seemed at a loss for once, for a moment at least, arms hanging loose and head tilted up against the arching wall.

She looked full at him. He'd taken charge since she woke or even before but was he conceding now? After a good two minutes he drew a deep breath and spoke—

—My gut is it'll leave when the sun comes up. Probably just disappear. Fade away back to wherever it came from. We just have to wait it out. Have you got your cellphone?

She shook her head without turning his way. —Left it in the truck. What was the point? No signal out here.

—I know that—It's the *time* I wanna check. What about a watch?

—Ha! Not for years...

—I've got a watch but it's too dark to read it. I was hoping you had something digital. He dug out his own phone, flipped up the cover, cupped the screen's glow with his left hand and angled it away from the entrance best he could. —3:37. Does that seem right to you?

—I guess.

—I don't know. It feels wrong somehow. Too late, or too early. Anyway my battery won't last much longer so I'm shutting down to conserve power. We can check the time again in an hour or so. Right now it's all we got. *We* are all we got. Each other. We've got to work together to survive.

Sue-Min hugged herself. She knew *she* was all *she* got, the only one she could trust, and she had to rely on herself. The rest of Pete's ideas made some sense though. Wait and see what happened at sunrise. And if the thing was still there at that point, well at least she would see better what she was dealing with.

—What time does the sun come up?

—This time of year, 6:00? 6:30 maybe? But we're in a canyon, so it may take another hour or so for it to shine down here.

He stared at her as if expecting her to run calculations in her head and announce the results to contradict him, but she neither replied nor met his gaze. After several seconds passed she felt him turn away.

—We should take turns keeping watch.

—Fine, you first. Her response came without hesitation, and she spun at once and crawled back to her bedroll. She had to think these things through. Lie down, maybe rest. Maybe sleep through it all if she could, wake come morning, deal with what was left to deal with then. From one side she heard Pete's mumbled —Okay. I'll wake you after what I think is an hour.

—How about you don't wake me *at all* unless it's life or death, or you find some sign of Ron. Turning away from Pete once more she bent and gripped the matched edges of the tandem bedroll she and Ron had shared, hands splayed wide as leverage allowed, dragged it toward the cave's back wall as far as she could get from Pete, though careful not to disturb the moth wing Sargasso.

Once arrived at this terminus she wriggled down inside the sack, back against the wall, head bent on bended knees, not caring if Pete witnessed her undisguised display of weakness.

She crouched and cried in silence. Thoughts of the thing outside never left. Thoughts of Ron never left. Sleep refused to come. Her tears oozed in slow soundless streams. She knew it was in no way logical but she felt abandoned, so much so she wanted to curse Ron for whatever stupid thing he must've done to draw the monster's attention. She pictured him cocky enough to try talking to it, same as he had with the ranchers. He thought he could talk to anyone if he knew even two words in their language—French and German tourists, an old Navajo couple in a truck stop near Thoreau, the waitress at a Greek restaurant in Albuquerque. Those occasions were awkward at best. Worst of all was when he tried speaking to her in broken Korean. That always ended in a fight. Could he have imagined himself a monster-whisperer?

More likely though he just staggered groggy and clueless to the cliff edge and unzipped, little LED light on his forehead, and then what? Maybe the thing snatched him up right then. Maybe it hadn't and Ron simply stumbled and fell when he saw it. Either way, wouldn't he have yelled? Why hadn't they heard? The canyon's acoustics? Perhaps Pete *had* heard and that's why *he* woke up. Or perhaps Pete had been there too. Perhaps Pete had pushed Ron. Would she really put that past him? Perhaps it was not an owl Pete saw dissolving but Ron…maybe Pete actually offered Ron up as some sort of sacrifice…

Maybe Pete had known this thing would appear outside tonight, *known it all along…maybe that was why he brought them here.* Why hadn't he sacrificed her too then? Was it because he wanted her for himself? How would the monster feel about that? Could she somehow offer Pete in *her* place? Would the thing let her go if she gave it Pete? What were the protocols for offering a sacrifice? Just pushing him from the edge didn't seem enough. Did she need to know some ritual, a chant, wave a crystal or a magic staff? In any such case she was fucked.

It wasn't fair to Ron for her to feel abandoned. Not if he really were dead. What if he were still alive somehow though, trapped perhaps on the opposite edge of the canyon, trying to get back to them. If the monster disappeared and she left at sunrise, wouldn't *she* be abandoning *him*? She remembered her birth mother handing her a worn and sweat-stained *Hanji* doll before retreating forever down a plain gray hall, not looking back, other women coming to fawn over Sue-Min, complimenting the doll, saying how lucky she was in a language she no longer spoke but still partly understood, sometimes heard in her dreams. She remembered that doll, its white smiling face, its tiny red kissy mouth. But she had no memory of it past that moment. What happened to the doll? When had she lost it—or when had it left her, who took it away? Had it even traveled with her out of Korea? She'd been nearly four then. Her next major memories were American TV, animal shows mostly—*Flipper*, *Lassie*, *Big Ben*. She needed one of those friendly entities to rescue her now, chase Pete away and lead her to safety past the creature in the canyon.

But no animal helper came. She was all on her own here.

Her mind cycled through every level of consciousness except sleep. She might as well have been cranked up on caffeine. Sleep was not going to come easy, not any time soon.

After what felt like several hours but was probably less than twenty minutes—and just as she slipped into sleep's first light stages—she felt Pete's hand on the back of her neck, his breath on her cheek. That awful sweat and Polo smell. She stiffened before he could speak, shook his hand off and wriggled away, the zipped together bags bunching about her right elbow and foot.

—What the fuck Pete? What do you want?

—Nothing. I just thought...you know...we're all alone here...and we may not make it out...I saw you shaking, like maybe you were crying...I thought I should hold you, help you get through the night.

—I don't need your help.

—I thought I could comfort you.

—We're not Adam and Eve here Pete, so don't get any ideas. If you were right before and this thing outside belongs to the night, then we're only trapped a few hours longer, and soon as the sun comes up we can make tracks back to our everyday world, contact the police or the Forest Service or whomever to come look for Ron. *If* we don't find him on the way out...

She felt his hand again, harder, tighter, thumb and fingers almost encircling her left bicep, even through the bag.

—Sue...

—My name is Sue-*Min*. Sue. Min. Let me go.

—Listen, Sue.

She struggled to pull free again but this time he tightened the cables of his fingers round her arm through the layered bag, squeezed.

—Listen Sue. We're trapped here at least till daylight. Maybe longer. Might be we're both gonna die here. We could help each other pass the time, help each other get to sleep.

—Pete, *please* just let me go, okay? She spoke in a strained whisper. In response he gripped her tighter, dragged her closer across the coarse cobbly floor.

—C'mon, don't be that way. Ron's not here, he's prob'ly dead. And I seen the way you look at me.

—Seriously? *How* do I look at you?

—You know, like—

She cut him off. —You know what? I *avoid* looking at you. And she knew right there she made a mistake. She had *engaged*. Offered an opening for his distorted reasoning.

—Yes you do. I seen you checking me out. You're sly, but I know you wanna give me some of that Asian persuasion…

Oh shit. Zero to rapey in sixty seconds, and her earlier intuitions all confirmed. At once she came wide awake, scattering any stray petals of Morpheus from her brain. Pete had crossed a line, and from here on she had to be not just hostage but hostage negotiator, had to argue her own release. But even successful where would she go? Pete had played his hand. Now she had to buy time, bluff.

—Don't you think we should focus on this thing outside, on survival? We shouldn't be looking for new ways to draw its attention.

She could name what Pete was angling toward, but that felt dangerous in itself. Best to leave some uncertainty around her recognition of his intent, degrees of doubt, not admit they were even discussing…*that*. She was certain Pete would take any overt mention of sex as a sign of deeper connection, an invitation.

She felt his hand slide up to her shoulder as he craned his head to look at her.

—What's wrong with you? You're Asian. Aren't you supposed to be submissive?

She bit back an exasperated scream. *No confrontation.* In an argument he would sooner or later find reason for turning to force. And the thing outside might hear their scuffle. She calmed herself best she could, then proceeded with her stock response to this and other stereotypes —Okay, first of all, I *am* Korean, but I grew up *here*. In the U.S.A. Baseball, hot dogs, apple pie, and Chevrolet. Just like you. *This* is my culture.

—What difference does that make?

Was he that dense, or was he consciously attempting to escalate, goad her into giving his threadbare conscience the provocation it required to increase his level of physical aggression? She needed a distraction.

—What do you know about the Korean War?

—Same as Nam, right? We fought the commies. Except we broke even in Korea, didn't lose the whole enchilada.

She cringed but continued —How much do you know about the side effects of the war—of any war?

—Casualties. MIAs. Some of our boys got left behind. My grandfather lost his best friend in that one. Still listed as MIA.

—Yeah, but do you know what war does to children?

—They didn't have child soldiers back then. Did they?

—I'm not talking about child soldiers. I'm talking about international adoptees. Do you know anything about them?

—You're talking about Korean kids?

His ignorance gave her a chance to assert a fragile authority. —Orphanages in South Korea were overcrowded and understaffed even before the Armistice. War orphans, G.I. babies... Then this missionary couple got the idea of offering the children up for adoption in the U.S. The Holts. They adopted eight Korean babies and wrote a book about it, started their own adoption agency. Holt International. The whole thing really took off from there. It was practically a fad for a while. Over two hundred thousand Korean children were expatriated altogether. An entire lost generation.

—What's all that got to do with anything? It's ancient history. I'm talking about now.

—It has to do with now. It has to do with *me*. *I* am one of those children.

—You were adopted?

—*Obviously enough.* Not one of the Holt kids—I came over later, in '71, and not as a baby, not from an orphanage—I was old enough I can remember my birth mother a little. I remember when she left me, gave me up. I didn't understand. Still don't understand. On some level I hate her. But I still love her too. How can I *not* love her—she's my mother? And I love my adoptive parents. How do you reconcile that? I don't even try, not anymore.

By way of response he rolled fast on top of her, pinning her legs once more with his bulk, his speed such she had no chance to react. He slid his left hand underneath her head, torqued her face toward the opening and the vast mass fixed outside in the night. —That! Look at *that*! We've got no time for flashbacks, for *This Is Your Life*. We've got life or death right outside. So what you're adopted? Big deal. Be glad you got to come to America, greatest country on Earth. American soldiers died to bring you that freedom.

—You think Korea is third world? *I've been there.* In some ways it's more advanced than the U.S.

—What are you trying to say? If you're gonna bash America, I don't fuckin' wanna hear it.

—What I'm telling you is whatever you think about Asian women doesn't apply to me. Whatever you think about *Korea* doesn't apply to me. Whatever you think about *Korea* doesn't apply to *Korea*! *Whatever wrongheaded racist bullshit,* but she didn't say that part aloud. —Please get off me Pete. Please? Her words came out as a wheeze because of the bulk he pressed against her chest. She could feel him twisting to align his hips above hers, his erection back and already grinding her hip. She groped in vain along the floor for a weapon to jab in his eye but here too the cave offered nothing but pebbles. Any more likely item was still in her pack or Ron's.

—*Pete NO!* Her compressed stage whisper came out almost loud enough to echo, but he hesitated less than a second at the sound. He did hesitate though. She didn't miss that. He was fully on her now, hands reaching for the edges of the sleeping bag to tug it down. As she fought back panic a last inspiration came.

—Stop or I'll scream and that thing will hear us! Won't it? I think you know somehow. You know more about that thing than you're letting on.

At once he clamped his hand over her mouth again, slid his hips over hers altogether. She could feel his erection against her belly now. Hard as it was, his cock felt small—compared to Ron's anyway—and Ron's was only average. She didn't want to feel any more of Pete's than she felt this moment.

Sue-Min struggled best she could, sought to squeeze out a scream between Pete's thick linked fingers. No luck. Her breath hissed heavily through her nose. The way he held her she could barely breathe.

Pete's free hand slid across her chest, groped at her breasts, left then right, his attempt grotesquely clumsy since she'd unsnapped her bra when she first lay down with Ron and it still hung loose beneath her shirt, cups crumpling under Pete's fingers and frustrating his efforts to reach her nipples. He arched off her a fraction as if to give himself room to maneuver. She floundered as he fondled her but proprioception identified her only free move as toppling to her right—which did not seem advisable as it would allow him to pin her facedown to the pebbly floor.

Pete fumbled for the metal snap at her waistband now, and this required him to rise off her a bit more. Within that interval she brought her arms up, pressed forearms to his chest and shoved hard, and once he lost his balance and flailed, she used his body for leverage to rise and jerked her legs from under him as well. He fell back as she shot up, only to catch her feet in the sleeping bag so she tumbled almost right back on top of him. He flailed his left arm across her chest but she rolled away, pulling free of the bag, ended on all fours several feet from Pete. Without thought she scrambled toward the cave mouth, ignoring the pain as the more jagged of the river pebbles dug under her kneecaps, into her palms. Pete rolled over as well and came after her. This time *she* was faster. A meter from the dripline she spun and flopped on her haunches, pointed both index fingers at her open mouth, said loud as she dared —*Come any closer and I will scream!* Pete froze where he was a few feet off, still crouched on all fours.

—This is *not* happening. It is *not*! She spoke with authority despite the continuing quaver in her voice. —Now back up against the wall or I. Will. Scream! *I will!*

—C'mon Sue…you don't wanna do that!

—My name is Sue-*Min* you asshole, and don't tell me what I want to do. I'll tell *you* how it's going to be from here out. Now back up into that south corner of the cave, past where the bats were.

Whatever Pete did or did not know about the hearing and habits of the thing outside, it appeared the threat of her scream held genuine sway over him. She knew it was likely a doomsday weapon, mutual assured destruction, but he seemed genuinely afraid she would deploy it.

—Okay, okay. Just don't do anything stupid. And he actually began backing toward the corner just as she had directed him, resembling some squat wretched sea creature on his hands and knees. If she could read his face in the gloom, what would she see revealed? Anger? Resentment? Guilt? Confusion? Fear? A mix perhaps, though she guessed mostly fear. She'd struck on something. But how long could she extract leverage from her threat?

Pete backed up, passive aggressive and slow, but after a couple minutes he reached the wall in the corner. There he sat and leaned his head against the stone's coarse arc, his eyes aimed toward the low domed roof.

Sue-Min brought her knees up and hugged them to her chest as if to muffle the sound of her galloping heart. This position helped some to still the tremors that shook her. How impossible could her situation be, trapped between a rapist and something a thousand times larger? She'd achieved a stalemate with Pete for the moment, but how long would it last? Certainly he'd be on top of her if she nodded off half a minute. Thought of the vigil she would have to maintain made her empty stomach acidic. Adrenalin had helped her thus far, still held her, and now it brought rage.

—Did you call that thing up, Pete? Did you summon it here?

His hesitation registered to Sue-Min as surprise…surprise she guessed the truth? Surprise at her accusation? Surprise a 114 pound woman got the better of him, backed him down? What had he done to women before, other women who had no threat to hold over him, no weapon for protection?

He didn't answer, simply stared upward. Not as if she expected a reply.

His silence made her nervous though, so she took a different tack — What's your phone say now?

He continued to stare at the stone ceiling for maybe five Miss'ippi, then pulled the phone from his pocket and flicked it on. After a minute its pale glow coated his face and he read aloud —4:19. We've still got a ways to go.

A pause.

—I wasn't going to hurt you, you know. Just the opposite. I could make you feel happy, help you forget this situation. Help us both. *If* you weren't so fuckin' uptight. How come you got to be such a bitch?

She considered his insult, its definition as he saw it—*bitch, (n)—any woman who declines sex with any man any time. Even rape.* Her reply was simple—she pointed again at her mouth with one hand, gestured toward the entrance with the other. As loud as she dared yet soft as she could she said —I *will* scream. Pete was barely a vague blur now, but she could sense the tension in his folded arms. Nod off for a minute though, and that's all he would need.

And outside was the creature, the thing, the unimaginable enormity that presumably devoured Ron. She sat now with her back to it. On its very doorstep even. This was not the best thought-out plan, but she hadn't had a whole lot of time to think. Pete had forced her to act and she had acted. Maybe she was lucky to be where she was. Or maybe she'd only scrambled out of the frying pan *fuck oh fuck oh FUCK this was all so wrong.* Yet except for the monster, it was nothing new in her life—how many times had she escaped one toxic relationship only to hurl herself into the arms of another? And creepy guys pulled this shit on her all the time.

The thought struck her—not for the first time—there was a discontinuity between her image of herself as independent, a free spirit, and her tendency to slide from one relationship right to the next. To define herself through relationships. Bad ones.

Ron, though…Ron was different. Not perfect—he could be neglectful, especially around Pete or his other male friends. *Especially around Pete.* Why Ron felt the need to impress this guy so much she did not understand. During the three months they'd been dating she repeatedly took a backseat to Pete. She'd come to see it as the price she paid to be with a guy who didn't hurt her, didn't hit her, didn't talk down to her. Seemed to like her for who she was, not for the shape of her eyes, her nation of origin. Never said *Five dollah make me hollah* when he wanted to fuck. She'd actually been with guys who waved a fiver at her in the bedroom and thought they were funny. More than a couple. She could picture Pete pulling that trick. But not Ron.

Adrenalin faded and she already felt drowsy, despite the menace behind and the menace ahead. She might as well talk to Pete, make conversation. At least that way she'd know he was also awake.

—What else did you see outside? Did you see what that thing did to Ron? No answer.

—What about this cave? Did you know it was here before we started out? Was this your destination the whole entire time?

No answer.

—C'mon Pete. You said we've got to work together to survive. If we're supposed to be a team, don't you think you can at least tell me the truth? How much of this did you plan ahead?

At last Pete broke his silence —You think you're so smart.

—No…

—Yes you do. You think you're like Charlie Chan's Number One Daughter. I'll tell you what—you don't know a goddamn thing. You can't see inside my mind.

—Trust me, I don't *want* to see inside your mind… All I did was ask you a couple questions.

—Well, they're stupid questions. How 'bout you focus on how we're gonna get outta here, okay?

She risked a glance over her right shoulder, up the wall of darkness to the shimmering pinwheel overhead. It seemed closer now, such that she viewed the veiny array almost from its lower edge. She turned farther, halfway round. The sections of the tremendous fan resembled the blades of a windmill, though its blades or petals were more numerous and didn't spin, only rippled a bit in a breeze she could not feel. Captivating, fascinating, like seaweed beneath a shallow sea. She found it hard to look away. She had to.

She spun back toward Pete. He'd made no move closer but seemed poised now, knees arched and knuckles pressed against the gravelly cave floor.

That was how it was going to be. All the way to sunrise at least. She needed a string with bells. Or a fence, preferably electric. And if she did doze off, would she awake as she fell? She needed some siren, some alarm, something that would go off if her grip relaxed. A sound grenade. The problem with those ideas was they would likely call the thing down on her. That and they were impossible from the start.

—What else do you know about this thing, Pete?

He turned to her slow. —Not a damn thing.

—Sure you do. You know it hunts by sound.

—I never said that.

—But you're scared of noise attracting it.

—Maybe I'm just being careful—like you should be.

—We've got to pass the time for a couple more hours at least. Why don't we play a game?

—Oh, what, like *I spy with my little eye maybe…something beginning with F—fucking giant monster?*

—I don't know, I thought more like charades.

—Please, Sue-*Min*, could you just try and keep quiet, and not make any sudden gestures?

—So you *do* know something about this thing and its habits…

—I'm just trying to be cautious. Maybe *you* could try too...

—Maybe I should've been more cautious when you were trying to rape me, how about that?

—Ha! You know you want it. Even now when you're playing hard to get. It's not rape when you're into it.

—How the hell am I into it?

—*You've been coming on to me from Day One.* I left you alone till now out of respect to Ron, but Ron's gone and we may not live to see the morning ourselves, so why not stop playing games and enjoy what time we have?

—How do you know for sure Ron's gone? Did you see what happened to him?

—He's not here. Where else would he be? Do you think he'd run away on us? Head back to the truck alone and leave us behind to deal with this craziness?

—Ron wouldn't do that. But now she wondered—could Ron still be alive? Had he found time to escape when the thing first appeared outside? Could it be he was going for help even now? But Ron didn't have the truck keys—far as she knew they remained in Pete's pocket. Who could he ask for help—the ranchers? They might just as likely shoot him on sight if he came knocking on their door at night. Ron wasn't leaving the canyon then.

She saw Pete nod in the gloom. —That's right. Where would he go anyway? Good luck with those ranchers. They wanted to shoot us the first time. How do you think they'd react if any of us showed up outside in the middle of the night?

—Let's change the subject. We don't know for sure where Ron is, so we shouldn't get carried away. Maybe he's waiting at the truck. Maybe he's trapped across the canyon. Maybe we'll find him in the morning.

—No, let's be real here. Ron is *gone*. Gone, gone, gone. Most likely *dead*. One way or another he ain't coming back. It's time for you to face that fact.

—You don't know that!

—It's obvious! How can you ignore it?

—Because I know Ron better than you.

—Oh really? Is that what you think? Who's known him since grade school? Who knows the name of the girl he lost his virginity to and where it happened? Who taught him how to shoot a .45? Who's lost count of the backcountry hikes we've taken together—up till now all without you?

As he said this Pete had begun to crawl forward on knuckles and knees. He moved slowly as if he thought she would not notice that way.

—Whoa right there Pete. Whoa and back up.

He froze but held his position, several feet forward of where he'd been before he began his little monologue.

—I'm only going to say this once. *Go back to the wall where you were before.*

He didn't move. She began to count in her head, wondering would she scream at ten, at twenty? She wasn't sure. She wasn't sure she could do it, trade a known threat for an unknown. The important thing though was for Pete to believe she would.

At twelve he hesitated, lurched and crawled back to the wall in reverse. Once he reached it she continued the conversation as if he never moved.

—Just because you've known him longer doesn't mean a thing. Who makes pillow talk with him? With whom does he share his deepest fears? Who knows his dreams? Do you know how he got that scar high up his right thigh? Do you know where his mother moved after she left them? Did you ever suck his cock? I doubt it. I know how he acts, what he'd do in this situation.

But *did* Ron have a chance? Or did that thing outside snap him up before he knew what got him? Slow streams of tears oozed down each of her cheeks. Perhaps their argument had no purpose other than to make her cry. She knew Ron was dead, despite all her hopes. She didn't know if Pete could see her crying, but she didn't dare look away. That might be a giveaway as to her emotional state, and if he saw her as vulnerable he might take it as another opportunity to advance. She knew now how fast he was. He was a jerk, a creeper, but he was in decent shape.

She fought her tears back till she thought she could speak clearly and returned to their conversation. —Look, Pete, let's not fight. It's not helping.

—No shit.

—Yeah, well I agree with you we've got to work together. We should talk about how we're going to get out of here.

—We're not going anywhere as long as that thing's outside. At least I'm not. You can do whatever you want I guess, but personally I'd prefer to have a witness when I tell this story to the police or the FBI or whoever. It's going to be way worse if I come back alone.

He had a point there. She imagined herself the sole survivor, telling the story to some detective in a gray room with a two-way mirror. Mental hospital, jail for life—that's how a lone survivor would likely end up. She considered again the possibility that Pete somehow sacrificed Ron to the monster. If he'd thought out the aftermath it would explain why he left her alive. One explanation anyway. Was it even the kind of monster that accepted sacrifices? And if it did, would that make it a god? She wondered what wishes or prayers it granted in response to a successful sacrifice. Wasn't Pete already looking for a pot of gold? Was this his plan to get it?

All this sacrifice stuff was pretty far out though. It was hard to picture Pete as any kind of priest or wizard. And what did she know about monsters anyway? Probably Pete's original story was true, how he'd gone to the cave mouth looking for Ron and spotted the gigantic night-obscuring thing instead. In that case she maybe should be grateful it hadn't been her—she might've rushed out there shouting Ron's name and that would've been the end for her *and* Pete as well. Disintegrated like the bat. Or maybe worse. Who knew what the unseen parts of this enormity might do, what claws and jaws were hidden in shadow?

—Hey. Pete spoke in a stage whisper. —Hey.

—Hey what?

—Why don't you come away from the entrance. You're going to attract that thing's attention. I don't think it even knows we're here so far. You don't need to be that close to the edge.

When she didn't respond he added —I'll stay right here. I promise I won't touch you.

—Yeah right.

—Honestly. Cross my heart and hope to die.

—Maybe you shouldn't hope that out loud.

—Whatever. Come away from the edge. It's not safe for either of us, you being there.

So far Pete's advice, his grasp of the situation, had actually been good. *Except for the attempted rape and all.* But he seemed to understand the monster situation. His plan to wait till morning made sense. If the thing didn't fade away with sunrise, they'd at least get some better sense of its dimensions, maybe spot some escape route or weakness. The ranchers might even report them missing if they didn't return to their truck by the end of the day. Or not—she pictured the hired hand using a backhoe to bury their truck in a trench. Next to a dozen others, all the way back to Model T's…

—Oh shit. *Don't move.*

Damn. What was Pete pulling now?

—Wha—?

—Shhh! Don't say anything, *and don't turn around.* There's something behind you.

Seriously? Just when she was ready to grant him a smidge of credence, he had to go and spring the oldest trick in the book? Yet he spoke slower and slightly louder than before, as if to give his words more gravity. And wasn't the point of that trick to *make* her turn around? Had Pete messed up his scheme or was there really something…

She turned. And saw—was it a *thing*, or an *effect*? An *event*? She could not be sure. It didn't help she'd turned from the wrong shoulder so she had to twist further at the hips to see it better. Now she was sideways to Pete, facing away, an alarm bell ringing in the back of her brain so long as he was out of sight.

Drifting in the air outside came a…ripple. A blur. She lacked the words. Approximately twice the span of her torso, the whatever it was had no distinct outline or shape. Or color. It hovered and twisted up the limited light like the air over heated pavement, the view through fountain glass. Not that there was much to see beyond the distortions themselves. It was as if a translucent flag drifted on its own, free of any pole, flapping in a nonexistent breeze.

Then as if she'd made eye contact or somehow caught its attention, it locked on a course and approached. She thought to scuttle backward but her muscles refused to respond. In seconds the region of ripples reached her…and passed right through her, so far as she could tell. She felt nothing as it struck, but immediately after she was convinced her flesh bore a coat of flat waxy scales, even beneath her clothes. She glanced at her bare forearms, saw nothing, ran her hands down them, felt nothing. By then the impression was gone.

She spun and saw the ripple or disturbance hovering some two meters past her, advancing no farther. Pete was huddled as far back in the cave as he could manage.

—Pete. Hey, Pete.

He did not respond.

—Pete, it's safe. It went right through me and I barely felt a thing. Don't worry.

He didn't answer, didn't move. She could see his face but couldn't tell if he was watching her or the drifting ripple. It hung a bit to the north, didn't seem interested in Pete at all—at least not yet. As she watched he raised his left hand just a few inches slowly and pointed toward her again. Then he hissed out one word —Others.

Sue-Min spun again and this time had to throw her left hand down to keep from losing her balance. It slid a few inches through the little cobbles till it found purchase then held.

Now she glimpsed a scatter of reddish hovering blobs, varying in size but all smaller than her head. A dozen, maybe two dozen. They advanced slowly, swirling about each other, swelling and distending, dumbbell to sphere to sausage and back. Flattening into discs. Other shapes. Flashing red to pink. When they reached the entrance they passed all around her on either side. None of them struck her or even came close.

Pete continued staring in what she presumed was terror—at the ripple, at the oncoming blobs, at her—she could not tell. Once inside the little cave the blobs wandered about while the ripple came to rest above the graveyard of moth wings. One blob drifted toward Pete and he contorted to avoid it, slouched backward to his elbows, almost to the ground. It exhibited no interest in him, stretching to a cylinder before reaching the wall above him instead and blinking out as it struck. But not quite all at once—it seemed to suck into the stone like a sloppy eater's spaghetti noodle. As she watched, the blobs all met the walls or floor or ceiling and disappeared one by one. One of the last wandered back, and before she could dodge, it struck her left shoulder. This time she felt a faint dampness, and the feeling lingered longer than the waxy sensation she experienced earlier.

The second the last blob was gone the ripple blinked out as well, sudden and complete, like a flat screen TV blinking off for the night.

The feeling of damp in her shoulder remained, though fading. She ran her hand over her shirt but it felt dry.

She found herself shaking. Maybe it was the encounter. Maybe it was just the early morning chill—no matter where you were, desert or jungle, it got really cold right around 4:00 a.m. Fieldwork taught her that. New Mexico,

Utah, Turkey, Belize—always the same, that's when the chill came. It was cold like that right now, which at least had to mean the dawn was almost upon them. She looked at her sleeping bag crumpled against the wall. Once you began to shiver it got hard to stop.

She brought her knees up, hugged them again to her chest. —Well Pete, you're the expert. Any idea what those things were?

A long moment passed before he answered —I dunno. Pause. —They must have something to do with the thing outside. Its breath, its spit, something it sheds? Its babies, its eggs? Some kind of parasites that slid off its skin? Hallucinations it caused us to see?

—Two of them hit me. The big flickering thing and one of the blobs. They all went right through me. I felt them though. I can still kind of feel where the blob hit. It feels wet but it's not. Whatever they were I don't think they were hallucinations exactly. Not the way I felt them.

—Whatever they were I think you attracted them sitting where you are. I wish you would come away from there before you attract something worse.

—I already did. I attracted *you*. And *you* tried to *rape* me. Better I take my chances with this monster and its friends.

—Don't talk that way Sue! I'm not like that! I swear. *I swear on my mother's grave.* I swear on the American flag. If you come back here I *will* leave you alone. No means no, *I get that now*, I know. I was lonely, that was all. And scared. I admit it, I was scared. I'm still scared. We're both scared. Not all men are like what you think. I just had a bad moment. I'm OK now. You're safe now.

—I'm scared of *you*, don't you get that? And I have very good reason.

She couldn't see his facial expression but she saw him hang his head. Bullshit acting.

—I'm sorry. I'm really sorry. Please come back this way. I won't touch you again. But we'll both be safer if you come away from the cave mouth. That much I'm sure of.

She regarded his vague huddled form in the rear of the space, tried to gauge his sincerity, his acting ability, the ratio of one to the other. His fear. Her fear. *A leopard doesn't change its spots*, something her adoptive father used to say. Fear could do a lot though.

Sue-Min glanced outside and up. Was the bat-melting blossom really closer now, larger? How much longer before it reached out for her? Her gut told her Pete was right at least about the danger of her location. Hadn't Ron most likely attracted its attention simply by standing in this very spot? She envisioned the pinwheel dipping and spinning, licking her up with a flick of one immense petal…

—Please Sue-Min? Please come away from there.

She waited, considered, weighed her fears. —Okay. First off you understand I'll scream as loud as I can *the second* you come near me, right?

—Yeah, no problem, I'll leave you alone, just like I said. I swear.

—Second, you need to move as far as you can into that sort of alcove behind you.

He immediately began wriggling the final few feet into the last rounded extremity of the shelter. He had to hunch just a little once he was all the way in.

She took a deep breath, said —All right. Not one move or I will scream like nothing you ever heard before.

—Yeah, yeah, okay. I get it. Just come away from the entrance.

She began to crawl toward the rear of the cave, the dusty cobbles wedging beneath her kneecaps again. She wished she had gotten her kneepads from her pack, but she hadn't expected to do any caving on this hike so left them behind. Not that this dinky rockshelter with no real dark zone counted as a genuine cave. She kept Pete in the corner of her eye the entire time, flicked glances at him every few feet.

At the wall she considered her sleeping bag. Her bag and Ron's, still zipped as one. She eyeballed Pete, looked back at the bag, decided not to slither inside. Instead she sat in the gravel with her back to the wall and tugged the bag up over her knees to her neck, smoothed it down along her sides. She wasn't going to get trapped again. Using it as a blanket, if she had to she could jettison it as a decoy, a distraction, like squid ink, a lizard's tail. If he just didn't get hold of her head or her hair…

—You stay there now.

Through the gloom she saw him cross himself, swiping his hand right to left across his chest, a casual-looking gesture, not the full Catholic way. —Cross my heart. I swear.

Too much adrenalin coursed through her yet to sleep. That and she knew she needed to pee soon. Which had been a problem the entire trip. Earlier she at least had Ron to keep lookout. Now? She could retreat to the corner opposite from Pete—or the entrance—but she had no way to keep him from staring at her all the while. She tensed at the thought of squatting, watching out for Pete spying on her, and trying to get low enough not to spatter. She'd almost rather pee guy style over the edge and take her chances with the monster.

And what about Pete? How long before he too needed to pee? Would he somehow exploit that necessity as an opportunity to expose himself to her—and that exposure to initiate something worse? Their situation made the simplest things suddenly unpleasant and complex.

She could wet herself under her cover, but she wasn't ready to go that far just yet. If they got out of here they were presumably going to the police or a ranger station, and she didn't want to go like that. Jeans pee-stained and reeking would not be an asset to her credibility. She considered her options. Pee herself where she sat. Pee at the entrance, which was probably how that thing got Ron. Get as far from Pete as she could to pee, which would not be far in this little cave.

She clenched against an urge fast becoming a throbbing ache, knowing she could hold it only so much longer before the choice would be made for her. Not much longer.

After several minutes fidgeting she turned slowly toward Pete. And just then, Pete spoke —I've got to take a leak, and I don't want to go up to the edge, not with that thing out there. Will you look away till I'm done? I'll do the same for you if you want me to. Promise.

That was unexpected. But he sounded sincere, so far as she could tell. As if *she* wanted to watch *him* anyway… Of course he could always rush her if she looked away. And why shouldn't *she* go first? Then again, if he took his turn without doing anything weird, wouldn't she feel safer addressing her own need? After a moment to ponder she said —*Okay, deal,* and faced to her right, cheek pressed against the vaguely moist rear wall of the cave. —Just tell me when you're done, okay?

She heard his boots grind over the pebbles, then faintly his stream as it spattered the wall. She pictured him trying to write his initials or some stupid thing, but knew that probably wasn't true, not under the circumstances. He spoke before he was done —Oh shit.

—What? She answered but did not turn.

—It just hit me. Arizona doesn't *do* daylight savings time. It's still an hour earlier here.

—What time is your phone set to? Mountain or Arizona? It doesn't matter unless you changed it for here.

—No. It's still set for Albuquerque. Mountain.

—Then sunrise should be around when we're expecting it. Pause. —Can I turn around now?

Faint, she heard him zip up. —Yeah, yeah, go ahead. I'm done.

—Check your phone. What's it say now?

She turned now, watched him struggle to dredge the device from his pocket. Then he found it, flicked it open and thumbed it on. And waited. For nothing. —It's dead.

He tucked it back in his pocket and slumped as he sat, for several seconds his outline dissolving even further in the shadows, and then he came straight again sudden enough to make her jerk backward even though he was nowhere close.

—I'm going to get something out of my pack, okay? I promise I won't come near you, so just stay cool. I'll go over, get it out, and come back here. No screaming, okay?

She could tell he was watching her, waiting.

—Okay. But go slow. Only not too slow. Get it done and go back.

He began to crawl toward the pack. She pushed back against the wall as far as she could go. It was only once he'd actually begun to rummage in his pack that she remembered he might have a gun. She sucked in a gasp just as he held up his prize.

—Got it!

—Got what? If he had a Glock out, she didn't want to play games. Best to establish new ground rules right away. They both knew he wouldn't dare shoot it here.

—Glowstick. He began to back up toward his corner.

Something drained from inside Sue-Min and she almost laughed. A spasm ran through her and she had to fight off the shakes, but when she realized he still might've got his gun out too, ice water welled up to refill the vacuum within her and she calmed.

When she looked over she saw the cold green glow already defining Pete's face, his knees up to block the light from the cave mouth all he could. Then he shook his head. —*What the fuck?*

—What?

—My watch says *9:12. No way* is that right. We haven't been here *that* freakin' long. The sun would be up, it wouldn't matter *what* time zone, *what* canyon we're down.

She struggled to process this new frustration. The only timepiece left to them and it had run amok. Nothing was working right. Everything was breaking down. On top of that she still had to go. *Now.*

—Okay, so while you're figuring that out, it's my turn to pee. Will you do the same for me?

—The same what?

—As I did for you. Promise not to watch while I pee.

Several seconds of silence then —Yeah yeah, of course. Fair's fair.

—If you don't I'll—

—You'll scream. I know. I won't look. Promise.

She doubted him but she had no more choice. She made her way around the wall, skirting the moth wings, to the place she calculated as farthest from Pete. She squatted so as to face him, keep some kind of lookout, but far as she could tell in the dark, he kept his word.

Finished, she realized the only paper they'd brought remained buried in Ron's pack. Shuffling over there dripping with pants around ankles was not an option, so with wiping a lost cause, she waited and wiggled as many long seconds as she dared before she tugged up her jeans and underwear and scuttled back to her sleeping bags, feeling that much more unclean.

Yet sleep still would not come, even with the urinary urge removed. Sue-Min continued watching Pete though she saw little more than a blurred dim form. Of all the people to be stuck with in this insane situation. Of course, she'd seen him enough to know that he *was* decent looking, in a cornfed white guy kind of way. Sort of guy who was destined for a career in sales if he didn't become a cop. Sandy blond buzz cut, bulked out biceps. He'd go to fat once he had a family, but he didn't and hadn't yet. Stamina would be his best quality in bed. This was a guy who could do pushups for an hour. If only he weren't such a creeper. Yuck.

She shuddered to shake off that train of thought and marshaled her mental focus back to priorities. They might both die here. How long could they survive? They had, she guessed, half a water bottle each plus maybe a backup liter stowed. She knew she did, was pretty sure about Ron. A handful of *Clif* bars stashed in their packs, possibly some other food too.

Her pack held a little Ziploc of walnut halves, another of carrot sticks. That was all. She was pretty sure Pete packed some jerky, and Ron had maybe brought a couple foil-wrapped single serving vacuum packs of salmon or tuna that should still be in his pack. And the worse than useless popcorn. Even if they could make a fire... She shuddered at the thought of those tiny explosions in their silence.

If they stayed trapped for long, water would be their problem before food. She'd noted several fuzzy streaks of algae along the back wall that meant slow trickling seeps, imagined taking turns with Pete licking dirty water from the wall, each of them fighting not to gag or puke. Could she even do it? Could Pete? How thirsty would they have to be first? And would the seeps be enough? No water pooled below them, so the flow could only be agonizingly slow.

Pete interrupted her speculations —I'm thinkin' if this thing outside isn't gone in half an hour, I'm goin' out anyway, gonna try to sneak past it, over it, under it, whatever. She saw the faint illumination of the glowstick brush his face. —I don't think it's even...

He broke off and slid to his knees then drooped as if deflating till his forehead touched the pebbly floor, groaning a low pained groan all the way down. Sue-Min rose and stepped toward him, closed the gap by near half, but went no closer. He might be feigning only to fool her —Pete? Pete, are you all right?

He took a long time to respond, groaning again before he half-rose and spoke. —My watch. Please tell me it's fucked up. It only says 9:15 now. It's been way more than three minutes since I checked it last time, and it said 9:12 then. What the hell? What's going on?

—Either way shouldn't the sun be up by now? Even down this canyon and on Arizona Time, we should have sunlight after 9:00 a.m.

—That's what I mean. We should have sun but we don't. It's like time is speedin' up and slowin' down. Maybe this thing outside is like a giant spider that builds its web out of time instead of silk.

—Now you're talking crazy talk.

—Am I? Then *you* explain this shit. First it's four in the morning, then all of a sudden it's *nine*. Then half an hour, maybe an hour passes, but it's only three minutes on my watch. What's causin' that? That thing might be weavin' a *web* out of time...or maybe it just inhabits some kind of *time vortex* it found, and it sits like an ant lion in its pit, waitin' for its next victim. Which tonight just happens to be us. Or this morning, whichever it really is…

—The sun's got to come up sometime. I mean, we *are* in a cave, in a canyon. It's going to take a while longer here, that's all. Don't you think the sky looks lighter outside now? I think it does, a little. Most likely your watch is screwed up. Maybe you bumped it climbing up here.

—I didn't bump it. And it was workin' fine before.

—Well whatever. Maybe these rocks have a high magnetic content, maybe they're messing with your watch. I've heard of caves in El Malpais like that, where a compass doesn't work right. Whatever it is, there has to be a natural explanation.

—Oh yeah? *Does that thing outside have a natural explanation?*

—Maybe. Maybe we just don't know the explanation yet.

—Bull-*shit*! That *thing* is a demon or an alien or something from another dimension. There's nothing rational or natural about it!

—Come on Pete. I'm scared as you are, but we've got to keep it together. Talking about demons isn't doing either of us any good. We should be talking about how we're going to get out of here.

—Okay, fine. Hey Sue-*Min*, do you know how we're gonna get out of here?

—I still think your idea of waiting till sunrise was a good one.

—Except maybe there isn't going to *be* any sunrise. Not for us.

—*There has to be.* It's just late because of our location, the canyon, the cave…

Pete rested hunched now, haunches on calves, knuckles of his clenched fists jammed down amidst the pebbles.

—What if the sun *never* rises? What if we're caught in this monster's vortex forever?

—What if we wait just a little longer and see if the sun comes up and the monster goes away? Isn't that worth waiting for, when we can walk right out of here, maybe even find Ron? It was your idea anyway.

Pete just shook his head and groaned some more. For several reasons she was trying to keep up a tough front but his apparent collapse wasn't helping. Not one bit. The truth was his comments had begun to get to her, especially his forecast of unending darkness. Shivering, she hugged herself, hoped he didn't see.

Sue-Min told herself Pete's watch was just bumped or broken. It might even start spinning backward next—and if it did, would it take them back to when Ron was still with them? Or were the movements of its damaged hands altogether meaningless, irrelevant to their current situation, the malfunction simply coincidence?

Pete rocked in place, spoke a cryptic sentence —*I say to myself that the earth is extinguished, though I never saw it lit.*

Sue-Min shivered. Her cave-mate was going fast from creep*er* to creep*y*. —What the hell was that about?

He turned to her. —It's from this play I was in, back in my UNM days. Beckett. I have this jones you know, for nerdy smart girls, and one I dated for a while was a theater major. She had this idea I'd be a good actor, kept pushing me to try out for plays she was producing. I finally did and got a part in this Beckett thing. It was weird shit—I played this guy in a wheelchair who kept a bloody handkerchief over his face most of the time. I still remember most of my lines though. My memory's good like that.

Sue-Min struggled to wrap her thoughts around the image of Pete the thespian but it was too much for her to process. Her mind was already overloaded and all she really wanted to do was go back to sleep, return to the sleeping bag whose upper half still smelled like Ron. Was this faint and fading fragrance all she had left, all that remained? She could not accept that. Ron was resilient, Ron was Ron. Unless she saw definite evidence of his death, she would keep holding out hope he was still alive. And probably needing their help if he was…

She shook her head again to clear it then asked Pete —What does your watch say now? She spoke without turning in his direction.

He did not answer immediately, did not turn toward her, did not even look at his watch. Sue-Min kept her peace. It was not as if she had anywhere to go right at the moment.

Finally Pete examined his watch as she observed him. She remembered it as an old school analog device, an inheritance she guessed, his dad's or his granddad's. He stared a long minute at the face beneath the crystal but neither moved nor spoke. Finally he said to her without turning —Still 9:15. The second hand moves but I don't think the other hands have even budged from where they were before.

—That's weird.

—You're tellin' me.

His voice was bitter, hopeless, beyond even cynicism. Sue-Min considered how much worse the betrayal of his watch would hurt him if it really were an heirloom. She turned away from him toward the opening and…

—Pete! Look! Look outside!

He turned slowly but once he faced the exit she knew he saw it too. The sky *was* lighter now, what she could see of it to either side of the silent immensity at least. No question. The shape of the thing did not resolve itself in relief and continued to defy her efforts to make sense of it overall.

—Do you see it? The sky is definitely getting brighter.

—But that thing is still there.

—Still here *now*… We don't know how it got here. We don't know how or when it might leave.

—*If* it leaves. How do we know it's not here to stay?

—Can you be a little less pessimistic? It was your idea anyway about it leaving with the light. Don't you want to test out that thought, see if you were right?

—I don't want to know if I was *wrong*. I just want to get out of here. We've got to find a way to escape.

—Let's see how bright it gets and what the monster does. Come on—if it's really after 9:00 now, we should definitely be getting sunlight down here, even if it's not direct.

It wasn't quite sunlight, but something *was* changing in the sky, a dim glow visible to either side of the enormous entity, an unusual brightness, neither the indigo of twilight nor the poet's rosy fingered dawn. Nor the sun's normal clean yellow-white. Something was wrong with this light. Something was *off*. She couldn't even put a color to what was more a decrease in darkness than any presence of actual light, and offered no direction of origin as far as she could tell. The central bulk that bore the blossom thing grew no clearer, even in contrast at its sides. The blossom itself grew no less bright.

She glanced at Pete again but he remained concentrated on his watch, his left wrist held close to his face, just below the green tube in his right. Without turning away from it he spoke —You really should come see this, Sue.

—I'll pass.

—Seriously. The hands are all running backwards now. Come see.

Sue-Min didn't like the sound of that but she was no way going to get close enough to see for herself. She was just going to have to trust him about the watch. She was pretty sure she could grant him that, at least from a distance. Even if what he said were true what the hell did it mean for them? She could see the sickly glimmer from outside spreading into the cave like a thin liquid spill, but it signified nothing to her yet.

Sue-Min watched the slow growing glow and Pete watched his watch. The monster remained shapeless, motionless. She glanced at Pete and back and the monster was gone. Fast as that. She missed whether it sank into the canyon or ascended into space. Or blinked out suddenly, faded away slow... No sound marked its departure, no flash of light. No wind. Shouldn't some kind of sonic boom have erupted as air rushed into the space it left empty?

Pete remained fixated on his watch. She called to him, a little louder than she would've dared before.

—Pete. Pete, look!

He looked. Paused.

—What happened? Is it doing something?

—I think it's *gone*. It was sudden. It just...blinked out. Well, *I blinked* and *it* was gone.

Pete scrambled toward her. She felt a fresh rush of adrenalin but held her ground. What could she do if he really came at her? She should've already grabbed the knife from her pack for protection, or even better the Glock from Ron's. Too late.

He passed her without a glance though, arrived at the entrance. From the dripline Pete looked every direction. —You're right. Holy shit. It's gone. Almost like we dreamed it up.

He stood and hurled the glowstick into the void. Its arc quickly dropped it from her sight, but she saw Pete's chin dip as he followed it down.

—Nothing. It's really gone.

He turned to Sue-Min. —Are you ready to get outta here? For all we know it might come back. We should make time while we can.

Sue-Min was not so sure they should leave the relative safety of the cave. If such a colossus could vanish with neither warning nor coda, how easily could it reappear, catch them in the open? Perhaps that was its plan.

Yet Pete already had his headlamp on and was over the lip, on his way down. —*C'mon! Let's go!*

She wanted to shout —*Wait*, call for some discussion of options, seek some consensus. But Pete was on the move and hadn't given her any chance for talk. And he had the keys to the truck.

She scrambled to the edge, hung over and called to him. —Wait! Give me a minute! I at least have to put my boots on.

Already twice her length below he looked up, nodded, said merely — Hurry!

—What about our packs?

—*Leave the packs.* We've got to move fast, travel light, get back to the truck as quick as we can. We can pick up our packs when we come back with the cops or whoever. Nobody's going to touch our stuff here meantime.

She grabbed her own light from where she'd left it by her pack—safe to use it now she guessed, hoped—and began lacing her boots. Pete was right. Her pack would only overbalance her on the way back down. They had a window of safety and they'd have to hurry through while it stayed open. However briefly it did. They had no way to tell how long that might be.

When she hunched over the edge she found Pete waiting in the same spot below. His presence gave her comfort, a surprise in itself. Her hands dug for purchase among the dusty pebbles but her feet found good holds, and soon she was below the rim, her hands on solid stone, heading for Pete. He didn't move. As she made her way toward him, he offered encouragement —C'mon, yeah, that's it. Right this way. His steady voice provided a beacon without her looking down.

Soon she was right above him, and for a moment she feared he might grab her ankle and yank her right off the slope, the last witness to whatever he'd done to Ron gone. That spasm of terror passed and a fresh impulse seized her, the desire to kick Pete right in the face, send *him* tumbling into the slot below. He would never bother her again if she did. Never bother *anyone*. But the keys... How badly broken might his body wind up, wedged in the crack below? Would the keys be accessible? What if they flipped from his pocket into the filthy pitch water? She'd never find them, shuddered at the thought of having to reach into that cold opaque foulness, grope blind amongst the sticks and bones. Even if she made it back to the truck without the keys, what could she do? She had no real idea how to hotwire a vehicle. Seek help from the ranchers? Hike out all the way on her own? What if the police found her bootprint pressed onto Pete's forehead?

The moment passed. She could not do it. She was no murderer. Her Baptist upbringing on the farm held that far.

Pete continued his descent and she followed. Though she had to feel with her feet for footholds, she found her handholds on the ribbed rock face with relative ease, and descended keeping just above Pete. They shared no more words till they arrived right above the coffee colored creek at the bottom of the crack, where Pete had to comment —Phase One done at least. And we're making good time I think…not that I can tell from my watch anymore… Now we've gotta get up and outta here. Are you ready?

—Yeah.

She was scanning ahead and behind for any remnant of Ron's broken body, but she saw nothing in her little headlamp's limited beam beyond the stony V, the stagnant water, the scattered broken ends of branches or bones. No Ron. And still no monster.

Pete began to chimney along the crack back the way they'd come, and two seconds later she followed. He didn't look back.

As Sue-Min rushed to keep up, her left hand slipped and her foot sunk half up her calf in the stagnant ink. Right off she felt the cold and cried out, an exclamation half gasp half yelp. She stopped her fall with her forearm, her submerged foot finding no bottom, and wriggled to brace herself anew, but before she could yank her wet foot free, Pete was there to take her arm, offer support. She would've shooed him off but her scraped palm already throbbed and the water was cold and who knew what worse?

—C'mon, he said, —Grab my arm, and she paused only a moment before wrapping first her right hand then her left around his bicep. She could feel the damage to her hand—after everything, she'd forgotten her gloves *again. Damn.* Pete raised her till her boot rose dripping from the black wet and held her in place until she could get her hands back against the sides of the crevice higher up. She shook her foot back and forth, for what little good it did. The water had run down inside her boot.

—You okay? Did you hurt yourself?

—Just wet. And angry at myself for slipping.

—Not your fault. It's dark and we're both rushing. Maybe I was rushing too much. Sorry. It must feel gross.

—Don't make me think about it.

—Yeah. Understood. Let's keep going then. I want to get up and out of this canyon as quick as we can. If that thing comes back, I figure it will show up here, and I want to be far away by then.

He led on and she followed, taking extra care now to maintain three points of contact with the walls at all times, grimacing each time she moved her left foot and felt her sodden wool sock squish inside her boot.

The limited beam from Sue-Min's weak LED light fell mainly on Pete's advancing back, the khaki shirt he wore a broad reflective canvas. As she watched his halting forward motion she considered the exchange they just shared, the way he helped her. He'd been civil, gentlemanly, even compassionate. The same guy who tried to force himself on her only a couple hours ago. Maybe being afraid a monster would eat him brought out the best in his personality. If only a giant monster were chasing him every minute in his life, he might become a decent guy, maybe even pick up where he left off on his theater career, learn to tap dance, acquire an interest in show tunes…

She almost laughed at her thoughts but caught the laugh in her throat so only a strangled hiccup emerged.

Pete didn't stop or turn around but asked —What was that? You okay? You need a break?

—No, I'm fine. Let's keep going.

Soon they reached a spot Pete identified as where they'd come down before, though it all looked the same to her in the dark. How hard would it be to retrace their route if they didn't come up in the right place?

But Pete was asking if she was ready, and why argue? They began their ascent, which was shorter and easier than their descent and did not take long.

Once at the top they followed the cliff edge back, scanning for landmarks in what terrain their lights revealed, searching for where they'd first come out on the canyon's rim, each suggesting this tree might or might not look familiar, that bush, this twisted snag. They could see only hints of the opposite face, and nothing of the chasm now far below. The odd gray light Sue-Min thought might have been dawn had departed, and the moon had set as well. The stars, though bright now, offered very little illumination.

Neither of them spoke about it aloud, but she was certain Pete shared her fear they had come up *past* the point they were seeking, and were now wandering further up Blossom Creek Canyon than they'd been so far—and if they were, how long would it be before they figured it out? They might go a mile if the canyon ran that long before it boxed off.

When Pete at last claimed they'd arrived at that spot where they first reached the cliff, Sue-Min was sure he was wrong. She would recall *that* outcrop, *that* juniper leaning out over the void. She didn't argue though. What good would it do? Following Pete was easy enough. If he were wrong, they'd still find their way in time, though they might have to double back. With her own volition exhausted, allowing Pete to lead was the simple option. Let him get the credit or take the blame if they got lost. She wanted nothing but to get going, get in the truck, get out of the canyon, get help. They progressed into the wood. She stopped trying to decide whether she'd come this way before.

They picked their way between outcrops and trees, leafless branches showing stark in their headlamps against the black background. Sue-Min began to consider just *how* lost they could get out here. But they had to hit the Blue River eventually, didn't they?

—Whoa! Pete stopped cold, spoke in his stage whisper again, left hand splayed out behind his back as if to hold her back. —You see that?

—See what? And then she did. A pale pink gleam backlit the trees ahead, shining the same hue as the blobs that wandered through the cave.

She took the two strides that brought her up beside Pete and halted, but she couldn't see any better from there, just the trees silhouetted against a strange stretch of rosy light. —What is it?

—Damned if I know. I thought it might be the dawn for a sec, but no, it's wrong.

—Is it that *thing*? What if all we did was walk right up to its lair?

—I don't think so. The color isn't right, and the light starts at the ground. That thing would have to be lying down. Let's get a little closer.

Together they picked their way to the edge of a clearing, saw ahead sheets of diffuse pink light rising from the ground—no, not the ground itself but from rows of stones. It was the same place they'd puzzled over the strange linear alignments of rocks. A cold light rose now from the rocks—or rather from the patterns they formed on the ground, as if these arcs and arms marked the foundations of translucent walls rising into the sky, not fading overhead so much as growing hard to follow from the angle of their height. Sue-Min wondered how the effect would look from high above.

She spoke softly —No way am I going near there. Not after those things hit me in the cave.

—You said they didn't hurt you, that you didn't feel anything.

—I said I didn't feel *much* but I didn't feel nothing either. I don't even want to think about what the aftereffects might be. I don't want to think about *anything* right now, Pete. I just want to get the hell out of here.

—Yeah. Damn. Well I agree. Let's not go close to that light. At least we know we're on the right track though—we definitely came by those stones on the way out. Now I'm kind of sorry we walked through them even then—if that's some kind of radiation they're giving off they might've been doing it before only we couldn't see it because the sun was too bright.

They skirted the open patch to what Sue-Min thought was the south, all but dodging from tree to tree and keeping a watch on the curving rosy walls as if the light might somehow notice them. The light did nothing but ascend and glow—it neither dimmed nor shimmered nor brightened nor moved. It showed no sign it recognized their presence, but they were glad to get well around it nonetheless.

As Pete said, at least they knew where they were. Sort of. They had passed the stones before, come right across them. Their path *had* come this way. Now if they could pick up its thread from here and follow it back.

Pete led the way until at last they came to the edge of a ridge. Sue-Min was sure they were somewhere near the spot from where she'd last glimpsed the truck the day before. Pete agreed. —Let's hope our luck holds out.

Their *luck*…the word struck Sue-Min as absurd in this context. How could anyone see their experiences as *lucky*? What prize had Ron won? Nothing held the same meaning anymore. Words had become as unreliable as Pete's watch.

They began following the ridge down. Though she could see nothing of the abyss to their left, and only the barest outlines of the mountains in the west, she was sure the hidden valley of the Blue lay below. They made good time down, the only mishap when Sue-Min stumbled once and fell against a trunk, scraping her hurt hand even worse. Again Pete came to her aid but this time she waved him off. Him touching her once was enough.

They reached the valley floor. They crossed the meager Blue. They did not find the truck. Pete cursed and kicked the ground, held his arms out, spun around. —It was right here. I'm sure! Those fucking rednecks! They took it!

Sue-Min shone her fading light on the ground. —I don't see any tracks. There should be tracks if the truck was here. The ground is damp enough from the river we're leaving tracks right now. See? She stepped with her left, lifted her foot, pointed at the shallow imprint of her boot sole fixed in her beam.

Pete stepped toward her, saw, turned to view the path of his own passage. —What the...?

Sue-Min meanwhile spun in a slow circle, and around 260 degrees caught a gleam as of chrome or glass. She saw it through the shadows of the shut gate. They were inside the gate and on the ranch. —Pete, look, *there*. She pointed. He turned and directed his light at the gate. Did he see the truck parked beyond? Was that what she had seen?

She turned again at a sound, a sort of grunt or huff behind her. Something rustled in the brush. She could not see much, but was that the golden glint of an eye in the night?

—Pete, I think a bull is behind us.

He looked back, and though he didn't say what he saw, he spoke softly but firmly —Run for the gate. And he ran.

Sue-Min ran too, hit the gate and grappled up its aluminum struts, always expecting a horn to pierce her kidney, her buttock, her thigh, toss her to the ground where she could be trampled and gored. Two strands of barbed wire ran across the top of the gate, the gap only a few inches. —Here, said Pete beside her, and lifted the bottom wire with a gloved hand between two barbs. —Go!

She levered up sideways, hugging the top rail, and slipped beneath the wire. Her feet hit the ground and she took two steps before she remembered Pete, rushed back to the gate and returned the favor, raising the wire with both hands.

It would've sucked to come all this way just to get killed by a bull. But they were over the gate, and no bull had rushed them. Now they'd be safe once they got in the truck. They'd escaped the monster, they'd escaped the bull. All they needed now was to escape the Blue.

The truck stood where they parked it. Intact.

Pete looked at her —I was sure those ranchers did something with it. I thought it would be gone, I really did.

—It looks okay. She walked around to the passenger side. Tires and windows all good. No visible damage.

—Yeahhh. Then —Let's get outta here.

—You've still got the keys, right?

—Hell yeah I do! He drew the keys from his right pants pocket and unlocked the driver's side door. He started the truck first then unlocked her door from the inside. Chivalry was dead for him once again. Sue-Min found this return to form almost reassuring after the out of character manners and kindness he'd shown twice during their escape.

The moment she joined him and had the door shut, even before she had her belt on, he swung them in a backwards curve toward the signs, then straightened the wheel and they were on their way out.

—Made it, Pete said. —Thank God!

Sue-Min had heard many examples of people lost or trapped then rescued only by the alleged *grace of God*. Those who called it that ignored all the people who didn't survive. What had God done for those folks? Were they denied his grace? What had God done for Ron? How was Pete more deserving than Ron? How was she?

They rode in silence at first, Pete navigating the twists and bumps, obviously going as fast as he dared in the darkness. After more than a minute he turned to her and said —Wanna see something really scary?

—Seriously? Are you fucking kidding?

—Yeah, I was kidding. It's a line from a movie. I guess you haven't seen it. Oh well, your loss. You would've laughed if you got it.

Half a silent minute passed, then —How about a joke?

She had no will to argue. —Sure. Whatever.

—Okay, so it's the Old West, on a train from Houston to El Paso. This beautiful woman is riding unescorted on the train, and they're barely out of the station before an obvious New Yorker turns to her and asks her if she'll get it on with him between cars for two dollars. The woman hides her blushing face behind her fan and says loudly —Will no man here defend a woman's honor?

About two seconds later this Texan gets up and without a word draws and shoots the Yankee right through the heart, then sits down again like it was nothing. The lady says —Thank you sir, for defending my honor.

—Honor, hell, the old cowboy says, and spits tobacco. —I'm not letting any Easterner come out here and raise the price of women in Texas.

Sue-Min stared ahead at the emptiness beyond their headlights while the truck jounced over ruts in the ungraded road. She took a series of long deep breaths. But she couldn't hold it in.

—That's your idea of a joke, Pete? That super-sexist bullshit? That's the kind of stuff you think is funny?

—Aw, c'mon, lighten up. That's a classic! And it's not against women—it's anti-Texan. Everyone in New Mexico likes to make fun of Texans. It's a *tradition*!

—Just when I began to think you might have a decent side, you remind me what an asshole you are. Are you trying to make *sure* I report your rape attempt when we get to a police station?

Right off she recognized her mistake. They were still in Pete's truck, still in a remote area. He could do about anything. She began to estimate how far a lead she could get on foot if she jumped out and ran when he stopped the truck.

—I didn't try to rape you! I flirted with you and you turned me down. End of story. Nothing wrong with that, except maybe your loss.

—I didn't *turn you down*! I threatened to yell loud enough the monster outside would hear! She imagined explaining this in her testimony, in a police station, in a courtroom. How much of her story was monster-dependent? Sue-Min clenched her fists, choked down her response, looked straight ahead. And without a thought she began to scream, pounding the dashboard with bloody palms as she allowed it all to pour out in a long wordless cry sectioned only by her necessary breath. Ron, the rape attempt, the monster…she howled it all out.

—Stop it! Pete shouted, —Stop it stop it stop it! You've *got* to lighten up! In her peripheral vision she saw him shake his head side to side, though he did not slow the truck.

She stopped screaming, though not because of Pete. She finally felt done.

—Look, I just want to get out of here, get to a police station, tell them Ron is missing, get a rescue op started. Anything else…it can wait. So please just drive, and no more jokes, okay?

—Sure, sure. You got no sense of humor anyway.

He paused then added —You really think there's a chance Ron is still alive out there?

—I don't know. If he's not we need to find his body at least. The image came to her unbidden—Ron's broken body, jammed into the crack, face down in the foul dark water.

—We don't know what happened to him. He might still be alive.

—True, I suppose, but what do you think the police will say if we talk about weird lights and monsters? We need to get our stories straight before—

The truck lurched suddenly, wheels rumbling against the undercarriage. Pete wrestled with the steering wheel.

—What the hell was that?

—I don't know! It was like the road surface shifted underneath us or something. Probably we went through some mud or sand or—

The ground buckled beneath them and lifted the whole truck suddenly upward. Metal crumpled, wheels spun in air and Sue-Min felt that sick too-fast elevator feeling—then the vast shimmering petals spread across the great dark bulk below and her stomach dropped out altogether. For a moment before they tumbled in they saw what opened at the center of the bloom. Then they lost all sight.

THE CROAKER

Michael cupped the steaming coffee mug in his hands to chase the chill his fingers caught on the walk from his father's house. He still hadn't found where the old man kept the keys to his car. Hoping to spot Donna the moment she arrived, he bobbed his head side to side for a clear view of the parking lot and any cars pulling off 22. But the windows beside his booth were painted up with some seasonal bullshit, making it difficult to see outside. Charlie Brown and the Great Pumpkin. Vines and pumpkins and sheaves of hay, the backs of the painted patterns flattened and drab. Charlie Brown, Jeez. Didn't that kid ever get old and die? He was older than Michael, yet he never kicked that football, never talked to the pretty girl. Why did people still watch that stuff? It was goddamn depressing.

The last time Michael sat in the Sunset Diner was the night his dad took him to dinner to say goodbye. The divorce and all that. Michael had only a vague memory of what the diner looked like then, still some resemblance to an old Pullman car no doubt, but the owners had obviously remodeled and expanded the place. His dad told him *order whatever you want* and Michael chose *Toasted Bagel with Butter and Jelly* off the dessert menu. When his dad said *That's not a dessert*, Michael showed it to him right there with the cheesecake, the puddings, the pies. The old man opened his mouth to argue or *talk some sense into him,* then closed it again and slumped in his seat.

Michael remembered that bagel. The waitress had served the two toasted halves on one plate, overlapping slightly like the bread beneath an open face sandwich, crisp and glistening with butter under a thin purple layer of translucent grape jelly. *He remembered it as the best damn bagel he ever ate.* And he remembered staring down and eating it at a condemned man's pace, severing little sections of the split toroid with knife and fork while his dad kept talking, asking him questions he ignored. The bagel remained in his memory but his father's words were gone. Now his father was gone too. Michael still ate his bagels with butter and jelly whenever he could, but they never tasted quite the same, the way they did in his memory. Nor had he seen a bagel served that way on any dessert menu since, this current incarnation of the Sunset Diner included. One more thing gone forever.

That was his past, a photo album with more gaps and empty pages than pics, like a map of the same Southwest desert his mom hauled him off to three miserable weeks later—a few cities, a few scattered towns, and vast uninhabited stretches of sand and scrub, mountains, national forest. Back in the jammed up Jersey burbs for the old man's funeral, he recognized a few of the streets but none of the houses, not anymore. As far as the snapshots in his memory remained, none looked the same. New siding, new paintjobs, new landscaping. New residents too, except for his dad, the last of the original owners on his block.

A childhood nightmare fluttered higher within him—driving down the street that should have been right around the corner from his family's house, the old man at the wheel, nearly home—only it was *not* the street around the corner from their house. The houses and the street looked almost the same, but they weren't, each house was altered, unfamiliar in some decisive way. Suddenly they were lost in a labyrinth of *almost*, where each turn they took only brought them to more streets and houses not *quite* the same as their street or their house, always promising the known around the next corner, never delivering. Though the denouement of his dream was long forgotten, neither it nor his wider distrust of suburban reality ever fully left him. As a kid, any time he biked out of sight of his own home, he eyed each house he passed for evidence of deception, shifting, impermanence. His route might grow unfamiliar at any time.

Donna Kuehner stood framed in the diner door when he turned away from the window. He knew her at once though she looked nothing like he remembered her. How long could you go without seeing someone and still recognize that person right away? Michael hadn't seen his dad in twelve years yet he knew him straight off in his casket at the funeral home. Same with Donna…only that was thirty-six years. *Thirty-six freakin' years.*

The clearest image his memory held of her was a hazed freeze frame from their last day together, a lean sandy haired tomboy squatting atop one low mortared rise of the stone-bordered waterfall in Tommy Crocker Memorial Park, hair cut in a truncated bell, edges feathered, smatter of freckles over her nose. High top Keds though he couldn't see their color, torn jeans with bare white fibers stretched across her knees, blue faded cotton T, peaked bumps beneath it the thickening nipples she steadfastly ignored. Ignored *then* anyhow. The outfit she wore today suggested her attitude had changed.

The two waitresses who accosted Michael right off when he entered allowed Donna to advance unchallenged. She squinted down the aisle till her gaze locked with his. No doubt or hesitation on her part either. Of course *he* had current photos up on his Facebook page, not just the generic gender avatar like hers, that gray empty vaguely female silhouette. She offered no smile, only a wave, a quick eleven to nine o'clock chop as she walked his way. Neither waitress moved to hand her a menu or follow, just milled about the register oblivious as she passed. He began to calculate his reduction to any potential tip.

This Donna's rich chestnut hair fell in waves well past her shoulders. Another new feature. He suspected the intervention of a curling iron. And at their age, dye…at least a touch. He'd made his own uneasy truce with the advancing gray that laid claim to his temples and all his facial hair but for a scattered fraction of his Van Dyke zone. That area was all he allowed to grow in anymore, though he kept it short and neatly trimmed. He longed for the dense dark shrubbery of his teens and twenties, even for as much as he retained into his thirties. Still, he was doing okay, better than some guys his age. Decent enough shape, still with most of his hair. Still *alive*. He could think of plenty he'd known who weren't…

Donna, a year or two older, was doing *better* than okay. The planes of her face were more deeply lined, but her skin was smooth, her once angular figure athletic but with added curves. Her outfit was seasonal, charming, and it showcased her figure. Lightweight gray cardigan, open and loose, lavender tank beneath, knotted dark purple silk scarf. Black jeans faded artfully half to gray. Simple black sandals, a bit unseasonable perhaps. Weathered gray leather satchel tucked beneath her right arm. She elbowed it behind her back as she approached. She damn near could've been a model, and she claimed the aisle like a catwalk.

Had she modeled? The gap in his knowledge of her past was enormous, all but absolute. She could've done anything in all that time, and their hometown *had* spawned two famous photographers, Margaret Bourke-White and Clayton Nelson, so why not a model? Nelson shot New York fashion models to this very day, though Bourke-White died right before Michael left Middlebrook, back when Nelson was running with the Crazelwoods, a local gang, and barely hanging in at MHS. *Running* the Crazelwoods, from what Michael heard. If Clayton could make that transition from teenage hood to fashion big shot, could be Donna modeled, too. He only just reconnected with her via Facebook. He knew damn near nothing of what she'd done since she was twelve. True he stalked her page on and off almost since he set up his own account in '08, but either she didn't have much there to begin with or she kept most of it blocked. Only with his father's death and the necessity of return did Michael feel he had sufficient justification to contact her. *Coming to town for my father's funeral. Wondered if you would like to get together?* And she accepted his friend request, messaged back *Sure*.

Modeling past or no, Donna commanded his full attention all the way down the aisle. Even decades back when he hardly knew what went where, he had already fallen for her, longed for her, for an intimacy he only vaguely understood. It was a different story now. They were both adults. And look at her. *Just look at her!* She had held up well. He fixed her in his gaze, slid his eyelids down, sought to burn her image against their twin screens, save it permanent.

Seeing Donna again he suddenly felt as if he had a second chance on it all. If he played things right he could restore a crucial missing photo to the scrapbook of his past. A do-over for his broken life—a reboot—seemed almost within reach.

Donna slid in opposite him, even that simple motion seductive. She left him spellbound.

—D-d-donna K-kuehner, he stuttered, though he was not a stutterer.

In reply she spoke his name as if mildly amused, made it almost a question at the end.

THE CROAKER

—Been a while, he said. Stupid *stupid!* Could he be more generic? —I mean, what've you been up to all these years? You already know I moved to Arizona with my mom, right. *Shut up! Let her talk! Her! Her!*

But he carried on, helpless. His parents' divorce, the move, his mom's death by heart attack his sophomore year at ASU. Dropping out, drinking, AA, cleaning up, return to ASU. His fifteen year marriage commencing with Catholic Carla's first pregnancy his senior year. Their three kids. His career teaching English at Phoenix Union High and then Desiderata. He left out the scandal. Passing reference to his and Carla's divorce. How Carla got full custody. How he should've got a better lawyer. The tiny apartment he occupied now, the limited visitation rights even before Carla took the kids to Nayarit. Drinking again, and losing his job on top of all that. Not from the drinking though. The economy. Retail slow, folks afraid to leave the house for a while…his dad's sudden death, the bereavement flight, handling arrangements while staying alone in the dead man's home, the house of his childhood.

Donna asked to see his menu and he slid it over. The interruption was just enough for him to correct course, shut his mouth and scold his mind in silence.

The older waitress returned the moment Donna set the menu down and he ordered for them both—Reuben with Taylor ham for him, and a Sunset Salad for her. And a coke for Donna too that the woman brought and set before Michael with a straw she drew from her apron. He passed it to Donna. —Sorry. I don't know what's up with her.

He was about to start in on the story of his days as a waiter when something called out within him again *Her! Her! Let her* speak! With an effort almost heroic for him, he capped off his monologue, asked for the second time —So. What about you? What've you been up to all these years?

She shrugged.

—Well, I don't know if I've done anything as exciting as you…

—What have I done that was exciting?

—You moved across the country when you were just a kid, lived in the desert…not to mention you've had your share of drama!

—It wasn't that exciting, believe me…

—Sure it is, compared to my life, stuck here in the same little town…

She continued, outlining a few semesters at Old Queens cut short by the death of one parent or the other, a timely entry into personal computer sales, opening her own shop, investments good and bad…Michael zoned out, pretended to follow her words while his gaze lasered over her form, the visible upper half at least. The angular tomboy he remembered lingered in her bone structure and tan and an underlying lean athleticism. No ring. On that he could be sure. And her name remained the same on Facebook.

Friends first, far back from an early age, met on the narrow bike trails of one of Middlebrook's undeveloped lots, he'd come to love this girl, then to lust after her in a vague and virginal way, she already in Eighth Grade and he in Sixth, a time when he lacked any real grasp of how to talk to a girl, let alone of the mystery dance. Way back when the older boys could leave him confused when they teased —Shut up kid, you still think the hole is round.

Almost two years older, she must've been more knowledgeable, if not possessed of genuine experience. One evening in her garage she showed her worldliness when she mocked him for liking another neighbor girl, one who lived nearer. Nancy Pitt. Nancy was the pretty blond sister of Michael's sometime friend John who lived just around the block. John was the guy Michael hung out with when Donna wasn't home. Michael had little interaction with Nancy, beyond asking *Is John home?* once or twice through the screen door.

Apropos of nothing, Donna commenced a pantomime of Michael and Nancy's projected future marital routine, first scooting out to the dripline of the open garage door then announcing her return from work in a pretended adult male Michael voice. From there she swaggered over to where Michael sat as dumbstruck spectator, walking as if she had a pair of potatoes jammed in her pants. Hands on hips she paused to address a vacant point just above the low lone row of cinderblocks around the staircase down to her basement from the garage. *Take your clothes off Nancy. I had a long day at work and I need to do the sex thing now.* That line delivered, she spun about and dropped to a squat atop the blocks, splayed her denimed thighs to suggest Nancy's spousal submission.

Her little skit confused the bejeezus out of Michael. The subject of his crush just addressed him with her legs spread wide, only she did it under the persona of another girl. Donna laid her hands high up her thighs, moaned —Oh Michael, give me your *bo*-ner!

They had discussed sex before, but always in the third person. Donna often wondered aloud what it would be like to be a man, have a cock, talked about older women's boobs and how she was curious to touch them. All this was easy for Michael as he shared most of these feelings, though more and more during her soliloquies, he watched as a vague and sourceless glow spread behind her head, isolating her from the background. Now Michael felt she already knew the object of his real attraction, his secret desire, felt she was mocking him for it. Mocking his feelings for her. Tears welled at the corners of his eyes as he said —*What do you know, you, you…jerkoff?* He stood and staggered back, caught his bike off the garage floor by one worn grubby handlegrip and paced it a few steps till the wheels turned and he leapt on. He did not look back. He did not want her to see his burning red face. His tears.

That was on a Sunday in late September. They didn't see each other in school afterward because he went to Middlebrook Middle and Donna attended Alma Prep at Pillar of Fire in Zarephath, an obscure little religious school of which she rarely spoke. Confusion and shame burned too bright within him yet to seek her out the following weekend—or the next after that—but come Saturday afternoon three weeks later he psyched himself up to visit her house again, and when she answered the door neither mentioned the events of his last visit.

She proposed an itinerary right away—ride their bikes to Tommy Crocker Memorial Park and attempt to spot the Croaker.

Michael had doubts about this plan from the start. The park was at the west edge of town, near the corner double border with Deep Brook and Pisgawawa. He was supposed to ask his parents' permission before he rode anywhere half that far, but he knew this time they'd say no. He might make it back before dark but no way before dinner. If he went without asking and sans permission, his return would likely involve interrogation, serious penalties…

Donna said —C'mon, Michael. It's still nice out now but you know if we wait another week, it's gonna get too cold. What if you fall in the water then?

How could he decline? This was Donna's most adventurous suggestion yet—and even that far back Michael had some ill-formed awareness of adventure as aphrodisiac. The Croaker was a local legend, Middlebrook's outdoor answer to old mirrorbound Mary Weathers. It was said to be the real reason for the name of the park, rather than local World War I casualty Tommy Crocker as alleged. It—not Tommy—supposedly inhabited the broad concrete tunnel that engulfed narrow Amber Brook before it reemerged to join the Deep Brook and a little further over the line in Pisgawawa, the Raritan River itself.

Others said *the* Croaker and Tommy *Crocker* were one and the same, that Tommy returned from the war so disfigured he went to live in the tunnel under the bridge. One version even had it that Army doctors gave Tommy gills to compensate for lungs reamed out by chlorine or mustard gas.

The invocation to the Croaker was simple. *Croaker, Croaker, hiding in the dark / Croaker, croaker, come out in the park!* You were supposed to stand on a certain flat rock in the middle of the brook and turn around three times while you repeated the words thrice as well. With your eyes shut. The goal was to open your eyes facing the bridge just as you completed the third recital. If you timed it just right, you would see the Croaker in the tunnel for a fraction of a second. If you timed it wrong, finished facing back or sideways, you would miss him. And if you *fell* while you were spinning and chanting with your eyes closed…then *you* belonged to the Croaker, who could rush out and drag you into his tunnel…if he so chose. You took that risk. Thus far Michael never dared, never even went close to the bridge. It was plenty dark and creepy down there anyway, Croaker or no.

Their ride took over an hour, so day was fading when they hit the park, sun grazing steep treetops beyond the road that marked the east edge of town. They came up from behind the old stone boathouse that must once have been the centerpiece of the park, jaunty young chaps in straw hats and striped jackets rowing out to serenade their ladyfriends with ukuleles, spread out like fireflies here and there across the lake. All long gone, and the building stood boatless now, gutted, blackened by log fires and scarred by graffiti, a palimpsest of random names and phrases gouged into the soot layered walls. A desecration. Michael pictured the parties that must go on there now at night, hippy girls in headbands dancing topless 'round bonfires, smoking marijuana and drinking whiskey, probably with Clayton and the Crazelwoods. Those guys were having all the fun.

Beyond the boathouse and down a dirt bank lay the Duckpond, stinking, green and foul, surface filmed with stagnating duck poop in slicks and whorls. Closer to the falls the water cleared up some, but not enough that fish could live in it. The only real fishing was below the dam and downstream. He and Donna had learned that the hard way following several wasted summer afternoons.

A bit to the east was the lake's lone island, half its dozen or so odd angled trees already converted to the colors of fall, brown and yellow, one tall oak a bright red. No more than 100 feet out, but unreachable with all the boats sold or sunk or burnt for firewood. Unless anyone wanted to swim through the scrim of duck shit. Beyond the island on the opposite bank rose Suicide Hill. In the winter the Tommy Crocker Duckpond mostly froze low and left a concave overhang between slope and lake. This meant a sled ride down the Hill offered an airborne jump of four vertical feet or so onto dense scraped ice. Michael never had the guts—or the sled—but he loved to watch for wipeouts. The trees atop Suicide Hill were turning too, some already losing leaves, dribbling down the hill, coloring the yards of the string of houses along the ridge, all homes among the largest and fanciest in town. Their fenced yards left a thin strip of public access along the heights. He never knew anyone who lived in one, but he could picture the dread and resentment with which they anticipated sledding season and the kids who clustered just outside their property lines. But as long as you stayed outside their fences the owners couldn't run you off.

Michael and Donna rode round the boathouse and past the stone benches, green paint peeling from their board seats, wood splintered beneath. And here—he almost flew off his bike. On one seat lay a copy of *Playboy*, the July issue, its full voluptuous stapled fold all but calling his name. His dad had a subscription but this was the issue at which Michael's mom finally caught him peeking. She'd taken it, hidden it, Michael had yet to uncover where. Or maybe she threw it out. For sure it was the last issue of the magazine she allowed in the house.

The cover showed the torso of a woman in a red top, no neck no face no hips, ring-pull zipper tugged down near to her navel, hemispheres of her boobs almost half exposed, edges of her nipples revealed on the diagonal. He could grab the magazine easy if there weren't people here, women with strollers and little kids fishing with plastic poles. And Donna.

—C'mon. Donna half turned and sped up. Had she seen the *bait*? They flipped together through his dad's old *Playboys* more than once, her idea as often as his. He was torn, divided, but saw how the setting sun caught in her hair, crowned it with a skullcap of burning gold. Maybe he could grab the *Playboy* later, stuff it up his shirt in front or back and when he got home rush right up the stairs to his room, stash it under his mattress. Maybe. He would eventually find his dad's copy if it was still in the house, but here was one he could have all to himself.

Donna was relentless, and with her longer legs working Michael had to pump his pedals hard just to keep up. Lucky for him she stopped at the dam. As he reached her she dropped her bike and scuttled atop the stonework to assume the exact pose his brain snapped as the last happy shot of her in his mental album of remembrances. If only he had convinced her to turn back then. But he didn't even try.

—You wanna leave our bikes here, or carry them across?

Michael hadn't considered the final approach. The dam itself was as far as he usually went, as the deep foamy pool at its foot was supposed to hold sunnies, crappies…some said even trout. He'd never caught the least little fish with his bread balls and worms, but he had seen sunnies there leaping brief and bright in the afternoon sun.

He knew at least three sets of uneven stepstones crossed the brook between dam and bridge. He'd never brought his bike across before, but after a few bewildered seconds he understood how easy it might be, how they could push their bikes along beside in the shallow water as they balanced on each stone in turn, the bikes even providing tripods of stability. Unless the water ran deeper than he remembered, or they hit a deep pocket. Then a bike would of a sudden become a problem. An anchor. A loss.

She didn't wait for his answer —Let's bring them across. We'll get to the bridge more faster that way. I know you need to get home soon. Don't wanna to get you in trouble with your folks.

He was already late, so what did it matter? No way he'd make it in time for dinner. He was gonna get grounded—and oh!—over Halloween. Plus who knew what else?

Donna was already pedaling down the dam's low slope, past the small memorial area where blunt squared pillars of mortared brook cobbles formed a pavilion of sorts, something his dad once called a poor man's Stonehenge. You could tell the structure belonged to the same era as the boathouse and dam. Either the memorial never had a roof or it fell or burned or both sometime way back. From there a narrow dirt trail cut the grass, winding along close to the bank except where trees or dense brush rose in its way. Gnarled roots rutted the path here and there, smoothed by years of feet and wheels. They had to slow as they bumped over the worst.

Michael followed Donna. The concrete embankment of Main Street ascended soon to their right, a high wall with chain link fence along its top, pressing steadily closer as they progressed. Between trees, brush, and wall it was already twilight, and he had to swat mosquitoes each time he slowed.

They came to the head of the first set of stepstones, but one glance showed the water here was way too deep to cross. They couldn't see the bottom, only ancient great olive-green carp drifting between the stones further out, the largest looking thicker and longer than his legs. The motions of the slow cylindrical carp reminded him of the submarine in *Voyage to the Bottom of the Sea*.

Pedaling ahead through the constricting frontage they reached the second row of stepstones. Here they could see the bottom but it looked at least two feet deep. No way that was going to work with their bikes. Michael was about to suggest they leave their bikes on the north bank—who was going to come along and steal them, anyway—but Donna was already threading her way onward between embankment and brush.

At the third set of stepstones the water ran shallow and slow. They could see most of the way across and nowhere was it more than a foot deep. Donna thrust the tires of her bike in the brook on her right and took the first step, wheeling the bicycle slowly alongside. As she hopped to the fifth stone, Michael began to follow.

Their meals arrived while Donna was still speaking. He had long since let go her thread though. The waitress set both plates in front of Michael then hovered a long silent moment beside the table, hands on hips. What the hell was that about? He gave the uniformed woman a weak glare as he slid Donna's salad across the table.

They began to eat, which choked off the convo a while. Finally Donna looked up, stared him straight, said —You're still thinking about that day we went to see the Croaker, aren't you?

Several elements of his autonomic nervous system cycled up, complicating his response. He froze a moment, then looked over at her, thought. At first all he could do was think. He spoke at last, softly —I'm sorry.

—It was a long time ago, she replied. —Why are you sorry?

—I should've...should've...I...

She looked at him long. He felt her eyes slicing deep.

—Seriously, how much do you remember from before you took off that day? Tell me.

—I don't know...I...

—Do you remember when we got to the bridge?

He nodded, picked up from his memory as he spoke, starting with their arrival on the south bank. The thin dirt path that ran there roughly paralleled the brook, and they peddled their bikes along it as they wound through weeds and trees, came out close to the bridge.

The Raritan Avenue Bridge marked the end of both the park and the Borough of Middlebrook. Its open underpart was long and low, a broad concrete arch absorbing the brook into darkness. A corrugated conduit alone came out the Deep Brook side, lost right off in a dense undeveloped tract, above or below ground from there Michael did not know. Poison ivy was almost rain forest thick there, wrapping the trunks of half the trees and coating the ground in rolling torrents of oily-sheened green.

Maybe five yards back from the bridge lay the final row of stepstones, their route bowed upstream, irregular in both spacing and shape...a lone angled slab near the center the obvious platform for the revolving evocation.

Donna spoke as they lay down their bikes —Who's gonna go first? I will if you want me to.

One of those moments came to Michael. He knew she didn't expect him to go. Not first, probably not at all. *She* wanted to do this and he was just here to watch like always. To bear witness to her endeavor, her tomboy daring. Not this time though. He saw his chance to shine in her eyes, same as the way she shone in his.

—I will, he said, and stepped toward the first stone before she could protest or he could fall prey to his own second thoughts and fears. He wasn't thinking of the green hidden figure beneath the bridge, its alleged webbed hands and feet, what rumor told of its claws and spiky teeth, but of how Donna seemed to glow whenever she smiled at him, haloed in the nimbus that rose behind her head for only him to see. That was real. Love. Love was real. Not the Croaker.

He arched and swayed from stone to stone. The first few were rounded cobbles but he caught traction at their high centers and continued on.

THE CROAKER

Dried silt gave each stone a khaki blush, dark scuffs marking the paths of previous feet. He wished for his bicycle—the tripod system really worked. He made it though. At the center slab he balanced and looked back at Donna. —Okay. I'm here. Are you gonna watch?

She stood and stared, her face somewhere between expectant and bland. —You're sure you want to do this? You don't have to, you know.

—*I'm the guy here.* I should go first. Watch me now. She stared blankly back, made maybe the slightest shrug. He faced the bridge, closed his eyes, gave the three count, took a deep breath, began the chant —*Croaker, Croaker...*

Right off he felt his words moving faster than his feet. He adjusted to match each repetition of the words to one complete rotation only. By the second time round he thought he had it right, but during the third round at *dark* Donna shouted his name and it threw him. He reopened his eyes to find himself turned back in the direction they had come, toward the dam now hidden beyond the trees, not the bridge, a filthy little blond troll in overalls standing almost close enough to touch.

He staggered away from the apparition and fell backward into the brook, his right elbow striking a rock, his left only muck. Suddenly he was wet and muddy, his right arm smarting from impact, shocked by the water's unexpected cold. Consumed by confusion, he heard Donna laughing. Laughing at *him*—how could she? Then he looked up at the troll. It had not moved, and he saw now it was only a shirtless dirty boy. He registered the familial resemblance to Rich Barone, a kid in his grade he'd once been friends with way back in First Grade and Kindergarten, but whom he rarely saw now that classes were tracked. This had to be Rich's younger brother. He was a weird little kid though, that was for sure. As if to confirm this a voice called from behind Michael, somewhat muffled by the bridge.

—Hey Little Mickey, why aren't you helping? Leave those kids alone and come help with the fish!

Little Mickey Barone splashed past Michael, kicking cold water in his face as he struggled to his knees against the muddy streambed, his hands splaying in the pliable muck like Play-Doh. Once he was half up he realized Donna had stopped laughing. Now she only stared past him toward the bridge. Squatting in the water on all fours like a frog, Michael turned to follow her gaze.

Company was coming. Three figures emerged from beneath the bridge as Mickey stepped to join them. None of them were gill men or fungus men. Though they came from shadow, Michael saw clear the three were boys he knew at least by sight, though all were older and taller than him. Toting a net between them, they nearly spanned the width of the culvert's low arch.

Mickey scuttled to the north end of the net and worked south, nabbing three long shining leapers from the mesh. *Trout!* Michael always knew there had to be some in this brook. The boy had to hold one in his mouth before he reached the left bank, where a scuffed white plastic utility bucket now stood, covered with a damp dirty cloth under a flat slab of slate. Mickey lifted this cover and slid his catch into the bucket one by one, spitting the last fish free from his teeth. Michael heard fishtails slapping the plastic from inside.

All the way on his feet now, Michael sloshed toward the bank, no longer concerned with the stepstones, wet as he already was. The boys from beneath the bridge headed the same way, folding their net one to the next as they came. Michael recognized the guy on the south end as Hodge Broussard, a hulking bully who was actually in his class, though he supposedly stayed back three times to land there. Over six feet tall and an opportunistic menace, he fortunately gave most of his attention to the girls. Michael once heard their P.E. teacher Mr. Walker complain to some Eighth Grade jocks —*Goddamn Broussard ain't even in high school and he gets more pussy than a bicycle seat. Hell, he even gets more than me.*

According to the Internet, Broussard was a permanent guest of the great state of Tennessee nowadays. Since 1987. Murder, murder, rape, attempted murder. His rap sheet had circulated through several Middlebrook themed groups on Facebook. His hair had gone all silver-white. Prison life did not appear to suit him.

Yet despite the occasional shove against the lockers of the Sixth Grade hall—even once a good solid shoulder punch for some forgotten offense— young Michael felt as if the rules were suspended for the moment in this place, bully and prey become casual, familiar, approachable, something apparently verified as he heard Broussard say —*Hey kid, you want for see what we catch?* Which was already Michael's wish. He wanted someday to be a marine biologist and loved to look at fish, especially still in water with all their electric colors on display.

THE CROAKER

He reached the bank and had to crawl some to get onto it, then approached the bucket. —Wayne, show these kids what we catch so far, said Broussard. Wayne, a nearly shirtless all but shapeless blob in cutoffs, obliged, lifting the cloth—a sodden square of flannel—and tilting back the hunk of pink flaking stone. Michael peered in—and saw eight or nine trout, hovering one above another in several gallons of water. These guys were catching their fish with a net like pros! Where did you even get a net like that?

—For the dinner, you know? Our family, they must eat. Broussard spoke as he wound the net in a loose coil beside the bucket. The boy who held the net's far end arrived beside him now. Michael recognized him as Devlin, last name unknown. He was tall and muscular like Broussard, but with dark hair and a face oddly equine in shape. Wayne was so fat his rolls bulged through the straining holes in his wifebeater T. Michael knew nothing of Wayne, other than his name, but Devlin's rep pegged him as an even more random and vicious bully than Broussard.

Donna waved a forkful of salad at him —The way you fell over when you opened your eyes and saw little Mickey Barone in front of you was priceless. I maybe shouldn'a tried to warn you he was standing there, I mean, I didn't want to mess you up—but he was *right* there. No way I could know you'd react that way though. And really, I didn't see him till he was next to you even though I was watching the whole time. He was one slippery little character. But go on with your story—I didn't mean to interrupt.

—You sure you want me to...

—Yeah, yeah, go on. I'm listening. You know what first though? Let's blow this taco stand. Got no ocean view.

Her knees brushed his beneath the table. She caught his eyes and held them. Michael watched as the luminescent nimbus of hopeless desire recreated itself behind and around her face. It was happening again. After all these years. He felt lightheaded, giddy...

He paid the check at the front register and she followed him out the door.

—You said you walked here. I've got a car. Let's go for a ride, see how much of the town you remember. What's left of it from back then anyway. It'll be fun.

Donna drove a silver-gray Ford Escort, the interior clean enough for a rental. He noted the lack of children's toys, the absence of a booster seat in the back. Nothing that might belong to a husband or boyfriend either, or an older son. No evidence of masculine presence. True, *absence of evidence was not evidence of absence.* But still...

They drove past the house where she once lived, other houses where they used to ring the doorbell and run, hide in hedges. He told her how where he lived now, kids called that game *Ding Dong Ditch.* Past his once and current place of residence. Past the filling station on the corner where the owner used to run out and teach them new cuss words whenever they crisscrossed his bell hose on their bikes. It was a garage for foreign cars now, and the bell hose was gone. They drove by the developments standing where the wooded sections once stretched, tracts where they rode their bikes along a maze-like set of trails. Talked of memorable sights they saw on those trails, infrequent and sometimes strange. Most often teenage couples making out in the woods beyond the path, but also the dark procession of people in robes they'd seen marching through the woods one evening. Or the tree that walked, the spiders that glowed, the vast pale bird too big to be a hawk or owl...

Michael got turned around and lost his bearings along all the back streets they took so he was surprised when they found themselves pulling up at Tommy Crocker Memorial Park, parking in a little lot he couldn't recall behind the boathouse. But he hadn't driven when he came here several decades back, had he? And like everything else, the route itself and the houses along it must have changed...

Other differences were more obvious. The boathouse seemed cleaner and polished up on the surface, and its blue metal roof looked altogether new. An unmistakable addition was the wooden boardwalk running along the near bank, wide enough for lovers to walk side by side, though its railings were already weathered and rough. On top of all, the restrooms he remembered as bolted shut were open now. He needed that. And as he relieved himself he realized this was the first time he ever did so here. The park had been all but derelict in his youth.

Where were all the ducks though? He saw very few, far fewer than he recalled. He remembered the Mallards best, the iridescent chevrons on the males' wings, and the black and white Muscovy ducks he couldn't find in any field guide. Only later did he learn they were imported.

As if telepathic, Donna said —Big chemical spill in '89. Killed most of the fish, then the ducks ate the dead fish and died too. They never really bounced back. He was about to ask whether she meant the ducks or the fish or both but what did it matter?

The life rings hung in what he was certain were the same places still, and he could swear they were those exact same ones that hung there in his youth, only more bleached out, their attached ropes gone stiff and gray. The rings seemed so flattened and brittle he could not imagine them saving anyone's life. How deep was the lake anyway? Had anyone ever drowned in it?

They walked the paved way that led from boathouse to dam as they couldn't find the access to the gray grainy wooden walkway without climbing the splintery railings. Michael pictured Donna posing atop the dam again, but when they reached it they found chain link fence arching over the low stone rises on either side.

The little dedication pavilion had a sort of roof now, though nothing that would ever keep the rain out, simply a series of overhanging boards, ends cut at angles, all slathered in creosote. He noted this addition as they passed.

Thus far their route was all but empty…over near the boathouse a stroller-pushing mom on the boardwalk, farther back on a park bench a gaunt older crewcut man whose head still bore the dimples of delivery room forceps. Michael shuddered, as sometimes when his mom cut his hair too short kids at school suggested he carried the same stigmata. His parents always assured him his head was *just shaped that way* though, that no obsolete machinations had wrenched him into this world.

The stepstones crossed in different locations now, intervening floods having no doubt washed the old rows away. Bikeless this time they chose to cross at the very first set. They couldn't see the bottom so they took each step with extra care, their efforts at balance successful if somewhat awkward, even comical. Any carp were either gone or obscured in the murk.

On the south bank they made their way toward the bridge, once more dodging the ubiquitous sheen of poison ivy that rose in clumps and wound round the trunks of trees, its triplicate leaves still green even as the trees turned above them.

—Finish your story now. You said you would.

—Huh?

—About those boys we met, from underneath the bridge.

—You sure? Maybe I should just let it go. What's it really matter now?

—No, I wanna hear it from your side, even if it's thirty plus years later. You left off when they were showing you their fish.

—Oh. Okay. Truth is, I mean I gotta admit…I was afraid of them. Broussard and Devlin most of all. I had trouble with Broussard before at school, and Devlin was just…scary. *Creepy.* But then Mickey called out to me.

—Hey kid. What are you doing here? You come to steal our fish?

He was crouching just under the low overhang of the Raritan Avenue Bridge, on the south side and facing us. I was afraid he might set the others off so I didn't want to ignore him. I said —No, we just ran into you guys by accident. I walked in his direction. I used to be friends with his brother so I thought that might help. This next part is gross. I don't think I should tell it.

—I already know, so go ahead.

—You sure? Okay. When I got about five steps away from him, I saw he was squatting there with his overalls all the way down in the water. He was taking a dump. Right there in public, more or less.

The memory returned to Michael with unwanted clarity, the blank faced squatting boy, thick khaki curls of his turds floating behind him, drifting slowly downstream toward Deep Brook on the diminished current.

—I was so shocked. Nobody I knew would ever do a thing like that, and it was a shock to realize that kind of people lived in our town. I don't think I ever went to the bathroom outside. Not number two anyway. And then I heard another sound, a kind of squeal, and…

He looked at her feet. —Maybe I should stop there?

—No. Go on.

—You sure?

—Yeah. I'm sure. Go on now.

They had reached the bridge, and were standing in pretty much the very spot where he had seen Broussard holding her, one hand over her mouth… the other fondling her chest as the two older boys approached. He told her as much, and she nodded.

—And then?

—Then Broussard said *You should go home now, little boy.*

—And what did you do then, Michael?

His heart raced. He felt near to tears.

—Michael?

—I took off. I was *scared*. I ran to my bike and rode all the way to the footbridge at the other end of the pond. I was afraid they'd get me too. Back then I thought they might kill me, feed me to the Croaker.

—Did you tell my parents? Did you tell *your* parents? Did you call the police?

He stared at the ground, eleven years old all over again. Eleven years old and terrified.

—No. I was scared.

—I was scared too.

Michael began to cry. —What happened? What did they do to you?

—I'll show you what they did.

She locked eyes with him as she raised each foot in turn, kicked off her sandals, and stood barefoot on the dirt path. He stared at her confused and she stared back.

She spoke —I learned something about the Croaker that day. I found out if you really want to see it you've got to go all the way under the bridge.

Those were the last words Donna ever spoke to him. Then she turned and stepped into the icy brook, her gray pants changing to black where the water reached them. She strode with purpose till she disappeared deep under the arch and was lost in the shadows. He called after her —Donna! Donna! What the fuck? But she neither answered nor returned.

She was gone into the darkness, just like that. For a moment he considered attempting to call her out with a version of the Croaker chant, subbing *Donna* for *Croaker* but rejected that plan. It felt ridiculous, wrong. Stupid even. Instead he called again from the bank, just her name and *Come back!* And of course she had the car keys...

Then he did hear something, a voice, but not Donna's. *You should go home now, little boy.* How he recognized it all these years later he did not know, but he did. It was Broussard.

Michael panicked at that point, torqued about and ran, caught up his bicycle where'd he left it, and once he got on, pedaled back down the path, wobbling wild side to side, eyes smeared with tears. He had to get help. He had to get away. *He had to get*...a polished root in the path almost threw him, caused him to throw out his left foot and come to an awkward panting stop after a series of unexpected short hops. He tugged up his T-shirt to wipe his eyes and looked back. No one followed. No Broussard, none of his gang. Not Donna, but those big boys, if they ran for him now, they might catch him yet. And then what?

He bike-walked past the root on the packed dirt path, pushed hard on his right pedal and straightened, rode on past all the stepstones, past the dam, past Suicide Hill on his right, and the island, on toward the blue painted wooden bridge that hid beneath ancient drooping willows at the far side of the park. He bumped over more roots with equilibrium intact. One smooth gnarled root, two, three, then the rickety bridge. He thudded across it and pushed back toward the boathouse. Perhaps some adults were still there, someone he could ask for help.

When he found no one at the boathouse it was at least half a relief. When it came down to it he was scared to talk to some strange adult. What would he say anyway? My friend is under the bridge? I think those boys are hurting her, doing *things* to her? *What kind of things, son?* The same things he wanted to do. He was sure it shone on his face plain as the sun.

The lone *Playboy* was still there on the bench, in the same place he glimpsed it before. No visible witnesses this time and he was alone, so he squeezed hard on the handbrakes, pulled up a few feet short and walked his bike to where it lay. One last look around and he reached for the magazine. Except when he stooped to scoop and grip it by its wide end it went flat in his hand. It was only the cover. Someone else had already popped the two staples, made off with the real goods. He looked all round again but saw no one there laughing at him so he didn't know who planted it.

Face afire he dropped the empty sleeve back on the bench, pedaled away around the boathouse and onto the street. He thought hard whether Donna's parents knew who she was with, where they'd gone together, where he lived. Did they even know his name? He thought not—she always met him outside the door, never brought him in. He told himself she'd be okay though. The boys were just gonna scare her and let her go. That was all. And she was tough, she'd get away. Maybe the whole deal was they just wanted to scare *him*. Maybe Donna was in on the scare, maybe she was getting back at him for the cold shoulder he gave her that other weekend...

It was already twilight. He still had a while before he got home, and when he did his parents would not be pleased at his lateness. The closer he got to home, the more he worried about his punishment, the less about Donna.

THE CROAKER

His parents *were* waiting for him, cornered him and sat him down soon as he came through the door. He expected questions, punishment, but they didn't even notice he was wet and muddy, and when they spoke they described their own failings, his father's especially, though they left it all vague. Their words were mechanical, as if they read from a teleprompter just outside his sight. *Sometimes people just stop loving each other. It's no one's fault.* He could no longer remember which of them said that, or how many times. He forgot all about Donna as he cried.

after

Once they were all inside and the bus driver closed the doors, conversation faded to a fraction of the chat fest they shared waiting in the lot. Colleen had gone gangbusters with a couple from up the block, Grant and Ken. Before Sandy she'd barely known them, only enough to wave and say Hi. She'd been shy or they'd been shy, she couldn't remember, maybe just obeying some unspoken etiquette limiting interaction for neighbors more than four doors apart.

They turned out to be quite charming. Interesting too. Ken—*please don't call me Kenny*—worked for NASA before he retired, did math for the Voyager probe. Grant did…what? She'd already forgotten. And as if they had also forgotten her, they'd selected seats eight or nine rows back and didn't meet her eyes when she walked past. A different etiquette already prevailed. Well, they kept her preoccupied throughout the long wait for the bus. And they'd all be in Seaside soon.

The smell of the bus grew loud in the silence. Funky sneakers, dust, the tired stale aroma of the faux green vinyl seats. The fear of all the people crammed together with their empty luggage. Luggage to fill with what tchotchkes might survive amongst their prized possessions. In the long queue to board, longer than the line of buses itself, they'd come mostly two by two, as if for the ark, though the flood was over now. Colleen was the only singleton she saw at least ten slots either ahead or behind.

Most dragged bulky rolling airplane bags to pack with personal treasures, and some lugged five gallon work buckets and pink or blue jugs of cleanser. Sewers had overflowed, they all knew that much. Seawater and sewer water and who knew what else had invaded their homes. If their homes were still there. Few had any clue yet whose made it and whose didn't. They would all find out soon.

Many gasped when they crested Pelican Island from the bridge on 37 and saw the debris pile ahead. Colleen herself stared in blank dismay. The heap was higher than the house she hoped still stood. At least part of her hoped it still stood. *Might solve some problems if it didn't...*

Shattered planks from the Boardwalk comprised most of the towering bulldozed mound. She wondered which broken tarry parts of boards she'd walked over the course of five decades with her parents, with her friends, with old boyfriends, with Derrick, with her kids. With Paul.

She'd neglected to charge her iPhone 4s in the car but borrowed a backup phone charger from Grant, got it up to 86%. In line for the bus she called Derrick, let him know she was headed in, promised to call again once she saw the shore house, share how bad the damage was. Hung up without a goodbye.

Colleen kept silent on the ride. Apprehension stifled the entire bus. She herself felt heavy, weighted, as if the storm had flooded her lungs and filled them still. The date was Nov. 10, almost two weeks after Sandy first made landfall on the Jersey Shore. Colleen and Derrick had barely gotten TV and power again at their home in Sourland Hills, and when they did, they found the rest of the world had moved on from the storm. Yet *they* were still in it, their friends and neighbors were still in it, though by now it was old news to the networks and the rest of the world.

Colleen stared out the window and twisted her wedding band round her finger. It was loose enough now it turned almost freely. She had no more idea than any of her silent seatmates what she might encounter in her neighborhood, at her home. Could be some had learned from aerial photos whether their homes survived, but even those few could not yet know the extent of any damage beneath their roofs.

The bus departed from the Tom's River Mall, a trip that most times took just fifteen minutes by car. It felt like an hour. She would've been okay with two hours. With three, four. With forever. She rode alone, far from Derrick.

after

Where for a while he couldn't hurt her, couldn't hit her, couldn't loom over her. She was keyed up about the house but no matter what the damage she'd be alone and could feel safe there, would not have to walk on eggshells, watching always over her shoulder.

Other buses arrived from other locations. Today was only the second day FEMA allowed homeowners in, selected by street. Her bus stopped at Hamilton and Boulevard. The driver cranked the lever to whoosh the door open. He hadn't said a word the whole way, so that was the first sound he made. Colleen wondered if he also had a home here, or how the storm had affected his life to leave him so solemn. Had he lost someone as well?

A fire truck faced them outside, and a man standing on the back spoke slowly through a bullhorn, as if addressing children or people with limited English proficiency —Go only to your own home. Do not attempt to enter anyone else's house. *Do not attempt to reach the beach.* The beach is not safe. All beach access points are blocked. Your bus will depart at four o'clock on the dot. Return to this spot before that time. *You must be on your bus! No one is permitted to stay in Seaside Heights overnight!*

Was that the mayor? She could not be sure. She never voted in those elections. Regardless, Colleen took no issue with any of his directives. All she wanted was to inspect their house, manage what damage she found, gather what valuables she could carry, secure any unsecured windows and doors. If possible.

As the passengers scattered in different directions, Colleen proceeded north on Boulevard toward her maybe yes maybe no home, wheeling her own empty suitcase down the center of the empty street.

Right away she noticed a couple things strange. First, no birds. There were never not gulls over Seaside, gulls and a few terns, the gulls ever ready to pounce on the least scrap of dropped food, not only on the beach but for several blocks inland.

Then the sand. Most days a thin coating of it dusted every street in town, but Boulevard was clear of sand today. Clean as the main drag of any town an hour from the shore. She'd seen a snowplow clearing sand from other streets on their way in, but no plow could scrape the roads and sidewalks fine enough to catch the eternal sand in their cracks. More like someone vacuumed the road. Then hosed it down and vacuumed it again.

Yet she saw sand coating the side streets despite the tracks of plows. Sand there rose up around road signs and heaped against house fronts in drifts like low snowbanks a foot deep or more. Why not Boulevard as well? Why was that one road so clear? Had Sandy done this, was there some pattern in her chaos, her fury? Had her winds blown only north to south, or the reverse? Colleen and most of New Jersey had gone without news throughout the storm and would have missed any such weather report, but she found the concept hard to swallow. Didn't hurricanes spin in circles or spirals, like giant tornadoes?

Seaside Heights, the Town That Fun Built. She'd never heard it so silent, seen it so still, even during the offseason. Not only no tourists or birds—no dogs, no wildlife, no animals of any kind. No cars.

One by one the other passengers from her bus disappeared into the grid. As she passed each cross street and looked toward the Boardwalk entrances on her right, she saw a lone police car at the end of each, parked facing out. No sign remained of the Boardwalk itself or its entrances, just crude high berms of sand behind the cruisers, and beyond those, nothing but pale sky, which though mostly blue and clear above, was hazy and clouded over the sea to the east, as if some remnant of the superstorm still lurked offshore, waiting only till they entered their homes to strike once more.

Soon she was one of the last handful of homeowners trundling down Boulevard. The farther they traveled the wider the space they opened up each to the next, till by the time Colleen reached Hancock, her own street, no one walked closer to her than half a block. She cut down Hancock and was alone except for the dark police car between her and the beach, the sea.

Now she saw sand. A plow had passed over and left a thin layer dusting the road while burying the curbs and the verge and the roots of parking meters in mounds like drifts of khaki snow. The wheels of Colleen's suitcase crunched and ground along in the grit. She examined the houses she passed. Sand piled against the fronts of each. No broken windows that she could see, but flood debris scattered across whatever few feet of frontage passed for each home's front yard.

She spotted the high water mark first on the facade of a home three houses up from her own. Right away then she saw it everywhere. It marked each home several feet above street level. The height of the flood. She knew now what she might face once inside, and the probable fate of the basement apartment they rented out in the summer, a decent source of extra income, especially helpful after Derrick forced her to quit her substitute teaching job. She dreaded to see the damage Sandy and the sea had done downstairs. She recalled the long litany of friends in Deep Brook who'd lost homes to the flooding a decade back, businesses too and in some cases both. That downtown had never recovered.

Colleen arrived at their home on Hancock, a robin's egg blue two-story Cape. She saw no obvious damage to the house, no signs of Sandy's power besides the sand drifts and the waterline. The latter crossed the front door to the basement apartment more than halfway to the handle, suggesting the downstairs had suffered, suffered hard. She decided to leave the basement for last. She wasn't ready yet to see the worst the flood had done, the memories it had erased. That space had sometimes been her refuge while otherwise unoccupied. And more than once while occupied as well. It was there she came to know Paul, the two summers he rented.

She and Paul never made any plans. They *lived in the moment* as the old phrase went. But those were the moments the lights came back on inside. And he told her it was the same for him. Told her without prompting. Said he'd been dead inside since cancer took his wife five years before. *Dead inside*, those were his own words. Now he was dead inside and out. That's what they said.

Colleen glanced at the parked cop car. It was a split block distant and dark inside. Looked empty. She turned left and saw a man paused on Boulevard, standing next to a silver-gray clamshell suitcase standing upright in the street. The man was staring down Hancock, staring down her street. Staring at her. Despite the distance she knew he was watching her. And after a second she was sure he was that creepy guy Derrick drank with sometimes. Jordan or George or something. She usually locked herself in her bedroom if Derrick brought that guy over—something he only did *against* her objections of course. Jordan or George supposedly lived a couple blocks down. Derrick said they met in a bar.

As soon as the man saw her returning his stare, he turned to face forward and towed his luggage quickly out of sight. Well, if he really was Jor/ge he already knew which house was hers. She didn't like that thought. Of all the people to see her here, to know she was alone. She stood in place till he was gone and counted to twenty before she moved again.

Just past their house lay the wide gravel drive they shared with their neighbor, its width mostly free of sand after the first few feet, though strewn with debris along its entire length. House rule was use the back door if your feet were wet or sandy, and she decided to stick with that rule today. That, and she suddenly preferred the back door. Who knew what eyes might be upon her still?

Colleen made her way up the shared drive, dragging her suitcase through the sand drifts closest to the street. The little wheels left zigzagging grooves beside the blurry prints of her feet. Once through the initial drifts she saw the storm's scattered flotsam more clearly. Obvious some of this stuff came all the way from the Boardwalk. First thing she noticed was a stuffed lion from one of the prize stands, half hidden under a ragged scrap of tar paper. Then a pair of sunglasses. The bulbous figure of a plush Holstein cow. *The lion and the heifer shall lie down together*, she thought. Then a water-stained white cardboard tube the width of her wrist still wound around with three friendship bracelets. Prizes from the Boardwalk all—from Spin the Wheel, Shoot the Clown, Pop the Balloon. Skee-Ball at *Sonny's and Rickey's*, or maybe *Lucky Leo's*. She didn't feel lucky today, and she doubted Leo did either. Carried here on wind or flood—or both? For a moment she saw and heard it all again—the lights and mirrors, the barkers' pitches, the ratcheting number wheels, the clatter and clunk of skee-ball games, the hydraulic rush of the big rides, the teenage squeals…and the rage of Sandy's assault on their home in Sourland Hills, the house lit by candles and flashlights alone. How loud had the storm gotten *here* as it steamrolled in right off the sea? How hard did this house shake?

She bent and slid the bottom bracelet off the tube, tugged it over her right hand and on to her wrist. It was a mostly green affair, with a trace of gold thread twisted in. Who knew what toxic stew had buoyed it here, but it was only a slender thing, could not have soaked up too much sewage, and she decided to accept it as a gift. Maybe it was the storm's way to compensate for all it had taken away. Hardly a fair exchange, but a token at least.

Debris in hefty measure had washed in around the back deck—a huge roll of tar paper, a cracked orange plastic trash can, one side of the railings off the neighbor's back stair. And the worst surprise awaited her here, a sign things might've run amiss beyond even any flooding. The back door to the basement apartment hung open, swung into the dark interior of the space. They always had trouble getting that door to lock right. No matter how many times she reminded the tenants they left it unlocked. Even Paul. But who closed it last and should have latched it? She or Derrick? Had the flood alone forced it open, or was it the victim of some battering ram from the logjam of wreckage? What if someone already got inside? She kept a .22 pistol under her bed in the Sourland Hills house. Twice she'd even had to pull it on Derrick when he was drunk and threatening. She'd left that behind, alas. Here her best bet would be a hammer or knife. Knives were in the kitchen drawers of course, and they kept the tools in a closet off the sunroom. But who might be between her and the front of the house?

Colleen calculated how long it might take her to reach a weapon if someone were already inside. Which floor? Stalker or squatter? Would the intruder show aggression or simply hide? She wished the basement no longer communicated with the main floor. A stairway still connected them. Derrick had promised for several years to wall off the basement end of the stairs and remodel the passage into closet space, but all he'd done was put deadbolts on the outside of the upstairs doors and the interior of the door downstairs. If an interloper really was inside, she'd have a temporary measure of safety if he remained downstairs. Worst case scenario was the person reclined even now on her bed upstairs, knife or hammer or some other weapon of his own already at hand.

Colleen considered walking the two extra blocks to the squad car, requesting a police escort before she entered her home. But the car had looked empty. How far might she have to tramp till she found any actual cops—and would they even help her? She doubted it. They'd laugh off her concern as female hysteria, excitability, nerves, tell her they had other, more important priorities.

Normally noisy Seaside was so quiet now Colleen felt she needed to muffle her steps in some way as she clumped up the back deck stairs, her suitcase thumping along behind her. The town had that creepy vibe of all deserted places, the way you never really felt entirely alone whether you could see anyone else or not.

Another surprise as she paused at the threshold, this one more positive. Her cellphone showed four bars. She tapped in 911 on the keypad before she drew out her door key but didn't make the call, just kept the phone in hand and her thumb above *send* as she unlocked the door. She inhaled deep, exhaled, stepped inside.

The light was dim, just what leaked in through drawn blinds and curtains, but she saw nothing different or out of place. Kitchen and dining room same as she left them in September. The dining room table still bore its undisturbed wooden bowl of pinecones from her yard in Sourland Hills—just as the table at the Sourland house held its corresponding centerpiece bowl of select seashells from Seaside. A pair of pale blue candles in pewter stands flanked the bowl.

She locked and chained the back door behind her, and leaving the suitcase beside it, hustled into the sunroom, still clutching the phone, thumb at ready. The kitchen was closest but the thought of brandishing a chef's knife herself invoked too many images of doomed women in slasher films. A hammer was her weapon of choice if she didn't have a gun. She was good with a hammer and so was her aim—her dad taught her how to pound a nail in just three strokes, a skill she retained all these many years later.

Colleen advanced through the kitchen and living room scanning side to side, moving as quickly and quietly as she could. It only took her a minute to round the corner to the sunroom inside the rarely used front door. She found the steel-handled claw hammer on a wicker shelf right where she remembered it, picked it up and flexed her fingers over the molded rubber grip. She allowed herself to lean half a minute against the east jamb of the doorway, panting softly. From there she could see most of the first floor. The back door was still closed, her suitcase where she'd left it. With a last deep breath she arched away from the doorframe and made her way toward the stairs, just around the corner from where she stood.

The light grew dimmer here and she counted the stairs each as she took them…five, six, seven, eight…then she stood on the landing outside her upstairs bedroom, Graham's room before he went off to college in Washington State and she stopped sharing a bed with Derrick, here or in Sourland.

She entered her own room first, hammer out, phone at her side, checked everywhere even under the bed and in the closet, then repeated the clearance in the full bath, the small bath, and the small bedroom. Nobody anywhere, no sign either of intruders or storm damage.

Colleen sat on the floor of her upstairs bedroom, back against the low rise of the futon bed, hammer hand aiming out the room's open door toward the head of the stairs. Her hands shook, but only slightly.

After several minutes passed and no one rushed up the stairs, she pushed herself to her feet and descended to the main floor. She finished clearing each room and closet with the hammer out before her in a two-handed grip, feeling ridiculous, but also feeling safer by increments.

So no one hid on the two upper floors, and neither storm nor intruder had shifted so much as a bar of soap. That left the basement apartment. Where she'd seen the door wide open. Whatever awaited her there, it would not be good. Flood damage, looter, someone still sleeping in Goldilocks' bed, Colleen really didn't want to know. Better to find out now though.

She dug Derrick's Maglite out of a kitchen drawer, stowed the phone in the pocket of her jeans, and held the light alongside the hammer after she unlocked the door and stepped outside. Her hands hardly shook at all anymore.

Standing before the open basement door with hammer cocked before her and light pressed against it she felt first like an action film star. Then she just felt ridiculous. She was a housewife inspecting flood damage, not Samuel L. Jackson or Angelina Jolie. The damage was going to be bad no matter what, but she couldn't pound the shit out of the storm in retaliation. Sandy had packed up and left, already died of natural causes somewhere far inland. Fizzled out eventually over the Midwest.

Before she took the four steps down from the threshold she played the light around the room. The furniture was all rearranged, scattered randomly throughout the room. Hither and thither, flotsam and jetsam. The fridge lay on its side, doors hanging open like the lolling tongues of dogs. Salt and foam scum stained it all, and a layer of milk chocolate pale mud covered the floor. The flood had churned the deposit into rough sinuous whorls, but the waters themselves had receded. She remembered the floor was concrete beneath the linoleum, with a brass drain set into it somewhere she couldn't recall. Apparently the drain did its job and didn't clog. Or maybe the water just seeped into the floor and the ground below. Or away through the walls.

Something odd about the doorjamb caught her eye, and she turned the Maglite on it for a clearer look. A sort of scurf or crust stuck to the edge of the doorway, almost colorless but shimmering a faint silver-blue beneath the Maglite beam, extending from near the threshold almost to the level of the latch, maybe an eighth of an inch at its thickest. She ran her left index finger up a bit of it and it crumbled at her touch. The remainder sticking to her fingertip might've been tiny scales or hairs. It felt powdery at first, and then her fingertip began to tingle faintly. She rubbed her hand against her jeans to get the stuff off, struck suddenly by the recognition it might be the residue of some toxic waste borne in on the flood. She spotted similar deposits now on the inner doorjamb and the edge of the door itself. As if flood damage wasn't bad enough…what toxins had the overswollen ocean poured into her home?

Once this house seemed the achievement of a dream. Not yet thirty and she owned two homes, one at the shore. Two mortgages true, but she had a set of keys to each house, and that was all that mattered. A summer house at Seaside, the Jersey version of the American dream. No ocean view but less than two blocks to the boardwalk and the beach.

The massive disparity between her dreams and the truth slammed down on her all at once. She felt something fracture inside, paused and shut her eyes, slipped into stillness as her protective armor tumbled down within her, toppling into the woman-shaped void she left where she stood. All her protections, her pretenses, the appearances she struggled to maintain. Two decades back she and Derrick had been young, married…optimistic. They owned a prosperous neighborhood liquor store, a wedding gift from Derrick's parents who'd built the business up for decades and were ready to retire. With the twins still in preschool and the world their oyster they'd felt confident purchasing the shore house, a dream they each held since elementary school. A dream most every suburban New Jersey kid had at some point, walking down the beach hearing the rumors about which celebrity owned which beachfront luxury home, arguing especially about which was Springsteen's, thinking how cool it would be to own property there too. Only there weren't enough shore homes to go around. She and Derrick got one though. Not beachfront, not next door to The Boss, but pretty decent nonetheless. True, Derrick drank, but most everyone she knew back then drank. Could she have foreseen how much worse he'd get, the violent rages, the abuse, or the way the neighborhood would change around their store, the big box retail outfits opening nearby in three directions, the years of counting quarters? The times she had to pull the .22 on Derrick? And all the other times she slept with it under her pillow. Mostly she kept locked doors between them at night and sometimes even by day when he started in early on the booze, her gut gone acid even though she covered her ears not to hear the threats and curses he thumped out on the door in the Morse code of drunks.

after

Their dreams had died long before Sandy, but till now they'd hung on, held together, first for the twins and afterward on inertia. Now the commitment of real estate replaced earlier bonds. Empty as all three structures were most of the time, two homes and the store offered obligations that kept them going even with the boys off to college on opposite coasts. Enter Sandy. This might be the end, the final straw, flood damage their insurance wouldn't cover, most of all if coupled with some kind of toxic waste contamination. The loss of the extra rent… They were barely making both mortgages, and sale of either property was unlikely given the current housing market and the damage she was examining now.

That first night in the shore house was where it all went south, way back when. Celebrating together with a five dollar bottle of Sutter Home Zinfandel, Derrick had moved on to bourbon and left her in the dust. When she suggested he apply the brakes as he stood to pour another two fingers from the bottle on the counter, he snapped, called her a whiny bitch. Then a whiny *fuckin'* bitch. Colleen rose furious from her seat, had just begun to call him out when he smacked her shoulders with both hands, palms flat, shoving her back into her seat hard enough she would've toppled if the chair hadn't struck the lower tier of cabinets. He'd gotten ugly before when he drank. But never this ugly.

Then Derrick backhanded her casually across the face, the first time he ever struck her. Not the last. She ducked to the side in advance of his second swing and he overcompensated and lost his balance, fell heavily to the carpet, cursed anew in Polish — *Ty pizdo*! She found out later what that meant, was not surprised. Colleen, already up and moving, ran for the room of the sleeping twins before he could get back on his feet, locked the door behind her. She expected Derrick's curses and pounding assault on the door any second, soon as he arose, but they never came. Concern for the twins most like. She clung panting in confusion to the siderail of Alexander's crib, tears dripping in silent rhythm onto the child's coverlets. Blood from her nose was staining the boy's blanket as well but she didn't realize that in the dark. There was no adult bed in the room back then, so she shoved together the two childsized comfy chairs and slept spanning them best she could in a compressed fetal curl.

Neither she nor Derrick mentioned his assault the next morning. First she slept in late, late as she could manage, then played with the boys until they grew bored with their own room and the few toys it held, beginning to mutiny at their unjustified confinement.

In the kitchen she found Derrick struggling to prepare an unburnt breakfast of bacon and eggs, toast on the side. Observing their father at the stove confused the twins, but given how rarely he made any effort in the kitchen—or with cleaning or any other housework for that matter—it was no surprise he drew attention. She had some idea what he was up to here. This could only be a guilt-meal. Though his culinary repentance held no interest for her, breakfast itself did. She hoped he correctly estimated enough for them all.

When sit down to table time came the bacon was plentiful but pale and flabby in random spots, still half raw, the gray and rubbery overcooked eggs lacked salt and pepper or any other seasoning, and Derrick had made the toast too soon which left it leathery and cold. Yet it was all essentially edible, and the boys paid no mind to the meal's shortcomings, gulping down barely chewed mouthfuls like pythons with distended jaws. Technically, their breakfast was probably no less nutritious than if she made it, though not half as appetizing, and she decided to keep her mouth zipped about its quality. Zipped for now, except to eat what little she could stomach. Later they would discuss his violence of the night before. No bribe of a single mismanaged meal was going to change what he'd done.

Only somehow they never had that talk. Meals, cleaning, the boys, the beach, exhaustion. Tomorrow, she told herself, but tomorrow came and went as well. Then Sunday night and back to Sourland, where other routines reasserted themselves. She chalked up his transgression to drink and the stress of the second mortgage, convinced herself it was a one time thing.

It was not. Three years later he began abusing her again, sometimes at the shore house, sometimes at Sourland. Sometimes even sober, least as far as she knew. Eventually in front of the twins. Intervals between incidents ranged from weeks to years, his triggers rarely clear. Each time she thought she'd learned just what not to do or say, he exploded again over something else. She began her own quiet metamorphosis, speaking less, moving slower, keeping to corners, wearing drab clothes.

He only hit her twice after that first incident down the shore. Yet the threat was always there. His pattern of abuse shifted instead to the verbal front, the psychological and emotional, cursing her out in both English and Polish, especially when no one else was around. A troubled coworker translated what Colleen could remember later of the Polish, grimacing at the phrases Derrick used, shaking her head and prefacing each translation with —No man should say these things to his wife.

Colleen learned not to trust his occasional morning kindness, serving her coffee or tea, sometimes toast with jam. Such gestures were already the downstroke of a pendulum that always bottomed out by afternoon and made a minefield of the day later. She also knew never to shut the TV off with Derrick in the room, even when he seemed to be passed out on the couch. So simple a flick of that switch always brought him right to his feet, swearing angrily, sometimes threatening her life. Such an incident was one of only two times she ran to her room and grabbed the gun down from her closet's top shelf, pointed it at Derrick as he entered the doorway in pursuit.

As the boys grew older—and taller—he toned it down some. By the time they grew taller than him he cut it out altogether, except for a certain sort of targeted glare. Now that the boys were gone however, she felt his rage and violence percolating close to the surface again, sensed the warning signs, kept herself prepared to cut and run, knew always the distance to the nearest door. And the .22. And which was closer at any given moment. She'd thought the eruption was going to come this morning, when she asked him to let her take the bus to Seaside alone, suggested he put in a full day at the liquor store instead, take an interest in the receipts. He glared, but that was all.

So it was that her visit to the shore house offered a sort of relief, despite apprehension over the confrontation she anticipated when she returned home, or the damage she expected to encounter here. But though the basement looked almost a total loss, the rest of the house seemed more or less as they'd left it. Their worst fears had not come to pass—no torn roof, no broken windows, no water damage on the upper floors. No evidence of looters. Really, they were getting off easy. A blessing.

As for the basement, she already knew she couldn't do much there now. No way she could repair the water damage or drag the ruined fridge or furniture out herself. They'd have to come back together, she and Derrick, maybe even bring additional help.

Colleen closed the downstairs door but could tell the latch didn't set. She pushed it back open a few inches, closed and tried it again. No good. That latch was always tricky, but the door seemed to be warped now as well. She didn't feel like wrestling with it at the moment—she'd lock it on her way out. And if she didn't, what would looters take anyway? If they even came. Seemed the police and Coast Guard had kept everything safe so far, despite everyone's fears. Back on the main floor she re-parked her suitcase upright beside the sofa, collapsed on the cushions with a muffled *whoof*. So the basement was a complete write off, and maybe contaminated…the upper two floors seemed untouched and likely to stay that way. Meanwhile at least she was actually safe here. Safe from Derrick. If only until 4:00 p.m. or so.

She kicked off her sneakers and stretched out on the couch, cradling her head on her folded hands. What essentials did she really need to gather? She might as well leave everything right here. Just as it was. Anything that survived Sandy and maybe looters wasn't going anywhere and didn't need to now. But a pure unfrightened rest? How much was that worth? She wriggled her stocking feet beneath the decorative pillows at the other end of the sofa and arched her back against the upright cushioned roll behind her. Her position was not the most comfortable but her feeling of safety more than compensated and she soon fell asleep.

***

When Colleen woke the light through the windows was sepia, dim. Was it after 4:00? Had she missed her bus? She dredged her phone from the pocket of her jeans, thumbed it on and waited, checked the time. 3:26. Wow. She still had time but she'd have to hoof it. Slipping on her sneakers she left the suitcase behind, rushed out the back door, locked it, remembered the unlocked basement, but what the hey? Let looters make off with the sodden contaminated junk down there—they'd be doing her a favor if they did.

She jogged alone up sandy Hancock to sterile Boulevard, hurried toward her bus stop. The bus was not back yet but the passengers sat in a row along the curb. Red Cross volunteers walked up and down the line, passing out plastic takeout boxes of what appeared to be food. Suddenly she felt ravenous so she took a seat in the line, gestured to a shapeless man carrying four stacked white Styrofoam cartons. He changed course and handed her a meal off the top along with a plastic fork wrapped in a single napkin. Neither of them exchanged any courtesies. Only too late did she realize that

after

Geor-dan or Jorge sat on her right, had paused from eating his own meal to stare right at her, free from shame. She turned back and fixed her gaze on the Styrofoam lid in her lap, lifted it and found in its four compartments…

…chunks of canned pineapple, cubes of unrecognizable meat dry and brown, the bottom half of a burger bun, and a splat of dark orange paste that might've been either applesauce or pureed yams. Or maybe even refried beans.

Colleen felt her appetite whirl away like water down a drain. All at once she couldn't be one of these people, couldn't eat their food or get on their bus. Couldn't go back.

Closing the lid of the repugnant meal and setting it on the pavement between her feet, she turned to George. —Will you watch this for me? I forgot something. I'll be right back.

He gaped several seconds before responding then said —Yeah, sure. Okay.

And then —You know, if you don't want the food, I'll eat it for you.

—That's fine, go ahead. I'm not that hungry anyway.

—Are you sure you're gonna be back in time? We're leaving as soon as the bus gets back.

—Of course. I'll probably just get in at the end of the line though, so I may not see you again. You go ahead and eat that stuff. I won't have time when I get back. Thanks! Thanks so much!

Colleen was already up and moving, sensing Georgie-boy staring after her, probably at her ass, but no one else noticed her departure so far as she could tell. On Boulevard she took the sidewalk on the east side of street, and at Hancock she slipped between the two houses at the end of the block, looking as casual as she could, then picked her way through the shared mostly unfenced spaces that served for backyards here. If Jordie kept his mouth shut and no one saw her on the street, she ought to make it home free, out of sight of the cruiser down the beach end of the street.

She reached the back of 46 Hancock unchallenged and took the deck stairs in a rush. Heart pounding she fumbled with the keys but soon had herself inside once more. She paused there, back against the wall beside the door, waiting for the thump of FEMA or the police, but that thump never came. She pulled out her phone, stared at the tiny white time at the top of the screen…4:05, 4:06, 4:07…4:11. At 4:15 she decided the bus must be gone. She walked to the sofa where she'd napped and sat down. The indoor light had grown quite dim. Her battery was down to 28%, but the phone was wonky and might die any second. She drew a deep breath and dialed Derrick, their home number in Sourland. It took him seven rings to pick up. Drinking.

—Hey. It's me. I wanted to let you know I decided to stay here awhile.

—How long is *a while?*

—I don't know. A few days. A week maybe. Till everybody else comes back, I guess. Till the power comes on again down here.

He didn't answer right away. Then —Will they let you? I don't think that's even legal. Aren't the evacuation orders still in effect?

—Doesn't matter. I'm here in the house already and no one saw me come in. I'll keep out of sight during the day. You might want to pick up the truck at the mall though. It's in front of Macy's more or less. I'll let you know when I want to come home.

—What the hell Colleen? Don't they have like, martial law down there? You might get shot or tasered or something.

As if he really cared. —I'll be safe. Oh, and the house…the basement flooded pretty bad, but the rest seems okay. I think all the furniture and the carpet down there are ruined. The fridge is lying on its side. Stinks too, like low tide and chemicals. Later on you'll have to come down and help me haul it all out. They've got construction dumpsters on the street for that stuff. But not now, okay? Anyway, this phone's gonna die so goodbye for now. Don't forget to pick up the truck. It'll look suspicious parked at the mall overnight. I'll be in touch when the power comes back on.

—Wait, look, if this is about…

She ended the call and shut off the phone at 17%, powered it down. Who knew how long that final fractional charge would last? Or when she might need it. Or why.

She'd really gone and done it now. How long was she stuck here? And what would happen if the police *did* catch her?

But she was safe from Derrick, safe from his words and safe from his fists. Safe from the hostile glares he gave her. Reasonably safe even from the memories of all he'd done to her, at least all he'd done in the Sourland house.

She was safe to sleep anywhere she wanted in this house, even to sleep with her door open, or at least unlocked.

after

Colleen began an inventory of the food in the cupboards and tiny pantry, mentally cataloguing what she found. Precious little. They'd cleaned out the fridge when they left for the season, taken most of the dry goods with them too. Once her list was complete, she immediately started slashing it down to only those items she could prepare without water, gas, or electricity. Why did they have so much pasta? But no jars of storebought *sauce*—her mother would roll over in her grave if Colleen didn't make her Sunday gravy from scratch. Their stores also included several cans of diced pineapple. She felt no urge to crack those open any time soon.

Then there was the matter of light. The Maglite *devoured* batteries, big D cells, and she'd be lucky if Derrick kept even one extra set in the house. With just that and a handful of candles she'd have to stretch what she had or find more somehow, at least till whenever the power came back on. Or maybe she would have to get used to the dark.

She'd also need a bucket for her latrine. A bucket and some sand. For a moment she thought seriously of the bright orange trashcan wedged beneath the deck. Then she envisioned it tumbling over as she straddled it mid-crap and scrapped that plan at once. What bucket in the house could she sacrifice? She wished she'd brought a cheap cleaning bucket like some of the other folks who came in on her bus. Eventually she settled on a battered blue plastic mop bucket from the kitchen closet, set it in a corner of the upstairs bathroom with a plastic bag liner, several sacks of sand she'd scooped up around the house beside it. Then tried to forget it all for the time being. She'd face that necessity soon enough. They'd done the same the last couple days in Sourland after the generator gave out and the well wouldn't pump, and when at last the power and water came back on, she and Derrick sealed the bucket they used inside two layers of trash bags and chucked it in a public dumpster several blocks from their house.

She learned the sand trick from her father. He did his best to teach her to be an outdoor girl. For a moment she thought of calling him later to thank him if that plan worked out for her here...then she remembered how long he'd been gone.

The blinds she decided she'd best leave down. They'd likely block the light of the Maglite beam from outside view well enough, but open windows would not. In the daytime enough light would filter through she could move around.

So this was her home for the next how long? She would need to get used to moving around in the dark, navigating like a blind woman with neither dog nor cane. She figured she could at least go out at night if she took care. She'd have to keep inside and quiet throughout the day.

What the hell had she gone and done? It was really sinking in now. Panic sent up a shudder but she steadied herself, reminded herself *why*. This was going to be a kind of vacation. Almost. A vacation from the volatile arena of her daily life.

She groped about the cabinets while a tenuous remnant of daylight remained, relocated a lone can of Chef Boyardee ravioli, something Derrick must've bought for himself because she sure as shit wouldn't feed that stuff to her kids. Probably it was six or seven years old or more, but it was canned, right? Intended to survive a nuclear holocaust anywhere but ground zero. She found the can opener and a fork, sat down at the table and ate the cold ravioli right from the can. They tasted better than she expected, evoking school lunches of her childhood, though she always ate them hot on a tray back then. Could be hunger and her glimpse of the free Red Cross meal made her more welcoming of the venerable chef's wares.

They had books and board games and cards in the closets, but she couldn't do much with those in the thickening dark. She recalled the moon as a dirty toenail sliver the night before, so there'd be little help on that front for a while. It was going to get really dark tonight, and that meant her and the Maglite and little else. Candles, if she were careful. The two on the table and maybe half a dozen others scattered about here and there.

Colleen took another nap, this time on her own bed upstairs. When she woke the blackness stretched extensive and deep, slit only by dim parallel lines of glow from between the slats of the blinds. She groped for the Maglite on the floor where she'd left it but didn't turn it on right away. Precious batteries.

She was going to need more batteries. Soon. They might run out before her food did. With nowhere to buy them—on the ride in she'd seen the only supermarket boarded up—she would have to become a looter herself. Must be some of her neighbors had batteries. Batteries, more canned goods, another flashlight or at least some more candles. And bottled water. She stripped the pillowcase off the pillow she'd been using, looped it double between belt and waistband of her jeans.

after

Downstairs she retrieved the hammer where she'd left it on the table, shoved the handle into her pocket as far as it would go. The result was awkward, the head and over half the handle still protruding. Removing it she worked it through her belt till the head pressed against her hip. Utility belt. She could be Batman now, or Batgirl. And the night was hers to roam.

She waited a while yet, wanting the darkness to harden—and any police to go home. Once she was certain it was close to 8:00, she stepped out through the back door, which she was careful to lock behind her. No need to let looters into her own home while she herself was out looting someone else's. That would be an unfunny irony.

She wished she had the .22, but really, what would she do with it in this wasteland? And would that make it Armed Robbery if she got caught with a gun on her? She'd seen that movie *Old Boy*. A hammer was good enough for him. It would have to be good enough for her.

Her eyes were well adapted to the dark by this point so she had little trouble traveling down the deck stairs without turning on the Maglite. Once at ground level she decided to cut between houses, come out on Fremont, the next avenue to the north. Her *borrowings* would be discovered eventually, so she would be wise to target houses at least a couple blocks from her own, muddy her trail as much as she could.

On the south side of Fremont she looked side to side, recognized the home to her right as the Van Nests', an older couple who had Derrick and her over for pinochle more than once. And on the left was the Maxcys', with whose youngest daughter Alexander had a summer fling not so far back.

She looked toward the shore and saw no more cruiser parked before this street's berm either, decided to chance a crossing. From there she made her way again between homes to Kearney, the avenue behind Fremont. She couldn't remember anyone on this street, so no one who lived there was likely to know her either.

Kearney, presumably named after the town in north Jersey, since the next street was *Carteret*. Most Seaside residents pronounced it *Kear*-knee, *kear* like *ear*, but they were seasonal and came from all over the state, some from New York and P.A. Colleen knew in the actual town they pronounced it *Car*-knee. Her one year at Old Queens a girl across the hall on her dorm floor came from there. Colleen took a shot at saying something nice about a town she'd never visited, just to make conversation, but the girl scoffed in response, said —You wanna know how bad Kearney is? *Guidos from other towns come to hang around in Kearney.* Well, plenty of Guidos came to hang around in Seaside too. Some even made it on that stupid MTV show *Jersey Shore.*

Fact was they shot that show right round the corner from where she stood. One night several friends had called to tell her she and the boys had appeared in a scene. Apparently a somewhat drunken *Snooki* had staggered by them as they walked toward the beach, the boys escorting her away from Derrick, who was also getting drunk—and ugly. They hadn't even spotted the camera crew. The incident afterward became a joke between them, but thereafter they also kept an eye out for MTV cameras. Well, not tonight. Small blessings.

Colleen decided to target homes close to the *Jersey Shore* house, thinking any break-ins thereabouts would be attributed to the show's low denominator appeal. Let that TV trainwreck at least be good for something. Police would likely think the looters were seeking souvenirs from the show house and got their addresses mixed up in the dark.

A pair of motels dominated a chunk of the southeast section of Kearney, but a bungalow between them had a fenced backyard, no doubt to keep out the motels' guests. Holding the Maglite inside two layers of the pillowcase and beamed at the ground, she made her way down the debris-littered drive on the little home's west side, came around the back and hustled up its low deck.

She discovered a door there with six glass panels set above the knob—oh thank her lucky stars. She fumbled at the knob, hand jittery with adrenaline. Right, left. Locked. Unlikely it was unlocked but foolish not to try first. She shut off the light, drew it out from the pillowcase, and slipped the hammer inside in its place. Firm grip around the handle, she thrust it against the lower left panel with what she hoped was just enough strength, had to pull back in time so as not to shove her hand through the jagged glass remaining in the rectangular frame.

The shattering glass made less noise than expected. Some small relief. She used the head of the shrouded hammer to snap loose any shards of glass still protruding, then reached inside and worked the latch. And she was in.

She swapped light for hammer again, looked around. This house was not so different from her own, though smaller, a bit more constricted. She'd come in through the kitchen, so she began to rifle the cabinets. A couple pointless cupboards of dishes pots and pans then she hit pay dirt! A half dozen cans of sockeye salmon and just as many flat tins of sardines in oil, five more of green beans, three of creamed corn. Another four of Campbell's chicken and stars, her childhood favorite. All better than anything she had at 46 Hancock. She stuffed the cans one by one in the pillowcase, the trembling of her hands much diminished, then set the sack down and drew out the light. Cupping it with her hand so her fingers more or less covered the lens, she began her search for spare batteries in drawers and closets. On batteries and candles she struck out.

Her sack had gotten hefty, too awkward anymore to hold with the light inside. A sea green linen napkin and a rubber band from an odd and ends drawer did the trick instead. She had enough food already for what? A week? A while at least. Her first B & E had paid off, bought her more time, justified the risk. No spare batteries or water but she could hunt for those tomorrow night…if the cops didn't get wise and hunt *her* down first.

She left the house through the door she'd entered, even latching it again through the little broken window panel. The pillowcase tugged at her arm so she wrapped its open end twice around her wrist. With the hammer through her belt and the switched-off light in her left hand, she stepped back out on Kearney.

Colleen decided not to return the same way she'd come, to obscure her route a bit, for what that mattered. And here her curiosity about the beach got the better of her, with the Kearney Avenue berm only a short block away. So it was she scuffed quickly down the sandy sidewalk on Kearney, across Ocean Terrace, and came to the head high ridge of sand where the boardwalk had been. The long mound was dense and damp, packed by a bulldozer it appeared, and it sloped enough on her side she felt she could manage a sliding climb over it.

First she slipped the hammer and the darkened lamp into the bag with the cans, then swung that sack onto the top of the wet compressed ridge. It rose just above her head but not beyond reach. Hands free she dug in, kicking footholds and clawing with her hands. Yet every attempted hold slid down half or more its height before catching, and she felt first like one of those guys from Greek myth, Sisyphus or Tantalus or such, her labors leading her nowhere except back to her start. After a solid minute of failure her feet finally found purchase. The sand was wet enough to hold together some, which helped, and digging in with her elbows in support of slipping hands offered more traction.

Soon she had herself sprawled across the damp bulldozed sand dike, the wet of the sand soaking into her clothes. She felt it against her knees, her hips, her belly, her boobs. She should've zipped up her coat before beginning her climb. Hugging the top of the heap she wiggled her way over till her feet found air, pushed off in that direction and let herself slide till she struck the beach. Eazy peazy.

She set the pillowcase sack on the sand and drew out the light, brushed herself off best she could. Ahead to the right the starlight revealed the dim silhouette of Casino Pier. So strange to see it all dark, out there where lights of every color usually lit the rides deep into the night. She thought of those rides she'd known since childhood, her favorite the Himalaya with its full time DJ and his infamous catchphrase *The louder you scream the faster we go*. Silent now. Every ride dark and quiet. The pier seemed too short somehow though perhaps that was only her angle. She wondered which attractions survived the storm intact, especially those farthest out, considered a moment walking the full length of the pier to see. But if there were guards anywhere they'd be on the pier. Not likely it'd be safe out there either, guards or no guards. Getting caught with her haul would compound her problems. The best thing would be to head home with her contraband quick without any fooling around. No time for serious sightseeing in the dark. No point either.

She walked out just as far as the edge of the surf, let it lap at her sneakers till her toes felt wet cold. Though the rhythm of the waves even now seemed somehow *off*, a flood of memories washed over her still at the sound. Standing in the shin deep surf holding hands with her dad, learning how to travel down the beach without a single step, trusting solely in the slow repetitive power of the tide. Or that April night they'd all come down from Old Queens so buzzed she'd lost her shorts to the tide after leaving them too close to the edge. Telling those stories to Paul as they walked along the night beach just this past July, hand in hand, her shorts soon to come off again.

As a girl she stared out from these shores, certain she saw the edge of England waver ever so faintly at the uncertain juncture of sea and sky. Staring out now along the edge of the pier, she spotted the skeletal steel Beziers of the rollercoaster barely silhouetted against the bruise-hued sky. Only the coaster no longer rode the end of the pier. It appeared instead to rise direct from the inky sea, its iconic form distorted, bent, no longer true. Another piece of her past stolen by the storm.

She looked down, watched the white edge of a wave just miss her already wet feet, walked forward until she was well within range of the surf. The water ran over her sneakers and she felt its iciness ascend her ankles, but she didn't mind. It made her feel close to fully alive a moment, in a way she hadn't since she'd last seen Paul, back in September. But Paul was dead they said, crushed under a tree during the attempted rescue of a husband and wife pinned in their car by a previous treefall. *They* survived. Sandy oh Sandy, why oh why? Like 9-11, she'd been hell on first responders. And hell on those who loved them.

Colleen tramped along the high water mark, came up even with Hancock before she knew it, the negative space of the street showing in shadow. From the surf she turned to face the berm…and almost backed farther into the sea. A group of men milled atop the heaped up sand. No, *not men*. The vertical elements were too thin, displayed no arms. A fence then? The kind you saw sagging between beach and dunes at Ocean City or Sandy Hook, rough red-stained slats rolled out in a wire mesh, not good for much except the message to KEEP OUT and being awkward to climb over. When had anyone put that up? She was sure it wasn't there when she first walked down Hancock that morning—and the berm at Kearney had been clear as well. She'd have to backtrack now, but how far? Was the motion she saw a sign some crew was putting it up right now? How long then before FEMA or whoever fenced the other street ends, and in which direction were they working? She didn't want to get trapped out here on the beach, wet and sandy and without dry clothes.

But as the fence rippled and she watched, she realized it wasn't either a fence—nor was it anything she recognized in form. Neither men nor fence slats but rows of bowed staves or spears or…*spines*, all shifting and bristling in suspect motion. Was this some security device installed for the night, like the clusters of wires on buildings meant to keep off pigeons, only here meant to keep out the likes of her? And she on the wrong side. Were they putting them up on every street? Would she get trapped and have to spend the night on the beach?

Colleen held her breath and watched, slowly hunkered down close to the waves, which soaked her sneakers fully now and splashed up her calves, splattering even her hunkered butt and thighs. She held the cold lumpy pillowcase across her lap.

The lower angle improved her view of the rippling rows enough she could see how the spikes all seemed to rise off something like a dark corrugated pipe or tube several feet thick that ascended the berm on its south side and ran along its upper ridge. Was this the latest innovation in emergency security fence, some humungous hose that needed only to be rolled out and inflated? But then the whole assemblage of spikes and tube rippled and rose a foot at least above the berm and she saw beneath in silhouette… were those *legs*? Dozens of thick stumpy legs? At this point she could no longer deny she was watching the movements of a living thing. As a long time—if part time—resident of the Shore, one whose sons at some time or other had dragged home the rotting corpse of most everything that lived in the ocean and died on shore, blabbered about things they knew only from TV or books—she ran through her mental inventory of possible legitimate identities of the creature on the berm. Oarfish was the only choice she lingered on—the only thing long enough—but Colleen knew this was no way an oarfish. Oarfish didn't have spikes near that high and didn't have legs at all. And though no expert, she was certain they couldn't live long out of the water.

The thing began to advance across the berm, and Colleen felt a cold fear seep in from her limbs. It had to be fully thirty feet in length. Maybe more.

Jointless, squat and thick, the maybe legs still appeared to support the horizontal central trunk. It was all one creature. It was nothing she knew. And she knew right then it was nothing known.

She almost swore aloud but bit back her *Fuck!* And bit it back a second time as the light from a vehicle turning far up the street backlit the thing. A state police car most like. A second only or less, but in that flash she saw the lumpy globe at its north end, the two curling tusks that hung beneath it. And she saw the same silver-blue sheen she'd seen off the crust on her downstairs door. She did swear aloud when she recognized *that*.

The thing moved then, dropped down from the berm. It moved in her direction. She rose and ran, splashing through the fizzling waves to solid sand, looking back then flat out sprinting. She couldn't be sure but the shadows suggested it had turned to head her way. She *was* sure it heard her, was just as certain it did not want to be her pet.

The sack thumped her thighs so she hefted it and held it against her chest, causing her upper half to shimmy slightly side to side while she ran but not upsetting her balance. Looking back she could see the creature coming toward her on the beach, but it was not gaining ground. Soon she reached the unencumbered Kearney berm and struggled over it in half the time she'd needed to cross before. Experience and the knowledge that something so big pursued her made her almost helium light.

On the street she considered a moment hunting for a cop…but unless she knew where they were that would be a crap shoot, and she didn't know. Would a cop even believe her? Could a cop even protect her from—whatever the hell that thing was? And what would the cops do if they caught her out here after hours? Send her back if not something worse. She imagined a patrol officer interrogating her, instructing her to calm herself, while the thing from the berm came closer, rose above them. Like a scene from some horror film, it would attack the hapless cop first, giving her just enough time to run. Maybe at the end of the movie she would find the cop's keys and escape in his abandoned patrol car. But this wasn't a movie.

She decided to follow her own route back so ran toward the house she'd barely just burgled. Cutting off Kearney she glanced back and saw the dark shape of the crawling thing rising over the berm. Pale starlight silhouetted its front against the sky, spiral *tusks* uncoiling and coiling. Not tusks then. Appendages of some kind. If the round part was the head they might be fangs. If. What the hell kind of thing was it?

Whatever it was, it *was* following her, she could not deny that. And though she had a lead, it was also making decent time. Fuck oh fuck. She scuttled along the fenceline of the site of her recent minor crime, considered a moment hiding out in that very house but the thing was likely close behind. She had to do more to give it the slip. Nor should she be caught inside the same house she robbed. What if it trapped her there all night and the rightful owners showed up on the morning's bus?

With the fence past she duckwalked through dark backyards, avoiding debris she barely saw, hoping not to step on an upright nail, slipped between the homes of folks she didn't know and likely never would, came out on Fremont's sandy walk, jigged to avoid a parking meter she almost slammed. There she glanced side to side—no cruiser, no foot patrol, not that she could see—then shot across the street without further thought. Standing above the sand covered curb of south Fremont she looked back between houses along her route. Nothing moved in the shadows but could she see it if it did? Then starlight flickered a second over something silver-blue and writhing and Colleen turned and ran through the dark. Not six feet on she tripped over some scattered hunk of wreckage she could not see. She found the ground hard, her shins smacking the unseen obstacle and throwing her torso forward. The pillowcase full of cans broke her fall only so far, her forearms grinding the shallow sand, cans and hammer pressed against her chest, one can edge jamming into her left breast hard enough she knew it would bruise. *Same place as that bitemark she had to hide from Derrick last June.*

She released an involuntary grunt of pain then scrambled to her feet. Evidence so far suggested the creature possessed excellent hearing. She had no ideas about its sight or sense of smell. Colleen looked back again and saw only the shadows, but unless the thing caught some random glimmer between houses once more, it might make it almost to the sidewalk before she would know.

Up and moving again she passed down an alley on the Fremont side of the block, then picked her way up the dark center aisle till she stood behind her own home. Up the deck struggling to muffle her near panicked steps, fumbling for the key at the door.

Inside.

Door closed behind her and locked. Her primary line of defense. Sack dropped on the table except the hammer and the light—what good the hammer might do her she didn't know—but just to have some kind of weapon in hand. She wasn't going to go down without a fight. Not that she knew at all what might go down. Her breath came fast and she knew she was near panic.

Up the stairs to the second floor, she selected the master bath for best chance at a last stand, and with the door locked behind her she hunched in the tub, clutching the hammer handle in both her hands, awaiting the sound of the creature forcing the first floor door below. Her whole form trembled with adrenalin, full-on fight or flight. Yet she'd flown as far as she could, probably couldn't put up much of a fight if it came to that. Her and her little hammer, against…whatever it was? Even if she did have her gun, she doubted .22 rounds would have much stopping power against something that size.

When the creature came to her house—and it did come—it was not the deck door it forced. She heard it entering the unlocked basement instead. She knew the creak of that door's swing well, especially learned to listen for it this summer past, every time Paul went in or out. That space had become almost sacred to her. *Tonight the part of Paul will be played by this gigantic spiky monster the Superstorm washed up.* Because that's what it had to be. What else? But from what deep impossible part of the sea? Why was it still alive on land? Shouldn't such a thing have died on shore, burst by the time it was churned up to the surface? What was the expression—explosive decompression? Unless it wasn't a sea creature at all.

Colleen curled in on herself, a struggle to stop the shaking. She heard sounds of the monster shifting around downstairs, but not of it squeezing back out through the door. After a while even those odd muffled noises stopped and all that remained was a faint sort of wet repetitive wheeze. The thing wasn't coming for her. Not yet. It was just camping out. *In her basement.*

The meaning of the residue along the downstairs doorframe became clear. That creature had visited her home on Hancock more than once before, denned up in her very own downstairs. Damn the sketchy lock on that door! If the monster had settled in for the night she would have to sleep in the tub. Not that she was going to get any sleep with shakes like she had now. But she couldn't risk alerting it with some new sound if she moved around. She was trapped but she had reasonable certainty now it didn't know she was upstairs. Not yet. Colleen was becoming convinced its presence below was no more than a horrible coincidence. It might even have lost her trail as she cut across the blocks…and yet tracked right back to the house it had been using all along as a lair.

She wondered where it went in the day, since it hadn't been there when she arrived. Did it hide in some other house or return to the sea? It couldn't have been wandering Seaside freely by day—there were police and other emergency services on patrol. But for some reason it kept on coming back to her house at night, the house where she herself had chosen to hide. Could her luck get any more fucked than this?

Colleen set the hammer softly between her knees and drew out her phone. Could she, should she call 911? *There's this enormous monster in my basement, I think it wants to eat me but it forgot I'm here for now, it's just hanging out.* They'd be way more interested in the crazy woman hiding in Seaside overnight. And with her luck the thing would be gone before they came. She set the phone on the floor.

Inching up slowly and stretching she reached the towel rack, tugged a thick one down and folded it double for a pillow. There were worse things than a night in the tub. She'd done it several times at parties in her youth. She could do it now. If the thing stayed down below till the morning she'd have time to consider more options. There ought at least to be more cops around then.

But if she got the police involved how would they react to her prohibited overnight presence in *The Town That Fun Built*? Probably escort her back to Tom's River at least, where an angry and likely inebriated Derrick would have to drive out to pick her up. Or maybe they'd just taser her and then *dump* her on the opposite side of the bridge.

If the thing stayed downstairs overnight she might wait it out, lock the door behind it proper whenever it left. The basement no longer communicated with the upstairs except for that stairway. Derrick had fit it with heavy deadbolts on the doors up and down once they started renting the space out. If the creature attempted to force those doors…well, at least she would hear and have some warning. Maybe then it would be time for 911. Or running out to Boulevard to wave for a cop. She estimated the drop from the bathroom window to the ground, the likely location of any possible patrol. She didn't think the Creeper could fit through the window behind her so it would have to backtrack. As long as she didn't break an ankle during the fall she could pick up a lead.

She vowed to keep her vigil all night long, or at least until the creature left, but sleep seized her soon as her adrenalin rush faded and held her till dim light through the blinds woke her, not the noise of her unexpected tenant departing. Was it still down in her basement, or had it left before the sun came up? And what was it waiting out down there? For the sunrise or her to get careless? Where had it gone if it left? The basement of some other home? Back to the sea? The sewers? Down into some tunnel deep in the dunes?

after

Colleen weighed her options. Staying in place did not seem a good plan. She needed water badly and would need more food as well. At least if the thing came for her now she should have time to call for help—out a window, over her phone—and hope someone heard.

As full consciousness returned and she felt more alert, she listened. The slow sucking wheeze she'd heard last night through the vents was gone. Did that mean the monster itself was gone? Or just deep in whatever passed for its sleep? She held her breath as long as she could, directed all of her attention to her ears. Nada. Of course the thing might be playing 'possum. Who knew how patient a predator it might be? And if this monster had really washed up with Sandy what had it eaten since the storm? What…or *who*? Was it starving now? Maybe it finally finished starving to death just this past night. Was the corpse of some species unknown to science lying crumpled in her basement even now? Would that carcass be worth some reward like the corpse of a sasquatch? Or was its advent more ominous, something the hurricane wrenched out of the sky, left stranded in Seaside once its ship sunk offshore? Would government men in Tyvek suits come to haul it into an unmarked truck, threaten her never to speak of it under the National Secrets Act before they drove off with the limp mass of mystery flesh, leaving her only unanswered questions and a trashed out downstairs? She'd have to think hard before reporting it in.

And that was only if the beast still lingered below. Might be it left while she was conked out, in which case she'd seem crazy making any report. Any contact with the law was not likely to go well for her in that scenario.

Colleen rose and stepped out of the tub, still holding both the hammer and the light. Standing, she wriggled her shoulders, flexed her arms to shake out all the cramps, then stretched her legs to clear the stiffness. After two full rounds of this she stared at the floor and listened. Nothing. She shrugged her shoulders in a full on —*Fuck it then*, and stamped her left foot flat against the tiled floor. Once, twice. Listened some more. No sound came from below. She unlocked the bathroom, advanced to the bolted door of the stairs and slapped it twice with her left hand, hard. Froze and listened. Still nothing. If the thing were still down there it did not seem to care. It was either too wily or too weak. What if it was injured, if it had come here to die? How would she know it was dead in the end? Again she considered trying to sell its body for some bucks. Could she pull that off? Would she need Derrick's help? How would they get it out?

Right then it hit her how little *she* cared for her own fate. Her life had dwindled down to this pitiful dissipated point, Paul dead and gone, leaving her with Derrick, a man for whom she knew she'd never have feelings again. With whom she'd never feel safe. The boys were departed to their own separate destinies. How often would she honestly ever see them again? Parts of summers and occasional holiday visits, growing less frequent as the years passed like in that old Harry Chapin song she thought so corny growing up. Anticipated emptiness left her absent of motivation and attachments, and much of her fear fluttered away with her cares.

Clutching both light and hammer, Colleen started down the stairs. From there through the kitchen and after a long pause hesitantly out the back door, squinting into the sunlight and scanning the back lot for cops. Despite her detachment her heart pounded harder as she descended the steps of the deck. Sure enough the basement door hung inward. She froze several yards back and listened close as she could but heard no sound from within—no shifting bulk, no sucking wheeze. It took a minute or more before she mastered her shakes enough to stagger forward half the distance and shine her light toward the open door.

Initially Colleen saw nothing inside. Sunlight, contrast, the beam diffusing before it entered the door. She had to move closer. One shuffling step, two. Three and she stood directly before the dark rectangular void, too close to dodge any monsters that lunged her way. She felt detached again, and her hands no longer trembled. What she observed was little different from the day before. A fresh layer of the powdery silver blue silt was plain around parts of the jambs, and some of the toppled chairs had shifted position though she didn't think the heavy fridge had moved. The broad arabesque swaths in the layer of floor muck seemed changed, but of that she could not be completely sure.

She saw no huge spiny crawly tube with legs. Nothing alive in the totaled room, not the littlest stray sparrow or wayward prancing crab. An enormous creature *had* pursued her to this house though, no doubt, and she *had* heard it enter the apartment below. All that she knew. So it left before sunrise, sometime while she slept in the tub. Was its initial pursuit and subsequent camping out in her basement an actual coincidence? Why should it not be? Sandy had made a shambles of conventional cause and effect. Strange synchronicities, unexpected conjunctions…sorrows that could only be suffered in silence. Most likely the creeping creature hid in her basement out of recent habit and had no notion its mislaid prey crouched and quivered two floors above.

If today the crawling thing followed a timetable similar to the night before, and came back to her house sometime after dark, it meant she herself would have only a few hours to gather necessities from her neighbors' homes before it returned to her doorstep. She hadn't checked the time last night but was pretty sure she'd be safe out from dusk to 8:00 p.m. at least. Still didn't leave her much time for what her father used to tell her they called *midnight requisitioning* in the army. She'd have to score some bottled water on her first or second try and get home before her uninvited guest.

She considered leaving, riding the bus back to the mall, calling Derrick to pick her up. Sharing the house with this mystery monster was not in the deal when she decided to stay. The question though was where she'd be safer, here with the thing in the basement, or back in Sourland with Derrick? Her gut told her *here*. All the signs said Derrick had been preparing to explode. The hell with that old saying about the devil you know.

Colleen reached out to close the basement door, paused. How intelligent was the Creeper? Would it recognize deliberate interference if she locked the door? She hadn't locked it last night but she *had* closed it, though she neglected to latch it tight. What if the thing suspected it was not alone and chose to search the upstairs? She guessed it had the mass to break down locked doors if it desired.

She began to withdraw her hand, opting to leave the room as it was. The decision left her feeling lighter…only now she had another thought. Leaning inward she grasped the knob, her fingers slipping in the slick dust that smeared it, and pulled the door within six inches of to. This way she could tell if the beast beat her back to the house in the evening. Also a wide open ground floor door was likely to attract cops, looters, good Samaritans. Best if everyone just left the house alone, even those who only sought to help.

That done she rushed to get inside before she herself drew attention.

Back in the kitchen, door locked behind her and panting, it was first things first. Scrubbed the dust from the doorknob off her hand with a dishtowel. Next she had to eat what she could. Withdrawing the cans from the pillowcase she chose cut green beans and one of corn. Beans and corn combined made protein, right? And the beans would be packed in a weak brine she could drink. Good thing they kept a neglected manual can opener in the drawer of random utensils.

She dumped first the corn and then the beans in a large salad bowl, stirred the mixture with a fork, then strafed the mass with the pepper grinder. No salt. Nothing salty or added salt on anything until she managed to stock up on water.

Her impromptu succotash offered little flavor despite the coarse grains of fresh ground pepper. She churned through the mix in under five minutes nonetheless. Hunger cut the blandness some, almost as reliable a condiment as the munchies. And how long had it been since she'd gotten stoned? Since her year at Old Queens she was pretty sure. Almost thirty years since the last time she'd smoked a joint, but she would spark up in a heartbeat if she had any now. And not just to increase the edibility of food from cans. Maybe she could find some in another home. She added dope to her illicit mental shopping list. Why the hell not? She was already living dangerously, more dangerously even than she intended when she turned back from the bus.

With the vegetables gone she guzzled the final ounces of their mingled juices from the bottom of the bowl. Even that did not taste so bad, though it hardly began to assuage her thirst. She was facing a long and dry-tongued day. She pondered her pantry but little there would yield liquid excess. All that pasta, what a pile of useless crap without water to cook it. Not even any ramen noodles she could crunch and chew like crackers in a pinch, a trick she'd turned to on more than one camping trip.

If Colleen had no immediate hope of adequate hydration, her next highest priority was some form of low-impact distraction. It was going to be an empty drawn out day. She sought the front closet where they kept most of the board games, surveyed her options. *Life*…at her age that game wasn't so funny anymore. *Monopoly, Clue. Trivial Pursuit. Sorry. Checkers.* Solo play of any family game would leave her more downhearted than she already felt.

She scoped a lone deck of Bicycle cards atop a battered *Yahtzee* box and groped for that. *Solitaire* offered a neutral outlet to occupy her time.

Carrying the deck to the dining room table Colleen shuffled the cards, cut the deck, dealt out Klondike's prescribed seven rows, began her first game. Midway through she realized two cards were missing, a red Jack and a black

after

Seven, so she substituted the Jokers from the pack by suit. She thought of the old song about the guy playing *Solitaire* with a fifty-one card deck till dawn. The substitution done she scrapped her first game and started over. Although she had no way to track the time it took her to win, she guessed it was under ten minutes. After her second and third full games concluded even quicker, she switched to *Klondike Three*.

She found herself stymied a while in her second round of *Klondike Three*, the Four of Clubs blocking her progress and refusing to budge. The substitution of the Jokers didn't help. She had trouble remembering the missing cards they replaced. Nonetheless she won that game in what she guessed was barely forty minutes, but in the next round she found herself constantly drawing cards off the aces' piles, the thing that annoyed her most in *Solitaire* of any sort.

At some point Colleen returned to conscious awareness staring at a card in her hand, no idea when or where she'd picked it up. Her hand and forearm that held it dipped and bobbed. She set the card down, and after a disoriented moment, stumbled over to the nearest couch where she curled into a fetal position, shielding her eyes best she could from what thin splintered sunlight slipped between the slats of the blinds.

So began the dreary and dismal routine of that day and the duration… *Klondike*, naps, scarfing down the unheated contents of various cans. All in the diffuse sunlight of the drawn Venetian blinds. Colleen could tell the angle of the light altered over the course of the day, but she could not follow closely the position of the sun outside. She recalled a lesson from her Psych class in college, a psychologist who sealed himself up inside some cave, attempted to determine how deep the human diurnal cycle ran. About three months inside the man became suicidal after accidentally crushing a mouse he contrived to capture for a companion, and his crew had to extract him. But all that time he'd kept pretty close to night and day outside in his routine, only gone off an hour or two. She almost wouldn't mind the company of a mouse right now. The thing in the basement, the Creeper, that was never going to be her pet. More important was that she never became its dinner. She would have to determine its patterns and learn them down cold if she hoped to survive. Just as with Derrick, she would have to decide when it was safe to move, and where. And she would have to work around the worst danger hours with only a vague concept of time. Despite that she felt safer than she did with her husband. How crazy was that? Was a monster worse when it wore a human face?

Several times she heard voices from the street outside, the latest batch of neighbors to ride in on the bus, and twice passing cars she presumed were police, patrolling for looters or just to keep everyone in line.

Night came in its time. She knew when it arrived. The light through the blinds faded and died, left her smothered in smoky dark. She'd taken some time to prepare, and now with coat on she stood, commando-prepared, with Maglite, pillowcase sack, hammer, and a kitchen knife for which she'd fashioned a crude scabbard out of cardboard and duct tape. She felt silly with her jury-rigged utility belt but she also felt to some degree outfitted for the night's excursion. She wore the remaining roll of duct tape round her right wrist like a gauntlet. The best she could do would just have to…do.

Colleen had been listening intently for any sign of the Creeper's return. She heard nothing. Slowly she unlocked and opened the deck door, peered into the gloom pooled between houses, deepest close to the ground.

The dark back lot between buildings was absolute black in its depths, but her eyes were well adjusted now, and she could pick out some relief in all but the most profound patches of shadow. She spotted no one poised or on the move, neither neighbors nor cops. No one and *no* thing. Not yet.

At that point she weighed the safety of leaving the deck door unlocked behind her. She might return to find someone or some *thing* inside. But how would anyone know it was open if they didn't know she was hiding out in this dim silent house? Only by chance if they took to trying multiple doorknobs to multiple homes. On the plus side she could get back in quick that way if the Creeper were on her tail. She decided in the end to shut the door behind her but leave it unlatched. What she'd do if it broke through the door behind her she'd decide at that time. If it left her any time.

Descending into the darkness she followed mostly her route of the night before, crossing Fremont, emerging farther east on Kearney to avoid the scene of her previous crime. Not stopping there though. She knew she would have to range a little farther each night in her B & E's. On to Carteret. She crossed that too and chose a yellow bungalow on the north side, worked around the back and—*Yes!*—the door there bore the same six convenient little glass panes as before. This time she applied a duct tape X to her target before she struck. The few fragments that fell inward made hardly any sound.

Inside the bungalow the smell of rank decay assaulted her at once. Had she stumbled onto a preexisting crime scene, the site of some unreported murder? *Fingerprints, fingerprints, had she left any on the doorknob, the tape?* Or was it some unfortunate undiscovered victim of the storm, rotting and forgotten here all this time? Should she just back up, get out, find another house? If the Creeper kept to last night's schedule, she didn't have time. She needed to get at least two blocks away before she chose another target, and that would mean cutting it too close timewise with the Creeper. Not a chance she could afford to take.

Colleen switched on her light, played it slowly over the floor. The decomposed corpse with visible ribs she pictured so distinctly failed to appear, but she found the answer once she reached the fridge. There she observed a dark pool on the floor, took it first for old blood till she saw the inky streaks of brown grease trailing down from the freezer's bottom edge. The occupants must have neglected to empty their icebox before Sandy hit and the power went out. Whatever they left had burst the freezer door open several inches, no doubt with the gassy exhaust of its own decay. They probably left a lot of meat in the freezer. Or fish. Ugh. She'd skip the fridge here. Not as if she'd find anything there she could salvage for her own.

Colleen spotted what passed for their pantry instead, the last couple cabinets in the corner, down below the end of a long marble counter. No water but she recovered a 12-pack of Sprite. Enough to keep her hydrated and alive a while longer, even if buzzed on sugar the entire time.

She decided to cut and run right then, be satisfied tonight with the oblong box, make it back to 46 Hancock ahead of the monster if she could. After thumbing the flashlight back off and jamming it into her belt, she hooked her left hand through the oval slot on top of the box and dragged the soda out.

She continued to see fairly well in the dark—well enough to make her way back to the door and out. She considered stuffing the whole box in her pillowcase, the box or the loose cans, but concluded the mass was less awkward as it was, and cradling it in her right hand she commenced her awkward return. No visit to the beach tonight—that had not gone so well the night before. The Creeper had followed her back, though she was now fairly certain it would have returned to her basement in the end regardless.

Perhaps it was best she had glimpsed it stretched across the berm, got some sense of its size, not simply heard it crawling through her downstairs door. What if she'd thought it was kids or raccoons, gone down herself to check out the sound?

On the watch for cops and monsters both, she crossed Carteret, Kearney, Fremont, approached her home. The door of the basement apartment remained as she'd left it. For a moment she considered locking it now she was back, but she could not decide on such a move as wise. Colleen rushed up the deck stairs to the main door instead, shouldered her way inside and locked it behind her. Then she set her spoils on the table, deposited tape and empty pillowcase beside the Sprite while keeping the other tools in her belt.

She tore the cover of the 12-pack back toward herself, fumbled out that first can and snapped open the lid. Her thirst made the sickly citrus sugar water taste almost divine, and she beat down the urge to guzzle the can's entire contents at once. She set it down half drained and stood clutching the table as rush and relief poured through her form. Her stomach knotted briefly with cold and acid then relaxed. Ohhh…plain fresh water would've been better for her but the sweetness sure hit the spot. She gulped down another quarter of the can and shivered in simple and innocent joy.

Colleen had only just kicked her soda habit two summers back. But that had been diet. She'd developed a Diet Dr. Pepper dependency, in part due to Derrick who drank it to get on his feet during the day after drinking, taunted her with —*C'mon, try it, try it, just a sip*, till the one July night with the AC down for four days she succumbed. Hooked ever since and gone to two liters a day, she'd only given it up once she began to feel spells first of tingling then total numbness in her hands and feet all the way out to her elbows and knees. Finally a Facebook friend passed on an Internet article about aspartame. If the article ran true, her symptoms meant she might be headed for heart disease or MS or even the Big C. Colleen went cold turkey from that moment on, not just DDP but any kind of soda, switched to water, coffee, tea, juice, sometimes broth. And the symptoms did vanish, starting the very next day.

This was regular soda though. High fructose corn syrup maybe, but no aspartame. Even if it were diet she couldn't afford to be picky here. She needed fluids, needed water. She drained the can and licked her lips and—

after

—heard something moving outside, faint scrape as if a chunk of debris had shifted against the pavement, the sand. She froze, listened, checkboxed possibilities in her mind. Cop. Creeper. Looter. Dog.

The deck creaked with a weight on the stairs. Again, higher. Colleen stood with empty can in hand, not daring even to breathe. One more creak then long seconds of nothing, then—

The downstairs door slapped open, and she heard the creature wheezing and squeezing its bulk through the frame. Terror shattered the spell of immobility binding her and she made a snap decision, scrabbled out another Sprite in each hand, tiptoed first toward then up the staircase, keeping her steps close to the walls to avoid making the stairs creak, skipping the third stair on purpose because she knew it was a noisemaker no matter where she trod. She had to get all the way inside the bathroom while the Creeper was still making its own noise to cover. Lucky it was long and its passage through the downstairs door took time.

She latched the bathroom door softly as she could, set her precious cans of Sprite on the floor, then climbed into the tub, careful not to let the Maglite or hammer handle strike the faux porcelain sides. The tub would be her bed again, here where she kept the most locked doors between her and… *That.* Considering the naps she'd taken during the day, the sugar or syrup rush from the Sprite she'd just sucked down, and the fight or flight adrenalin that still made her ticker pound, she doubted she'd get much sleep tonight. Knees half up in the tub, head against a pillow of two folded towels, she allowed her mind to move from theme to theme. It didn't so much wander as leap, as if crossing a row of stepping stones planted in a creek.

About the fourth stone on her stream of consciousness wandered to her father, twenty-four years gone now but remaining a regular remembrance and reappearance in her dreams. Tom Ellery had taught her the outdoor survival skills she would need to live through her current situation. Distant as her alcoholic mother always was, Colleen had been daddy's girl till cancer took him in her twenties, ending her brief excursion to Old Queens. A decisive man and strong, she compared all other men since to him. Derrick came up short of course, drinking habit or no. He just couldn't measure. Had she driven him into dependency, always considering him less than Tom, who never took any drink stronger than Sanka in her sight? No. Derrick already drank before they married, and full-blown alcoholism had been his decision alone.

She pondered weakness and handicaps, recalled the time she and her father saw a man out walking with his seeing eye dog. She called on Tom to explain the dog's odd halter. She'd been about six at the time. Once she understood she'd asked her dad whether there also existed sniffing nose dogs or tasting tongue dogs for folks who'd lost those abilities, but after a thoughtful pause her dad told her *no* and explained the likely reasons why not. She pondered the possibilities for some time nonetheless, and her speculative conception of the tasting tongue dog never left her altogether. This imaginary canine grew gradually more grotesque over the years her thoughts served as its host, till it became a thing more immense lolling tongue than recognizable dog. She contemplated its image anew.

The irregular rasp of the Creeper's respiration reached her ears through the vent. Colleen envisioned what aperture might serve the creature for a mouth, dagger-ringed pucker perhaps, beyond that the extent of its bulk, the rows of wriggling spines or spikes or feelers above, its stumpy feet or legs below. She pictured it pressing heavily against her overturned chairs, their toppled ruined fridge, constructing its own comfortable muddy nest amidst the wreckage of her basement while she lay all night in her upstairs tub.

In this home where she sought refuge she now hid not only from Derrick but from a monster. And from the police. On the other hand both cops and monster appeared to follow regular patterns without any of Derrick's unpredictability, his sudden eruptions. If she kept quiet during the night and out of sight during the day she ought to stay safe. True, a hard winter was headed for this unheated home, but she felt certain she could survive it, even if it meant setting fires in the tub and sleeping beside it to stay warm. It was a reasonable assumption too that power ought to return sometime soon. They already had power again in Sourland Hills, so it couldn't be much longer in returning to Seaside. She could manage till then. Meanwhile thoughts of the encircling array of obstacles kept her awake. What if Derrick drove down here too? Would he believe her stories about the thing below?

Her troubled insomnia waned after only minutes though. Whether lulled by the arrhythmic wheeze of the creature's breathing or the final fade of her own sucrose and adrenalin rush, she slumped into slumber all at once. At some point she woke sputtering, suspecting she'd begun to snore—one of her husband's perpetual complaints while they still shared a bed. In the silent house the muffled puffs of her sleeping breath might pop like cannon shots, attracting the Creeper's attention, its hunger. It might come for her, be upon her, before she even awoke.

Yet her squatter below had gone silent. Had it heard her? Or perhaps it slept a deep sleep too. If it heard her, it was making no move to investigate. Colleen wriggled onto her left side, adjusted the pillow and towels beneath her head. Less comfortable but less likely she'd snore in that configuration.

It took her a while to find sleep a second time, wriggling in a new position. After an unknown period she woke in darkness, disoriented, scared that Derrick was with her in the room. Then she heard what must have wakened her, the rough brush of her downstairs guest squeezing out through the basement door. What time was it? Her internal clock and the tenor of the light through the blinds told her sunrise was coming soon. Where did the monster go during the day—into the sea? What did it do there? Did it feed? She envisioned it gobbling down a helpless struggling dogfish or shark, a half dozen skates and rays, multitudes of smaller fish. All defenseless against its tusks and bulk. Unless the fish had split with the dogs and birds, said *fuck this* as the storm blew them all about, abandoned the local waters and left them barren for how many miles out?

Next she heard it crawling across the debris in the back lot between houses. These sounds came muted and brief and then disappeared altogether—the beast had either traveled out of range or ceased to move. She did not expect its return till night, but she kept to the tub till full outside sun nonetheless. Ensconced within her enamel well, she considered her situation. She returned to this home seeking refuge. Had she only traded her domestic hell for enrollment in some inconceivable game of cat and mouse?

She thought of Paul, how he gave her hope, showed her she could still feel. She thought of him inside her, gripping her hipbones. Thought of him in her mouth. His mouth on her. No more now, none of it. Never again.

Yet the creature, *the Creeper* as she had come to think of it, had ignored her in the house, even if it had pursued her outside. She'd kept as quiet as she could, as she suspected its hearing was quite acute. Still, the Creeper at least had discernible rhythms, a pattern, a timetable of sorts, and she was already learning that schedule. Derrick she could never fully predict. She was certain he recognized this haphazard behavior manifested as threatening to her all by itself, that his unpredictability was therefore deliberate, a major part of the daily agenda of intimidation he practiced against her.

Only after she was sure the slivered sunlight slipping through slits in the blinds of the bathroom's single window signified full-on day did she rise from the tub, stiff-legged and gripping the towel rod while she shook her circulation back one leg at a time. Hesitantly, listening attentively at every step, she made her halting way down to the kitchen again. There she downed another Sprite for breakfast, along with a small bowl of raisin bran, dry. She considered pouring some of the Sprite over the cereal—cereal box instructions always said add milk *or* juice, but *Sprite*? She could not bring herself to do it in the end. Better to crunch the flakes and raisins on their own like uncooked ramen, use the soda to wash it all down.

After her makeshift breakfast came more Klondike. She wished they'd left more books in this house, but all she could find were a few scattered paperbacks she'd already read, mostly Stephen King, the titles not really what she needed in her current situation. *It. Gerald's Game.* No fucking way on either of those.

If this was a day when other homeowners came in she might go out and walk the streets a while, though not too far and not for long. Nor could she mingle much—she was already getting scruffy and noticeably ripe. Soon she would look and reek like a bona fide bag lady. And that would attract the wrong attention. Colleen considered the strength of the Creeper's sense of smell. She had no way to know.

She thought of a song from her early '90s line dancing days. *Where did it come from, where did it go? Cotton-eyed Joe.* If the Creeper even had eyes. She had not yet gotten close enough to see, suspected it would not be healthy for her if she ever did.

Strange that such a thing could survive ashore, but then strange might as well be the thing's middle name. Strange as hell. Living on land by night, returning to the sea by day, leaving ahead of the first true light. Then back to her basement to make its den after dusk. She knew from her sons how some forms of plankton rose toward the surface each night, and the creatures that preyed on the plankton followed. From what deeps had Sandy swept the Creeper? Was it stymied now by the continental shelf, an unexpected obstacle blocking it from sinking back to its home in the depths? Or had the storm torn it down from orbit and left it like Gilligan, Crusoe. Did it spend the daylight hours in search of its shattered craft?

Why couldn't the Creeper give her more time after dark? Nights should have been *her* time to have the whole town to herself, what was left of it anyway. Except for a couple cops maybe, who probably never got out of their cars and were easy to dodge if she kept to backyards and shadows. Instead, by her clockless chronologically challenged estimation, the Creeper allowed her barely two hours each night for breaking into her neighbors' homes before she had to beat it back to her own. The cost of encountering it outside or already waiting camped out in her basement was unknown but serious cause for concern if it was genuinely carnivorous. She had no doubt it was, and hungry too. It had pursued her from the beach with unmistakable intent. Nights in the tub were cramped, but chancing an outside run-in with the Creeper was no alternative. She'd already formed a mental image of it gulping her down whole. And the reality might be even worse.

Would it keep to the schedule it followed so far? For her sake it had to. She still hoped to *requisition* bottled water, powdered milk, more food, some better paperback books perhaps. But she would need to range farther afield each night, all the while without crossing Boulevard, the place she'd most likely be exposed to patrols. Colleen became concerned about creating a semicircle of break-ins right round her home. Wasn't that the main clue in *Silence of the Lambs*? She remembered Jodie Foster finding the killer after realizing that his home was in the center of the circle of his victims.

That night she cut even farther to the north, crossing Carteret to backyards on the south side of Sampson. Let the arc of her minor crime wave curve in to pinpoint someone else's house. The home she hit was no jackpot, but she did liberate two tins of tuna and a half dozen copies of *National Geo*. Hustling back she barely made the tub before she heard her roommate stuffing its bulk once more though the downstairs door. Too close.

Most of her neighbors had left little or no food over the winter. She was discovering this fast. By the fifth night she'd added only half a plastic sack of stale Frosted Mini-Wheats, a full bottle of Jägermeister, five liters of water, a paperback copy of *Up Above the World* by Paul Bowles, palm trees on its cover suggesting some tropical setting very welcome right now, one of those wooden puzzles that were as hard to reassemble as they were to take apart, and two extra decks of cards, but the batteries in her flashlight were painfully low and she had yet to locate a replacement set. Lack of batteries was about to become a catch-22, no matter how well she got around in the dark.

The sixth night she found batteries but not until after Bad Thing Number One. Late that afternoon, while she nodded over Bowles and Klondike, someone tried the knob on the front door, the door she never used. Softly at first then in forceful alternating torques. Her first thought was the Creeper was out there trying to get inside. But after the torqueing and a pause came human footsteps on the deck. Had the police arrived at last? Or had some other hidden recluse come to B & E her home in turn? Oh, the irony of that. The footfalls traveled east to west along the deck, following the long row of windows fronting the room. Colleen scrunched down at the table low as she could, though the angle from the sunroom to her seat was a thin slice at best.

It wasn't the Creeper and it wasn't the cops. Someone wanted in, someone without any right to enter.

Another pause then the steps retreated down the deck. Once off the wooden planking she had no way to tell where whoever was out there had gone. She waited for a creak on the back deck stairs but it never came. Had her prowler already scoped out the view through the back windows? Had he seen her slouched at the table? He might have.

Colleen counted to twenty, rushed up the stairs to Alexander's old bedroom that overlooked the street. Peering carefully through the blinds she saw no one at first. But then at the edge of her vision, making toward the shore, she caught sight of George's retreating back. George or whatever his name was.

She saw him only for seconds but she was sure it was him. Of all the people to have seen her bolt from the bus stop. She had not thought out her original flight so well.

That night she waited long as she dared before embarking on her desperate quest for additional batteries. Just in case the pervert had returned and hid outside for her somewhere. Yet her daytime stalker did not reappear.

Colleen met success in her battery quest at last, though she had to venture all the way to Hiering Avenue, five blocks from Hancock, and just across Central, farther than she'd gone before. She made it back ahead of the Creeper but it returned before she even reached the stairs to the living room. She'd heard its approach while she was still on the deck. Huddled in the tub she sensed a decelerated pace seize the creature's wheezing breath, followed by its restless rattling of the latched lower door to the old stairs ascending from basement below to the second floor. Colleen wondered how badly she was about to regret not nagging Derrick more often about sealing off that stair. In her rush to the tub she had failed to lock or even shut the bathroom door. If the thing made it up the stairs and through the door at the top, no other barrier protected her.

She twisted to stare at the room's lone window, facing west above the foot of the tub. How fast and how safely could she throw it open and wriggle out? A story and a half drop to the drive? Headfirst. However she did it, the fall was gonna hurt. Almost certainly a broken arm or wrist, and if she could manage to rise and run after that, how long before the thing made its way outside behind her and gave pursuit? Broken leg or ankle and she was dead for sure. At least the Creeper couldn't fit through the window, she was near certain of that, which meant it would have to backtrack down the stairs. That might buy her a bit of time, but where would she run to even then? She considered again whether any cop would believe her tale, whether a cop could protect her from the Creeper.

She listened to the door of the downstairs stairwell creak and strain as the creature pushed and probed with its bulk. After several iterations the sound slowed in frequency till it finally ceased. Slowly the wheezing resumed the pattern she'd come to know these past six nights. It shocked Colleen that Derrick's shoddy handiwork, the cheap latch and bolts of the stairwell door, had held. Perhaps the creature considered the door a more solid barrier than it was. She recalled in her preschool years watching Mutual of Omaha's *Wild Kingdom* on Sunday nights before Disney, how Marlin and the other guy, the one who took all the real risks, sometimes used a blanket fence, how some animals accepted it as solid, unable to distinguish between blankets and brick. Could it be the Creeper suffered a similar shortsight? Might do her good to remember if it did. She knew from that first night she moved faster than the thing, if not by much, but outrunning it was no longer the issue once it turned out to be her houseguest. Of course she could just relocate into any other empty house, but then she'd risk discovery by the owners or police, and right now there was no worse word in Jersey than *looter*. Didn't the cops have orders to shoot looters on sight? She'd make the headlines even if she didn't get shot. Definitely not something she wanted the twins to see.

Colleen shifted slowly, soundlessly in the tub, working the towel pillows into place beneath her shoulders and head, found her position of comfort, pulled the doubled comforter she'd tugged from her bed up to her chin and tucked its edges in best she could. Only the oddly cycled wheezing rose now from below. Could it be the Creeper was faking sleep? Or maybe its attention span was brief. She'd heard of animals like that though she couldn't remember which. Frogs, maybe.

She took up the bottle of Jäger, which she'd set beside the tub, propped it in her quilted lap. Twisting the lid to snap the tax stamp, she debated this move a moment. She'd taken no strong drink since her Old Queens days and no drink at all since Derrick began his drunken abuse. She tried to keep it out of the house. Both houses. Cried when she caught Graham with a bottle of Jack Daniel's hidden in his room. But different rules applied now. She welcomed anything that might help her sleep.

With a silent *fuck it* she gulped down a slug. It was every bit as noxious as she recalled from college, over-sweet licorice and lawn clippings and just plain gross, generic store brand cough drops and black jelly beans half-chewed, sucked, and spit in her mouth, hint of burning rubber underneath it all. Add the inescapable flavor of ethanol once the rest began to fade. The rough measured shot sat and burned in her gut, a caustic liquid lump. Simultaneously she felt the first wave of drowsiness spread from gut to limbs. She gagged down a second shot, barely kept from retching it up as her stomach contracted into a protesting knot.

Colleen shivered. She didn't think she would drink the Jäger again, but if she recovered maybe two more bottles of the stuff she might hold enough liquid for one legitimate toilet flush. She set the bottle softly on the floor beside the tub, real sleepiness sliding over her just ahead of nausea. Had she not been so exhausted she might have barfed, but within a few minutes she slipped into fitful slumber.

In sleep she dreamt, the dream sectioned off by moments of unwelcome half waking. The first dream was of Paul, hiding him in her Sourland Hills house, a place he'd never entered in life. Colleen dodged about trying to keep Derrick and her lover apart, the whole scenario a bad sitcom plot. She woke before she and Paul found a place to be alone.

Some internal spasm had brought her back. An impulse within her called for more Jäger but lingering nausea told her no. Thinking of Paul she clutched her knees close under the covers, began crying in silence. To see him again, even in a dream…why couldn't it have lasted longer, why was their time together so damn short?

Sleep reclaimed her quickly and she dreamt again, this time of a house she had to break into seeking some item of necessity to her survival. But it turned out the Creeper was already hiding inside that house so this time she had to dodge it from room to room. The police were right outside but she couldn't yell to them because all the windows were boarded up. The house had an unlimited array of rooms extending farther and farther away from the street, like that famous mansion in California. She moved deeper and the Creeper followed. Random people appeared to guide her but she waved them aside for their own safety and continued on alone. Derrick, Paul, the twins, even Snooki and her camera crew, she passed them all by. Over time the rooms became a series of shuddering empty train cars, and she worked her way down the aisle of each in turn, struggling to stay ahead of the creature she assumed still pursued. At one point she wondered how the Creeper operated the buttons to open the doors between cars. Was some human accomplice helping it along?

She traversed car after car not knowing whether she was headed for engine or caboose, nor which would serve her best in her efforts to escape. Both were dead ends after all. If she reached the caboose first, could she detach it from the rest of the train, escape that way as in an old Western movie? Only wouldn't it then slow to a stop in time? In that case the Creeper might follow her down the tracks and set upon her at its leisure. What if she arrived at the engine instead, could she convince the engineers to uncouple—was that the right word?—the rest of the train and carry on? In such a case she might escape, put good distance between her and…

She awoke again, groggy and confused. Once she recognized her location anew, remembered why she hunched in the tub, she studied the blinds for any ooze of morning sun through the slats. She saw none. Her stomach had settled and her queasy buzz was gone, but the thing in her basement still breathed its odd irregular wheeze.

She listened and as she listened slumber took her a third time, but if she dreamt this go-round those dreams stayed sealed within the walls of sleep once she woke. She still recalled the dream of Paul with clarity though. The dawn was definite behind the blinds now and she heard no sound through the vents from below. The Creeper was gone. She'd made it through another night. Perhaps only barely.

She thought of that old song by America, *A Horse With No Name*. She wasn't crossing the desert but there *was* sand and she *was* alone. So far she had no difficulty recalling her name. How many days did it take before the singer let his horse run free? It came back to her only as *After blah days in the desert sun...* And the song said something about the ocean as well, she knew that but she could not recollect what...

Downstairs she played Klondike, wrestled with the wood puzzle, grew discouraged, gave the Bowles book a shot but three pages in it bored her. She had a long day ahead, and a longer night. She'd decided not to venture out tonight. She'd recovered enough food and fluids by now to feed herself and keep hydrated for at least a week, and last night she and the Creeper had come way too close.

Seeking adequate light in her failed stab at Bowles, she'd settled in on the spare bed in the sunroom, seated back to the wall, which meant her shoulders pressed against the window and its sealed blinds. The day had not gone on long before she heard voices outside, the latest busload of homeowners arriving to inspect whatever was left to inspect, to salvage what they could. Would any of them discover evidence of her petty thefts, report the break-ins to the police? And would any of the cops then undertake direct action in their hunt for the looter? How long before they searched house to house and came to her door? How long before they broke it down? Things might turn interesting if they came at night when her guest was home. Might turn interesting real fast. Should she put up a sign outside? *Beware of Thing? Beware of Sea Monster? I Don't Know What The Hell Is Down There, So Just Please Beware...*

Soon she recognized the voices of Grant and don't call me Kenny, considered stepping out to join them, mingle, say hello. Not a good plan and she knew it. Her hair was a hopeless matted mess now, and even through her coat and clothes she could smell each of her armpits, left and right distinct, despite her regular use of baby powder as dry shampoo. A public appearance might ignite suspicion, and if the cops already knew they had a looter on their hands, they were sooner or later going to do the math and come right for her. She would become *a person of interest*, no longer fit for human company, her only companion an equally wretched creature tossed up and stranded by the storm. How had the Creeper found itself in such a similar situation? She thought of the way mother birds ignored their hatchlings after a human being touched them. Could the Creeper be merely a child of its kind? Was she herself a victim of the unpleasant reality behind *E.T.*? If the Creeper were Junior, she did not want to be around when Mom and Dad came to rescue their lost offspring. Sea monsters, space aliens, or mysterious creatures from Dimension X, how long would their journey require, and how hungry would they be when they finally arrived?

Colleen slumped against window and wall, considered again how she'd stayed behind here to avoid Derrick just to find herself a prisoner once more. She pondered her situation. The Creeper was horrifying, but unlike Derrick it was consistent, and sharing her house with it appeared manageable if she worked around its timetable, kept to its blind spots. For that matter, could the creature see at all? Perhaps she'd found the reason for its heightened hearing. Didn't blind folks develop such amplified senses all the time? If it could not see, what kind of senses did it have, what lonesome concessions did it make to the world? Colleen knew now there were no service dogs for those who lost their sense of taste or smell. They were on their own, no long extended canine tongues to taste for them.

Voices outside came and went. In time she heard only the weather, faintly the still disrupted surf. Little wind blew today so Colleen mostly attended a backdrop of faint white noise. At some point though the almost-silence broadcast a wrongness wholly beyond the subtle pattern of disoriented ocean waves or the intermittent currents of the birdless breeze. Her troubled gut read an indefinable distortion riding the sparse mélange of silence and sound. Not as if any crickets had been chirping and suddenly stopped, but it hit her as if she heard them and they had, which gave her a shudder she recalled well from camping trips with her dad.

Colleen shoved herself up the wall along her back, adjusting only her legs and shifting slightly to her right to avoid ruffling the blinds with her shoulders. Once her head was well even with what she guessed was the upper sash of the lower storm window she twisted about and pressed the wall with her left hand. With care she slid three fingers over one edge of the blinds and slowly drew them down only so much as she needed to peek out. Dead center outside 46 Hancock stood pudgy creepy Jordie, paused at the verge of sidewalk and street. She knew at once the clamshell case beside him held mainly booze. Store brand vodka probably, or a couple sixers of MGD. Nothing higher quality than that.

Though she'd been certain the man outside couldn't see her, he smiled, began to raise one hand in a wave. —*Oh no no no!* She jerked her fingers free of the blinds, spun back against the wall and slid once more onto the bed. *Georgie Porgie, Puddin' and Pie...* Had he seen her? Did he now know for sure she was hiding in her house? Did he know she was alone? Why did she have to go and give herself away? How long had he been waiting for exactly that error?

Colleen knew no way to undo her mistake. She began to ponder what the next move would be for Geor—whatever his name was. At least the doors were all locked, except of course the back door to the basement. The Creeper's part time home. She didn't dare go out to lock that—not by day, and not by night. Different situations, different dangers, but the downstairs door was best left alone. She would sit here in her darkening home, shift from spare bed to tub, sleep if she could but stay on guard. She feared the narrative of her already precarious scenario was headed down a *cul de sac.*

Once more Colleen considered sneaking out of her own home, spending the night in one of the houses she'd robbed, someplace she could sleep safe from both Geordie and the Creeper, on a borrowed bed like Goldilocks. Yet that way she risked arrival of the rightful owners, her worst case scenario running out into the dark to encounter right off who—creature, creeper man, patrolling police? In another house, if she even made it safely to one, how was she to secure a damaged door behind her? She might yet latch it, but any human pursuer could open it right behind her. And the Creeper? How smart was it—could it work a lock? How had it really entered her basement after the storm? She remembered the dream in which it traveled between locked train cars on her tail.

If her last stand were upon her, she wanted to make it in her own home. She wished again she'd brought the .22 from Sourland. She considered various makeshift weapons, settled on an aerosol hairspray can coupled with a butane match. Her improvised little flamethrower offered only a few feet of reach, and would depend on near perfect timing and the element of surprise to be any real use, but she set her hopes on fire nonetheless. And she had the hammer in a pinch.

Colleen ascended to the upstairs master bath, still the most secure space she knew in this unfortified home. She paused along the way, downed a can of salmon and a Sprite without sitting down, slurping the brine off the pink crumbly fish chunks before she discarded the lid and dug into the rest with a fork. Everything tasted better when you had very little to eat. No sauce like starvation.

Comfy in the tub, Colleen counted passing hours best she could, sought for slumber though it would not come. Restless, she kept up her vigil instead.

Sometime before her estimate of 8:00 p.m. her uninvited guest returned, squeezing through the lower door, spikes on its back clitter-clattering against the wooden frame. She listened as it shifted and got comfortable, much as she herself had done in the tub, followed by the uneven pattern of its respiration—or was it snoring? Did it even sleep? She was sharing her house with this enormous thing, but what did she really know about it? Other than its general size and shape, the times it came and went…nothing.

Less than half an hour by her guess passed before she heard a voice from the deck. —Colleen? Mrs. Budny? It's me, your neighbor. Jordan. You know, Jordan Georgina? Your husband's friend? You remember me, right?

Colleen could tell by the rhythm of his words, the overlong pauses in awkward places, that he'd been drinking. She acquired that sense as a survival skill, all those years with Derrick. Of course he'd been drinking. A guy like Jordan would have to get his nerve up for what he had planned tonight. Drinking, but not drunk though. She wished he *was* fully drunk. She might have more of an advantage in a physical confrontation then. And a real shot at outrunning him if she made a break for it. She was pretty sure she could outrun the Creeper too, so long as she could get around it in the first place. If it stayed in the basement while she ran out of the house.

A pause, and then —I know you're here. It's okay. Your husband sent me. He sent me to check on you. Derrick sent me. He's worried about you here all alone, so he asked me to look in on you.

Colleen knew immediately he was lying. Jordan might've talked to Derrick, and Derrick might even have told him she was holed up in the shore house, but Derrick would never have asked this man to check in on her. Even he was never that cruel. Or stupid.

She heard the deck boards creak as Jordan crossed to the door and the rattle of the latch as he twisted it. —Mrs. Budny? Are you there? Are you all right?

Colleen tensed in the tub. This guy was not going away on his own. She had the sense things were about to happen rapidly now. She gripped the hairspray and the butane match tight.

—Mrs. Budny, I'm concerned you may have injured yourself, that you might need assistance. Can you make any sound at all? If you've fallen and you can't get up, just try to pound on the floor or something so I can hear, so I know where to find you.

She guessed he had his ear pressed to the door at this point. She held her breath, froze motionless. She knew no matter what she did, Jordan was not going away. He knew she was inside, and he was seeking to assess her weakness, her vulnerability. Well, she would show him. She was not as helpless as she maybe thought.

And if she successfully blinded Jordan with fire, what might her next move be? She could make a break for the front door, but if she ran out of the house at this hour she could run right into the Creeper. She hadn't heard it stirring but it had to be listening. Unless she were wrong about its senses. Yet it also waited. Why? Her instincts told her Jordan would come barreling through the back door the second he heard her move.

—Mrs. Budny, I don't know if you can hear me, but I'm terribly worried about you. I'm concerned you might be injured, maybe badly, so I'll need to force the door. I'm going to do that now, okay? Please don't be frightened. I'm only here to help. Derrick sent me to check on you, remember? As soon as I'm inside I can help you out however you need. Don't panic. I'm here to help. Just give me a minute.

He slammed against the door almost at once. Colleen felt a tremor run faint throughout the house. So much for his minute. Yet she did not hear the door pop open.

Jordan cursed in a muffled burst then struck the door again. This time she heard the double crack as it gave, flew open, smacked the interior wall. He was coming. He was coming for her.

Inside, he spoke softer. —Okay Mrs. Budny, I'm here to help you. If you can just give me some sign where you're trapped, I can get to you faster.

Trapped. How long had she been trapped? From the first night she'd spent in this very house? Her wedding night? Or even earlier? How many years? Since she first met Derrick? And she'd never fought back, never tried to escape. Well tonight she was prepared to fight.

after

She'd been scared but now that Jordan was in the house Colleen felt a strange icy calm. She still trembled some but even that was subsiding.

She knew she had to get up, at least prepare to meet the menace on her feet. Taking care not to clank the hammer handle against the side of the tub, she rose, stepped softly on shaky legs to a spot on the right just beyond the inward swing of the door, raised and aimed the hairspray can with the butane match at ready, index fingers on their respective triggers.

She could hear Jordan moving about the first floor, calling —Colleen? Mrs. Budny? She pictured him with his own flashlight, peering into corners, spotting evidence of her presence in the house and nodding silently to himself. How long before he figured out she was upstairs? She stared at the gap beneath the bathroom door, awaiting the beam of his light to shine through. Nothing yet, but that made sense if he were still downstairs. The angle would not be right till he reached her floor.

She heard Jordan's first steps on the staircase, his asking if she was hurt upstairs, the Creeper brushing out through the downstairs door, creaking up the deck, then back into the house through the first floor door. It was moving fast. Jordan must have left the door open behind him, but so far as she could tell, he hadn't noticed the approach of this other intruder. Perhaps his position on the staircase muffled the sounds she heard so clearly from above. Perhaps he had no frame of reference for such a thing. Perhaps he was just drunk enough to miss it.

Jordan continued calling out to her, acting convinced she was hurt or hiding somewhere upstairs, the tone of his voice something he must've thought reassuring, though its effect was altogether the opposite.

At last Colleen saw the expected glow of a flashlight playing under her door. She prepared to defend herself in a way she'd never done before.

Everything happened suddenly then, suddenly and almost all at once. Jordan must've spotted the closed bathroom door —Are you in the bathroom, Colleen? Are you injured? He spoke louder now, and with confidence, just as the Creeper hit the base of the stairs and came up fast, an arrival she recognized from the way the stairs creaked, a sound she'd feared since her very first night back. That had to be when Jordan finally got wise, realized he was not the only predator in the house tonight. His —*Whatthe...?* broke off in a thump as he slipped or stumbled, probably losing his balance when he spun, the real exact measure of his inebriation. He shrieked briefly—his voice as high as a little girl's—and then came several minutes of sounds that made Colleen grind the heels of her palms into her ears, for what little good that did, still clutching the halves of her makeshift defense, the chill of the hairspray can stinging her skull even through her hair.

Slowly the chewing and slurping sounds died into silence outside. Everything was quiet a while, then the stairs began to creak and groan again, and the whole house quivered slightly as the Creeper climbed higher. Her mind supplied unwanted images of a thing she'd barely witnessed in motion, and suddenly she saw it as a much larger version of the *Very Hungry Caterpillar*, something from a book she'd read to the twins when they were small. Colleen began to shiver. Her coat no longer seemed to hold off the cold. She wanted to wrap the comforter around herself but it lay crumpled in the tub and she didn't dare move toward it and risk making any sound.

She lowered her hands to her waist. There was still the thing's breathing, though muffled now, the scattered tapping of its spikes or spines against the stairwell walls, the creaking of the stairs themselves beneath its bulk.

Would it go back to the basement now that it had…fed? Or would it decide to camp out on the upper floors? What if it got comfortable and chose not to leave in the morning anymore? No matter what it did she doubted she could secure any doors against something that size. If Jordan had kicked the deck door open he had likely splintered the jamb, in which case only a carpenter could repair it now. She might still keep safe in the bathroom for a time, but the limits of her prison were contracting. Her options as well.

The floor beyond the door popped and crackled as the Creeper heaved more of its mass up the stairs. Soon Colleen heard the thing's wet sucking wheeze right outside. Her hands shook so bad now she pressed them to her stomach, fought to keep her breathing as quiet as she could.

On the other side of the door the creaking floor sounds eased till only the wheeze came through. The sound grew lower in register and more ragged, and its pacing slowed. Was the thing preparing to go to sleep right there? Did it need time to digest perhaps, like an anaconda after swallowing an Amazon explorer? What if it stayed outside her door right into the day and didn't depart at its usual hour? What if it knew she was here and decided to wait her out? She wished she'd already climbed back into the tub to lie down. She couldn't stand up all night, but she didn't want to make the slightest sound while the Creeper remained right outside the door. Maybe she could ease her way down and into the tub, but for the moment she held still, staring at the door and listening, studying the semi-silence outside.

After several minutes passed without any change Colleen heard a rustle near the floor, a soft sound, almost squishy. Peering down in the dim light the window admitted she saw a wide dark band sliding under the bathroom door, several inches across and already far enough inside it was questing toward the edge of the tub. Its mobile tip dabbed at the floor as it passed, the entire appendage quivering along its entire length as if with hidden transmissions of hunger and need.

For a moment she froze, then regained the agency of her limbs. She crouched in one smooth fluid motion and waited for the flat dark feeler or tongue to come close. When it did she thumbed the hairspray toggle while fumbling the trigger of the butane match. Hairspray hissed out but failed to light, and the intruding appendage changed direction at the sound, came straight toward her face and fast. She almost dropped the match but held her position, adjusted and got the butane right, thumbed the hairspray in tandem with the flame. A plume of ragged orange fire ignited and flared out all at once, nearly blinding her dark-adapted sight and making her panic and release both triggers. She closed her eyes and shook her head to get her vision back. When she reopened them she saw the thing was only inches from her chest. She aimed the flame almost straight up and fired, jerking her head back as she did.

Sparse blue sparks arched up where the fire struck the thing. The Creeper's tongue sizzled and writhed, jerked away from her and began squeezing back beneath the door at once, bunching and pulling under a few inches at a time. Colleen rose to her knees and gave it another shot of burning hairspray then collapsed back onto the rim of the tub. She didn't want to take her gaze off the thing but layered afterimages of the flames remained in her sight. She was spraying fire around her house while she could barely see. She closed her eyes and counted to five. Opened her eyes. Closed them and counted again.

Once Colleen's vision was clear enough she saw the questing extension had withdrawn beneath the door. She heard the wheezing outside increase again in frequency, a sort of buzz or hum joining it as an undertone now. This was the moment of truth—had she genuinely injured the Creeper, hurt it enough to make it back off, or had she simply pissed it off? Was it discouraged or was it minded for revenge? Would it simply use its bulk to smash down the door now and reach her? She doubted her makeshift blowtorch would help her much then. Nor the hammer.

The floor creaked. Colleen envisioned the Creeper rearing to attack? She turned toward her lone little window, considered once more how long it might take her to open it and clamber out, calculated how bad she'd be hurt in the fall to the ground. Then she heard the Creeper moving on the stairs. Was it…going down? Had it chosen to retreat? Did it really hate fire as much as she hoped? Had it perceived the door as a solid obstacle?

It *was* going down. She strained to listen as it reached the main floor, paused almost ten minutes, then crawled back along the deck same as it entered. At last Colleen heard the familiar sound it made squeezing into the basement. After an interval of several more minutes it grew quiet except for the erratic wheeze that carried up faint through the floorboards and vents. The *Very Hungry Caterpillar* was going to sleep.

Colleen twisted and settled into the tub, set her simple armaments between her knees and bunched the pillows up behind her head. Strangely her heart only now began to beat fast, when the danger was apparently passed. Both dangers. What had almost happened to her? She could manage a pretty good guess regarding Jordan's intentions. And his fate. How close had she come to sharing the latter? At what point would the Creeper have smashed down the door? And when would it be back?

She hugged her knees and scrunched up her eyelids, struggled to project herself into the inhuman mind below. Pain, anger, hunger—which would drive the Creeper most? She had never dared defend herself against Derrick that way, not so far as pulling the trigger, but then she had only twice feared him enough to pull a gun on him—and she'd never been concerned he might swallow her whole. She considered the consequences of threatening Derrick with the flamethrower can. Of using it. Such a tactic would probably only enrage her husband. If he could swat it out of her hand that might mean her end. The threat of the pistol had served her better those times. As for the Creeper, she half regretted hurting it. After all, it had saved her from Jordan.

Colleen listened. The Creeper drew rough wet breaths, the only sound. Maybe it was full for now, true. Or maybe it was only saving her for its next meal. She wrestled long hours with insomnia, tortured by thoughts of another attack, considered escape out the window or even the front door and where she might go, went so far as to contemplate calling Derrick if the phone still had any charge…but she'd left it downstairs, on the table by her soda supply. She thought a lot about Paul. Sometime after midnight she slipped into sleep.

When she woke the next morning no sound came from the basement. Still she waited nervous over an hour, all attention given to her ears. Nothing. Must be her weird guest already left for the day. She waited longer, slipped back into sleep. When she woke again she let the sun outside get brighter before she rose and unlocked the bathroom door, hairspray and butane match at ready and aimed toward the stairs. She prepared herself to fight or seek refuge at the least stirring from below.

In the poor morning half light she saw dark serpentine streaks smearing the bathroom's tile floor where the Creeper's tongue had probed, guessed these were dried blood. Jordan's. If so, these marks were almost the only sign the man had left. No such mark of him remained outside the door. Colleen found two things on the stairs though. The first, on the top step, was a wrinkled yellow ShopRite bag holding a roll of duct tape and half a dozen of the widest size zip ties. Several other zip ties had slipped out onto the second step down.

On the fourth step from the top lay a pistol. Saturday Night Special, snubnose .38. She picked it up, opened the cylinder the way her dad taught her and ran her fingers over the ends of the cartridges. Then on impulse she curled a pinky over the front of the cylinder, slipped it into one two three chambers in turn, felt the cool indentations in the tips of each round. Hollow points. What did the guy have in mind that he needed a gun to deal with a lone unarmed housewife? He obviously had not expected the Creeper, so had he planned to use it on *her*? To threaten her? To force her? Or for after? She suspected leaving her around to testify, or even to tell Derrick, had never been part of Jordan's plan. Yet he had no time to squeeze off a single round at the Creeper. It must've come at him quickly once he slipped. She had no sympathy for the man. Would-be rapist. Fucking drunk.

Just how fast *was* this creature though? Yes, she could outrun it on open ground, but at close quarters it might have the advantage. Colleen shuddered, dropped the hairspray and butane match in the bag with the zip ties and tape, and holding the revolver out in front, began to pick her way slowly down the stairs, always ready to turn and run back to the bathroom.

A blue-gray residue dusted the stair rail and the right stairwell wall, the same flaky powder she'd seen on the doorframe below. She descended the stairway stepping down its center, careful never to touch or brush the tainted walls or rail. The stairs themselves showed no further sign of either Jordan or the thing that followed him up, nor of the struggle that transpired there.

On the main floor she encountered even fewer signs of the two intruders. One toppled chair at the dining room table, smudged with traces of the mackerel colored dust. And of course the back door, hanging open, also dusted, long scar of bright raw pine marking the sockets of deadbolt and lock where Jordan had forced it and torn a section of the door jamb free. She shut the door softly and after several minutes searching in the shadows found the jagged wooden fragment under the overhang of the lower kitchen cabinets. Maybe later she might nail it back in place, if the nails didn't split the shard altogether. She had the hammer handy, just needed to scrounge for nails. It would be a crude fix but she couldn't leave the door as it was, not if she intended to stay.

Colleen was convinced the Creeper had gone off to wherever it normally hid during the day. But she was equally certain it would come crawling up the stairs again tonight, and maybe this time her little flamethrower and the bathroom door would fail to hold it off. Once more she thought hard about hiding in some other house, but what if the monster pursued her there and she had to make a stand on unfamiliar ground? And there were always the actual residents and the cops. As a possible looter she might even get shot if caught. The irony of that would be way too much. She didn't want to die an ironic death. She'd had too much irony already in her life. Her best choice was still to stand her ground in the place she knew best. And she did have a gun now of course. How much good it would be against a thing the Creeper's size she had no idea, but it might at least buy her some time. Shots fired were also likely to bring police if they were on patrol, and she might call to them out the bathroom window if they drove down her street. They would come equipped with additional firepower. Encountering the Creeper in action ought to make it easier for them to believe, respond accordingly. Who would come out on top in a battle of cops against monster? She didn't know, but she thought the cops ought to have a chance, especially if they came equipped with riot guns. They'd have a better chance than she would anyway, and if not, they might at least distract the thing long enough for her to escape. She felt a twinge of guilt at the thought of setting the Creeper up after it saved her from a rapist, but shook it off. She knew the monster would gulp her down the same as Jordan given the half a chance. Why else had it probed beneath the bathroom door? Shouldn't she let the professionals handle it instead?

She ate a cold breakfast of Sprite and raisin bran, then hunted up a pair of the narrowest nails she could find and hammered the broken fragment of doorframe roughly back into place, working hard not to split the wood as she did. The door itself now stuck when she tried it, but she'd at least secured the house against any ready egress.

Now came the dragged out day to wait, bide her time till the night. Books and puzzles let her focus drift, so it was back to Klondike. *Klondike Three.* Even there she found herself off her game, constantly drawing from the aces' piles once more. She even lost twice out of seven games, far more frequent than her usual rate.

Her mind kept flashing forward to the coming night. Would the Creeper come upstairs again? Colleen considered the potential imminence of her mortality. She had a gun and thanks to her dad she knew how to use it, but where in the Creeper's anatomy would she need to hit it? If the little revolver was even going to do any good, regardless of its ammo. The thing might have no brain but a dozen hearts. Or no heart at all, not in the sense she thought of a heart anyway. Perhaps she ought to leave a letter in the tub…*If you are reading this I have probably been swallowed by a giant caterpillar thing that lives in the basement. I don't know what it is or where it came from.* She wouldn't mention Jordan. In his case oblivion was an ideal fate.

To whom would she address her letter? Derrick? Her sons? Ruthie, the *best friend* she spoke to only once in the past two years? The police, perhaps? She wished Paul were still alive. She had so much she wanted to say to him. How he made her feel sexy, made her feel loved. How she wanted to take off with him, leave this place behind, leave New Jersey, start fresh somewhere far away. How much of that had he sensed on his own? How much had he thought himself? She hoped those thoughts hadn't distracted him the moment the tree fell. No, the tree was all Sandy. Such harm could not have come from the love she felt—the love she hoped Paul felt the same.

Paul was gone though, and he was the only one to whom she might have left such a letter. So no letter. Let mystery claim her memory if she disappeared, like Judge Crater or Amelia Earhart or Jimmy Hoffa. Perhaps the police would discover the Creeper too late to save her, defeat it in some one-sided gun battle, discover her half-digested corpse inside. Then everyone would know her fate. Would she then find a kind of posthumous fame? She pictured tabloid headlines— *Giant Centipede Devours Jersey Housewife*, or *Sandy Sea Monster Claims Woman as Seaside Snack*. She'd show up in that magazine the boys used to bring home. *Weird NJ*. They used to go with some odd girl from Middlebrook to visit the sites it mentioned. Kirstyn Something. Derrick eventually put a stop to that. How would they feel when their mother and their own familiar shore home popped up in the pages of *Weird NJ*? What a sad irony that would be when it was Paul who should have received recognition, Paul who died in the line of duty, fighting to save others instead of himself. Everyone should know his name, remember his sacrifice. Instead he only managed to become a statistic.

After scattered naps, Klondike and two short chapters into the boring Bowles, Colleen watched through the blinds as the evening thickened and drifted down outside. No way she would venture out tonight. The Creeper might ambush her anywhere. She turned to return to the upstairs master bath. Though the thing already knew to look for her there, it still seemed the most secure room in the house. If she had to make a final stand she might as well make it there. *The hungry and the hunted…* Like the Boss sang in "Jungle Land."

Colleen considered barricading the bottom of the stairwell with whatever furniture she could move. Problem was, she would have to finish the job from the inside. How could she snug up heavy items to the outside of the doorway by herself, heft table and chairs to cover the upper part of the opening? And how easy for the Creeper simply to shove aside any barricade when it arrived? Best to trust the .38, her makeshift flamethrower, the locked bathroom door.

She sat in the gloomy restroom tub, pistol, hairspray and butane match arrayed beneath her angled knees. The next move belonged to the Creeper. She could only wait. She was prepared as she could be, at least without military grade ordnance. With a couple grenades or a rocket launcher she might have a chance, but such weapons would probably kill her too if used inside. If not at first, in the ensuing fire. Though the thought of destroying the house was not altogether bad.

Colleen kept watch in silence, in dark. Hours passed and the rush of adrenalin she'd been riding faded away. She struggled against the weight of her eyelids, her head, but she could not win in the end, and sometime before midnight she slumped in the tub, chin on chest.

***

Sunlight filtering from behind the blinds woke her. She arched her head up and regarded the door. Unbroken, unopened. The entire night was gone, and the monster had not come. Why? Had her awkward fix to the back door kept it out? Or had the memory of her little flamethrower on its tongue kept it downstairs? Perhaps Jordan had satisfied its appetite for a while.

She strained her ears to hear it wheezing below—but heard nothing. Had it already departed? Had it come and gone without her notice? She doubted that. Or could it be the creature never returned last night? Perhaps it had to return to the sea to digest, or to a burrow somewhere in the sand. She needed to use the bucket, and she was hungry, but she wasn't getting up or going anywhere just yet. She had to be *absolutely* sure. What if the Creeper was clever and attempting to draw her out? Could it be that intelligent?

For almost half an hour Colleen fought her fear, hoping to hold off another adrenalin rush so long as she needed to keep still. No sound came from beneath her the entire time. Or from outside. In the end she rose, climbed out of the tub, did her business, opened the door with agonizing care.

No new signs of intrusion marked her floor. She advanced down the dismal stairs, .38 always out front, cocked and ready. On the first floor, nothing. The back door? Intact. Her quick inspection for enormous monsters found no sign. If the thing had returned late in the night, it hadn't invaded the upper floors. She doubted the broken door could hold it back if it really tried...so had the creature even made an attempt to enter? Had it ever returned to her home last night? If it did not lie curled quietly in the basement below, she'd have no way to be sure it had come back in the last twenty-four hours at all. The Creeper's comings and goings had been so consistent this far. Colleen had grown almost comfortable with its presence. What would she do if the creature changed its schedule now, became erratic and unpredictable? Like Derrick.

She couldn't handle dry cereal this morning. Her stomach was a tightly clenched acid knot. She breakfasted on tinned fish instead, sluicing the contents down with a can of Sprite, the brine and shredded fish flesh, the steamed down to softness bits of spine and bone.

Having temporarily addressed her nutritional needs, Colleen considered the options ahead. She could stay inside till nightfall, or she could step out and check the basement, see if the Creeper had in fact returned. And if it did wait below? How quickly could the creature rush the door? How fast could she aim and fire? How fast could she turn and run away?

Stepping outside in the daytime brought additional risks unrelated to the Creeper, the reason why she'd avoided such excursions so far. Someone might report her, and then the police would come. She had her ID but not a copy of the deed. Even if they believed the house was her own, she remained in violation of the curfew. She saw herself cuffed and hauled off, if they did not do far worse. Colleen wondered if they were using the Seaside jail, or were they shipping prisoners somewhere else? And her one call? That would have to go to Derrick. If he even decided to bail her out, things would not go well back in Sourland Hills. She'd ignored his directive not to stay overnight in Seaside, and she could see him wanting to punish her for that choice. She doubted she'd get a chance to prove him wrong. He'd start in and the only question then was how far things would escalate. Without the boys at home she would not be safe.

After an unmeasured duration of probably half an hour or so, Colleen stepped toward the door, patting the Maglite in her belt, now positioned opposite the .38. Her pants had grown so baggy the accessories actually helped keep them up by tightening her belt. And she might need both revolver and light as she inspected downstairs.

She left the door unlocked behind her, cracked open only half an inch, and crossed the deck with agonizing slowness, assessing the sound of each of her steps, listening for some response, any response, from below. Nothing came so she continued out.

Once she'd reached the sandy ground she prepared herself to run away rather than back upstairs. She'd passed the point of no return. If the thing was down there and came after her, she'd have a better chance on open ground. Leading it back to the house where it could corner her seemed suicide now. Colleen held no confidence locked doors could hold the Creeper off, especially the deck door now that its frame was already damaged. Nor was she convinced the gun would stop it. Maybe only make it mad. *The Very Angry Caterpillar*...

She shuffled toward the basement door at a measured halting pace, pistol pressed against flashlight in her unexpectedly steady hands. Even with fresh batteries the sun erased the Maglite's beam entire until she got within a body length of the door. At last the cold light she cast began to reflect off surfaces inside the room. She took one more step closer, another, played the light around the interior in an extended arc.

Colleen saw only the upended furniture and appliances as before. No bus-length sea monster with spikes down its back and a suspicious bulge somewhere in its middle. She stepped closer, took a deep breath, and stepped right up to the doorway. Swinging the light all around the basement she saw nothing other than walls and furniture and floor. A toppled easy chair made her think of Paul, how she dared one time to meet him down here when Derrick was passed out upstairs and the boys were on the boardwalk, how she gripped the back of that very chair while he tugged her shorts down her thighs and slid smooth inside her. She'd been so wet already. But Paul was gone, and now the Creeper was gone too. Did it slip out before she woke this morning...or had it never returned at all last night?

She'd come to rely on the creature's regular schedule. Had she come to count on its protection too? It had taken care of Jordan for her, hadn't it? She didn't plan things the way they played out, but wasn't she also now considering luring Derrick into its grasp? The notion floated in her mind below the surface of consciousness, but it *was* there. Invite Derrick to meet her, tell him she was staying in the basement, time his arrival right... another problem solved. She wondered if she could do it.

But if the Creeper really was gone, if it wasn't coming back, well so much for that plan. She had no idea where it might be hiding out. What if it picked another house? Or maybe now it roamed the neighborhood at night. That meant her nocturnal expeditions just got a whole lot more dangerous. She might come upon the creature anywhere, at any time. What if it trapped her in an unfamiliar home, a place where she didn't know the floorplan? Just how clever a predator was the thing? It had taken an armed man down without a fight. Could its temporary disappearance be a deliberate plan to lure her out and trap her? Or did it even care? How well had Jordan satisfied its hunger? Perhaps it had gone off to digest him for a week the way a python did. Or it might be recovering from the burns to its tongue, though she did not think she'd hurt it all that bad.

Colleen calculated how long her current cache of canned goods would last, how many days before she had to venture out again. She had batteries finally, Sprite and water for at least a week. Food was running low, but couldn't a person go much longer without food than water? She was certain she read that somewhere. Wasn't that how hunger strikes worked—water, but no food? She still had the canned pineapple. A last resort.

What if the Creeper was behind her right this minute? She spun and scanned the narrow lot, saw nothing suspicious, no giant monsters, nothing moving. Yet the thing could be right around any corner, or lurking in any of the houses within or out of sight. She never discovered what it did during its days. She'd seen it that first night, striding along the berm at the end of Hancock and the verge of the beach, and since then she'd come to know its patterns of going and coming from her house but not where it went. Her general assumption was the Creeper returned each day to the sea, to hunt for food she supposed. Yet she had no firsthand evidence of any of this, and for all she knew the creature might simply be switching houses while the sun was up, perhaps to a home with no eastern or southern exposure. What if she stumbled into its other lair during one of her own excursions?

That was if it had even gone far. It could be lurking right nearby, bunching up to rush her the very next moment. Would it know her as the one who torched its tongue? Would it recognize her by the sound of her breathing, her particular smell? Colleen considered her exposed position and hustled back up the deck stairs. Once inside she locked the door and collapsed into a kitchen chair, stuck the light back in her belt but set the pistol in her lap. She listened close for any sound from outside, kept her gaze on the kitchen door, ready to aim and fire the moment it burst open.

Minutes. Nothing. Longer. Nothing. Maybe it only waited for her guard to drop. Just how cunning a hunter was the Creeper? The consistency of its movements so far had created a sense of safety for Colleen, but now that it deviated from its punchclock routine she felt a familiar discomfort creeping in. She'd begun to feel a degree of ease with her reliable basement squatter, but now that she could no longer predict its movements it would be like dealing with a much larger, deadlier version of Derrick. It was *déjà vu all over again*, as Yogi Berra used to say. Just when she'd begun to consider the monster almost a friend. After all, it saved her life. Probably not on purpose, but that action had to count for something.

Though it remained only morning Colleen climbed back up the stairs, locked the bathroom door and settled once more into the tub. Bored enough already she actually made some headway in the Bowles, she read till she encountered the line *This was the sort of room where there could be spiders and one would not see them.* That was too much. Way too close to home. She flung the book behind her latrine where it fell to the floor with pages splayed. Possibly still to the spider page. Bowles had betrayed her, whoever he was. *She* was trapped right this minute in a room, in a house, in a *town*, all of which had become the room where something worse than spiders hid. Or was she herself the spider, hiding in shadows? She thought of a possibility she had not considered before. What if the Creeper was not alone? What if others of its kind had also invaded Seaside Heights? She had only seen it one time after all, and that was in the dark. How many similar creatures might be loose in Seaside, perhaps taking turns occupying her basement? Maybe they knew she was upstairs all along and had set her aside for some special kind of feast. Who knew how many of the monsters were out there, or what they got up to during the days? Perhaps *her* Creeper had only gone off this morning to call for help or hunt for a mate.

Colleen spent most of the day behind the locked door of the upstairs restroom, uncertain when her Creeper might return, alone or with friends. She ventured downstairs only twice, once for food and drink from her meager stash, and later to the sunroom for an old board game whose lid she could use to lay out cards for *Klondike*, a thing with many plastic parts called *Mousetrap*. She remembered the game as missing several pieces but couldn't remember which. The diving board? The bowling ball? No one had touched the dusty faded box in years, not since the boys were still in grade school. Wedged between her ribs and thighs its cardboard lid served well enough as a makeshift card table.

She napped. She played cards. Sometime in the afternoon she set *Mousetrap* on the floor and hung over the tub, struggled to assemble the multicolored components based on blurred recollections. The game's instructions were one of the components gone AWOL. Despite her memory of lost parts, all the other pieces appeared present, and after some trial and error she had the entire Rube Goldberg contraption put together and began catching plastic mice. Which got boring fast. She wished they had *Boobytrap*. That game might prove more suitable for solo play.

Dark at last began to seep between the blinds. Colleen set the cards and game aside, checked the position of the .38 in her lap, pointed toward the door. In an hour or two the Creeper ought to return, but it might come back early. And it might bring family, friends. The question was whether it would come after her again. If it did—was raw firepower going to hold it off as well as fire itself had night before last?

Colleen kept her vigil to the hour of the Creeper's expected return and beyond. Close to midnight her head collapsed on her chest.

She woke several times before sunrise, and each time strained to hear the wheeze and rustle of her monstrous squatter. Yet beyond the natural creaks and pops of any old house at night, she heard nothing. Could it be she had 46 Hancock all to herself? Hadn't that been her plan at the start?

Another night passed sans sign or sound of the Creeper. Once the sun at last began to ooze through the closed blinds above, Colleen stood shaking then shook the cramps from out her limbs, sure as she could be the creature was not in her basement.

Her new morning ritual came next, padding down the stairs with the pistol outstretched. Stopping to listen after every step. Hearing nothing.

Once she checked the basement and found no evidence of the Creeper's return, she felt a fresh wave of melancholy. A massive and dangerous monster had been hiding in her home. She ought to be happy it was gone. Instead she considered the routines she'd built around it, its disposal of Jordan right at the moment he'd gotten close enough to threaten. Likely it never knew she was in the house until it got upstairs. Likely it would have gulped her down same as Jordan if it got the chance.

She missed it. She *owed* it. And now she was feeling…what? Empty monster nest syndrome? Yet if she grew lax in its absence, careless in her habits, there was always the danger it might return unexpected, come upon her unawares. She might not think so kindly of it then. Colleen had no way to know if the Creeper was gone forever. Perhaps it simply went off somewhere for a few days to finish digesting Jordan, down into the sea or a hole in the sand, in which case it might be back after the bulge of its big meal dissolved. And if she got sloppy in her schedule, stayed out too late or forgot to lock up, would she become the Creeper's next meal?

Since Colleen no longer knew the creature's whereabouts, she abandoned her nighttime outings altogether. She had enough food, enough soda if not water, an adequate supply of batteries all to last a few days. She couldn't risk entering a home where the Creeper was camping. Not to mention the danger of an encounter with the cops. She considered the increasing likelihood they knew by now they had a break-in bandit on their hands. She'd been lucky thus far but best not to push it. How much longer anyway before water and power came back on? That would solve a big part of her problem. Even help with food because running water would allow her to prepare pasta. At least if the power came back on as well.

She kept to her refuge in the upstairs tub, kept that door locked, kept the gun close at all times. And she kept to this pattern four days after the Creeper dealt with Jordan and disappeared, saving her whether that was its goal or not. The last two days she began to hear more vehicles on the street, not just police patrols at night. A few glances through the blinds told her FEMA was letting homeowners drive in now. Seaside had taken another step toward normalcy.

Close to her guess as to noon on the third day post-Creeper she heard tires crunching over the sand and debris in the side gravel drive. She drew herself half up the edge of the tub, shook out the pins and needles and stretched against the cramps in her legs. She stood when she could, and once she could walk at all she staggered out and toward the little kitchen on the east side of the upper floor. Shoving aside the blinds she looked down and saw what she knew at once she'd been expecting. A maroon Dodge Ram. Derrick's truck. Derrick's or one just like it. Derrick's.

Already someone knocked on the back door. Four times, in two paired raps. Standard Derrick. If she had any doubt it was him at that point he spoke —Hey honey, open up. I forgot my housekeys. I came to take you home. I've been worried sick about you all alone here you know. It's not safe. Do you remember my friend Jordan, the one you didn't like? He disappeared a few days ago and they say it probably happened here. When I heard that it was the last straw. I knew I had to come check on you.

A pause and then —Come on, Colleen. I'm gonna be really fucking worried if you're not here and I'll be pissed if I hafta fuck up the door. Come on, you're making me nervous.

She stepped down the stairs as if in a trance. Halfway to the door she called out —Hold on. I'm coming. Don't do anything—just wait. She'd been about to say —*Don't do anything stupid* but she didn't want to set him off.

—Okay, I'm waiting. And then she was unlocking the door, opening it—ever so briefly wondering whether the Creeper could imitate voices—maybe it could but could it drive a truck?

Derrick stood on the deck, full six two, possibly three in work boots, wearing the black North Face coat she'd bought him two years back, bald spot tucked under a Yankees cap, graying temples revealed at the sides. The coat hung open and she noted the white work shirt he wore beneath it seemed clean, same for his jeans. Was he actually doing his own laundry now that the water and power had come back on in Sourland? That would be something.

She was a different story of course, and it was her appearance he picked up on first.

—Aw honey, you look like hell. Like some kind of old homeless hag. Let's get you home and get you cleaned up. Alex is coming back for Thanksgiving soon and I don't want him seeing you like this. Let's get the hell out of here, come on. It's not safe and you don't wanna be here no more. Let's just go right now. Do you have any stuff you need to grab?

Colleen thought of the pistol, abandoned in the master bathroom tub alongside the hairspray and the butane lighter. Would she need those now? Maybe the gun, but she suddenly found it hard to care.

She nodded to Derrick, said simply —Okay. Let's go. Her voice came a hoarse whisper. She stepped out before he ever entered and locked the house with the keys she'd carried in her pocket the entire time. Numb, she allowed him to lead her toward the truck. She sat tense all the way up Boulevard to the Pelican Island Bridge waiting for the Creeper to rush the truck, topple it and suck them both from the wreckage like marrow. It did not come. Once on 37, Derrick began to talk, first in snippets then a torrent. All the way to Sourland Hills, Colleen never heard a word Derrick spoke, never looked up from her lap where she spun the green and gold friendship bracelet she'd taken from the tube in the driveway and worn on her right wrist ever since.

lók'aa'ch'égai mountain journal

Date: Wed, 8 June 201—
Subject: the journal
From: yrekachica96@gmail.com
To: faakthe49ers95@hotmail.com

Hey babe, so here is part one of that LONG email I told you was coming. Sorry you had to wait. I wish you were here so I could just show you what I found. It took me a while to get all the pages from the journal scanned in. Do me a favor please and read EVERYthing with all the attachments before you write back. Take your time too, but I want your opinion. I'm still trying to decide what to make of it all myself or even whether to say anything about it. But I really need to know what you think so I'm sharing it with you. I haven't showed this to anyone else yet. Honestly, I'm pretty weirded out. You'll see why soon enough.

OK, so you already know I never met my biological father. He ran out on my mom when she was five months pregnant with me, told her he needed time to think, drove out to Arizona to hang out with one of his friends and herd sheep on an Indian reservation. Only he never came back. As far as I'm concerned, Angelo is my real dad. He always treated

177

me like his own daughter. I never wanted to know anything about my biological father and I never cared.

Well, remember last month, my eighteenth birthday party, and my Grandma Phyllis came? I've always been cool with her—it's not her fault what her son did to me and my mom, and I actually like having an extra grandmother, especially since my dad's father died of cancer right before he married my mom. And I feel bad for her, the way her son ran off just like her husband before him. I'm all she's got, right? She can be uptight but she's basically good to me. I wish she would stop nagging me about going to church though. Ain't happening, no way no how. Other than that though, she's cool.

Anyway, we talked for a while. She asked me about my college plans and seemed happy I was going to Chico State even though it's where her son met my mother. Then the church thing but she didn't push too hard, thank God. And she gave me a card which when I opened it later had a check for one thousand dollars. NOT GOING TO COMPLAIN ABOUT THAT!!! Only then she says I'm going to send you some of your father's things. It's time I passed them on to you. And she gives me a big hug and a kiss on the cheek and walks away. I don't know if you saw me talking to her. You were busy talking baseball with Angelo I think.

Sure enough a box shows up about four days later. Not so big, about a foot all round, and not too heavy either. At first I didn't want to deal with it, so I just stuck it in the corner of my bedroom and tried to ignore it. But it was getting to me more and more until that Sunday I was acting all restless, and Angelo said, Why don't you just open the box? And that he'd be here for me no matter what was inside and how it made me feel. That's what I mean about Angelo. He knows when something is bothering me. He's a good dad. A real dad.

So I opened the box. Inside is another box but there's a letter on top. From Grandma Phyllis, on her pink and blue art design stationary. Kandinsky, I think.

lók'aa'ch'égai mountain journal

Dear Rachel,

I received the enclosed package about five months after your father disappeared. An Indian man sent it to me, along with a letter. Although I read his letter at the time, I have never looked closely at the rest of what was inside. I think you will understand my reasons. Now that you are old enough however, I believe these items should belong to you to do with as you wish. Probably you will just want to throw them away. I doubt you will find many answers, and although I myself no longer have any need of them, if you come across something you feel I should know, you may tell me. You have been raised and grown up well in most regards, and now it is time for me to trust your judgment.

The box inside was hardly smaller, but obviously older. The cardboard was wrinkled and the tape was peeling and coated with dust on what used to be the sticky side. The return address was a Mr. Ervin Redhouse in Lukachukai, Arizona. I opened it up without taking it out of Phyllis's box, and the first thing I found was another letter, this one on old notebook paper. The ink was a little faded but I could read it all right.

Dear Mrs. Wilson,

The objects inside this box belonged to your son Daniel, who stayed in my sheep camp until July 23. Some time during the late night of that day or early morning of the 24th he left in his car and we never saw him again. I can not say exactly when because the other sheepherder and I were attending a ceremonial event that night and did not return until after sunrise. Several days later we drove down the mountain to shower and purchase supplies at a trading post, and at that time I reported Daniel's disappearance to the Navajo Police. They showed no concern. It was not until you contacted them in September that they returned to ask questions. My confidence in them is low, so I chose not to hand over the items in the box. I felt they belonged to Daniel's family, and you would never get them if I surrendered them to our police. I am sorry if I made the wrong decision.

Please contact me if I can be any more help.

179

Yours truly,

Ervin Redhouse

I could see inside some books, a journal, an old flashlight, a folded pair of socks that were all dried out and stiff now, a toothbrush, some odds and ends. At that point I set the box aside and tried to ignore it for another day. But I kept looking at it every time I went in my room. And I started making up reasons just to go in the room. Finally that night I couldn't sleep because of it. So I got up and turned on the desk light, then started taking everything out and laying it on the carpet.

There were three books. *Japan and India Journals*, by Joanne Kyger. *The Way to Rainy Mountain*, by N. Scott Momaday. *Back Roads to Far Towns*, by Basho. A little black address book, two dozen old envelopes with a few brown shreds of the rubber band that must have held them together, a roll of stamps from before we were born, and a couple dried up ballpoint pens. The flashlight was dead, and pukey corrosion was crusted around the end. Four funny shaped rocks. And the journal. That was the main thing.

The journal was one of those black and white composition notebooks they give kids in school. On the cover it said Leonard Washburn. English 1. Mr. Sharp. The first sixteen pages were by a student from the reservation. Grammar exercises, stories about what he did over the weekend, stuff like that. I skimmed over those pages but nothing seemed relevant. One of the few things I knew about my dad was the guy who hooked him up with the sheepherding was some college friend who went to teach on the Navajo Reservation after graduation. I didn't remember his friend's name but I guess the journal was recycled from one of his classes.

After Leonard's entries came three blank pages, and then a header, in black ballpoint, overwritten several times and underlined. *lók'aa'ch'égai mountain journal*, just like that. My father was not big on capital letters, which is going to get obvious real fast. And that's where his journal starts. The handwriting is different from there. Leonard Washburn actually had

better handwriting than my father. Way better. I will let you look at the
journal now. The first few pages are attached. I'm going to have to split it
up over more than one email, OK?

jpeg file: lokaajournal1

lók'aa'ch'égai mountain journal — day 1 — July 11(?)

got lost chasing a lost sheep
(the blackfaced one, the one from Colorado, the Rocky Mountain sheep,
the one from the prep school, the one that thinks it is a cow, the stupid one)
think I cut back too far west at one point finally asked directions from
an older woman who was with her own little herd. she gave me the kind
of directions I'm already getting used to here: pointing with bottom lip
instead of finger. My son saw you, said there's a man out there who's not
Diné, looks like a white man.

found my way back after that, Ervin asks Where have you been? I tell him
Everywhere. I wish.
the best word I learned today is that for watermelon: *ch'ééh jiyáán*: in vain
one eats it.

Studied the location of the camp better after I got back. it runs right up
(or the clearing in which the camp sits runs) to the trees at the base of the
easternmost

jpeg file: lokaajournal2

of the two hills between which it ~~lay~~ lies also remembering the shape of
the hill
and the large brown-weed-covered pond by the road alongside the camp
and the locations of other nearby camps

day 2 afternoon

already I am becoming uncomfortable from the dirt, having gone two mornings without a shower, probably a record for me since puberty. my scalp itches. I am unhappily anticipating the growth of rashes on scalp, armpits, chest, and possibly groin. there should be some way, combination of practices and mindset, that could help me avoid this, but I have no inkling. just hope I will reach a certain threshold and things will not get worse. if the situation does become acute, I will just have to say fuck it and drive into town. Gallup maybe, or Farmington. I should have talked to Stan and Dayglo and Becky more when I was in Frisco about their experiences in the communes and how they handled

jpeg file: lokaajournal3

personal hygiene with limited access to water. my situation at least should be less of a thorn once the women leave, although it sounds like Ervin's three sisters may be periodic visitors here.

my time with Ervin has been minimal so far, mainly due to the German contingent. That woman grates on my nerves, her and her bratty kid and that pale wimpy boyfriend who never speaks. They don't belong here. Volker is all right. I don't know his story yet but I at least figured out he is not with the others.

I did get to herd sheep with Ervin for a while this morning. first we had to find them. he must think I'm a teacher like Jim, as he gave me a whole lecture comparing sheepherding to lesson planning. I didn't say anything. who knew what wisdom he might share. at least I can pass it on to Jim when I see him again. here's what I remember: Everyday when you're sheepherding something like this happens. yesterday we couldn't find that Colorado sheep, today we can't find any of them. it's like when you're lesson planning and the kids don't follow your lesson plan. if you try to be rigid, you get frustrated. you have to be flexible. I said lesson plans are hard to follow. he just looked at me.

we still haven't found that Colorado sheep. stupid sheep.

evening

there is quite a variety of livestock here—cows, horses, and goats in addition to the sheep,

jpeg file: lokaajournal4

all tooling about the whole day long. right now a small herd of cows is casually making their way through our camp after spending the last couple hours chomping away in the dip just behind us.

night is coming on and I will have to make do with my rough Mexican rug for a blanket. I had a sleeping bag, but I left it in Volker's tent when he and Ervin drove down to the Seven-2-Eleven. the wind was kicking up, and I thought the sleeping bag might help weigh down the tent since he hadn't staked it too good. then I saw the tent really coming loose, so I ran back to the shade house for the hammer. only once I turned around with the hammer in my hand, I saw the tent floating in the middle of the stock pond and slowly sinking. Volker tried to make frybread inside the tent on his hotplate once, and the oil spattered and melted a hole, so that's probably where the water was coming in. He's a real city boy, even worse than me. so I had to take off my boots and pants, wade out to the middle of the muddy pond bareass and drag the whole thing back. the same pond all the animals drink out of. I probably got sheep spit on my nads. horse spit. cow spit. goat spit. worse. don't want to think about it. now my sleeping bag is hanging up behind the big tent to dry. I hope it doesn't blow all the way down the hill.

the wind is fading and night is coming down pretty heavy now so I can barely see the lines on the paper. it's easy to imagine the

jpeg file: lokaajournal5

emergence of a whole separate set of animals, coyote punching in as sheepdog punches out. although Funny is pretty much useless. Funny the sheepdog. seems totally useless, to be sure.

Night is coming on so dense now I can't see the lines on this journal, so it's time for me to punch out too.

Day ?

(can't remember if it's been one or two days since I last wrote in here. they weren't good days)

I can smell my armpits some of the time, my asshole most of the time, and my jeans smell like sheep, though I hardly notice that. Everything smells like sheep.

good news is the Germans are gone, Uta and her crew but not Volker which is cool. Volker is alright. Ervin had me drive them down the Kerr-McGee road to Red Rock Trading Post. that road is way shorter than the main road on either side, though it's not maintained even half as well. deep washouts cut inward several places from the edge, and random fallen rocks and boulders require tricky navigation. the dropoff under most of the out-side edge is hundreds or maybe a thousand feet into pristine stands of old growth pine.

I'm keeping this journal because Joanne Kyger told me to at her reading I went to in Bolinas with Becky. I told her I was leaving to spend the summer herding sheep on the Navajo Reservation, and she told me Keep a journal. So I am. The main idea was to write some poetry, so here goes.

blue damselfly lights on swamp grass tip
many painted lady butterflies on
yellow daisies

locusts ~~clickety click~~ clackety looping flights
                    around the shade house

a killdeer or plover plucks
          screechy violin strings
                    inland sandpiper

clouds east, maybe over Jim's school

jpeg file: lokaajournal6

lók'aa'ch'égai mountain journal

light up nuclear lightning flash
        again
    and again
every minute or so

you get the picture
Volker working on his bike, when we came back
from the Enemy Way (Squaw Dance)
the parking light was on
might be someone tried to hotwire it.
horses in the boggy pond
water weed streaming from out their mouths
the water up above their knees
move like dinosaurs
      in a Hollywood movie

lightning flashes dimming
      growing farther apart
stars coming out
      killdeer gone to bed

there goes one last flash
    a big one
nighty-night

Date: Wed, 8 June 201—
Subject: the journal(2)
From: yrekachica96@gmail.com
To: faakthe49ers95@hotmail.com

Starting a second email cause I think that was about all the attachments
one message can stand. So my biological father was some kind of poet, only
the non-rhyming type. I guess his stuff is OK. Kind of like haikus but with
too many words. Probably he planned to polish it up later on.

The next half dozen pages of his journal are attached.

jpeg file: lokaajournal7

next day — Monday maybe

Ervin says Did you hear that noise last night?
(the noise the dogs made at the Archies'
corral)
something might have gotten into their herd
it would have been a bear
      if a bear gets into the herd at night
                    pull your car up to the corral
          put on the high beams and honk the horn
      it won't give up the one it's killed
             but try to keep it from killing another
         or it won't stop
                 don't get out of your car
no shit I won't get out of my car. not till I'm all the way down the mountain and drinking a beer in Farmington.

later we herd the sheep all the way to the
east edge of the mountain
          see Shiprock
   and its wings
             past there
     nothing
        just haze
   but in the dusty road
             bear tracks

I didn't sign on for this

jpeg file: lokaajournal8

as I was writing the above two small birds invaded the shade house making insect noises. I could not identify them.

(wish I had field guide, binoculars, chopsticks, gun, running water, other things I will think of later.)

Volker is not back with the fish yet, if he actually caught any.

Ervin asked me to help him tie up the sides of the tent we sleep in. It's a huge army tent like in *M*A*S*H*, maybe forty feet long. When we do a shit-ton of beetles go scrambling, big black beetles with Popeye legs. They must have thought the tent was one big rock for them all to hide under.

The beetles have a jerky sort of walk, and if you get close to one, it stops and sticks its butt in the air. a drop of orange goo comes out, and you do not want to get that stuff on you. no matter how many times you wash your hands in the pond, the smell will not come off.

next day + 1

> Approaching sunset
black & white swallows circle my head
> à la cartoon tweety birds
but I haven't been hit
> propelling themselves with ~~snaps~~
~~of the wings flutter flutter f~~ flutters and snaps
gliding between motions past my head and
if I turn at just the right speed
> I can see them as if motionless
not as jewel~~ish as~~ as bright as the blue & orange

jpeg file: lokaajournal9

barn swallows I know from back home
same cigar-shaped body though
same snappy flight patterns
> zooming down to eat the bugs
around my head
> fill the same ecological niche

as bats, different time slot though
they punch out when the bats punch in
        (remembering again the Warner Bros cartoon
where sheepdog and coyote punch the same
time clock then beat each other afterward)
        all those old cartoons are just
fun with the food chain funnies

saw a log across the mountain that a bear had rolled over
and clawed, hunting tasty grubs.
proud of myself I didn't freak out

slowly the mountain is making itself known to me
in little things I see.

jpeg file: lokaajournal10

Next day

what I have learned is the obvious
the land writes itself if
        you just hold the pen.

no erotic dreams last night
no witches
        at least not that I remember
didn't mention that when it happened
                best to let it be

from the large flat rock where I sit
        size and shape of a legless grand piano
I have a spectacular view off the mountain's
edge as far as the Shiprock
Tse'bit'á'i
        the baked lava butt of an ancient eagle
sits out in the desert

lók'aa'ch'égai mountain journal

losing tail feathers year by year
tips of wing feathers (pinions?) visible as well
stretching out

jpeg file: lokaajournal11

     lava rills and dykes
array of other volcanic extrusions
          also visible
     but best not to mention as
          at least one is a place of witches
               (got lectured on that already

a live eagle soaring now before it
     banked off behind some aspens and
gone as quickly as I could write this
down into Red Valley
(James says his students pronounce it
Rat Valley)
the waves of pine break there
     one or two roads very faint beyond
Red Valley Trading Post a greenish dash
Hills and the shadow of clouds

     nothing visible of the town of
Shiprock, largest town on the Diné Nation
known to Navajos more often as Tó. Water.
For the San Juan River that runs through its heart
Why would anyone refer to the place they live
as a sacred place nearby? —Ervin Redhouse

jpeg file: lokaajournal12

long gone the four horses — three chestnut one
        coffee w/ cream
     that suddenly appeared as I sat here

preparing to write
        watching me nervously
                because I was too close to the road
      but when I got up to step back and
           give them room to pass
        they vanished as quickly as they appeared

easy-come easy-go as
    the objects of my vision
        engage my attention
    I take note
a wide variety of insects dominate
        most notable a lone Jerusalem cricket, the
    infamous child of the earth or *chacho de la tierra*
      The ugliest thing you'll
ever see Jim called it
    most folks think this fetus-shaped
monster is a venomous spider but
it's harmless to everyone except trees

as I'm examining it a visitor comes, one
of the Archies' grandkids, a

jpeg file: lokaajournal13

    little girl, maybe six or seven, dressed
      like a tiny cowgirl
she speaks to Ervin very earnestly in Navajo five minutes
    or more. Seriously and rapidly. he
asks a few questions. I
        can't follow any of it
    except *ch'įįdii.* several times.
      I recognize that one. devil. or ghost. Navajos
take that shit very serious
    after she's done she runs right off. All
Ervin says is We've got to go over the Archies

later. and then it's back to biz. I don't
    ask him to explain. they're probably
        having a ceremony. Ervin
might be invited, but not Volker or me

saw my first reptiles up here
yesterday, (~~was~~ beginning to think there were
    none this high)
a two foot garter snake
    which I was almost on top of before
it poured itself beneath a rock
scanning after crossing the meadow past the outhouse
    a horned toad
                first ever I have seen in the wild
         and the last thing I expected to see
up here
    scuttled under a bush
          so unsure whether
seen for real
    but several hours later when we got back from

Date: Wed, 8 June 201—
Subject: the journal (3)
From: yrekachica96@gmail.com
To: faakthe49ers95@hotmail.com

Continuing here. The journal has over thirty written pages so it's going
to take a couple more emails. Sorry about all the emails and attachments.
Thanks for reading this stuff. You know it means a lot to me. I love you
babe.

  jpeg file: lokaajournal14

    Red Valley Trading Post
(really Red Rock but that's another…)
        I went back and there it was

this time let me pick it up and hold it
    in my hand
looking a little like a cute Lorne Greene
body fringed with tiny spikes
    Ervin said We have so
many stories about them
                then I put it

back where I found it
but sad to see it go

later, herding sheep with Volker
we saw another garter snake
              just a baby
    Volker said it was the first snake he
ever saw
            I ask him Don't you have snakes
        in Germany? Yes, but…
Ervin comes over then, says we need to visit
    the Archies says

jpeg file: lokaajournal15

       something killed one of
their sheep last night
he walks on past us, Volker
    and I look at each other,
          follow along
      the road to the fork that leads to
      the Archies' camp
we pass their herd in the big meadow, the
    little girl and a teenage boy watching
      them. Ervin already put our herd in
    the corral for the night. the Archies
have a serious herd, maybe 500 strong, not
    like Ervin's little hobby herd, a
mere 124

lók'aa'ch'égai mountain journal

the rest of the Archies are in their corral, with
a few goats, the old man and the younger
couple that must be
  his son and daughter or spouse I never
got it straight. we have to climb the
    fence because the gate is closed
  the gate is the rusted rectangle of wire and
springs left over after a mattress burned or

jpeg file: lokaajournal16

    rotted away. smart recycling
inside we find them all standing around the
deflated carcass of a sheep. I mean
  it's like a balloon someone let the
air out of, seriously the saddest
     sorriest thing I've ever seen
the old guy talks to Ervin and there's that word
  again. when he says it he glances at
      the setting sun, already under the
  treetops in the west
Ervin looks at Volker and me, says They need you to carry
it out. because a *ch'įįdii* killed it, Diné
cannot touch it. but you can because you are
bilagáana. they already dug a hole.
and he points with his lip across the road
at the hillside
I don't want to touch the flattened sheep, it's too
wrong. I look at Volker for support but
his face is blank. the corpse has bloodstained
wool around its neck, but no blood on the ground. Ervin
   should have told us to bring gloves, some kind of

jpeg file: lokaajournal17

tarp or canvas to carry it on. but no so we grab the

dirty hooves two each, even the legs limp as
        jello. boneless. the Archies open the gate and
   we carry the wretched thing across the road
to a pit about three feet deep and lower it
     in. there's only one shovel so
I get a rake. after, we
both look at our hands I
    want to wash them or rub them on my pants but
       only hold them stiff at my sides
back at our camp we scrub them in the stock pond with
Ervin's biodegradable soap but I can
   feel the filthy lanolin coating them still

that night the coyotes yip on the hill different
from before, stopping altogether, exploding in wild chorus
I heard actual panic in their cries
    could be a bear but they had to know bear. they
kept me up late and then
     my dreams were a mess
one I remember had a rattlesnake poking straight out
   at me from a hole in a tree, the snake
     patterned with the swallows' colors in bands
   spoke to me I think but I can never remember
      what anyone says in my dreams, snakes
    included it seems
          clear now

jpeg file: lokaajournal18

   the colors of this place have crept
    into
      my dreams
        and accompany me wherever I go

Volker wakes me up, all panicked, Come
quickly, zere iss something wrong vith

lók'aa'ch'égai mountain journal

Funny.
Funny iss licking his penis!
fuck. he's serious! I roll over,
  disgusted. with Volker, not the dog. Volker,
dogs do that. it's normal. you'd
      do it too if you could
he takes some convincing. after
  that I can't go back to sleep. Ervin
    and his Germans.
he went to some prep school out east. talks
  a lot about this one German I
    think was his boyfriend there. Lukas.
that's why all the Germans. he tries a few out
every summer. turns out they have

jpeg file: lokaajournal19

clubs there where they dress up like Native Americans.
build campfires and sleep in
  teepees. teepees aren't Navajo
surprises me really Ervin would
hang around with such people. maybe he's sick of
them by now, maybe that's why he acted so chill
to Uta. Volker is not from one of
those clubs. I think he knew Lukas personal
somehow. I got in cause of Jim of
course. Ervin is a consultant at his school
I have to say he is an interesting guy. kind of a douche
  sometimes, but highly educated. also very
traditional, carries himself almost like European royalty. not like I hang
with European royalty
  much. but he's got that deep sense of history. his own, his family's,
his people's. not all Diné are like
that. I never know what he thinks of me. hard to read. he
    seems to like Volker well enough. I wish
  I could introduce him to Becky but he probably

wouldn't like her folks. he's said one or two
    things negative about hippies. so

jpeg file: lokaajournal20

that's probably out

[in this space would be notes from a day I skipped because Volker went
to Towaoc for the Sun Dance, which he missed anyway, and I was busy
with the sheep all day until he came back, after which I put them in the
corral and we talked until the sun went down. but we didn't talk about the
Archies' creepy dead sheep]

Sunday I think, because Ervin is due back tonight

fly poem — an essay

a cold wind blows up my ass in
the outhouse
disturbing the flies from their positions
        recalling
~~Finally I~~^read the sign on the Kerr McGee Road
DANGER: POISONOUS GAS IN THIS AREA
        H2S
    when Ervin comes back he says

jpeg file: lokaajournal21

            All these years they told
us there was nothing to worry about
        then they put those signs up just two years ago

~~I knew~~ there was an oily rotten smell
    around that ~~oil~~ pump
                ~~where I looked for the sheep~~
        but I thought it was only

196

lók'aa'ch'égai mountain journal

the smell of the thing itself
    and its hydraulics, natural
        perhaps for ~~an~~ oil pumps
    using the word natural here in a limited sense
          ~~I noticed that~~ several pines
      ~~were~~ dead around it standing with their
    needles still clinging, ~~but~~ brown and dry
~~and beside it, another~~
~~and~~ in the grass, another
     sawed up ~~where it lay~~   side
so broken down ~~it didn't st~~ I was standing in ^ it before
I saw ~~it, and~~ fanning out
    Bleached white, a whale's bones. like Typee

Date: Wed, 8 June 201—
Subject: the journal(4)
From: yrekachica96@gmail.com
To: faakthe49ers95@hotmail.com

So you can see the whole thing is starting to get freaky. Who is this Becky with the hippy parents? You know that's not my mom's name. He NEVER mentions my mom or fetus me, not once. I think I'm glad I never met him. But read on.

jpeg file: lokaajournal22

I have not much mentioned the flies yet
    ~~they are~~ not so handsome
or brilliant
        as some ~~of the~~ other insects
    but they have their place here nonetheless

    most ubiquitous are the horse
            and outhouse varieties
but my favorites, ~~although have~~ even though they

~~always~~ make me uneasy
 are the robber flies
  ~~which are~~ larger
 an inch to an inch/ and a half
   ~~which and~~ do the same hairy
leg basket catch as dragonflies
  ~~but as a more recent entry in~~ but more recently
  ~~the geological record~~ evolved
they come in black red and gray
   with long tapered bodies
and unlike dragonflies fold
  on   their wings flat
 ~~over~~ ^ their backs

jpeg file: lokaajournal23

they are prone to land on my shoulders ~~and back~~
   ~~in fact~~ one landed
on me as I climbed this hill
 where   I write this a heavy buzzing behind
and then ^ I took my hat off   monster
 to see ~~and there was~~ a big black ^ ~~beastly~~
~~one~~ holding a fat hairy moth
   their name implies
can't they steal other predators' prey
 ^ ~~I cannot~~ vouch for this but I will say
   ~~that~~ among all flies
these robbers are the only I know
 ~~at least~~ that aren't scavengers or parasites

The Navajo Nation doesn't monitor these wells
I think Kerr McGee is ripping us off
to which I replied Don't forget
they're the people who killed Karen Silkwood
   whose story it turned out
he did not know

lók'aa'ch'égai mountain journal

though he'd heard of the film

jpeg file: lokaajournal24

Volker didn't know it either
      so I explained it to them both
they were not surprised

day whatever

fucking Volker wakes me up early again this morning is this guy still on
some time zone in Deutschland? he's kind of an odd calm though this time,
not all fired up like he was about Funny. tells me I need to come look. I get
up and follow him outside the tent. the Archies and their sheep are moving
down the road, the kids and elders on horseback, the horses loaded up with
gear. the young couple walks and waves sticks to guide the sheep. they've
got three sheepdogs, all efficient, and the dogs are helping move the herd
down the road. down the mountain. toward Lukachukai. that can't be right.
before we even came up here Ervin explained how traditional it was to take
your sheep up the mountain for the summer. down below there's no water,
little grass. and it's hot. who takes their sheep down to the desert in the
summer? I look for Ervin but he's not around. Volker tells me Ervin said
they're leaving because of the *ch'įįdii*. that's crazy. a bear or coyotes killed
that sheep. a thirsty bear. but down the road and down the mountain they
go. not one of them looks at us. even their dogs ignore us.

jpeg file: lokaajournal25

        one more thing
~~then~~ last night Volker asked me
      what I wrote on the hill ~~and~~
I told him about this poem
      only partway finished
              It's about Kerr-McGee
and the outhouse flies
after he read the first three lines he

told me a story

            when I was in the Boundary Waters

they had an outhouse like this too

                  no door

no flies but there are lots of mosquitoes

       and they fly up and stab you

               in the butt

                      but you can't cover your

           butt

                  because

       you have to take your shit!

~~at which I laughed and wrote down because mosquitoes are in the order~~
~~of flies and thus have their place at this primal feast~~

jpeg file: lokaajournal26

also one more quote from Ervin

      everyone up here has

given in

            let them drill on their land

       except me and the old lady

the old lady only has a little herd. I haven't seen her or her sheep since
that day I got lost.

the next afternoon I drive Ervin down to Winterplace

      to get some stuff. Volker stays to watch

       the herd. first time they didn't stick me

     with that. Ervin's got the only two story house

in Lukachukai. electric but no running water. from

        there we go all the way to the store in Navajo

       a single lonely mountain sticks up by

    Navajo. Ervin calls it *Tł'ógí* Mountain. he says

some people call it Fuzzy Mountain but

not him. he says people see lights

on top of it sometimes. says they've been seeing

lók'aa'ch'égai mountain journal

lights up there lately. when they do they
stay inside, lock their doors. what the hell?

jpeg file: lokaajournal27

Ervin takes his own ragged truck up from Winterplace
     I follow in my car
at one point he stops by a dirt turnoff and we both
                     get out to stare at
          a sign, painted plywood propped on two bales of
straw
BANANA MILKSHAKES 2.00. One day
                we're going down there. he laughs then,
     something he doesn't do much. but you've got to
be ready either to drink a milkshake, or a whole bottle
         of GD. Garden Deluxe. cheap wine popular with
     inebriates here. at least we don't go down
             that road today. this afternoon my
stomach's not feeling up to either

almost right away back at camp Ervin and Volker
     start ~~getting ready~~ preparing to leave
again they're going to a Fire Dance won't
     be back for two more days. thanks for the
warning guys. so it's just me and the
           sheep and useless Funny
if I can find him
haven't seen him for several days either.

jpeg file: lokaajournal28

but he runs off a lot. not a real sheepdog anyway I
know now. just a stray Ervin took in. basically
         all Funny does is run around while you're
     herding, probably doing more harm than good, but
he is a cute little fellow, although like me he

201

needs a bath. still AWOL today so I'm soon
    alone. I put the sheep in the corral early. fuck it. that's what Ervin
gets for leaving me alone. this extra
  hour gives me time to write a letter to
Becky. I write in the shade house and finish just
before the sun starts to set. that
 happens fast up here. now I
              am going to try to capture the
      sunset in a poem, like a painter, like Kyger
on her back porch in Bolinas. here goes

Date: Wed, 8 June 201—
Subject: the journal(5)
From: yrekachica96@gmail.com
To: faakthe49ers95@hotmail.com

Warning, he goes full on poetry here, and he's not very good. I'm glad I
never wanted to be a poet. It's obviously not in my blood.

jpeg file: lokaajournal29

tuesday or something, sunset

moon ¾ full over the hill
crows cawing beneath it
in Navajo gąągii —
the one that goes gąą
pink hitting the clouds
headed fast this way
from the east really a
rather washed-out sunset
horses sloshing in the pond
got up and left
three brown and one white
followed the sun
animals getting ready to

trade shifts for the night
last daybirds calling
the crows have stopped
one cow mooing
off to the north
the pink is setting too
I'll just let the fire go out

jpeg file: lokaajournal30

shit. need to describe what just happened. I'm writing in the tent now it's around 11:00 I think. should've brought a watch. shitshitshit.

I went to the outhouse and when I was coming back I heard a sound from the south side of the clearing like click-click. like someone clicking a pen but louder. I shine the flashlight over there. nothing at first. then I see there's like a black space in the air several feet across, a rough kind of triangle shape. The flashlight beam stops dead there like it hit a rock only the spot is at least my height above the ground. has kind of a ripple to it, like over the pavement on a hot summer day.

as if that isn't freaky enough something inside it reflects the light, a kind of almond-shaped yellow spot as big as my hand. it turns and shows the same kind of spot on the other side and I realize I'm looking at two big eyes. like insect eyes but a foot apart. like the head of a giant mantis maybe. I take off running and don't stop till I'm back at the tent with the flaps tied shut from the inside. not for the first time I wish Ervin had a gun, but no, he says he never needed one. he can talk to the bears and shit. only what I saw was no bear. I don't know what the hell it was.

I am writing this down in case something happens to me. I am seriously close to panic right now and I'm not ashamed to admit it. I'm looking around to see what I can use for a weapon but the best thing I can find is the stick we use for a poker in the woodstove. a stick! a fucking stick! it's not even pointed!

I listen but I don't hear anything. it's been like half an hour

jpeg file: lokaajournal31

now. maybe. I don't know.

next morning I don't know what day

I fell asleep eventually. what else could I do? never heard any more noises after I got back to the tent. really nice day when I go outside. take my time though, restart the campfire from some embers, make myself coffee in the blue enamel pot. nothing like coffee cooked over a campfire — even if you've got to spit out the grounds with the last couple cups. make myself oatmeal too. there was one brownspotty banana left in the food bucket hung up in the tree, so I slice that over my oats with the side of a fork.

kicking back in the shade house now. perfect morning really, except for what I thought I saw last night. maybe it was nothing, maybe just fog. maybe it was a cow. cows look really creepy if you shine a light on them head on in the dark. like aliens. but it wasn't a cow. the sheep are bleating like crazy in the corral. probably need to take them out let them eat, but I'm not in any rush. stupid sheep. shut up and wait!

I checked the meadow south of the outhouse. everything the same. my little horned toad bud gone, but no surprise. I didn't have any corn pollen to put on him the way Ervin taught me anyway. one more missed blessing I guess.

jpeg file: lokaajournal32

ohh fuckfuckfuck! when are Volker and Ervin coming back? I herded the sheep down the Kerr McGee road. kinda wanted to see if the old lady or her son were around. getting lonely up here and I thought I'd ask them if they've seen anything strange. the old lady speaks some English, so I figured her son does too. The sheep got past the oil wells no problem, and I hugged the far side of the road while I was going by. but when we got close to the old lady's camp they stopped short and the sheep in front turned around and pushed back so the whole herd got jammed up in the road. I cursed at them but they weren't going anywhere right then so I jogged up toward the old lady's little camp.

I spotted the corral first. some kind of black fog hung over it. not fog. thousands of flies hovering about three feet off the ground. three feet but no closer, like there was an invisible barrier. could hear them buzzing. got a little closer and first I thought the corral was blanketed with sheepskins which seemed both excessive and creepy for a sheep corral. then I saw it wasn't sheepskins but sheep inside, all dead and flat like that one at the Archies'. at least two dozen, about all she had. and her sheepdog next to the corral, nothing but a fuzzy empty skin. I looked over at her cabin, saw the door stuck open and another cloud of hovering flies through the gloom inside. I thought about going closer to look then the smell hit me and I couldn't get away from there fast enough. a wave of deep rot with this sour chemical undertone. worst thing I ever smelled in my life.

I got the sheep moving back down the road, looking over my shoulder and listening the whole damn time, but we made it back to the big meadow no problem. that's where I'm writing this now. no need to worry about mixing Ervin's herd up with the Archies' anymore at least.

when Ervin and Volker get back will tell them what I saw, all of it, and then I'm out of here. take the fastest way down, the Kerr-McGee road on the east side. hit up Jim in Farmington for a place to stay. I'll be coming down the mountain, like the Jane's Addiction song. wish I had a boombox with me now — but I need to listen out, keep my ears open for that clickclick.

the herd circulated around the central meltpond a few hours but now they're starting to scatter. still plenty of good grass left here so I guess they just got bored. stupid sheep.

sheep are back in the corral now. even they know it's early so they're bleating like hell. fuck them — unless Ervin comes back early and then I'm fucked. hope they shut up before dark. Need to keep my ears open for clicks or any other strange sounds. I'm

jpeg file: lokaajournal33

going in the tent where the herd won't sound so loud. stupid sheep.

oh fuck. not good. I fell asleep a while but now the sheep are going crazy. I didn't know sheep could scream. Volker and Ervin, where are you? I know something's in there.

just heard that clickclick again. sounded right behind the tent. I've got my car parked close to the tent in front so I picture the sprint from here to its door. keys already in my pocket. I could do what Ervin said with the highbeams and horn, or just get the hell out of here, take the Kerr McGee road down. damn road is unstable and cut up by washouts but it's the shortest route off the mountain by half. I can find some police down below or just wait till Ervin and Volker make it back. but FUCK THIS.

leaving the flashlight. taking the stick. moon is bright enough to see where I'm going but I'm afraid whatever is attacking the sheep might spot the flashlight beam. counting down from 10 then making a run for my car with keys in my hand. play it by ear from there - if I make it. on the count of 10...

Date: Wed, 8 June 201-
Subject: the journal(6)
From: yrekachica96@gmail.com
To: faakthe49ers95@hotmail.com

And that's it. The journal ends there. I went through all the blank pages just to make sure. All I found was that nine pages were torn out from the end, and between the second and third torn remnants, a page dated July 11 at the top in my father's handwriting, and two lines down, Dear D——. My mother's name. The only place it appears anywhere in the whole journal. I'm guessing the missing pages were letters he sent to other people while he was up on that mountain. I told you I found an address book in the box too, right? My mom's old address is in there, yeah, but I also found Rebecca Deigh. In Berkeley. I searched online, found two Gloria Deighs, one in San Francisco. North Beach. The other in Texas. No Stanley. An Ervin Redhouse shows up in Lukachukai. I found too many James Sharps to even start. I haven't tried to contact either Ervin or Gloria, and right now I don't plan to.

OK babe, here's where I need to hear from you. In my opinion this whole journal was nothing but a BS scam to convince my pregnant mother that her boyfriend got eaten by some kind of chupacabra or something. If he did then what happened to his car? Probably he ran off to be with this Becky, but probably abandoned her too later on. I don't even want to think of him as my father anymore. From now on he's nothing but a sperm donor.

Do you agree, baby? Or do you think I should try to track these people down, get some real answers? Should I say anything to Phyllis or my mom? I say no. I think they've both got closure on it either way, and this journal story will only open old wounds. They don't deserve that, especially my mom.

True, my sperm donor might still be alive somewhere. But I don't care. Should I do anything? Should I care? Tell me no. I think I should just throw the journal away.

Really, that's not the part that freaks me out the most. Please don't think I'm paranoid, OK? But I thought I heard a sound outside my window last night while I was reading the journal. A quick double click. Of course I saw nothing when I looked. My crazy imagination, right? Maybe I've got a little bit of poet in me after all. I wish you were here though, babe. For lots of reasons. I hope you miss me as much as I miss you. I love you.

THE ANODIZING LINE

They sat at the flat gray tables in the drab gray room, twenty-two kids from central Jersey, mostly male, mostly white, while the man from HR with the armpit stains played a ten minute videotape about proper lifting technique. Afterward he monitored them one by one picking up a bulky but empty cardboard box and marked checks on his clipboard to verify they each lifted with their legs, not their backs. Then everyone printed their names on time cards, and as they punched in at Azotype for the first time he read off the list of their assignments by department. Anodizing. Flashbulb Room. Dye Kitchen. Almost half the group was assigned to the General Manufacturing Floor. Kelly and someone named Robert Ferrante were last. Judging by his response to the name, the athletic darkhaired boy at the end of the table was Robert. They both got Maintenance. Did that mean they were going to be janitors?

The HR man lined them up and led them through a door in the corner of the sad little cafeteria. Beyond they traveled a narrow hall that veered quickly ninety degrees right. Photographic enlargements in cheap plastic frames decorated the walls, pictures of the plant from different time periods, black and white but for the final two. The first of these looked to be from the '50s while the second was an artist's vision of the company's future, broad-shouldered strong-chinned men in three-piece mylar suits consulting blueprints underneath a towering complex of spires and arches with rocketships streaking overhead. Each frame hung crooked at its own unique angle. Kelly quickly fell in alongside his new workmate at the end of the line. Robert glanced over, looked Kelly up and down —You Kelly Keslo? and after Kelly's mumbled response he stared a moment longer before nodding curtly. —I'm *Bobby. Not. Robert.* Call me Robert and I'll beat your ass. Got it? Kelly nodded at once.

Bobby wore a PROPERTY OF DEEP BROOK ATHLETIC DEPT T-shirt with *BASEBALL* screened in a central cartouche. The shirt was old enough or washed so often the letters had begun to flake away and peel. He wore the shirt tight around his biceps and chest. Deep Brook High was the primary rival of Kelly's hometown team, the Middlebrook Bluejays, though Kelly had never gone out for sports. Bobby obviously did. Football, baseball, maybe wrestling too. He had the air of a triple letterman.

The hall ended in another door, a windowless gray rectangle the HR man opened for them all to file through. Just before they crossed that threshold Bobby reached over and gripped Kelly by the right bicep, pulled him close and whispered

—Wonkaland…

…as the ceiling shot away overhead and they stepped into a jungle of pipes branches creepers runners of busbars cables conduits ducts trunks of dull steel woven round and encrusted with plastic and cable vines rising toward and right up to and even through the roof, extending along the length of the floor, the all of it alive with sliding conveyors and pistons and lifts and bottlecappers and somewhere deep amidst the crab claw mangrove thickets of machinery a great cogged wheel spinning like the underwater sun. The space was enormous, easily three times the size of Middlebrook High's gym and a full three stories high. Men in brown shirts and women in blue smocks stood or scuttled along and between the separate assembly lines. Everyone wore the same squarish gray plastic glasses. Black and yellow forklifts whizzed and whirred through a narrow open corridor ahead, mostly toting pallets of boxes though some bore their blank dark forks exposed and threatening.

HR stopped short and the group bunched behind him. Bobby released his grip on Kelly's arm and let go the door at the same time. It swung shut behind them. As HR began reading off the names of the dozen or so consigned to the General Manufacturing Floor, a tall man in khaki chinos and a white shirt hustled toward them, clipboard clapped between bicep and side. The moment the man came close enough, HR said —Here are your summer college temps, Mr. Jeffries. And he motioned like an orchestra conductor for the assigned group to peel off from the body. Bobby shot Kelly a brief and unreadable sideways stare as they both turned to examine Jeffries.

The floor boss, if that was his role, gave his new charges a quick up/down inspection then said to HR —I hope they're more on the ball than the group you sent us last summer.

—I'm sure they will be, if you will simply give them the opportunity. They completed the orientation with flying colors, every last one.

Jeffries grunted and waved his group to follow him into the mechanical ecology of the G.M.F. HR in turn led his own now much diminished crew along the edge of the operation until they reached another door, a garage-sized opening wide enough for forklifts. Thick plastic strips hung to cover this entry, translucent but too scuffed to reveal more than degrees of light and dark.

Once through the strips the group stood in a long corridor stretching near to the edge of vision, neither so narrow nor so low as the hall from the cafeteria, but far smaller than the G.M.F. Normal-sized doors led left and right from this passage, and at several but not all HR stopped, read two or three names from his clipboard, then offered up that many student workers to whichever minor boss approached.

Before long only Bobby and Kelly remained with the man. He led them around a bend and all the way to the last door on the left then ushered them through.

The room inside was large, though no more than half the size of Wonka-land. Two stories maybe. Not quite the width of a high school gym. A potbellied man in a blue pinstriped shirt spotted the intruders and trundled over to meet them, shaking his head and huffing as he came.

—Are you sticking us with these two, Ackerman? Didn't you have room for them in Manufacturing or somewhere else?

Ackerman. That was the HR man's name. He introduced himself at orientation but Kelly had let the name slide right by.

—Karlin's orders, Mr. Winston, so I suggest you make the best of it. And after all they're only here for a couple months. This is Kelly Keslo and

Bobby *Ferrante*. Ackerman spoke Bobby's surname with emphasis, spoke it slow, then looked to Winston to see if he'd gotten the message, whatever that message was. Kelly tried to remember if he'd heard either that name or Karlin before from his dad but drew a blank.

Winston rolled his eyes. —All right you two, come with me. He walked away without checking whether they followed. Bobby strutted after him and Kelly leapt to follow a moment later. Ackerman was already on his way out behind them, no goodbye.

Winston led them into the first of several small partitioned offices along the same wall as the door. All were roofless and windowed from waist height up. Once inside, the man tugged open four of the five drawers in a battered beige metal desk before he found what he wanted. Hand still in the drawer he looked over his shoulder at the boys' faces, nodded, drew out something or some things, then shoved the drawer shut with his knee.

In his hand he held two pairs of glasses with thick gray plastic frames and little shields attached to their sides, identical to the pair he wore and which Jeffries wore before him. The workers on the manufacturing floor had worn them too, though Kelly had not seen any of them up close. Safety glasses, he realized now. Ugly damn safety glasses.

—Put these on right now, you two. And I don't want to hear any guff about how *they're uncool* or *they don't fit*. Also, if I even once see either of you without these on, even in the Break Room, you're finished here, understand? I don't care who anybody's father is.

Bobby and Kelly took the glasses, put them on, turned toward each other. Bobby asked —How do I look?

Kelly shrugged. —You look okay.

It was true. Bobby was still handsome, only now he was handsome in cheap awkward glasses. If anything, his almost perfect face made the glasses look out of place.

—And me?

Bobby stared back, shook his head slowly. —Trust me dude, you don't wanna know. Just stay away from mirrors as long as you're here.

Something sank inside Kelly. Good news, for once he got to be on the same team as the hot guy. Bad news, he had to wear these dorky glasses the whole time.

—This way, said Winston, and he led them back onto the Maintenance

Floor. They crossed between workstations, some vacant, some occupied by mechanics working at desks and tables, red rolling toolboxes the size of upright pianos beside them. Other mechanics had no desks and labored over immense freestanding chunks of machinery perched on metal racks or pallets. Welding torches sparked and sputtered behind a low wall to their left.

Winston led them all the way to the far wall and up a flimsy flight of stairs. The stairs did not inspire confidence. Crafted from greasy plywood and hanging from the ceiling by metal cables, the staircase rocked slightly with every step. Boxes of random machine parts lay to either side, stacked two or three deep near the top and spilling over.

The balcony beyond was even more a mess. Pipe fittings, switches, and coils of colored wire cascaded from plastic bins along the walls to cover most of the floor. The balcony extended along two entire sides of the large room, and its floor was covered to the corner at least. They couldn't even reach that turn without grinding and crunching over a layer of mounded parts.

—The storage balcony hasn't got organized in…*a while*, said Winston. —Sorting it ought to keep you fellers busy a while. Maybe all summer. Come and see me if you finish before then so I can inspect your work. You know where my office is now. And he was gone back down the stairs without further instructions.

Bobby sat down on a pile of pipe corners and wire. —Winston's a dick—look at this shit! How are we supposed to sort it all?

Kelly stepped closer to Bobby and the wall, so close his outer thigh almost brushed Bobby's shoulder. He inspected the upper bins, found his initial suspicion correct. —It's only the bottom bins that are really disorganized, at least over here. I bet we can get the whole thing done in a week or two. Winston may not like us now but if we pull this project off in record time he'll have to give us better jobs next. He bent to retrieve a T-shaped pipe connection and deposited it in a third tier bin that already held maybe two dozen of the same.

As Kelly scanned and marked the contents of the upper bins he began rearranging their contents while bending to retrieve and add pieces from the floor. Most were connections and corners of metal pipes in varying widths. At first Bobby just watched him, a skeptical expression on his face, but after Kelly had placed nearly a dozen pieces in the upper bins, Bobby rose slowly and brushed off his jeans, front and back. —Fuck it, why not? He began to follow Kelly's lead. By lunch break they had cleared the stairs nearly as far as the balcony proper. The more junk they moved off the floor the easier their task became.

As the two boys worked they began to talk and joke, beginning with more in-depth introductions and wandering on from there. Bobby was headed into his junior year at Old Queens. Kelly would be a freshman at Middlebrook Community, the best his family could afford for now. Bobby had worked here the two summers prior, always on the manufacturing floor. —What a bunch of doonwads, he said. —I don't miss any of 'em. Doonwad was a new term to Kelly and he laughed at the epithet perhaps a little too hard. Bobby said —You like that? I got plenty more where that came from. Dinglehoffer. Dorkhauser. I deal with lots of dipsticks. Gotta be prepared, you know? Call a spade a spade.

Bobby seemed pleased with the younger boy's approval and paused to look him up and down again. Kelly felt a warm sudden rush at his partner's inspection, starting in his chest and spreading out toward his hands and down to his groin. They gave him morphine when he had his appendix out at twelve, and this feeling was a bit like that. He struggled to pack both feeling and memory back into whatever interior boxes from which they escaped.

—So what's that shit on your shirt? Some kind of graph? School's out for summer bro, didn't they tell you?

Kelly pinched the front of his T-shirt in two spots atop his nipples and plucked it outward. —This? It's the radio signal of a dying star.

—So you wanna be an astronomer or some kind of science dork?

—No. It's from the cover of an album by a band I like.

—You gonna tell me their name? 'Cause it ain't on the shirt.

—Sure. Yeah. Joy Division.

—Never heard of 'em.

—They never played the U.S. Their lead singer killed himself on the night before their first American tour.

Bobby raised his eyebrows. —Damn, that's pretty dismal. Are you into anything less depressing?

—Yeah, sure. Echo & the Bunnymen, The Teardrop Explodes, the Violent Femmes, The Cure…

Bobby fanned his hands palm down between them. —Whoa. Stop right there, you're weirding me out. Just tell me you're into Springsteen or AC/DC, anything normal.

—Yeah, sure, Springsteen's okay.

Kelly could barely tolerate The Boss, but he didn't want to alienate Bobby. Little white lies, why not? Was taste in music all that important? Couldn't they still be friends? Of course they could.

Bobby broke from their project for the moment, seated himself on another mound of mechanical rejectamenta. —Fucking Winston. He basically banished us here. I know it's because of my dad. Bobby shook his head. —There's some cute girls this year. Did you see the ass on that brunette they sent to the Flashbulb Room? Now we won't ever see her except at lunch. When she's sitting down. He turned to Kelly. —Anyway, dibs, that one's mine. But the black girl that works with her is pretty hot too. You know what they say—

Kelly cut in. —What does our assignment have to do with your father?

Bobby looked up at him, his expression puzzled. —You do know who my dad is, don't you?

Headshake.

Bobby showed exaggerated shock, shook his own head on the bias to express disbelief. —You never heard of Tommy Ferrante? He paused to observe Kelly's face, shook his head again. —Tommy Ferrante, the assistant general manager at the Big Building?

—Sorry.

—Well, he draws a lot of water 'round this place. But Karlin and Winston must be thinking a little distance means they can fuck with me like this. Pause. —Who's your dad?

—Eugene Keslo.

—Never heard of him.

—He works at the Big Building too. Does some kind of drafting, I think. He's only been here a couple years. He came to Azotype after he got laid off from his last job with Lehn & Fink.

—I'll ask my dad if he knows him. If yours is far enough down the totem pole it might even be they put us together as a joke. But the joke will be on them. They think Karlin will protect them but they've got another thing coming. Don't worry though. I'll look out for you too. We're in this together now.

A bell sounded somewhere outside in the room. Bobby pushed himself to his feet. —Lunch. Come on, let's blow this pop stand. We've only got half an hour to make our move. You can have the black girl if you want—you okay with that?

—I'm not prejudiced, if that's what you mean.

—Fuck that. Who cares? You're going to bang her, not marry her. It's all pink in the middle, right? All pussy is good pussy, some is just better. Know what I mean?

Once they were out on the Maintenance Floor they fell in with a loose formation of about a dozen mechanics, all headed into the corridor and toward the cafeteria. Other groups emerged from the doors to either side, but none mingled en route.

Two bored women in hairnets slopped their meals on trays once they arrived. A flattened breaded chicken breast, a lone scoop of watery corn, quivering orange Jello, a roll. Sliding his meal along the metal rails, Kelly wondered if he was back in high school. The brown compartmentalized plastic trays were identical to those from his four years at Middlebrook High. He looked away to clear the thought. He was glad to be out of that place and never going back.

Bobby led him to the table where the crew from the Flashbulb Room sat. They couldn't find seats right across from the two girls he mentioned, but they came close. The brunette of Bobby's interest was lean and athletic, her chestnut hair worn short beneath her hairnet. The black girl seemed to have more of a figure, though it was hard to tell with her sitting down. She also wore glasses. Real glasses, not safety glasses. Kelly learned later that no one had to wear safety glasses in the Flashbulb Room. It was the only area besides Admin where they were not required.

Kelly noticed then the entire Flashbulb Room crew was female. All wearing hairnets. None of the teams at the other tables wore hairnets, except for the cafeteria staff. Most everyone still wore their safety glasses.

Bobby launched his opener after only two forkloads of corn. —You guys are in the Flashbulb Room, right? No one responded but Bobby nodded as if they had, said —Is it as cake as they say? I've been on the Main Floor past two summers, but they stuck us in Maintenance this year, can you believe it? Oh yeah, this is Kelly, my new partner. He really got screwed, right? His first summer here and *boom*, Maintenance. At least he's got me to look after him, you know?

Thus far the brunette had glanced up at Bobby only twice between bites. No one else acknowledged his monologue. Bobby swung his thigh against Kelly's and jerked his chin half an inch in the girls' direction, apparently the signal for him to join the uneven discussion. He struggled at first but not wanting to disappoint his new friend said —So do they treat you all right in the Flashbulb Room? Our new boss seems like kind of a jerk.

Both girls looked up, their faces blank.

—They treat us okay, I guess, said the brunette. The black girl shrugged and returned to carving her chicken with the edge of her fork.

Bobby nodded encouragement so Kelly went on. —Do you really make flashbulbs in there? Do people still use those?

Both girls looked up again, along with several of the regular employees who sat within hearing. The brunette regarded him a moment, said —No, and returned to her food. Everyone but Bobby and Kelly looked down. Bobby slammed his leg against Kelly's beneath the table and shot him a frown.

They finished their meal in silence and it was not until they rose to return their trays that Bobby directly addressed his target once more —Well, see you tomorrow I guess.

—See you tomorrow, she replied. Her voice was flat and she did not look their way.

Everyone from their table walked out together but somehow the older members of the Flashbulb crew got between Bobby and Kelly and the two girls, so they traversed the corridor in silence.

Once back on their cluttered balcony Bobby shot his partner the stink eye. —Why'd you have to go asking that, you fuckin' dickstain? Don't you know anything?

—What do you mean?

—The Flashbulb Room is a government contract. Everyone in there has to sign a nondisclosure form. I'm surprised they put summer temps in there. I've never seen them do that before. Even I don't know what they make in that place, but it sure as shit *ain't* flashbulbs.

—I'm sorry. I don't know anything about what goes on anywhere here. I just assumed—

—Never assume anything, right? Your father must be way, way down the chain. Just let me take the lead from now on, okay? Don't worry, I can fix this. At least those chicks were digging us already. They were *really* digging you, even though you had to go be a total dillhole. Did you see how they both looked up any time you said anything, no matter how defective? Looked like they were checking out your weird spiky hair. They probably think it's *cute*. Without warning he punched Kelly's arm. Hard. —Stu-ud! Kelly lost his balance and had to grab the edge of a bin to steady himself. —Next time just follow my lead okay? And try to be a little less retarded. We'll be rolling in pussy before you know it!

Kelly nodded, turned to face the rows of unruly bins lining the left side of the stairs, began sorting and shifting, focused on emptying the overstuffed and torn cardboard boxes on the floor. —I guess we should get back to work now, huh?

Bobby bobbed his head like a dashboard dog, noncommittal, sighed and said —Yeah, yeah. Slowly he stepped to join Kelly at his task.

The two boys fell quickly into a comfortable common rhythm, bending, rising and reaching, swapping brittle switches and chilly lengths of pipe, pointing out to each other concentrations of like items in one bin or another. They spoke little but the pace of their progress improved.

Twice mechanics appeared on the stairs seeking particular parts and interrupting them. The first time Kelly knew exactly where to look, had the piece of pipe in half a minute. The mechanic showed blatant surprise. The second request left them in the dark. Some kind of *ballast*. All they could do was shrug and clear the way as the burly red-bearded man crunched around the corner and out of their sight. They drew apart once more when he returned ten minutes later, toting a long black rod with trailing wires. The man departed between them without a word. Kelly felt guilt he knew was undeserved. He wanted to be helpful but how was he to know what a ballast was, or where to find one in this free-for-all? Next time he would have a better idea.

By the end of the workday Bobby and Kelly were finishing the stairs and beginning to sort the chaos on the first stretch of the balcony. Kelly hoped Mr. Winston would stop by to witness their initial progress and be impressed, but the time bell's chime alone released them. Kelly said —Well, see you tomorrow I guess. Bobby only nodded then said —Remember the plan for lunch tomorrow. Then he thumped Kelly again with his fist—softer this time—and took off across the Maintenance Floor. Kelly watched him all the way to the door before he followed.

Eugene Keslo was waiting outside the main door in the family's dented red station wagon. Before Kelly even buckled up his father asked —Well how was your first day?

—Okay, I guess. I got assigned to Maintenance, but I'm not a janitor. At least I don't think so. Listen, is there a guy at your building named Tommy Ferrante?

—Yes. He's one of the big big bigshots. Why? He didn't come over here to inspect, did he?

—No. I'm working with his son, Bobby.

Eugene examined his own son then turned back toward the dashboard and spoke in a toneless voice —Don't mess this up, okay? Tommy Ferrante has a lot of juice around this place.

—Sure sure, don't worry. We're getting along real good already.

His father's hands stayed whiteknuckle tight on the wheel. —Just keep it that way, please?

—No problem Dad. It's only for two months. What can go wrong?

Neither spoke again the whole way home.

***

Kelly arrived early at Azotype the following day. He had no choice as to when his father dropped him off. Waiting for 8:00 in the caf he sat amidst a slowly growing cohort of silent summer temps. The regular employees mostly kept to themselves. Kelly scanned for Bobby. The Flashbulb girls sat near the door speaking softly with their own crew, but no Bobby, not until everyone, regulars and summer temps alike, stood lined up before the punch clock, waiting for the hour to strike. Only then did Bobby stroll in to join them, unhurried and unworried, just in time to join the line.

Kelly waited for his partner against one wall just inside the door to Wonkaland, pushed off to join the older boy once he entered, one of the last. The G.M.F. had only begun to stir, assembly lines jerking to life with metallic clunks and groans, forklift drivers finding their rides and waking them, the vehicles' small solid wheels squealing as they maneuvered curves in reverse. Bobby nodded when Kelly fell in beside him but didn't speak, and they marched side by side in weary morning silence down the corridor to the Maintenance door.

Ignored on the floor, they made straight for the parapets of their kipple-covered castle. The now orderly stair offered Kelly a feeling of accomplishment, but that evaporated the moment he turned the corner to the balcony's primary length, many times what they'd already cleared and heaped as high as their armpits in more places than one.

Bobby had come by a styrofoam cup somehow somewhere, thin steam creeping out the little nick in its lid. He settled on a mounded crate of shifting switches and sipped from his cup. Coffee, Kelly presumed, but hesitated to ask. They were both just around the bend and thus out of sight of the main room, so he found a seat across from Bobby on an already split box spilling gray PVC pipe. The next section of the storage looked to be mostly PVC.

Bobby sipped and said nothing. He seemed so natural and at ease, a king on his throne. Kelly stared at the grease speckled floor between them and said nothing. A thousand comments occurred to him but he squelched each one out. After several silent minutes Bobby upended his cup, crumpled it, dropped it beside the junk on which he sat, pushed himself to his feet and swiped his hands against his thighs. —Well, let's get to work.

Kelly leapt up at once. —Do you want to finish the metal pipe on that side and I'll start in on this PVC?

—Yeah, whatever man. This stuff is going to take some time. Might as well dig in, do what we can.

Soon they fell once more into their same coordinated rhythm of the day before. Back to back they sorted pipe and switches, turning only to pass stray components to one another in accordance with overall placement. They made encouraging but quiet progress, until after a while Kelly relaxed and began to sing softly —*PVC 15, oh oh, my PVC 15*, throwing in —*transmission, transition*, and —*jump down a rainbow*. These fragments were all he really recalled of the song.

Bobby spoke behind him —What the fuck are you saying? Is that supposed to be some kind of song?

—Yeah. It's part of a Bowie song, *TVC 15*, only I'm saying PVC 15 because, you know, I'm looking at a whole wall of it. I don't remember much of the song.

—I can *tell* that. Bowie, huh? Well go ahead. I never heard of that song but at least I heard of Bowie. Not like that gay-ass shit you tried to tell me about yesterday, Boy Division or whatever. Bowie rocks. *Let's Dance*, right? Chicks love that shit.

Kelly recommended his broken recital, awkward at first then with increasing abandon as Bobby joined in, and soon they shared the fragmentary chant, mostly *PVC 15, oh oh*, and a drawn out *Tran-n-n-sition* for a refrain. One would stop, the other would start, their intermittent anthem never fully living, never quite dead. Bobby had reached a section of PVC himself by this time, and that seemed to enhance his sense of engagement in both their jagged shanty and the work. And so they continued until the lunch bell sounded somewhere off their narrow ark's starboard bow.

***

Twice as they traveled the corridor Bobby reminded Kelly to follow his lead and not *fuck things up*. Yet once they reached the cafeteria they found Bobby's plan stymied from the start. The rest of the Flashbulb Room's older all female crew had closed ranks round the two targets and left the boys nowhere to sit but the table's ends, way too far from the girls for conversation.

Bobby growled softly then jerked his head toward Kelly to follow him away.

The two boys toted their trays between tables, searching out a desirable pair of seats. In the opposite corner of the room they found their counterparts from the G.M.F., nine boys and three girls occupying their own table. None of the regular employees sat with them, so Bobby and Kelly were able to find seats among their peers, though not quite together. The G.M.F. kids were most of them awkward in appearance and, as soon became apparent, manner as well. They spoke little to each other while they chewed their rectangular pizza and briny green beans. After five minutes of near silence Bobby opened a mostly one-sided discussion, starting with small talk, sharing and acquiring names along with mumbled descriptions of life on the Manufacturing Floor.

Kelly saw soon that his partner gave most of his attention to a round-faced blonde two seats to his left, a girl neither so heavy nor gangly as the two other girls on her crew. Her wavy hair framed a face almost lobster red from too much sun. Kelly saw but wondered if Bobby could see how the skin of her cheeks and forehead peeled in white-edged jigsaw shreds. Kelly kept his own counsel, never feeling any cue come along for him to step in.

As they shuffled back to Maintenance, Bobby said to Kelly, —What'd you think of beach girl?

—She was okay, I guess. She sure loves the sun.

—Yeah. From now on our name for her is Bahama Mama. She's gonna be part of our backup plan. Depending on how things go, she might be yours. When her face heals up she won't be so bad. She's got a nice ass at least. I saw that shit when we were getting up. But man that fuckin' Indian kid between us was pissing me off.

A brown-skinned boy had divided Bobby and the sunburnt girl. Inderjit. He'd gotten rather chatty and the more so as Bobby focused on the blonde. Kelly had actually found him the most interesting person at the table, intelligent and well-spoken with no trace of an accent. —I was hoping you'd distract him, talk about nerd bands or some shit.

—I was waiting for your signal. You never gave me a signal.

Bobby stared back a long five count, then nodded, said —True. Okay, next time just use your judgment. If you think I need backup, jump in. Otherwise wait it out. That's how you need to fly if you're gonna be my wingman. Clear?

—Okay. Clear. Sorry.

—Hey, don't worry about it. We've got all summer. Tomorrow might be a whole different kettle of fish if we can get to the Flashbulb girls again. That's our Plan A. If not, Bahama Mama for Plan B. Just hope she has a friend for you, or you're only gonna get to watch. Forget the rest of those dogs from the G.M.F. I'll find you something better, I promise.

Kelly mumbled —It's okay, really. But he doubted Bobby heard. Or cared.

***

They'd only taken their first steps up the greasy staircase to the storage when someone spoke behind them. —Where the fuck you two think you're going?

THE ANODIZING LINE

They turned to see a strange short man hustling toward them, a squat wide-shouldered troll in the brown Azotype uniform.

Bobby held his ground and clotheslined Kelly with a stiff steely arm across the chest before he could retreat down the stairs. —Back to work.

—Since when do you guys work here?

—We're college temps. We just started yesterday.

The troll paused, already close enough to strike them with his brawny caveman arms. —What are you doing on my balcony then?

—Winston assigned us to organize this mess. That's our *job*. The troll looked them over and they returned his gaze. He had bad skin and dirty blond hair that fell to his shoulders in greasy ringlets. The name cartouche on his breast pocket read *CYR*.

Cyr took a moment to process Bobby's answer, nodded, said —Ah, all right, that's cool. But why don't you hold off here a minute, okay? I've got something stored up there and I need to get it down before you two bozos lose it on me. So just stay here until I get back. Shouldn't take me long if you haven't messed with it already.

Cyr shoved between them before they could reply, stomped up the steps and was gone around the corner.

Kelly and Bobby turned to each other. —Don't look at me, said Bobby. —I never heard of this guy before. Just let him get what he wants and get out of our way. I can tell he's just gonna be a pain in our ass otherwise.

After maybe two whole minutes Cyr returned, clutching a small bundle to his gut. His prize was maybe the length of an average cucumber but somewhat more broad, wrapped in the same kind of crumpled yellow newspaper they were finding lining the bins. He pushed between them with neither goodbye nor thanks and was gone around the corner of the staircase onto the Maintenance Floor. Headed for the locker room Kelly supposed, to restash his whatever.

—What a fucking whacko, said Bobby.

—For real. What do you think he had there?

—Shit, I don't know. Drugs probably. Or a gun? Some mad scientist project he's been building in his spare time? Maybe a dildo he uses for his faggy fun. Whatever it is, he sure didn't want us to see it. And I'm okay with that. Let's get back to work, hope nobody else hid any damn dildos up here.

Back on the balcony they reattacked the PVC, returning to their chopped up Bowie chant at intervals though with less enthusiasm than before. Further interruptions came more frequently this afternoon, mechanics, welders, and electricians each seeking some switch or other part, or perhaps just a break from their work on the floor. The two boys helped them when they could, cleared the way when they couldn't, chatted with all who lingered. Each discussion taught them more about their new community. One of the electricians, Terry, gave them the full schmear on Cyr, first name Teddy. The troll was General Maintenance, a kind of glorified custodian. The boys were stuck with a job Cyr must have rejected. According to Terry they could keep busy all summer on Cyr's sloppy seconds.

Terry was younger than most of the crew, late twenties maybe, with a haircut like a Ramone. Kelly was desperate to ask him if he got into punk and new wave, but he didn't want to bring up the subject in front of Bobby. Another time. After all, they had the whole summer.

Another visitor, Chaz, one of the welders, seemed impressed by their progress but suggested they slow their pace, though he refused to give a reason when pressed, just said —Trust me. You guys maybe don't want to finish too fast.

By the time the final time bell rang they'd completed the region of PVC and entered a section of miscellaneous switches and parts. Looking ahead they made estimates as to whether they'd finish Thursday or Friday and considered how and how well Winston would reward them for their speedy work.

***

Bobby and Kelly continued making progress on the balcony shelves despite increasing visits from downstairs employees, most of whom obviously sought only to hide out for a while and found the boys' company a bonus to killing time. Chaz and another welder named Posey came often, though Teddy Cyr never returned. They saw him only briefly and at a distance on the Maintenance Floor. He never showed up for lunch in the caf either. As far as anyone cared to know, he ate somewhere unknown off by himself. If anything, he avoided the boys.

By Thursday afternoon it seemed clear they would finish sorting the balcony sometime the next day. Bobby considered how they might leverage their success with Winston. A better assignment—perhaps even to another department, perhaps *even* to the exclusive Flashbulb Room? An early release for lunch so as to give them some advantage in seating? An apprenticeship to the electricians or welders, with most of whom they were now on quite good terms? Bobby saw no limits to their soon to be enhanced bargaining position—or perhaps to his own negotiating power. He reassured Kelly any deal would cover them both, regardless of the option. Bobby *had his back*, they were *partners*, they were *together in this*. The bell rang and they made for the corridor, Bobby scanning for the Flashbulb girls.

Meanwhile Kelly's father all but interrogated him as they traveled home in the afternoons. He wanted to know everything but Kelly told him little. Really, there was little to tell. —Everything's okay Dad, all right? I've been working hard so please let me rest? Yet Mr. Keslo kept his questions running all the way down 22 until they took the turnoff to that last winding extremity of their homeward ride.

***

The next morning Bobby and Kelly strode the corridor like gunfighters in a black and white western. Though half a head shorter, Kelly felt equal to Bobby in height for the moment. Completion of a herculean task lay within reach, and a heroes' welcome would greet them after. Winston had thought organizing the storage would take the whole summer, yet they were about to finish the job in a single week. How happy would Winston be? Maybe he'd do a little dance. Kelly chuckled at the thought, and Bobby asked him what was so funny, fully agreeing once he heard the image described. —Not bad Keslo. Not bad. Get down, Winston. Let's dance. Put on your red shoes. Am I right? Can't you just see it?

They strode up the staircase side by side, something only possible now they'd cleared the boxes from the floor. Around the corner and onto the balcony, which shook ever more the farther out they traveled on it. The cables holding it were easy to see and looked way too thin.

No more than ten feet remained to sort on either side. Bobby took the left flank and Kelly the right, their unspoken division since the week began. Kelly made quick work of two columns of switches then came upon a region of...*ballasts*. Handling them he quickly recognized they were components

225

of fluorescent lights. Rectangular plastic ingots of assorted size, mostly black, some white and a few even blue, nearly half still in their packaging. Ballast to him meant something dumped off a submarine or hot air balloon, vehicles that needed to descend and rise. Jules Verne stuff. *Around the World in Eighty Days.* He brought the matter up to Bobby but the other boy merely shrugged. All that mattered now to Bobby was getting the job done and claiming their reward.

Kelly looked out at the fluorescents that hung above the Maintenance Floor, each suspended from metal rods. He envisioned the lights as rigid jellyfish, each suspended in place by the weight of its ballast. Could they possibly pop loose and pulse through the room with tentacles out to trawl the Maintenance Floor for meat? How safe would he and Bobby be on the balcony? Despite his daydreaming he kept on with the work. The ballasts were large and thus fewer per bin than switches or bits of pipe, so by 11:30 both he and Bobby had finished their halves of the task. The once cluttered balcony was tidy from end to end. Kelly suggested they report to Winston now, but Bobby recommended they wait till after lunch. —If we finish too soon he might get suspicious, think we cut corners. He's the suspicious type. Come on, let chill for a while. So they dragged two of the now empty crates back to the balcony's *cul de sac.* Perched on his crate Kelly listened while Bobby outlined once more his plans for both their next assignment and the Flashbulb Room girls. He projected confidence in practically visible waves.

Lunch put a damper on Bobby's enthusiasm some. Their primary targets remained blocked by the seating so the boys ate at the end of the G.M.F. temp table. Inder just would not. Shut. Up. By now it was obvious starting from the farthest department in the plant placed them at a disadvantage as to choice of seating. Kelly could see Bobby growing firm in his resolve to press Winston for an earlier lunch release.

Kelly noticed too that few of the Maintenance crew ate with the general staff. It wasn't just Cyr—not one of those he'd come to know sat in sight, and he could not recall having seen them in the cafeteria at all this week. Did Maintenance have its own break room he and Bobby had yet to find? He recognized two or three dudes who sat alone, but none he'd met or knew by name. A couple of the less social mechs, the old loner electrician known to his coworkers as *The Force.* Bobby said the man looked like Keith

Richards' grandfather. Maybe the Maintenance crew mostly went out for lunch. Or maybe he and Bobby were excluded from the team's secret eating place. He felt a sudden wave of alienation and neglect but shook it off. Nothing he wasn't used to from Middlebrook High of course.

The mousy haired girl beside him tried to open conversation but he ignored her. She wore nerdy glasses but had boobs the shape and size of Nerf footballs and was probably halfway attractive with her glasses off. Kelly only mumbled uninterested replies, just enough to avoid seeming rude. She spoke about how she rode her bicycle to work, a feat that had to require both a singular commitment and a spectacular sense of equilibrium in her case but Kelly didn't care and simply wanted her to hush. Why didn't Bobby show any interest? Was this one too overall curvy for his tastes? Too nerdy?

—The other day while I was riding here to work this man pulled up in a station wagon and offered me fifty dollars if I'd let him do mouth sex to me in his car.

Inder on her left replied —That's terrible. How did you respond?

—I said *No thank you, I'm not like that* and pedaled away! What did you think? He took off so fast I couldn't see his plates. Can you believe that? Right in the daylight out on Route 22.

Kelly only shook his head and went back to his chicken parmesan but Inder wouldn't let it go —You should contact the police, give them a description of the man and his car. A guy like that will only do it again, so you might be protecting the next girl he targets if you turn him in. I have a camera you can borrow, in case you encounter him another time.

The girl showed hardly any interest in Inder, no more than Kelly showed in her. The car she described sounded just like Kelly's dad's—the man inside it too. Mr. Keslo had the perfect alibi however. He would have been driving to work with Kelly at the time she alleged. Maybe she had seen their car and made up the description on purpose, was trying to get his goat. If so it wasn't working. She might do better with one of the other boys, Inder probably if not Bobby. He felt badly for her if the incident were real, but it certainly didn't inspire him to flirt with her or ask her out.

The end of lunch break came as a relief for Bobby and Kelly both, and they fell into lockstep as they left, hurrying side by side down the corridor toward Maintenance. They paused a moment once inside, pondering the ways in which their next assignment would be different from their last. In just one week they'd grown accustomed to the balcony. The cozy isolation it provided them and their rapid progress brought them feelings of accomplishment. Though they were about to move up in this world, their next task might lack such a convenient setting and definite end. Regardless they marched with confidence toward Winston's little cube.

Winston wasn't there and they couldn't see him on the floor, so Bobby plopped down into Winston's worn swivel chair, feet on the desk, while Kelly lounged cross-armed against the rear wall, the only one that was structural and wouldn't wobble. Bobby had just begun rummaging in the desk drawers when Winston waddled into the room.

—Who told you two jokers you could get comfortable in here?

Kelly snapped to attention but Bobby held his pose, although he slowly slid the desk drawer shut. Winston glared at him. —Get your goddamn shoes off my desk, you little pissant.

Bobby lifted his feet with exaggerated robot motion, swung them to the right, dropped them to the floor. He returned Winston's glare eye to eye.

—Well, whadda you two want? Don't tell me you lost your safety glasses already.

Obviously they had not. Winston wasn't blind.

—We finished, said Bobby.

—Finished what? Are you quitting already? Please say it's so.

—We finished the job you gave us, organizing that storage.

Winston's nostrils flared and his face turned red. For what protection his friend could give—his friend or his friend's father—Kelly stepped behind the taller boy and the office chair. Winston actually seemed about to lose it.

Winston looked them up and down both. —Well you can't be serious, so what's the punchline? It better be good, the way you're wasting my time. I'll burn you both to the ground if you're messing with me.

—No joke. For real, said Bobby. —We *finished*. Why don't you come take a look? We didn't mess around. *We got the job done. Just like you asked.*

Winston took one lone angry step toward Bobby. For a moment Kelly thought better of his association with the handsome older boy and staggered back against the wall but Winston came no closer, checked himself and held. The older man sighed and unclenched his fists. —Okay, okay, show me what you *think* you did with that mess. My guess is you only made it worse, but come on, let's have a look. He turned to exit the office, gesturing to the boys to follow. Bobby slid out of his usurped throne in no rush or hurry while Kelly shuffled uncertainly behind.

Winston led the way up the stairs swinging his head side to side as he ascended. Several times he swabbed the blunt tip of his index finger along the edges of bins, examined the oily gritty evidence there before twisting his fingers inside an aging yellow hankie. The man let out little sea lion noises throughout, soft incomprehensible huffs and honks and bleats.

At the top of the stairs Winston surveyed their handiwork to the bend of the hanging aisle and uttered a modulated grunt that might've indicated approval or surprise. Kelly wished they had photos of how the balcony looked before, floor heaped with split and broken boxes spilling pipes and machine parts, bins all blocked and cluttered with random junk.

As he progressed along the length of the storage Winston continued to smudge up dust and grime from the edges of bins and other horizontal surfaces. All the while Bobby played tour guide, describing the results of their labors, paraphrased the testimonies of mechanics, electricians, and welders who'd come looking for some part they'd finally been able to find. Despite the extent of their efforts Winston seemed more concerned with the cleanliness of the upstairs realm than its recent reorganization. Kelly began to worry. They had only sorted, made no effort to clean. Had he misinterpreted their assignment entirely? Would Bobby blame him if they failed Winston's inspection?

As they all doubled back from the end Winston spoke —Well, you did a good enough job sorting all this junk out, I've got to admit that, but the whole mess is still filthy from front to back. You need to wipe it all down and drag a shop vac up here to finish the job. That ought to take you another week. Once you do that maybe you'll be done.

Kelly asked —Where can we find a shop vac?

Winston shot him an angry look but answered fair —Check with Teddy Cyr. He ought to have one. Ask him to let you borrow it. You'll find him around somewhere.

As Winston reached the bottom of the stairs he spoke to them again, though he only turned his chin far as the line of his shoulder and did not face them. —All right, now you know what you've got to do. Don't bother me again till you've got it all done, understand? Then he was gone, leaving the boys in the middle of the staircase. Halfway up or halfway down? Kelly supposed that depended on whether you were an optimist or a pessimist.

Bobby stepped to the bottom stair. —C'mon. Let's go find that weirdo Cyr and get our vacuum.

Kelly cut in —Don't you think Winston is being a super jerk? I'm sure the first time he only asked us to straighten things up here, not to clean. Isn't that Cyr's own job? I don't think we've seen him back up here since he came to get his whatever it was.

—I'll deal with Winston later. For now, what the hell? We can kill some more time up here. We don't really know where they'll put us next.

In the end they tracked Cyr all the way out of Maintenance and down to the G.M.F., where he was speaking to an obese bearded forklift driver behind the other man's parked vehicle in a far corner of the room. Cyr first froze like a jacklit deer as they approached, but once they explained their mission he warmed some and allowed Bobby and Kelly to accompany him back to Maintenance. There he unlocked the janitor's closet, instructed the boys to wait outside, dragged out the shop vac, showed them how to turn it on and use it. That done, he closed and locked the closet behind him and wandered off.

The vac was basically a bulky gray plastic garbage can sealed and fitted with wheels, a pump, a plug cord, and a hose. They rolled it to the base of the stairs then hefted it awkwardly up, Bobby tugging the lid and hose end, Kelly gripping the base by two of its three dirty wheels.

They searched for an outlet after they reached the balcony. Nothing, nowhere. Another delay as they hunted down an extension cord. Good thing the cool electrician Terry had an extra power cord to loan them. Once again Kelly was dying to ask him about different bands, but he remained reluctant to bring up the subject in front of Bobby. If they were going to talk music, Kelly wanted to get Terry alone.

Cord attached and plugged into an outlet beneath the balcony, the bulky vacuum blasted to life. Kelly shoved the scuffed stained canister between the shelves while Bobby ran the nozzle over the rims and contents of the bins. The futility of their endeavor became apparent at once. The aisle was too tight for the vacuum, and Kelly had to rock it from side to side to wiggle it between the bins. Sooner or later it was going to jam.

Bobby dropped the still sucking hose and kicked it against the bottom row of bins. —Fuck! Kelly barely heard him over the wheezy roar of the vac but it was easy to read his lips on that one simple word. He flicked the power switch to shut down the machine, then pointed to the bins he'd already covered. Kelly saw the hose hadn't picked up the grimy coating that upset Winston. Not one tiny bit. —Lookit this shit, man. We're gonna have to wipe every one of 'em down with rags. We really *could* end up here all summer if we have to do that. The hell with that shit. Think, man. You're smart. How do we do this so it doesn't take forever?

Eager to please, Kelly pondered their plight, but it was Bobby who quickly figured out they could simply flip the contents of the worst bins, thrust the grimiest pieces toward the back, and replace them with fresher components dredged up from beneath. Kelly followed behind meanwhile and wiped down the bin edges with a pair of drab red rags from the big cardboard drum on the Maintenance Floor. They were fudging their assignment but they both knew this cleaning bit was bullshit from the start.

Once again they found a common rhythm, and despite the tedious wretchedness of their task, they finished well before the workday's end. Neither however, was eager to summon Winston up for another inspection. Instead they sat facing the shop vac, now shoved into the corner just above the stairs, their backs against the bins, talking haltingly in broken bursts. They swung the end of the hose between them in a lazy game of tetherball. Tethernozzle. Tetherhose.

Bobby spoke most —You know, this is my third summer working here and the first time anyone was such a dick as Winston. He must think Karlin can protect him but we'll see about that. Asshole. Sorry you got dragged into whatever's going on with these guys. Just remember, no matter what I've got your back.

—Hey, it's okay. I think working with you is cool—I mean, you've got experience which is a super big help—and we get along all right.

—Ha! Yeah. You and me, we're cool. PVC 15 and all that. It's Winston and his bullshit that's pissing me off. Guy's on a serious power trip. Like I said, I'm sorry he's targeting you too. Otherwise, I just wish we could get at the Flashbulb girls. It's like those old biddies they work with are blocking us on purpose. If we could only get near those chicks we'd be picking up on some primo action, I tell you.

—Well, there'll be other opportunities, right? We've got all summer.

Bobby said nothing. Kelly swung the hose back but Bobby only caught it and released it to hang in place, an unreadable expression contorting his face. Kelly made several attempts to restart the conversation but Bobby showed no further interest. Finally the bell chimed and their workday was done.

***

They met back up in the cafeteria Monday morning. Pulling Kelly in close Bobby whispered —I talked to my dad about this fucker Winston. Let's see what happens now. Might be that fat fuck is in for a little surprise.

Inder sat down with them just then so Bobby clammed up. Kelly kept expecting the other boy to have some kind of accent like Hadji on *Jonny Quest*, but he didn't. His English sounded the same as any other Jersey boy from the burbs, except perhaps a little better. The King's English, as Kelly's dad would say. —So how are you fellows finding Maintenance so far? Bobby didn't answer, showed no interest, so Kelly replied instead. —It's okay I guess. What about where you are?

—The work is very repetitive. But it is simple and the regular workers are friendly. So are the other college temps. As dull as it becomes we still have a decent time.

Just as Kelly opened his mouth to reply he felt Bobby's thigh slap against his own beneath the table. He glanced sideways at his friend and saw his look of disapproval, gulped down the extended response he intended and said simply —That's cool.

Inder seemed eager to continue but just then the regulars rose and headed for the clock, and the college temps scrambled to follow. Soon Bobby and Kelly left Inder behind on their trip back to Maintenance. Bobby only spoke again once they were an isolated pair —Do us *both* a favor and don't encourage the Hindude, okay? I can already see that guy is going to be nothing but trouble all summer. The less we have to do with him the better. Especially if we want to nail those chicks. He's guaranteed to fuck that up.

—Sure, no problem. I just thought he might be a good connection or something.

—Trust me, I know his type. Stick with me and forget about that douchewaffle. He's a dead end, pure poison. We let him hang around us and he's just going to get between us and any girls.

232

THE ANODIZING LINE

Kelly nodded and muttered a simple okay, afraid Bobby would ask him to sign some kind of loyalty oath or swear in blood. Or talk about girls. They walked on in silence till they reached Maintenance, where their first task was to locate Winston and take him on another tour of their neatened and now visibly cleaner upstairs storage.

The boys finally found their portly supervisor addressing a clot of mechanics, yet though they positioned themselves clear in his eyesight he kept them fidgeting while he assigned various jobs that needed doing on the Anodizing and A5 Lines. It took nearly ten minutes until all the mechanics scattered and they could invite Winston to examine their handiwork of the previous week...only to hear him decline their invitation. Winston showed no interest at all in the fruits of their labors. Instead he issued them new directives entire —Time to split you two wisenheimers up, at least for a while. Keslo, you help out the welders. Ferrante...I want you to shadow Steve and Carmine. They're probably out on the Anodizing Line right now. If they don't have enough work to occupy you, check in with the electricians or the plumbers—if you can find them.

Kelly glanced at Bobby before he left. Bobby shrugged. This unexpected change of plans caught Kelly unawares. After a glare and a nod and a —Well, what're you waiting for? from Winston, Kelly wandered over to the welders in the far corner of the huge room. Theirs was the only area of the operation other than the offices set off by partitions, waist high prefab walls. Bubbles of blue glow flickered and sparked from behind these walls, and Kelly had no sooner entered their realm through one of its gates when one of the men shut off his torch and hustled toward the youngster, shuttled him to a battered cabinet and outfitted him with a pair of dark tinted goggles and the directive to never—even with the goggles on—look into the blue light. Kelly lifted the safety glasses to perch on his forehead where they rested atop the newly added goggles. Could Winston complain about that?

There were three welders, all black. Two were in their thirties while the third was a lean and elderly Haitian man who kept mostly to himself. The younger welders were outgoing and friendly and quickly took Kelly under their wings. Posey and Chaz. Posey even knew Kelly's father a bit, the first person he'd met here who did, unless he counted the girl with the Nerf boobs.

As grateful as the welders acted to have his help they really didn't seem to need it much. Or at all. His only job was to hand them shit from time to time, primarily skinny metal rods. They were unhurried in their work and paused frequently to extemporize on one topic or another...what they'd done the past weekend, plans for the upcoming weekend. Family. Chicks. Posey was altogether eloquent when describing the buttocks of various women he knew. Music, especially P-Funk and Marvin Gaye. The best way to make great barbecue. According to Chaz, a cider vinegar marinade was key. Both men went out of their way to include Kelly in their conversation —What you think Kelly? Kelly, you ever have barbecue so good it make you cry? Tell me Kelly, you ever seen an ass like I'm talking about? It didn't seem to bother them he had little to contribute. —Ain't that right, Kelly? —What you think, Kelly my man? —Listen to Kelly, man knows what's what.

Kelly felt an easier sense of belonging with the welders than he had with Bobby. Here he didn't have to try. Over half the time Posey and Chaz actually answered for him, but they had a way of doing it that came off as complimentary and supportive rather than preemptive. His presence simply became a natural part of their routine. The experience was new to him, but welcome. Though they kept mostly to themselves on the floor, the welders seemed more cheerful than any of the other Azotype employees he'd met so far, almost carefree. They reminded Kelly of the three harpooners in *Moby Dick*, indispensable to the plant's operations and treated with obvious respect by the rest of the department, though like the harpooners, none of them were white.

The downside was lunch came way too early, and Posey and Chaz didn't eat in the cafeteria. They brought meals from home and ate on benches in their workspace, so Kelly was left to walk the long hall alone. In the caf he found and joined Bobby down the end of the table of college temps from the G.M.F. The day's meal was Salisbury steak and mashed potatoes drizzled thinly with chocolaty gravy. More watery corn. High school all over again, again.

Bobby seemed withdrawn so Kelly held off speaking to him until they both made some inroads on the miserable meal.

—So how is it with the mechanics?

Bobby shrugged, raised another chunk of gravy-coated mystery meat to his mouth. —Okay, I guess. They don't know why I'm there so they've got me doing random bullshit jobs.

—Well, the welders are pretty cool. I don't do much but it's kinda fun just hanging out with them.

—Yeah, I bet. Bobby eyed him. —Wanna switch after lunch? I could work with the welders and you could take the mechanics. Think about it. You'd learn even more that way...

—I don't know. Winston assigned us where we are right now. He might not like it if we switch on our own.

—Fuck Winston. All he's doing is throwing his weight around.

Kelly spoke staring down at his potato volcano, its low walls breached and draining gravy into the tray's rectangular well. —I know, but still I don't want to piss him off.

—True, but trust me that fat shit is going to have troubles of his own soon enough.

—I do trust you. I just don't want to make any waves.

—Yeah, I get that. For you *or* your dad, right? Don't worry. You won't get blamed for what's about to go down and neither will your dad. But it's cool if you want to stay out of it for now.

After that their conversation stalled until they carried their trays back to the counter. As they were scraping their uneaten scraps into the trash Bobby suddenly asked —Did you hear about Teddy Cyr?

Kelly hadn't, mumbled something to the effect. Bobby filled him in, suddenly enthusiastic. —He's in jail! Him and two of his brothers got drunk and raped their other brother's wife. Tried to kill her too, but they were so wasted she got away. The gang that couldn't shoot straight.

—No way.

—Yes way. What a sick fucking freak, huh? Anyway, I don't think we'll be seeing *him* around here anymore. The mechanics say they're glad he's gone. His old man still drives a forklift out on the main floor though. I wonder how he's takin' it.

Soon they were walking back down the hall, side by side but entirely silent. Kelly pondered the extent of his own exposure to the now incarcerated troll.

***

The boys parted ways in Maintenance, Kelly rejoining the welders while Bobby passed on through a door on the far side of the room. Other than this singular exchange of disturbing news, their week continued in much the same routine, with Bobby's efforts to get close to the Flashbulb Room girls at lunch frustrated daily.

They had no contact except lunchtimes till Thursday afternoon, when someone pulled a fire alarm shortly after 1:00. Winston led his crew onto the lawn outside the G.M.F. where all the floor bosses scuttled about checking clipboards to account for their charges. Jeffries, Winston, other department managers whose names Kelly did not know.

The heat and humidity together were intense and Kelly began sweating almost at once. The sun overhead felt like it was melting and pouring molten fluid directly onto their heads. *Doe, a deer,* he thought. *Re, a drop of golden sun...*

Suddenly Bobby stood beside him. The older boy threw an arm loosely over Kelly's shoulders and pointed with his free hand toward the immense unbroken expanse of brick. Speaking loudly, but not so loudly others could hear him, he called out —*Heyyy, Kool-Aid!*

Kelly laughed, imagining the impossible portly pitcher erupting through the vast facade ahead, dispensing its refreshing chemical beverage to everyone in sight as they gathered round their savior. Bobby had nailed it dead on again. With sweat pouring into his eyes, Kelly wished the vision were true.

***

Finally on Friday they received fresh orders. Kelly had just settled in to his now familiar rhythm with Posey and Chaz when Winston appeared outside the welders' enclosure with Bobby in tow. He beckoned Kelly to join them beyond the partition.

—All right, I've got another job for you two wiseacres, and I need this done right away today, understand?

Their new assignment was to go up on the roof and pump out the waste oil from a drum beneath the air conditioner. The door to the roof was inside the Flashbulb Room. Winston handed Kelly a tarnished key hanging from a battered chunk of wood, instructed them to find containers for disposal of the oil stacked in the janitor's closet.

Although Bobby perked up at the mention of the Flashbulb Room, Kelly felt repulsed at the necessity of entering Cyr's former sanctum.

The door to the closet hung open now so it was some small relief they didn't need to touch the knob. The boys squeezed in and past assorted junk and tools till they found a stack of cardboard cubes on their sides, each with the short neck and lid of a three gallon plastic jug protruding from its top. After brief experimentation they found they could each carry four apiece, though this method was awkward and meant they had to stop and retrieve dropped boxes several times en route.

They found the base of the metal stair leading to the roof right inside the entrance to the Flashbulb Room on their left. Only a few feet ahead was another door in a high wide wall. Both wall and door were painted the same battleship gray as so much else at Azotype. Yet unlike Maintenance or General Manufacturing, the Flashbulb Room refused to unfold to their view the moment they entered. Instead the wide wall rose right to the ceiling, cloistering them in a long corridor, three stories high yet only a few feet wide. If the girls really worked in the next room there was no way to tell, as any employees remained out of sight and the sounds of hidden people and machines came muted and blurred from beyond the door.

When Bobby stepped forward and grasped the doorknob Kelly called after him without thought —Hey man, I don't think we're supposed to go in there. Bobby spun back, a sudden strange rage flaring across his face. It only lasted a moment before he relaxed and nodded. —Yeah, yeah, you might be right. Bad idea. Fuck it.

Kelly's heart kept pounding minutes past. The unexpected expression of concentrated anger and hate on Bobby's face had struck like a kick in the gut.

The stairs creaked and clanked as they climbed, clattered each time either of them dropped a box, something that happened every dozen steps or so, but no one from the other side stepped into the odd narrow room to check on the source of these sounds.

The padlocked trapdoor at the top was the same plain and now-familiar gray, though paint flaked from its underside in ragged strips. Fortunately their key worked. Buttersmooth. Bobby shouldered open the door and they stepped into the summer sun.

The heat struck at once, and Bobby stripped off his shirt without hesitation, tucked it under his belt like a football flag. His torso was toned but only lightly tanned, hairless other than for thin twin whorls around his nipples and a tenuous trail extending up from his waistline. He looked across at Kelly and laughed. —C'mon man. Take off your shirt. It's super hot up here and you're gonna roast. Don't be a freakin' dorkheimer.

Dropping his boxes Kelly reluctantly shrugged his own shirt off and followed suit. Their T-shirts each hung like loincloths now. Bobby clapped Kelly on one pale freckled shoulder and laughed. —Damn, dude, you look like a frickin' titless chick! I guess you don't work out much, huh? Let's get some sun. You *really* need it!

Bobby laughed again, grabbed his set of boxes, spun, and walked off across the roof. Already self-conscious, Kelly wrapped his arms around his thin and undefined chest. As he hustled to keep up, Kelly heard his partner say —Don't worry. I'm sure you'll make someone a wonderful wife someday.

Kelly wanted nothing more that moment than to rush back down the staircase and spend the rest of the day hiding, in the locker room or down the end of the storage balcony perhaps. And never come back. He regarded Bobby's retreating back, wrapped in muscle and half again as wide as his own yet tapering to a sleek and narrow waist.

Yet he had no choice. He had to see this through for his father if not for himself. He followed Bobby in his path across the roof. His partner never looked back, not even when Kelly dropped two of the boxes and had to stop to pick them up.

The AC unit was easy to locate. A towering metal monstrosity taller and longer than Kelly's home, it rumbled and buzzed with concealed life. Approaching it the boys soon found on its unshadowed south side the rust-covered fifty-five gallon drum that served as receptacle for the beast's excess. A curling metal tube ran from the vibratory immensity to one side of the drum's lid, while a simple rusty hand pump rose opposite.

—Let's get going before we fuckin' cook up here, said Bobby. He unscrewed the lid from the first of his box-jugs and held it under the spigot. —You pump while I hold the jug, okay? I think that's safest. If either of us gets tired we can always switch.

Kelly worked the handle of the skinny pump. It stuck at first but he soon had it spouting short gouts of rotten brown oil into Bobby's jug. It quickly became clear to both boys their task would take time.

The smell of the waste oil came faint but foul, and Kelly's stomach threatened to disgorge, but he thought of Bobby watching and kept it in. No way he wanted to upchuck in front of his new friend. He could not bear the added disgrace.

It took at least fifteen minutes before they had one full jug. Kelly watched the muscles in Bobby's arms grow taut as he strained to hold it up and asked —Are we going to have to haul these all down those same stairs we came up?

Bobby replied simply —Wait. Watch. Follow me. Hefting the box he led Kelly toward the eastern edge of the roof, where he rested his burden on the wall for a moment while he scanned to either side below. Then he retrieved the box and passed on to the north with Kelly trailing obediently a few feet behind.

When Bobby stopped they stood high above one end of a long green dumpster that extended from the wall at ground level. Cardboard and wood scraps from broken pallets stuffed the bin three quarters full. The end below them rested not quite flush with the wall, maybe three feet out, with a rain-warped sheet of plywood stretching from the building to the dumpster's edge. Bobby hefted the cube to his shoulder, his hand pressed flat against its rear face, then shoved it out into open space with a shotput thrust. The box-jug arched and dropped and fell, landing a good third of the way out into the bin. It bounced lightly on impact and rocked the assembled trash but sprung no visible ruptures or leaks. The plastic liner had to be tougher than Kelly thought. They stared until the substrate of junk stopped wobbling then returned to their task.

This time Bobby worked the pump while Kelly held the jugbox, pushing his burden against the drum with his stomach to hold it in place. Sweat dripped into his eyes and stung.

Whatever Bobby's pumping method, his squirts came not only over twice the volume of Kelly's but closer together as well, so the box filled quickly and grew rapidly in weight. Once Kelly proclaimed it full Bobby screwed the cap on and Kelly hauled the vessel toward the spot on the wall his friend had found before. It was so heavy that he had to stop halfway and set it down.

Looking at the dumpster below, Kelly felt unsure whether he could make the throw. A miss that fell short or to either side would likely make a mess and bring down Winston's wrath upon them once they got busted. Stressing, he raised the cube to his chest, steeled himself to propel it out the best he could, but he felt Bobby's hand on his back before he could throw. —Wait, said his partner. —Let me show you the way.

As Kelly watched, Bobby pantomimed raising the box to his own shoulder, steadying it with his left hand while he pushed out with his right, palm flat against a box he himself didn't hold. After he observed the sequence twice Kelly raised his own very real cube to shoulder height, balanced it and before he could second guess, hurled it into the heated air where it tumbled end over end extended seconds before landing at last in the bin, not nearly so far out as Bobby's had fallen, only a few feet from the end of the plywood ramp. But he hadn't missed, and that was what counted.

Bobby high-fived him, and Kelly felt a little thrill. —Not bad, you puss. I thought for sure you'd choke. Not great, but hey, you made it. That's all that matters.

After that they alternated on pump and jug. Their second throws each exceeded their first, though Kelly's flew askew some and landed perilously close to the dumpster's left edge. Bobby's landed right on top of his first box like Robin Hood splitting his own arrow. Something inside the original burst and wet darkness stained the cardboard beneath it but did not spread far.

Kelly determined to make his own third shot count. Raising the box to his shoulder he cocked his elbow tight, breathed in deep, only to slip and drive the box straight down where it struck the top of wall just two feet below. As the box tumbled to the roof the lid of the jug within cracked and popped off and dark grease splattered both boys from waist to face. Some of the filth got in Kelly's mouth which meant several minutes of spitting and wiping up. At least the safety glasses worked. Since his bare forearms and fingers failed to clear his eyes enough he was forced to use his *Electric Warrior* T-shirt as a rag. Beside him Bobby cursed and did much the same. When Kelly looked across at the other boy he saw his face and chest still splashed and smeared. Oh, he'd really fucked up this time. Bobby was going to be *so* pissed.

—Pick it up! Bobby shouted, and only then did he notice the box on its side, still glug-glugging oil onto the roof and creating a spreading pool around their sneakers. Quickly he bent to right the broken container. He didn't want to look at Bobby again but he did. And his friend was laughing.

—I'm glad you think this is funny.

—C'mon man, you should've seen yourself. You threw that thing *right at* the top of the wall, and *BAM*! Yeah it's a mess, but you have to admit, that was some funny shit! Were you fucking around on purpose or what?

Kelly's mouth remained foul, his chest and arms greasy and brown. He spat into the gravel twice more. Bobby kept on laughing, so hard now he hunched over, hands on his knees. Kelly tried to let go, join in with his friend, but he felt too embarrassed. *Angry*. Stained. A potential bonding moment was passing him by but he could not relax enough to grasp it.

—Awww man, you look like some kind of skinny wannabe Rambo with that shit all over you. Your T-shirt barely got it off, just smeared it all around. Do I look the same?

Kelly looked his partner up and down, saw the oil streaks somehow only emphasized Bobby's athletic form. —Yeah, pretty much. Except it looks good on you—I mean I guess we both look kinda silly.

—Man, it was like you frickin' *aimed that fucker*—like you set it up!

—No. It was an accident 'cause I was trying too hard. I wanted to get this one way out there, but I didn't balance it right and it just shot down.

—Well it was pretty fucking decent! No way you could've done it that way if you tried.

As Bobby spoke he kicked the fine gravel coating the roof across the extent of Kelly's personal oil spill. —I doubt that fat lard Winston ever wheezes his way up here, but better to be safe, if you know what I mean.

Kelly nodded, then retrieved the half-drained carton at his feet. In a deft single motion he hefted and hurled it into the heated air where it arced perfectly and struck the dumpster dead center a good third of the way out. Not so far out as Bobby's shots, but an improvement for him, even if this one was only partway full.

Now it was his turn to pump while Bobby held and tossed the box. Shouldn't the drum be empty by now? Apparently not, as the black gouts came thick or thicker than before. He stared across the drum at Bobby's oil-stained torso, thought about how the chocolaty streaks and smears presented as failed camouflage, heightening the boy's muscle tone rather than hiding it.

Bobby's next throw flew flawless and smooth, landing out beyond his previous shots. Although Kelly held the box for the next round, his partner gently took it from him once time came to launch it. —No offense bro, but I don't want to take any chances. Your little trick was funny once but let's not go down that road again, okay? I can only swallow so much of this crap.

Kelly nodded. He had no desire to repeat his mistake. Let Bobby handle the rest of the throws if he wanted. All of them.

When at last they had the drum as empty as it would go, the pump sputtering and sucking air, Bobby suggested they hold off on trekking back down right away and instead conduct a circuit of the plant from above. After all they might likely never have a chance to explore it this way again. In no rush to explain his oil-stained torso to Winston or anyone else below, Kelly acquiesced. No sooner had he agreed than Bobby began to lead him around the building, clockwise if the rooftop was the clockface and someone was looking down on them from above.

After the roof of the Flashbulb Room they had to descend a metal ladder to a lower section. Neither of them knew which part of the plant they stood above now. Bobby reiterated the open secret that the purpose of the Flashbulb Room fulfilled a government contract and suggested that rumor might be only a front for some even more clandestine operation taking place beneath their feet right this very now. Kelly responded with a vague nod and grunt, unsure how serious his partner meant to be. They traversed this section close to its walls, not wanting their footsteps to be audible below.

Soon they reached a second three-story section to the southeast and followed the join of the two constructions until they arrived at another gray ladder bolted to the wall. Both ladder and wall were obviously newer than all the roof they'd crossed so far.

Once they reached this fresh section of roof they found themselves on a building barely one hundred feet wide, yet extending southeast and northwest into vanishing lines right out of their sight…which shouldn't be possible. The entire factory just wasn't that large.

Everywhere before when they looked down from the walls they saw short stretches of lawn pocked by dandelions and less identifiable weeds. Here below they saw only raw torn-up earth and the tread tracks of heavy movers.

—I bet this is that new A5 Line, said Bobby. —Goddamn, it's long.

—Looks like it's longer than the whole plant.

Bobby returned him a gaze he could not read. Kelly grew defensive.

—I mean, look. You can't see either end of it. Can you? I can't. It just gets hazy and goes off both directions into the trees.

—It's only some kind of optical illusion created by the heat.

Standing on this structure made Kelly uneasy. Though he felt no motion or vibration through the soles of his Nikes, the building seemed unstable and shifting in some indefinable way. —Let's keep moving, okay?

—Yeah, sure man. We need to get back anyway. Don't want Winston sending a search party after us. Assuming he notices how long we've been gone.

They continued along the edge of the infinite rectangle till at last they reached another gray ladder leading down to a lower portion of the plant. They took it without discussion, Bobby in the lead. He seemed just as eager as Kelly to get off this place.

From its side the A5 Line didn't look so strange. The upper expanse of its cinderblock wall offered visible ends to view now. The whole thing was long—but not infinite. Now it seemed just another wing of the overall plant, newer and longer than the rest, yes, but unremarkable in any other way.

Shame swept over Kelly, growing deeper once he remembered he was smeared with air conditioner oil and why. Bobby was filthy too but he showed no sign he cared. And he wore the filthy grease well.

They wandered the rooftops disoriented a while, searching for any familiar mark. Eventually Kelly spotted the AC unit they serviced and they made as much of a beeline toward it as they could considering the terrain.

***

Back at last on the platform above the alcove of the Flashbulb Room, Bobby locked the metal door behind them, moving quickly as if he thought something dogged their heels. They descended the clanky metal stairs, and only at the bottom did they realize they'd left their empty box-jugs on the roof. Kelly mentioned it but Bobby said —No fucking way, man. We done our job on the roof for today. Nobody knows how many boxes we took up there or how many we used. Nobody cares either. So fuck it.

Kelly acquiesced. His only real interest was getting to the restroom and scrubbing off as much of the oil that coated his torso as he could before he had to explain his condition to Winston or anybody else.

Bobby and Kelly made it to the men's without interference. The restroom was really a little locker room. The square front area contained the urinals, stalls, sinks, and taps, while battered beige lockers lined the walls of the adjoining room beyond. Once they'd both tugged their shirts back off Bobby looked at Kelly, at himself in the mirror, laughed again. Kelly forced a chuckle but folded his arms across his flat unmuscled chest. Bobby watched, shook his head, unzipped his jeans partway and let them slip several inches down, revealing the dark upper curls of his pubes, and when he turned toward the mirror, the first few inches of the crack of his ass. Apparently he wore no underwear. Kelly looked away blushing and began assembling the wads of wet brown paper towels in a row on the sink, enough he hoped to wipe the greasy film from his own flesh.

***

Fifteen minutes later they looked reasonably clean, enough to withstand all but close inspection, though their hard-scrubbed torsos were splotched pink and red from scrubbing. Then they put their T-shirts back on, both badly wrinkled and stained, though Kelly's, mostly black, hid the wretched filth better. Next they requested each other's inspection, spun 360 on their heels in turn to receive it. Their mutual verdict was *passable* unless anyone looked close. Kelly became even more conscious of Bobby's physical near-perfection and his own inferior physique.

Bobby led the way outside…where they ran into Winston almost at once.

—What are you two turkeys doing back down here already? And what the heck happened to you? The man's little pig eyes scrunched to slits. —You didn't tip over the waste oil barrel, did you? I give you a simple job…

—Simple, yeah, but it was messy. And *no*, we didn't tip it over, Bobby replied. —Listen, Winston, we need uniforms same as everyone else. We're ruining our street clothes with grease and grime and acid even. Everybody else on this floor has a uniform. Why not us?

Kelly had not expected this demand. He would never have confronted Winston himself. Though Bobby was right, what good would it do to piss off their boss?

Winston stared back at them and chuckled. —Not on my watch. For safety's sake we need to know who you temps are without hesitation. Our uniformed workers have skills you will never acquire, and the difference has to be obvious at a moment's notice. So it's street clothes for you and your other summertime pals, got it?

Bobby began to speak again but Winston shushed him. —Unless you've got something new to add, this part of the conversation is over. Now listen up, here's your assignment for the rest of the day and next week at least. You've got just enough time left on the clock today to talk to the mechanics and get instructed on how to pump out the sludge pond. You can start Monday if you don't have time today. That ought to keep you little shits out of my sight for a while. *Finally*. So snap to it.

With that Winston turned his back and waddled off. Kelly watched Bobby clench and unclench his fists, his face reddening.

—Hey man, come on, it's Friday. Let's just talk to the mechanics, see what they say. That's all we have to do for now.

Bobby looked over, angry at first, then sliding into an icy calm. —Yeah. Let's talk to the mechs. Let's do that *now*. He led the way to their work area. The mechs weren't doing a whole lot of work at the moment, though even those who were just lounging and gabbing had some unfinished task close at hand, something they could leap back into if Winston or another of the bosses approached.

None of the mechs seemed especially excited to discuss the sludge pond. Finally one named Claudio agreed to take them out there Monday morning. —Too late for all that today, but the sludge ain't goin' nowhere now. So you just wait, okay?

The boys stayed and listened to the mechanics' chatter for several minutes. Steve, who owned a boat, was discussing his plans for a weekend fishing trip, and that outing seemed to be the focus of conversation. Suddenly Bobby smacked Kelly's arm with the back of his hand. —Come with me. We're going to do something about this uniform situation right fucking now. Come on. And he took off toward a door in the nearest corner of the Maintenance Floor. Kelly had never been through this door before, never paid it any attention. Bobby opened it and stepped through, leaving Kelly to catch it and follow on his own.

The hallway beyond was carpeted, the walls covered in cheap wood panel. Doors opened along either side, each topped with a faux brass plaque. Bobby stopped at the third on their right. The plaque on this one read *D. Karlin*. Bobby shouldered through and Kelly kept close.

They entered a modest office with more wood paneled walls. A gray-haired man in a striped shirt and tie sat behind a heavy wooden desk, shuffling papers. The stripes on his shirt were straight and narrow, those on his tie diagonal and wide. Three framed pictures held pride of place on his desk, but Kelly and Bobby could only see their backs. A silver metal paperweight in the shape of a rocket held another stack of papers on the corner of the desk. The man looked up at them but did not speak.

Bobby took the lead. —Good afternoon Mr. Karlin. I'm Bobby *Ferrante*. I think you know my father, Tommy Ferrante.

Karlin was hard to read. Kelly took the look on his face for something between annoyance and curiosity but it could've meant anything. Homicidal rage, perhaps. He looked the boys over slowly before he spoke.

—Yes, I know your father. Did he send you here?

—No sir. We came on our own. As a last resort.

Karlin arched his right eyebrow and clasped his hands. —Do tell.

—Well sir, it's like this. Me and Kelly here are assigned to Maintenance for the summer, and we're getting all the sh— all the dirty jobs. But we don't have uniforms, so we're ruining our own clothes.

—Is that right?

—Yes sir. We were hoping you could help us get uniforms like the regular employees.

—And have you discussed your concerns with Mr. Winston? He is your supervisor, is he not? Have you followed the chain of command?

—Yes sir, we did, but he only blew us off. And next week we have to pump out the sludge pond.

—The sludge pond, hmmm?

—Yes sir.

—All right. Thank you for bringing this to my attention. I promise I will see what I can do. Meanwhile, you boys have a good weekend and stay out of trouble, okay?

Poised to continue, Bobby paused, said only —Thank you, sir, then turned and ushered Kelly out with a hand on the small of his back. In the hall a young woman in a white blouse and black skirt froze and stared at them as they emerged from Karlin's office.

A few minutes later it was time to punch out, and soon the two boys went their separate ways. Driving home, Kelly's father asked his son how his week had gone, but Kelly only shrugged and spoke in clipped generalities. He didn't mention the visit to Karlin at all. He didn't see any point. His father would only worry about it and he had enough worries already.

***

Kelly spent most of the weekend listening to records in his room...The Cure, New Order, T Rex, Roxy Music. Bowie. He'd acquired a bit of a sunburn while on the roof and he didn't want to aggravate it. He hoped it wouldn't peel. His folks were accustomed by now to his preference for solitude so they left him mostly alone, calling him out only for evening meals. His parents' conversation at the table was stiff and strained and had been that way since before he started high school so neither of them noticed much as he grew withdrawn himself. Kelly didn't know what was going on between his mother and father and didn't really care. He'd be off to college soon and hoped that distance would grant him additional insulation from their opaque and smoldering tensions, even if he'd only be commuting and would still have to come home at night.

His father became more communicative on the Monday morning ride to work. His main interest seemed to be how Kelly was getting along with his coworkers, his boss, and as always, Tommy Ferrante's kid. Had he met Tommy Ferrante? Kelly emphasized the positives in his truncated replies, emphasizing his friendship with Bobby and omitting any mention of his encounters with Winston and Karlin.

Kelly could understand why his father was nervous. His department had seen three sets of layoffs already. So far he'd survived but if another round came his number would probably be up. Initially proud he could get his son a summer job at the plant, he now seemed anxious as to how Kelly's performance might affect his own tenuous status. The volatile Ferrante connection only exacerbated that concern. Mr. Keslo obviously recognized his son's social awkwardness, had no confidence he could make friends at work...or anywhere else.

Kelly made an effort to set his father at ease, though in truth he cared very little for how the elder Keslo felt. His effort showed little or no success. His dad closed with —*Well, do your best to be sociable...* Looking toward the floor and shaking his head...

Back at the plant Kelly headed first for the break room, where the line for the time clock had yet to form. The Flashbulb girls were there and unescorted, but Bobby remained AWOL come 9:00 a.m. Kelly gave the girls a halfhearted and unreciprocated wave but made no attempt at conversation.

He punched in and walked to Maintenance with no sign of Bobby, and almost the moment he entered the door, Winston called him into his office. Two short stacks of folded cloth lay on his boss's desk. Before the man could speak, Bobby strolled in and shook the man's hand. —Hey Mr. Winston, how ya doing? My dad said to tell you *hi*.

—That's very nice, Mr. Ferrante. Please pass on my regards in return. He looked at Bobby with a mix of ugliness and satisfaction. —I understand you two visited Mr. Karlin on Friday and spoke to him regarding your uniform request. Therefore he has instructed me to find you both uniforms after all. So I have and here they are. He swept his hand toward the desk. —You get one set each. I'm sorry, but *these* are all we had on hand. You *will* wear them however. As of this moment, it is a *requirement* that the two of you be in uniform at all times in this facility.

Kelly muttered a thanks into Winston's smirk as they grabbed their new uniforms off the desk. Bobby didn't say a word. Wearing the same uniform all week long was going to be a joke. A really rotten joke. Winston's petty revenge. Getting the uniforms dirty, sweating at their work, they would have to wash them every couple days at least.

In the locker room they quickly stripped to skivvies. Bobby wore a jock strap today while Kelly sported boxers. Self-conscious of his scrawny legs and arms, his ill-defined chest, Kelly drew the new clothes on quickly. The shirt was loose even though the sleeves were too short. The pants were short but too wide at the waist. He hadn't anticipated this, though why he might've expected Winston to give them uniforms that fit he did not know. He gave the sleeves a double roll and cinched his belt tight around the extra fabric at his waist, saw Bobby doing the same. —What the fuck? said Bobby. —Who had these before? Then he glanced across at Kelly's shirt and saw the name in the cartouche. —Oh. Shit. Fucking Winston. That fucking scumbag motherfucker.

Kelly pinched the front of his own shirt and twisted the fabric of the pocket toward his face. Even upside down the three letters were easy to read. *C-Y-R*. How had the company not retired the troll's uniforms, burnt them in the incinerator even? —Man, said Kelly —Winston got us good.

Bobby laughed. —Fuck Winston. He leapt atop the wooden bench and cleared his throat theatrically, placing his right hand over his heart. —I swear to wear this uniform with pride, in honor of our fallen brother. If Teddy Cyr is not returning, it's up to us to share his legacy. No whining now, no complaints—Winston has given us a mission and we will see it through! Teddy Cyr lives on in each of us!

Kelly stared up at his partner, trying to read his expression, but detected no remaining signs of irony. Bobby looked as serious as General Patton.

—Dude, that's fucked up. How do we know anyone even *washed* these? I am totally grossed out, and I'm changing back right now.

Bobby jumped down from the bench, threw a powerful arm around Kelly's shoulders and held him in place. —Oh no you're not! Don't you get it? Winston thinks he has us trapped now. He's figuring no way we'll wear these things, and as soon as we take them off, he's got us. Well, let's show him. Plus I'll talk to my dad and he'll talk to Karlin, and in a couple days that asshole Winston will be giving us five brand new uniforms each in the right sizes and begging us to wear them even one day a week. Trust me.

Bobby swept up both sets of their street clothes and stuffed them in the first empty locker he found, slammed the door. —C'mon, let's go find Claudio. The new Brothers Cyr have work to do!

***

Claudio grimaced when reminded of Friday's promise, but he led them outside without dispute. They exited through a door behind the Anodizing Line and came out at the top of a gentle downward slope. Some six or seven yards below, a chain link fence surrounded an artificial pond and a tiny shack. A loop of heavy chain secured the only gate, but the padlock that held it was unlocked. As the mech opened the gate and led them through, he said —Welcome to your new home. 'Cause I expect you're gonna be here a while.

The pond was really four linked ponds, like swimming pools with still clear water. Pristine white sludge coated the bottom of each. A cement walkway circled the perimeter of the pond while a metal catwalk crossed all four pools at their center.

Claudio explained their new job. The sludge was silica powder from the Anodizing Line, a necessary element in the preparation of the aluminum plates. The workers there had to constantly hose everything down, as the powder, if breathed in, could cause silicosis, which was something like black lung. The drainage from that process ended up here in the pond, where the silica was allowed to settle out in the sun. When the layer of sludge grew too thick it had to be pumped out, though Claudio admitted he could no longer recall precisely the last time anyone had bothered. Years.

The pump was outside the little shack, the controls inside. Claudio uncoiled the wide corrugated hose from where it hung on the fence and demonstrated the way to plunge its mouth deep into the residue at the center of the first pool. Another hose ran out beneath the base of the fence in back and drained the sludge down a slope into a ditch mostly screened by trees.

—This is a really easy job, said Claudio. —Really easy as in *really boring*. Boring, and *long*. Depending on how well this damn pump works, you might be out here the whole rest of the summer.

He left them as the exhaust hose began to gurgle and burp its snow-white ooze down an already dead and silica plastered slope. Kelly wondered where the stream beneath drained. Probably into the river somewhere.

As soon as Claudio was gone Bobby shrugged off his shirt and hung it on the fence. —At least we can get some tan now. That's one thing that sucks about working inside. C'mon man, join me.

Kelly felt his anxiety rising at the thought of baring his chest to Bobby once more. —I better not. I burn really easy, you know, and I'm already a little red after our time on the roof. I think I'll just hang out in the shack, if that's okay with you.

Bobby shook his head in disgust. —Whatever, wuss. You might as well get naked in the shack since no one can see you in there at all.

There were no seats in the little building so Kelly sat on the bare concrete floor with his back against the wall that faced the pump. Bobby looked in on him one more time, gave another disgusted headshake, then wandered off. From time to time Kelly could hear the muted clink of Bobby's steel-toed safety boots on the catwalks. The monotonous chugging vibration of the pump began to lull him into drowsiness but just as he was falling asleep the sound stopped with an extended squeal and a pop.

Kelly struggled to his feet and inspected the faded gray control panel. He pressed the green START button once, twice, over and over. Nothing. He tried the red RESET. No luck. He stepped out the open door to look for Bobby and the late morning sun smacked him so full in the face he staggered back. Of a sudden he felt weak beyond the sluggishness of his glancing encounter with actual sleep. Was he getting sick? That would be bad—he didn't know what would happen if he missed even one day of work.

Shading his eyes he spotted Bobby near the far end of the catwalk, clutching the rail and squatting, staring down into the calm silent water and the sludge below. —Hey! Bobby! The pump shut down.

Gripping the rail Bobby swung to his feet. —What the fuck man? What did you do?

—I didn't do nothing. It shut off all by itself.

—Did you try to restart it?

—Yeah, of course I did.

—Let me try.

Bobby stomped over, holding the rails to either side and swinging himself across the catwalk several steps at a time. When he reached the shack he repeated Kelly's futile assault on the controls. —Shit. It really is seized up or something. He stepped back outside and examined the limp hose hanging into the pond, its throat submerged in the chalky sludge. —Let's go look for Claudio.

Bobby shrugged his shirt back on and they trudged up the short slope to the door. Which they now saw had no outside handle. Kelly dimly recalled Claudio propping it with a hunk of metal when they came out. Bobby cursed.

They began to circle around the plant, and past the next corner came upon a steel garage door halfway up. Bobby ducked under and inside, Kelly followed, and they found themselves at one end of the Anodizing Line. A forklift was loading a huge spool of aluminum sheeting onto a horizontal spindle while two workers they hadn't yet met sprayed the machinery down with green garden hoses. The men wore grubby dust masks over their noses and mouths. Bobby asked the nearest if he'd seen Claudio and the man gestured vaguely down the assembly line.

The room actually contained three assembly lines, or perhaps three parts of the same long line given that the sheeting moved toward them on their right but away on their left. They proceeded down the narrow alley between two seemingly infinite rows of machines. The components of the Anodizing Line looked variously like dumpsters, enormous metal looms, garbage trucks sans wheels, each thrumming humming and rattling to its own unique rhythm as the boys ran their gauntlet. At irregular intervals the broad gray ribbon of aluminum reappeared as it spun from one machine to the next, its unguarded edge vibrating knife-sharp at just the right height for decapitation. Their feet scuffed a film of chalky dust from the floor and Kelly wondered whether they should be walking here unprotected when the workers all wore those crappy little masks. More garden hoses lay discarded every ten yards or so, some leaking slowly onto the wet cement.

Suddenly the machinery on their right crunched to a halt, a stretch of aluminum bellying down to hang slack. Kelly spotted a knot of men ahead in the aisle. Bobby picked up his pace so he must have seen them too. Soon Kelly recognized Claudio and two of the other mechs, along with Terry the electrician and Alphonse, one of the plant's mysterious pair of plumbers. The men appeared to be arguing but all hushed when the boys walked up. The air here smelled sour, vinegary.

The mech named Carmine sparked up almost at once. —Hey, one of you guys want to do us a favor? He looked them over close then said — Not you, Ferrante. Kenny, how about you? You want to help us out? We'll all owe you for this one, big time.

—Kelly.

—Yeah, Kelly. Help us out, okay? Earn a major league favor to be named later.

All the men faced him now. He was for the moment the center of attention. Not Bobby.

—Sure, I guess so. What do you need?

Alphonse took the lead —You see the big etching tank here? He gestured to his left, their right, and Kelly realized they stood beside a vast PVC vat, a tank roughly the size and shape of a military tank. —Somebody drop a piece of plastic sheeting inside and it floats now on top. That means we no can restart the line until it comes out, otherwise the sheeting will get sucked down and clog below the surface of the acid, and then we have to drain the tank. Very bad if that happens, you understand?

Alphonse stared at Kelly and Kelly stared back.

—Here's the thing. All us old men are too heavy, too fat to hang in there and pick it up. But look at you, young and lean. We can hold you while you reach for it. It will only take a second. In, out, done. Just like that, boom, boom, boom. What do you say, kiddo?

Kelly said —Acid?

—Yes, here's the thing. This is the etching tank, so it's filled with eighty percent pure sulfuric acid. That's why everything PVC here, yes? The acid eats the metal, but not the PVC. But no worries for you. We will all have a hold on you, tight tight tight. Keep you safe. Will only take a second. Completely safe for you, trust me.

Kelly looked at Bobby. Bobby nodded and whispered —PVC 15, man. Go for it, dude. Be the hero.

Kelly turned to the group and said *okay*. He saw relief spread over them. Alphonse handed him a pair of thick black rubber gloves and they all climbed on top of the tank via a PVC ladder built into its side.

A row of trapdoors studded the gray expanse, squares of clear plastic on clear plastic hinges. Alphonse kicked the nearest one open with the tip of his boot and pointed inside. The surface of the sulfuric acid extended in every direction below, a crumpled sheet of clear plastic floating on its top, partly submerged but with a single broad fold reaching up.

—Okay, here's the thing, said Alphonse. Me and Carmine and Steve are all going to hold onto you while we lower you inside. As soon as you have a grip on that damn plastic, give us the signal and we'll yank you out. The whole operation will no take more than a second. Just try not to breathe while you are inside, okay? All you need to do is say you got it and we pull you right out. Right out. Zip zip zip.

Kelly got down on his hands and knees, gloved fingers curled around the lip of the trapdoor. Before he could say *I'm ready* he felt powerful hands grip his ankles and calves and lift him. Another hand hooked under his belt in the back, and together the hands shoved him out over the opening. Without thinking he allowed himself to slide over the edge and inside. He hung headfirst with his arms out but his fingers remained at least a foot from the offending sheet.

—A little lower, he said, then gagged on the sour air. Several quarters he'd brought for the soda machine in the caf slipped from his right pocket and plopped into the acid but fortunately didn't splash. He would have had no time to blink if they did. He dropped several inches more as he began to slide out of Teddy Cyr's pants, and his fingers found the protruding edge of the sheet. He called out —*Now*, gagging again on the acid fumes. Nothing happened and he called once more, louder —I got it. *I got it!*

The hands dragged him back out through the trap instantly and lifted him to his feet in a single motion. He felt all those hands and more clapping him on the back. He dropped the plastic on top of the vat. Alphonse soccer-kicked it away at once, down to the floor on the side of the machinery opposite from where Bobby, Claudio, and some of the others still stood below. Then the plumber flipped the trap shut with his boot. Kelly realized his pants were half down his ass and yanked them up by the belt loops. Carmine said —You done good, kid, and they all climbed down again.

Bobby looked him up and down, said —Dude, you got some real brass monkey balls. Too bad they would've dissolved if you fell in that tank, haha! Still, that was the gutsiest thing I've ever seen anyone do around here.

—All right, problem solved, said Carmine. —Let's get outta here. I hate this goddamn place.

The others nodded, picked up the few tools still scattered about. Carmine turned to the boys and asked —What are you two doing out here anyway?

Bobby answered, as Kelly was still gasping in the fresh air, not so fresh really but better than what he inhaled inside the vat. He noticed now all the men wore dust masks, though he doubted these kept out the acid fumes.

—We came looking for Claudio. Claudio had already begun to walk away but turned to face them. —We need help with the pump. It's seized up or stuck or something.

—Probably just a blown fuse. Okay, follow me. As the rest of the men scattered he led the boys around and through the other two production lines. Red lights on poles began to flash and the machinery restarted. Twice they ducked under the ominous racing razor of aluminum. Past the far side of the third line they came at last to a door that opened onto the familiar Maintenance Floor, and from there they followed Claudio up the stairs of the storage balcony they knew all too well.

The Anodizing Line

—It's déjà vu all over again, said Bobby behind the mech's advancing back, giving his voice a quaver meant to suggest some eerie condition.

Claudio plucked a copper tube from a bin Kelly half-remembered, paused as if with second thoughts, then clutched up a whole handful—and after the briefest hesitation, a second handful. He stuffed them all in his pockets. The little cylinders had the look of miniature explosives, which in fact had been the joke Bobby and Kelly shared while sorting that section.

From there they traveled outside and returned to the pond and the shack, where Claudio showed them how to throw the breaker, tug the hose mouth into clear water, replace the fuse, restore the power and restart the pump before guiding the hose back into the sludge. He drew the double handful of fuses from his pockets and held them out to Kelly. —Here. These are likely to blow a lot. You might as well be ready. And from now on if you run out, you know where to find more. You won't need to come hunting for me anymore, okay?

Claudio was barely out of sight before that first replacement fuse blew. Working as a team they changed it a second time, Bobby struggling to position the hose end where the sludge was shallow while Kelly worked the switches and breakers. This third fuse lasted almost an hour.

They changed fuses four more times that day but could figure no pattern to their failure regardless of where they positioned the hose. Bobby left Kelly to monitor the shack while he patrolled the catwalk. He claimed he was hunting frogs but they were always too fast for him to catch. Kelly wondered how frogs survived in this water and if they could, what they ate. No way there could be any fish. Then again the dust was safe so long as it stayed damp, so the frogs probably never had to breathe it.

By the end of the workday they'd made no visible dent in the first pond's sludge nor had Bobby caught a single frog. Tired, hot, and dusty they trudged all the way to the punch clock without a word.

***

That evening Kelly asked his mom to toss his sour-smelling Teddy Cyr clothes in the wash. An hour or so later she knocked on his door, asked to come in. She held up the uniform for him to see. First the shirt, which seemed all right, then the pants. The calves and thighs of the pants had

255

dissolved down the front. Pretty much everywhere they'd rubbed the rim of the acid tank there was next to nothing left beyond a few ragged horizontal threads. He would have to wear his normal jeans tomorrow, and he dreaded Winston's response. Would he get fired on the spot? If he did, how would it affect his father's job? How would his father respond?

Mrs. Keslo sat down on the corner of his bed. Roxy Music's *Remake/Remodel* spun on the stereo. She asked her son to turn the music down but did not speak right away when he complied. It was as if she'd forgotten how to speak to him.

—Kelly. Kelly, is this something that is going to cause you problems at the plant? Is it going to cause problems for your dad? His job is not much but it's all he has. Right now, it's all *we* have. I hope you won't do anything to jeopardize that position. All you need to do is make it through the summer without any…mistakes. This job is just a stepping stone for you but it's your father's whole career. You've got a bright future ahead in college. You'll meet others like yourself, you'll see.

Kelly's father had no higher ed, but Jill Keslo had attended Trenton State two and a half years. She left to marry before she could graduate and it was no secret she regretted that decision now.

***

Despite his anxiety Kelly walked right past Winston the next morning and the man said nothing about his return to jeans. No one at all noticed he was half out of uniform, or if they noticed they didn't comment so maybe didn't care. At home that night he threw the ruined work pants in the trash, wishing he could discard the shirt as well. Anything would be better than wearing the rapist troll's uniforms…anything but getting fired and taking his dad down with him. Remaining concerned about stains he tried to select his oldest jeans, Lees and Levi's he was proud still fit.

By Wednesday they'd reached the second pool but burned more than halfway through the entire bin of fuses. Bobby now carried a long wiggly spear crafted from a metal rod he'd gotten from the welders and ground to a point against the pavement. Watching his partner stalk the catwalk with it made Kelly think of *Lord of the Flies*, only Bobby was hunting frogs, not pigs. What was the point? There would be no feast even if he were successful, and hot as the pavement was they would not be cooking any frogs' legs out here. Kelly had yet to see any of the frogs for himself, though he did hear their croaking all right. He couldn't argue that.

Neither of them could explain what they might be doing differently that day but they got through the entire afternoon without blowing a single fuse, which meant high fives. Kelly felt a warm rush in his chest at the contact.

On Thursday morning the fuses blew twice early on, but Bobby finally caught a frog. He burst into the pump shack waving the miserable little dead thing on the end of his wobbly rod, bloody, green, legs still twitching. Though Bobby called for acknowledgment of his hunting prowess, Kelly felt only a sudden sadness, and without reflection said —Why do you wanna do that? Poor frog.

Bobby jabbed the rod with the dying frog into the floor at Kelly's feet. —*Because they bother me.* They exist without my permission and without my control. But now they know they can't escape *my reach*. You got a problem with that? If you do you better speak up now.

Kelly kept silent. Bobby said —Yeah, I thought so. He held his prey down with the toe of his boot while he pulled the makeshift spear free, then kicked the punctured bleeding thing into the nearest pool, where it bobbed on the surface. Bobby turned and strode out the door, away from the shack, and as he did Kelly heard him mutter a single word. *Faggot.*

So it had come to that, and so soon. Somehow Kelly had always known it would, but he blamed himself for hoping this time, told himself it was nothing new. There'd been a boy in high school, one of the stars of the baseball team. He'd been friendly to Kelly all on his own. But only when no one else was around. Came the day Kelly said *Hi Jeff* while Jeff was talking to a teammate in the hall…Jeff shot back with that same word and shoved Kelly against the wall of lockers, hard. They never spoke again. Jeff never even looked at him the rest of the year. Was his summer at Azotype headed the same way now?

Kelly sat in the shack the rest of the day, listening to the chugging of the pump while Bobby hunted frogs or did whatever he did outside. When the fuses blew—and they did, three more times—he changed them alone, as Bobby by then was absent from view, possibly taking his frog-hunt down to the polluted ditch below.

Friday Kelly continued entirely by himself, keeping to the shack even though the sky was overcast and dark. Best he could tell Bobby never visited the ponds at all. Whether his AWOL partner patrolled the plant or scouted the drainage behind the trees downslope, Kelly did not know. Briefly he considered reporting Bobby's absence, but the thought of Winston's reaction discouraged that plan. Not to mention that would pretty much be the end of whatever relationship he and Bobby had shared. That relationship seemed to be evaporating already, but maybe it wasn't too late to save it. No need to narc out his friend.

Bobby turned up at lunch though, first as a firm hand between Kelly's shoulders as he sought out a seat, guiding him toward a rare and unlikely gap beside the Flashbulb Room girls, whose guardians had somehow grown lax or were perhaps just late. Bobby tried to make conversation but as before the girls only acknowledged his efforts with shrugs and grunts. Kelly wondered how they could ignore him, his handsome face and his muscles stretching even the fabric of Cyr's odd-sized shirt. Perhaps they were a couple unto themselves. Kelly felt a flash of envy at the thought.

Bobby sent signals for him to join the conversation, sideways looks and taps on the hip, but Kelly had no words for the girls. Let them eat their grilled cheeses in peace if they preferred it that way. Why help Bobby try to pick them up when they consistently demonstrated such obvious disinterest? And if they did connect? Kelly considered the inevitable awkward double date, remembering Patty Koenig, the girl he took to senior prom, his only high school date. He and Patty had known each other since second grade and agreed to go together with the unspoken understanding that they went as friends. Kelly was relieved when she politely abandoned him early on for her own little group of female friends. He spent the rest of the night as a wallflower, at ease outside those moments when Jeff walked or danced by…which seemed too often not to be deliberate.

At last their awkward lunch came to an end. Bobby shot him a scowl but held back his words. Somewhere along the corridor the two boys drew apart, and Kelly returned to the sludge pond alone.

The sky was even darker now, and before long the first fat raindrops began to patter the shack roof and pock the surface of the pond. He heard muffled thunder from somewhere to the south, and a minute later Bobby swung in the door, his Cyr shirt leopard-speckled with spots of rain. —Shit man, I think it's getting ready to really pour.

Kelly responded tentatively, facing out the little south window —Well you can hang out here with me till it's over. At least the roof isn't leaking. Yet.

He felt the weight of Bobby's angry gaze on his back. —Man, you were fuckin' deadweight just now with those Flashbulb girls. Today was my chance, and all I needed was a little help, but no, you were useless. You totally choked this time.

Kelly hesitated, mumbled a sorry.

—I get it man. He stepped closer. —You know I do.

Bobby stood right behind him. Kelly didn't dare turn. Bobby stretched out a hand to touch Kelly's back. —I know what you are. And I know what you want.

Kelly's heart began racing and blood ran to his face. How many times had he fantasized a moment almost like this? Just as he imagined turning to meet Bobby's lips the hand at his back became an arm around his throat.

—And I know the only thing you're good for, you fucking little faggot.

***

Kelly lay curled two hours or more on the pump shack's cold concrete floor, drifting in and out of sleep. The blood and semen had long since crusted on his buttocks and thighs, he could feel that, but pain still pulsed out from his bent right arm, from the scrapes and bruises on his elbow, knees, and chin, from his anus. Most of all he felt an intense yet irrational compulsion to poop. Even once sleep would no longer accept him he continued to clench his eyes shut and made no attempt to rise. All the while his mind raced with insoluble contradictions and dead end options.

He fought off full wakefulness for as long as he could but the rain had begun driving in through the open door and the chill spreading puddle it formed soaked under his naked calves and knees. Slowly he pulled himself deeper into the shack. Irremediably awake now, he struggled first to his knees, then clutching his crumpled boxers and jeans, he stood and pulled them inch by inch up. He couldn't believe how bad it still hurt. Was it really supposed to feel like that? Would it be this way every time? Slowly he slid his pants all the way to his waist and buckled his belt. His eyes leaked fresh tears down dry trails he hadn't tried to wipe off. He bent unsteadily to retrieve his safety glasses from the floor and almost tumbled over because of the pain.

Really, how had he not seen this coming? How had he not realized about Bobby? And who would believe him if he tried to tell? How would they treat him even if they believed? Who could he even try to tell—Winston? The welders? Karlin? His dad? Kelly knew even while Bobby still held him to the floor he would be alone with all of this, all the knowledge, all the pain. He was going to have to deal with it on his own.

Starting the pump back up no longer seemed so important, but he supposed he ought to in case anyone was watching or came to check. First he took an oily rag from atop the control panel and unbuckled his belt. He could feel a fresh wetness where his buttocks met his thighs and he didn't need the embarrassment or explanations of a visible stain, so he carefully pushed the rag down to the bottom of his butt, flattened it as best he could, hoping it would do for now, hoping it left no visible bulge. A stupid joke came back to him the guys used to tell in mid school—this one dude notices his friend always gets all the girls, so he asks him his secret. His friend says —It's easy. Every time I go out I stuff a potato down my pants. Why don't you try it, let me know how it works? After a week or so the friend asks the first dude how the potato trick worked out, and the dude says —Terrible! I get even less attention from girls than before—they won't even come near me. His friend thinks for a minute then says —Don't tell me you put the potato down the *back* of your pants! Well, Kelly wasn't trying to attract any girls. Not now not ever. Right now he didn't want to attract any attention at all. Best to show neither lump nor bloodstain. Best just to get home and clean up then. If he could only do that much he might be able to think.

The ride home with his dad was uncomfortable in so many ways. Mr. Keslo wanted to talk but Kelly did his best not to respond. The questions about Bobby Ferrante were the worst. Kelly tried to imply all was fine without using any actual words.

Back home Kelly made for the bathroom and the shower as soon as he came in the door, pausing only to snatch up clean blue jeans and boxers from his room. As he dressed after his shower he pressed a fresh wad of tissue into the crack of his ass. He considered using one of his mother's tampons but passed on the likelihood it might be missed. Not something he wanted to have to explain.

THE ANODIZING LINE

***

He spent the entire weekend locked in his room, hardly even getting out of bed, only leaving to use the bathroom or eat meals. He played mostly Joy Division and the Cure, but sometimes let the needle spin and bump at the center of the record for hours rather than get up and change it or turn it over. He found he didn't really care whether the music played or not. His favorite albums were like sucked-out oranges, drained of juice and flavor. He no longer cared, they offered no comfort, he couldn't connect.

Vicious contradictions twisted in his brain. He never wanted to go back to Azotype, but how would that affect his father's job if he didn't? The very thought of encountering Bobby again made him hyperventilate. Most of all he wanted to tell someone, anyone, what Bobby had done, but he knew he was totally alone in his pain. No one would believe him, and even if they did they would only look on him with disgust. To expose the source of his suffering would mean revealing his true self, and that was something he was nowhere near prepared to do.

Kelly slept only in fits, shook in terror whenever his parents knocked on the door, actually snapped at his mom to *fuck off* when she called him down to dinner on Sunday night. He knew he'd hurt her and he regretted it, but he offered no apology as she jittered around him later at the dining room table. Meanwhile his father pushed pointless shop talk that Kelly deflected with monosyllables as he chewed.

***

Come Monday morning though, he was up and ready to go. He had no choice. He could not risk his father's job, their fractured and limping family's frail lifeline. He was edgy on the ride, edgier still entering the plant, but he made it all the way to Maintenance without glimpsing Bobby. Winston caught him as he was headed up the balcony stairs for more fuses.

—Forget about the sludge pond for now. Your pissant little pal Ferrante pulled some strings, got himself reassigned to the Flashbulb Room. Since you're all alone now Alphonse asked if you can help him change out a heat exchanger on Line 2. Apparently you made a good impression on him the

261

other day, who the hell knows how? Do you know where I'm talking about, where to go?

Kelly nodded and Winston dismissed him with a backhand wave. He quickly found Alphonse and two of the mechs clustered around a conglomeration of pipes on the middle of the Anodizing Line's three sections. The focus of their attention was a thick metal trunk, wide as Kelly's waist and rising nearly his entire height. Straps from an overhead hoist wrapped round it, but it remained bolted in tight and not going anywhere yet.

Alphonse handed him an adjustable wrench and pointed out the bolts that locked the heat exchanger in place, a dozen each ringing the base and the crown of the pipe, seven on either of the smaller side tubes. Some of the bolt heads were partway dissolved due to the acid in the air, and it was over these that the mechs shook their heads. But Alphonse attacked them methodically with WD-40 and a pipe wrench until one by one he drew them out while Kelly worked steadily at those more intact. The work was repetitive yet demanding enough to offer him adequate distraction.

With one bolt top and bottom both left to go Alphonse rechecked the straps, then signaled Kelly and they each addressed their bolt. Alphonse's bottom bolt cracked off almost right away causing Kelly's to snap in turn before he had it loose of the upper flange, and the massive pipe swung free to hang from the hoist. It only shifted a few inches but he was so startled he almost fell from his perch. He calmed his breathing as Alphonse worked the hanging control box on the hoist, raising the heat exchanger, moving it to one side, and lowering it gently onto a flat metal cart. Clear liquid like lymph dribbled out of it. Kelly hoped it was only water.

Together they wheeled the cart and its awkward burden all the way back to the Maintenance Shop, just Alphonse and Kelly, the skeptical mechs having long since wandered off. There Alphonse used another hoist to raise the pipe again and set it on a pallet. He replaced it on the cart with a fresh heat exchanger they tugged from a long cardboard box with agonizing patience. The plumber explained how the thing's innards contained a honeycomb of glass tubes through which heat passed from water to acid while the fluids never mingled. If they were careless and cracked even a single tube, they would ruin a three thousand dollar part and keep most of the Anodizing Line shut down a week or more until a replacement arrived. Kelly protested that Alphonse was wrong to place so much faith in him, but the plumber shrugged it off. —As good as anyone, you. Anyway, here's the thing. These mechs, they don't care anyway if the line shuts down. I get the blame and they take it easy all week. You do right so far. I watch. Good man. Alphonse motioned as if to pat him on the back but when Kelly flinched the plumber shrugged and lowered his hand. After that he was careful not to invade Kelly's space.

Kelly spent three days with Alphonse and found himself learning some actual skills. How to use a pipe wrench, how to clean the ends of a threaded pipe and wrap the threads with pink Teflon tape for a tighter seal. The manifold benefits of WD-40. The work held just enough interest to keep Kelly's mind occupied. Alphonse spoke little, but he was patient and seemed concerned that Kelly genuinely learned the techniques he took the time to explain.

Lunch was the bad time. His stomach knotted and he felt near to panic at the thought of seeing Bobby. The first day Kelly hid in the locker room at lunch, stretched along one of the hard wooden benches. His plan was to nap the full half hour but he couldn't rest one minute. Though no one came in he jerked up every time a change in air pressure rattled the door.

Tuesday and Wednesday he spent lunch on the storage balcony. Someone had already deposited another sloppy box of ballasts way down the end on the floor, and Kelly sat on this with his back against the bins. His mind raced with thoughts he sought to put aside but could not. Mostly Bobby. Bobby, Bobby, Bobby.

Thursday morning Winston changed his assignment, sent him to the electricians, Terry and Dean. Since Terry was the cool one Kelly actually felt a mild excitement at this gig. As much as he dreaded coming to work this week, it hadn't been too bad so far. He still spent his nights and evenings in tortured isolation. Yet once he reached the plant each morning the actual work made him feel he belonged. Even Winston began treating him like someone halfway worthwhile instead of an unwanted burden.

He found Terry and Dean with a mech named Connor, and the four of them walked together to the Manufacturing Floor where they commandeered a cherry picker. Terry called on Connor to drive the machine while he directed from the floor and Dean and Kelly crewed the faded blue cage. Their mission was to replace tubes and ballasts in the high fluorescent panels. Kelly jumped when the cage jerked and began to ascend, but a look all round told him no threats approached, and gripping the rails he rode it up. Nervous at first, he grew more relaxed as the cage rose higher. Perhaps because he knew its ascent meant no one but Dean could approach him unseen.

He wished he got to work closer to Terry but told himself there'd be other times. His role with Dean was to hold tools, ballasts, and other parts, hand them over upon request. Easy stuff, like a nurse in the O.R., except they were thirty or more feet above the floor. Not so easy for Kelly though. He began to panic at the thought of riding the rectangular blue cage with his former partner, but each time he got nervous Dean said something banal and the contrast helped Kelly calm down.

The team made slow but systematic progress across the lightscape over the G.M.F. The dead fluorescents were scattered at random, so Terry and Connor had to negotiate their right of way at times with forklift drivers, the crew on the lines, once even Jeffries himself. Kelly looked down on it all with detached relief.

By lunch they'd only replaced eight of the jellyfish brains but everyone on the team seemed pleased with their progress. Connor booked off for parts unknown while Dean and Terry invited Kelly to join them for lunch at the nearby McDonald's on Route 22. He hadn't known employees were allowed to leave the plant for lunch, but the electricians assured him it was legit so long as they returned in time, which they would guarantee happened. And they would even buy his lunch. *Forget that shit they serve in the caf.* Dean made a gagging sound and they all three laughed.

Friday went the same, only Winston stopped them as they were coming back in from Mickey D's. Stopped *Kelly* and waved the others on. This was it, Kelly knew it. Maybe the regular crew were allowed to eat out, but not summer temps. He felt a mix of terror and relief at the thought of his imminent termination from Azotype.

—Keslo, said Winston, —How'd you like to make a little extra money this weekend? The bulky man explained that Striker, the third electrician, was coming in the next day to do some work and needed an assistant. The job was Kelly's if he wanted it, and Winston went out of his way to mention how he would make time and a half for overtime.

—I'll have to ask my dad.

—I already called over and asked him. He says it's okay. And then he added, all on his own —It'll just be you and Striker. No one else.

Kelly agreed. Working with the plumbers and electricians wasn't that bad, so why not make some extra dough? At home he'd only spend Saturday moping around his room anyway. He didn't want to end up yelling at his mom again.

He rushed to catch up with his crew. When he joined them Terry asked —What'd Winston want? He didn't hassle you, did he, that fat man-boobs fuck?

—No, he offered me overtime. Tomorrow. Helping Striker.

Connor chuckled and said —The Force, while Dean wriggled his hand in the air chest height between them and spoke-sung the opening notes of the *Twilight Zone* theme.

—Cut it out, you guys, said Terry.

—Why do you all call him that?

—Because he's *possessed*, said Connor.

—He's a weird guy, that's all, said Terry. And you know how we all like to joke around. But he's a good electrician. He's been here longer than all of us and he knows his stuff. You'll be all right with him for a day, I think.

After that it was back up the cherry picker, so no more discussion about Striker, AKA The Force. Come day's end they'd finished their irregular circuit of the Manufacturing Floor and by Kelly's estimate improved the lighting over the enormous room by some twenty percent, though no one acknowledged their efforts or even seemed to notice them at all unless they got in the way.

***

Saturday morning Kelly's father offered to let him take the station wagon. The wagon was no Rolls but even Kelly's mother was not allowed to drive it. This overtime opportunity appeared to be the source of an odd kind of pride for Mr. Keslo, and he mentioned several times the way Winston had called him, praising the floor boss for his manners and forethought. Of course Kelly received instructions to —Come right home after your work is done though. No running off to parties in the car. As if that ever happened.

Past the unstaffed receptionist's desk most of the lights in the plant were off, so Kelly had to navigate back to Maintenance through a dismal gloom, relieved only by scattered skylights he never noticed before. He found Striker right away though, pacing just inside the corridor door.

—You Keslo? Must be, must be, of course you are. Hope you're ready because we have a busy day ahead. Busy busy. Lots of bulbs, lots of lights. Well what are you waiting for? Grab that sack and come with me. Let's go, let's go.

He spoke this all in a single uninflected burst without allowing Kelly to reply, pointing as he finished to a lumpy burlap bag on the floor. Kelly hefted the sack by its neck and rushed after the electrician who was already at the door.

Bobby's description of Striker as Keith Richards' grandfather still seemed apt. Gaunt and ever so slightly hunched, the man was older than any of the other Maintenance staff. Despite a full head of auburn hair his face was craggy and deeply creased. His gray eyes never seemed to focus long. And he was the only man in the plant Kelly ever saw smoking. In fact he never saw the man *not* smoking. A perpetual cigarette hung from his lips, regardless of plant rules and restrictions and the ubiquitous *NO SMOKING/NO FUMAR* signs.

Lugging the bulky sack Kelly followed the electrician down the corridor to a door he always ignored before. Striker unlocked it with a key off the sort of wide metal key ring frontier jailers used in old western movies. The room inside was so dark Kelly received only vague impressions of densely packed machinery in the limited light seeping in through the open door behind them.

Striker fiddled with a switch on the wall which did nothing but spit brittle clicks. —Well ain't that fine and dandy? Not that I'm surprised. Not surprised at all. Why don't you dig in your sack there and find me the flashlight? Kelly poked one arm in up to the shoulder, groped amongst the bulbs and boxes and wiry bits until he found the cold metal tube of a torch. Standing, he held it out, but Striker said —Are you daft, boy? Turn it on, turn it on.

Kelly thumbed the switch forward and The Force directed him along the wall until the beam revealed a gray metal box. Striker opened it and began to poke at its wires and relays with a screwdriver while Kelly played the light inside. Nothing happened for maybe ten minutes other than Striker rambling on about how painful his shoes were not these the shoes he wore when he went out to nightclubs they didn't use to be painful but either his feet had changed or his shoes had shrunk or something he couldn't tell which and it was a shame because he really liked those shoes. They were Italian. Leather. The best, you know? Got them in New York City and the shop isn't even there any—

A blast of orange sparks flew out past Striker's right shoulder. —Oh you cheeky bastard you, you think you can do that to me? *Hold that light steady, boy!* Hold it steady.

Kelly had staggered back when the sparks shot out, allowing the light to dip forty-five degrees toward the floor. He sucked in deep breaths and brought the beam back up. Striker continued his work and Kelly jerked only slightly at the next two bursts, the bulk of the sparks pattering softly off Striker's face and chest. Finally the electrician stuck a hand into the guts of the box, threw some switch or breaker with a dull sudden clunk, and the lights flared on in the room, so bright Kelly had to squinch his eyes shut and could only reopen them in stages.

The space didn't look much bigger than Maintenance to Kelly, though it was difficult to tell for certain because the machinery was packed so tight. Only by looking up at the ceiling could he get some idea of the size of the room. —What is this place?

—You've never been in the Pickle Factory?

—Nope.

—Well, this is the Pickle Factory.

—Do they make pickles here?

—Exactly where do they find you guys? Striker shook his head longer than needed, said —Come on.

They travelled through the labyrinth of electromechanical obscurity. Kelly could make no sense of either the devices or their arrangement. None of them revealed any obvious relation to any other. Few even displayed any connection. Striker stopped to work on the control panels of some, though his selections seemed random. Sometimes the machines shook briefly to noisy life beneath his touch while other times they slept on and the results of his ministrations remained obscure. The man maintained a wild disjointed monologue the entire time, discussing his perennial aches and pains, his dream of a Lamborghini, how he'd learned all he needed to know as an electrician while still in the Navy. Kelly allowed most of the words to flow by while the overall rhythm soothed him some.

Eventually they retreated down the main hall to the Flashbulb Room for a long tall stepladder stored there in the alcove beneath the stairs, and with that set up they began to change bulbs protected by high basket-shaped wire cages. Striker worked the lights while Kelly steadied the ladder, held the screws, and handed bulbs up to the electrician. The hardest part of the job was toting the ladder around the dense metal maze. All in all they spent a couple hours in the Pickle Factory. As much as Striker spoke he never explained the purpose of the place or of the work they did there. Over half the lights he replaced were already working.

—I usually skip lunch on a Saturday, clear out of here that much earlier. Are you okay with that?

Kelly was. His appetite had been all but absent of late and he hadn't brought anything to eat anyway.

From the Pickle Factory they traveled on to the Dye Kitchen, a space Kelly knew only slightly from the time he and Bobby had sought Teddy Cyr there. The room was comparable in area to the Pickle Factory but was packed with tanks and drums and tangles of pipes rather than random inscrutable machinery. A central aisle divided the territory though this walkway had several crooks and zagged to the right entirely before reaching the far wall. A chemical tang like paint or glue hung in the air.

—Reach in that sack and get me the cordless screwdriver. *The cordless.*

As Kelly groped about in the bag, Striker explained only cordless tools were allowed in the Dye Kitchen, as even a single spark might ignite fire or explosion.

—What about your cigarette then?

—Listen, kid, don't tell me my job. Don't try to tell me my job, okay? And he flicked ash on the floor. The gray flakes disappeared into the honey-combed cells of the black rubber mat that ran down the aisle.

Kelly found the requested device and together they raised the ladder, began again the routine of changing lights. Bulb by bulb they progressed deeper into the Dye Kitchen, hefting the ungainly open ladder from each to each Three Stooges style. Kelly kept expecting Striker to poke him in the eyes and say —*Nyuk, nyuk!* He was careful not to walk beneath it and incur bad luck. Several times The Force broke from this routine to tinker with control panels but he maintained his monologue the entire time, rarely seeking to engage his assistant unless requesting a part. Kelly remembered something a witty history teacher had said of an attention-seeking friend — *He could survive on a desert island so long as there was someone there to watch him.* Striker it seemed only needed someone to listen, or really, just to hear. Probably he was like this even when he worked alone.

It took an hour or more before they worked their way round the corner turn, found themselves facing a forklift door in the far wall. By now they'd worked into a rhythm of moving the ladder, steadying the ladder, handing nuts and bolts up and down, Striker's running patter their soundtrack, a substitute for the radio or cassette player Kelly wished he was allowed. Sometimes they had to maneuver the ladder deep down the narrow alleys between the tanks and struggle to find even footing and room to open. Other times their targets hung right off the aisle.

Eventually they negotiated the right angle turn and worked their way to within a few yards of the gray garage door. Around this time Striker asked from atop the ladder —You ever been to England, kid?

Kelly took a moment to answer —No, but I really want to go. A lot of bands I'm into are from there.

—Well you'd like it kid, I'm telling you. You'd like it a lot. When I was there in the Navy, the whores that worked the alleys in Liverpool had this neat trick, you know. A real neat trick. They'd cut a strip of inner tube and run it over one arm, behind their neck and around one thigh. All they needed to do was pull down on that arm and their quim was right there. Right there. They called that kind of fuck a *trembler.* Those were the days.

Motion to Kelly's left caught his eye, causing him to sidestep reflexively. The ladder shook, and Striker called down —*Hey!* Kelly stepped back to steady his grip while bending his head to the left to examine what he'd seen. A figure covered entire in a silver contamination suit approached down the aisle, toting a bucket of something bubbling and blue. The suit was complete all the way out to gloves and a hood with a rectangular faceplate riveted in place. The suited figure lowered the bucket toward a small trapdoor at the base of the wall less than two yards from where Kelly stood, raised the lid and poured its troubled contents *down the hatch.*

This did not look good. —Hey, said Kelly, —Are we all right being around that stuff without protection?

The silver-clad figure turned and looked up and down as if noticing Kelly,

Striker, and the ladder for the first time, paused then pressed a button below the faceplate and spoke.

—Nothing to worry about. Everything is safe. The voice emerged infected by an electric insect buzz, but Kelly could make the words out well enough. He thought to ask —*Then why are you all covered up like that?* but the figure had already closed the trap and turned to walk away and Striker was meanwhile calling from above for another bulb, which meant climbing partway up to meet him.

When Striker descended the ladder Kelly tried to tell him about the worker and the blue burbling gunk, but The Force shrugged off the information and *we're done with the Dye Kitchen anyway so grab your end of the ladder and let's get out of here if you don't like this place.*

From the Dye Kitchen they returned to the Flashbulb Room, and after they restowed the ladder, Striker opened the forbidden inner door with another key from his heavy brass ring. Kelly's anxiety flared again —Are we allowed to go in there?

—Listen kid, I wouldn't have the key if I wasn't allowed to go in there, would I? Would I? Just relax and follow me. You are one nervous kid, you know that? Very nervous.

Inside was a small room with bare walls and a low ceiling. Nothing there but a desk and the desktop was bare but for a black princess phone and a Rolodex. Kelly noticed the phone bore no cord. A second door led off to their left, this one heavy, metal, with a spoked wheel in place of a knob, like something in a battleship or a submarine. In his mind Kelly heard the sound of water splashing in torrents and some all-American TV actor's voice yelling —*Close all watertight doors.* The door was already closed though. Striker reached round the front of the desk, opened one of the drawers then closed it again. Opened a second, closed it in turn. As far as Kelly could tell, he didn't remove anything from the desk. Then he walked over to the metal door, and gripping its spokes, spun the wheel.

Kelly got as far as —Are we really supposed to go— before Striker cut him off with —Kid, what did I tell you? What did I already tell you? Goddamn nervous kid.

Striker opened the door and stepped into the room beyond. Kelly struggled to drive down his anxiety and followed, still lugging the lumpy sack on his back. Inside was a room as large as Maintenance, occupied solely by a two-story burnished metal cube. The side that faced them bore another door identical to the one they'd just come through but unpainted. Both visible sides of the cube were featureless except for the door and the lines of rivets that ran along bottom, top, and vertical edges. Each individual side seemed to be a single giant metal plate, aluminum or some kind of alloy.

Kelly steeled himself to see at last what was inside the Flashbulb, but Striker ignored the door and walked around the cube instead. Just beyond the side opposite the door an oblong metal box rose from the cement on three steely posts. Cables from the box ran along the floor both to the far wall and back to the cube. Striker opened the box, drew something from his pocket Kelly thought was a fuse, replaced the old fuse or whatever, jammed the little dead soldier back in his pants, closed the box again and said —There. There, that's done.

From the cube he led Kelly to the back wall of the room, bare but for a third battleship door, this one painted gray like the first. Beyond this door they came into a lengthy corridor Kelly had never seen before, lit by a wide-spaced row of caged red bulbs along the opposite wall. Striker had grown silent now, the first time all day. Kelly followed him down the hall. It went on what seemed forever without another door. The Force mumbled occasionally under his breath but never renewed his monologue. Just when Kelly was convinced the corridor somehow extended longer than the plant itself they came to a corrugated garage door on their left. A little red on white sign beside the door proclaimed CONSTRUCTION AREA / HARD HATS REQUIRED. Striker bent down, grasped the handle, and raised the apparently unlocked door with a clatter and a whoosh. He stepped inside.

Kelly hesitated at the threshold, called to The Force —Hey, should we be in here? Or at least have helmets on or something?

—I told you not to worry, kid. You worry too much. What a worrier. Now follow me.

Kelly followed, sensing himself at the edge of panic. Once he was inside Striker said —Here, let me have that sack now. Let me have the sack.

Kelly relinquished the bag with relief. His shoulder ached from its weight. Striker gripped the sack by the neck but didn't lift it. Instead he allowed it to slip to the broad concrete platform on which they stood and said —Okay now follow me.

A deep trench divided the floor ahead. Kelly could barely see the opposite edge in the light from the door. A pair of handrails curled over their edge several yards to the left, the same kind as in a deep in-ground swimming pool. Striker grasped the rails and began his descent and Kelly followed behind with only slight delay.

The trench was maybe ten feet deep and twice as wide. Railroad tracks ran up its center and construction debris lay strewn all over. Girders, conduit, 2x4s. Random pallets, some empty, some with shadowy machinery still strapped on top, others with stacked and strapped construction supplies. The Force stepped across the tracks and began to pick his way forward down the line, Kelly trailing him once again. There seemed fewer obstacles on the opposite side of the rails.

—What is this place?

—The A5 Line, of course. The A5. What's wrong with you, nervous kid, did you crawl out from under a rock?

—I'm sorry. I, uh, didn't know. I only heard of it a little. He paused, then asked —What's it do?

—Do? Right now it doesn't do anything. But it's supposed to replace the Anodizing Line when it's done. Totally automated and one continuous line, not that three-way zigzag clusterfuck they're running now. This is the future. So witness the future.

Striker grew silent again as Kelly followed him down the trench. This seemed strange after the man's all day running patter, but to Kelly's surprise he found the dark and quiet calming, and the shadows wrapped him like swaddling clothes. He shuffled to avoid the debris on the floor, picking his way with his feet because the third time he looked down he almost lost sight of The Force. Fortunately he could still follow the man's faint but immensely magnified shadow on some distant end wall way ahead.

The floor of the trench rose steadily till it grew level with the floor on either side, at which point the tracks stopped at a barrier striped diagonal yellow and black. Kelly drew comfort from the way the shadows hid him, confidence from his skill at making his way in the almost total dark. Really, this was the best part of the day. It was quiet, he was safe, and he was seeing something the other summer temps would never get to see. A piece of the future, even if it was a work in progress. He followed Striker's enormous fuzzy shadow and no longer cared he had no clue about their mission to this location. He presumed Striker would tell him when they reached that far wall.

Overconfident, he almost tripped over some unknown mass on the floor, and twisting to maintain his balance he lurched a little to his left. Striker did the same, or at least his shadow did the same. Fear fell over Kelly. He raised his right arm. The shadow raised its right arm. He lifted his left and the shadow copied his motion again. He wasn't following Striker's shadow. The shadow was his own. Striker was gone and he was following his own static shadow on the blank far wall.

Kelly tried to call out for The Force but he'd begun to hyperventilate and his voice choked out in strangled fits. He *wasn't* safe here. *Not safe at all.* With Striker gone anyone could be behind him. Maybe Bobby. *Maybe Bobby was working overtime too.* They came through the Flashbulb Room to get here. Bobby might've been following him ever since.

He had to get out or at least find a light. He staggered to his right where the wall was closest, hit it too soon and almost knocked himself down, bruising his already aching right arm and shoulder which began to throb. The wall was unbroken cinderblock. Somewhere in it there had to be a door! Kelly began to track along the wall, brushing against it with his left hand, the uninjured side. His heart pounded and his breath rasped in his ears. He muttered *Oh man oh man oh man!* speaking the words softly so as not to reveal his location to anyone or anything lurking in the dark.

His hand struck metal at last. He stopped and felt along the cool smooth surface, found the broad bar of a fire door, pressed against it with all his weight.

The bar depressed with a click but the door didn't move. For a moment Kelly was convinced it was locked then it burst open and he tumbled through.

He stumbled into sunlight as the door swung shut behind him. Swung. *Shut.* He heard it latch. The summer sun hit him full in the face, blinding bright. He threw his right forearm up to shield his already watering eyes, shoving his safety glasses up his forehead askew. He wanted to close his eyes but he had to see who might be close or coming closer. His eyes hurt, his nose ran, his side hurt, and he was in full panic mode.

Kelly spun in an awkward two-step, surveying his perimeter as best he could from beneath his forearm and through half-closed eyes. He stood on a neatly manicured lawn. The door he came out bore no outside handle or knob, not even a keyhole. Simply a smooth gray rectangle in an endless high brick wall.

As his eyes adjusted he raised his arm till it served him more as visor than shield, plucked off his safety glasses and placed them folded in his shirt pocket. He saw the treeline maybe ten yards beyond the wall of the plant. Glistening oily poison ivy enveloped most of the trunks. Kelly remembered the raw earth scarred by tread tracks they'd seen from the roof of this building and felt confused. Could he be outside a different section of the A5 now, something built early enough the grass already had time to grow back? Yet he felt certain he'd exited on the same side he surveyed with Bobby from the roof.

He smeared tears from his eyes and snot from his nose with the crook of his elbow and peered around, his head still tilted downward but slowly raising his gaze to see farther, higher.

No one approached him, that much was good. No one whatsoever in sight. The little strip of lawn extended empty along the side of the plant as far as he could see, paralleled off to his left by the edge of the forest, artificially sharp. His panic subsided some and his breathing began to slow. Raising his eyes a little higher he saw the treetops—and far beyond them, tall buildings. Insanely tall buildings. Which was impossible. This part of Jersey had no big cities, and Underbridge was far from both Philly and New York. It was not as if either Poroth or Flemington had urban skylines, and those were the only large towns even remotely close to the plant.

Even the buildings themselves were strange, crystalline and glinting. Immense translucent tubes connected them in a web that could not, should not exist. And was this city on fire? Great serpentine smoke fingers waved slowly amidst the structures. Waved and trembled but never moved up or down. Some of these blunt gray pillars reached even above the highest of the buildings, all of which appeared taller than the Empire State Building or World Trade Center towers.

Kelly felt his breath racing once more out of control. Where the hell had he come out and what the hell was he seeing?

Unable to process this vision he raised his eyes higher. Best to let himself stare into emptiness a moment. The sky was icy cloudless blue just as the air was stagnant with furnace heat and still. He caught glimmers at the edges of his sight that disappeared when he tried to look direct.

THE ANODIZING LINE

Holding his eyes and head still with effort he saw in his side vision immense iridescent cigars and spheres, pulsing without rhythm as they drifted about. Beyond these he witnessed the sky divided by veins, a complicated irregular web of flickering light. As he grew more skilled at observing the jagged glints he saw how some conjoined with the distant spindly crystalline towers, while others wove into the poison ivy vines climbing the trees nearby. Background and foreground ceased any separation at that recognition and his vision flattened into a single canvas seeming close enough to touch. Swinging his head away to his left—*the south?*—he saw the sun draining straight into the grid, droplets of yellow fire pulsing into the pattern. *What the hell all was he seeing?* He was hallucinating, he was panicking, he was going crazy. He fell to his knees. *Oh man. Oh man.* Closed his eyes. Took deep breaths.

When he opened them again he saw a little deer emerging with tentative steps from the trees directly ahead. Because his entire range of sight appeared as part of a single plane the animal seemed to grow larger rather than nearer. *Doe, a deer*, he thought once more, but this was only a fawn. Spitting image of Bambi, or almost. Strangely fearless it approached as Kelly knelt and gasped. Here was something innocent, something pure. Something uncontaminated. If deer had no fear of people in this place, didn't that mean he was somewhere safe, somewhere good? He stared at the fawn as if it had come to his personal rescue.

The fawn finally halted its slow approach just a few feet away. Kelly looked right at it and it stared straight back. Then its mouth dropped open— dropped farther than could be normal—utterly unhinged and gaped was more precise—and a thick band of dense gray smoke emerged and began to stretch toward him where he knelt. The vapor trembled in the windless air, its forward end twisting and turning like a blind snake's face. The fawn stood frozen while the smoke sought for Kelly where he crouched on the grass.

Stumbling to unsteady feet he first shuffled backward then turned and began to run, heading north along the building's flat and featureless wall, away from the fawn, away from the animate smoke, away from the ensnared and complicit sun.

He became aware of a faint buzzing background hum. Usually this time of year the cicadas were crazy loud but the hum he heard was neither cicadas nor crickets nor birds. Nor the wind. It pulsed with its own peculiar rhythm and he was certain he heard the whisper of voices within it though he could not make them out.

Kelly ran alongside the high wall close enough to touch it, convinced the fawn pursued, along with the smoke, Bobby, and whatever made the hum. Each. All. All in one. He didn't dare look back, didn't dare surrender an inch of ground. Didn't know where he was going, other than away.

Suddenly he saw another door. Another blank rectangle, no latch no keyhole no knob, but a door. He threw himself at it, clawed at its edges, hammered its smooth gray surface with both his fists. Beneath his futile thumping he half felt half heard an intense mechanical vibration and roar from the other side.

It only took a few seconds before the door burst open, knocking him sideways and nearly to the ground in surprise. Striker stood in the aperture, a humungous olive drab cylinder behind him now occupying the trench they walked down before. Could it be in his flight from the smoke-mouthed fawn he had run as far as some part of the line where the machinery was already installed? It didn't seem that way but he no longer trusted any of his impressions anymore. The cylinder thrummed and rumbled, incomprehensible arrangements of lights pulsing along its visible side.

The Force blinked, scanned, hunkered down and caught Kelly by the left wrist, yanked him up and over the threshold as if he only weighed a scant few pounds. —What the hell were you doing out there, you nervous kid? You really are one crazy nervous kid. Striker pulled the door shut with a solid *thunk* and a click of the latch.

Kelly was outright sobbing, only realized it now. He made an effort to thank Striker, tried to hug him, but the odd old man held him back with his strong wiry arms. —One crazy nervous kid. Okay, okay. It's okay. You're okay. Everyone's okay. Just try and calm down. What the hell were you doing outside anyway? Why in hell did you want to go out there?

Kelly couldn't answer, was panting too hard. First he fought to wrestle his sobbing under control, then struggled with his breath. He felt dizzy and possibly close to a faint.

It was then he realized the concrete trench was empty again. No vast rumbling tube, no flashing lights. All he'd seen and heard when Striker opened the door was gone. The A5 Line lay quiet, cool, incomplete, and void, just as it had before he stepped out the first of the fire doors.

What he'd seen outside and what he'd seen inside when Striker opened the door had both been so intense and clear. So *real*, as unreal and impossible as all of it seemed. If what he saw through the door while he was still outside was gone, did the nightmare he just escaped remain beyond? He decided he didn't need to know. At least not yet.

—Come on nervous kid, get up. We're done here, so let's go.

Kelly looked to The Force, expecting a hand up, but the man had already turned his back and was headed for another metal swimming pool ladder descending back into the trench. Kelly struggled with legs gone wobbly, forced his feet forward as Striker disappeared over the edge, baby steps first then shuffling in pursuit, determined not to find himself left behind in this place a second time.

They retraced their steps to the entrance of the A5 Line with neither detour nor delay, other than Striker stooping without stopping to retrieve the sack from right where he'd abandoned it. They soon found themselves in Maintenance again, where the main lights remained off. —Listen kid, I can tell you're pretty shook up by whatever you saw outside, so you probably won't be good for anything else today. Why don't you go home and I'll finish up alone?

—What about the punch clock? It has to be like three hours early. I don't want to get in trouble. Or lose my hours.

—Ha! said The Force, his voice more growl than laugh. —I'll take care of that, don't you worry. I know how to work that punch clock better than a fifty cent whore. I'm not staying here much longer myself, but I guarantee we'll both get paid a full eight hours wages. And why shouldn't we? We did the work we were supposed to do. All of it. You go on, nervous kid. I've got this under control. Trust me.

Kelly hesitated, frozen a moment, then mumbled —Okay, sure, thanks man. He wasn't certain he trusted Striker but he *was* certain he didn't want to argue with him. He was even more sure he wanted to get the hell out of Azotype A.S.A.P. He'd take his chances with Striker and the clock.

He executed a sloppy about-face and headed for the door. Neither he nor The Force said another word, nor did they ever see each other again. He felt a twinge as he passed the Flashbulb Room door, now that he knew about the corridor behind it and all it led to. Another shudder as he passed the

Dye Kitchen, recalling the man in the hazard suit and his chemical burden. On through the strangely silent and motionless G.M.F. to the punch clock and caf. Facing the clock he hesitated long but left his card alone in the end. If Striker didn't punch him out for 5:00 he'd just claim he forgot, trust to The Force to back up whatever bullshit story he told.

At the front doors he froze again. What if the vistas and patterns of madness manifested outside here as well? Why should they not? What kind of mutant animal might await him out there—a 'possum, a muskrat, a feral dog? He peered with fear through the polarized glass. All appeared normal, the parking lot, his father's car, the lawn, the line of trees all round. He stood staring out but observed no anomalies. No zigzag jigsaw sky, no crystalline buildings, no gigantic waving fingers of smoke. No suspicious creatures, no fawns.

Breathing deep and slow as he could manage he opened the door. The view grew brighter but everything otherwise stayed the same. He picked his way toward the station wagon like a soldier traversing a battlefield ringed by snipers, eyes fixed the whole time on the upper edge of the tree line that bordered the lot.

Finally he reached the wagon. There were only three other cars today in the usually full lot. At first he tried to guess which was Striker's but quit right off. He wanted to forget The Force and everything else about this day. He unlocked the dinged and dented door, got in and sat down. Mr. Keslo had explained his trick of taps and timing to avoid a stall, but Kelly had not paid attention. Still the damn thing started instantly. *Oh thank you Bowie, thank you thank you!*

On the entrance road and out onto 22 the views remained cozy and familiar, the same as he had seen outside car windows his entire life. As the road and his driving found their own easy rhythms he felt his panic start to drain, his racing heart begin to slow. He considered the likelihood the strange things he had seen were nothing more than afterimages invoked by the summer sun's glare. Coming out of the shadowed factory like that into such intense direct brightness, couldn't the sunlight have had its full merciless way with him? There was also his low blood sugar to consider.

Kelly continued east on 22 and out of Underbridge, along the north edge of Winterville, past the Stavros Brothers Quarry on his left and on into the northern outskirts of Deep Brook, the foothills of the Watchung

THE ANODIZING LINE

Mountains sloping always to the edge of the westbound lane on his left.

Beyond Deep Brook the Watchungs pulled back a bit, the bordering forest broke up, and businesses began to line the road, as they would close to continuously from here all the way to Newark, growing more and more dense until they extended into near-constant ribbons of commerce on either side and expanding into the median somewhere around Springfield. First a short strip mall on the right. Strike and Spare Bowling Alley with its circle-themed Fifties portico of suspended disks and concrete mushrooms on the left. His exit approached and he was changing lanes to make the turn when the heavens fractured into that jagged golden web, the towers of crystal and smoke appeared ahead, the bright burning lines from above wove into the bowling alley's odd façade and into the median and into the hood of his father's car and his hands and the steering wheel and everything out the windshield lost its depth and condensed into two dimensions. Right before he swerved off the road and struck a utility pole he realized how much it all reminded him of that cheap glass painting behind the counter in the pizza place down the street from his house, the one where a flickering hidden bulb created the illusion of a moving waterfall between poplar trees and partially toppled Roman pillars.

The next time Kelly opened his eyes was in Winterville Memorial, a needle dribbling morphine into his skinny wrist to blunt the waves of pain from fractured skull and ribs, the raging fire where his right leg ended just below the knee. He'd known the needle before but now he recognized it as a true and honest friend. Before long he came to know it as his only real friend, and the only thing that ever dulled the brightness of the shining lines and the inescapable city no one else could see with its wriggling questing fingers of smoke, dulled them just enough to hold them all at bay, enough to keep this old world from flattening into a frozen false front, a dead glass door he might any moment trip into and shatter and fall through for good.

THE GREEN EYE

The seven o'clock sign was our siren song. I read about sirens in the Ulysses book I got from Scholastic. My dad said that book was not the real *Odyssey* but I liked it all the same. I mainly liked the monsters. The cyclops and the squid monster. And the sirens.

The sign sounded so much louder from Cousin Milo's house that it had to be coming from his side of town, which was why I got the idea to look for its source. He lived on the south side, near the train tracks and all the factories.

I wanted to see the sign. When I was little my mom used to say, "Be home by the seven o'clock sign," and ever since I always had this picture in my mind of a steamwhistle stuck on a billboard. Mitch Pataki's brothers said the sign marked a curfew but all us kids stayed out past seven in the summer and we never saw any police. Or if we did, they just drove by without saying anything. Mitch's brothers were bullies and said a lot of crap to scare younger kids. One time Greg Pataki told me the police would come around when I was eighteen and give me a cardiac arrest. I already knew from books a cardiac arrest meant a heart attack so he couldn't fool me, but I played along to be safe. Those brothers were mean and Greg was the oldest and meanest. Even Mitch was mean. Arguing was only gonna get me an ass-kicking so I kept my mouth shut.

I didn't usually hang out with Milo, but my best friend, Danny Kirkpatrick, had gone camping with his family for I didn't know how long. Danny was one year older than me and went to school at Zarephath Pillar of Fire, but he lived right the other side of my block so we'd been best friends since he moved in my second grade year.

Milo was a year younger than me and not too cool, but he had his moments, like when he showed me the springfed pond behind the old dump and taught me how to catch snapper and painter turtles there using chicken legs on a fishing line. And I didn't know till that day at Milo's that my Uncle Jacob built an aboveground pool in their backyard. Danny had a pool once but it turned all green from algae and his parents got rid of it. It was gross. Like pea soup. It got that way because they never put chlorine in it. His mom said chlorine was something from the government. One time before they took the pool away we peeled off our swimsuits underwater and skinnydipped because you couldn't see anything below the surface anyway. It probably would've been cooler if we'd gotten Danny's sisters to come in with us but we only did it because they weren't home. I suppose it might've been weird for Danny, but I had a bad crush on his sister Samantha back then.

Me and Milo spent the afternoon swimming. He showed me how we could drop in from the branch of a big tulip tree that hung over the pool. Instead of *Cannonball!* we yelled nonsense stuff from old *MAD* comic books when we jumped. *Portzebie!* and *How's your mom, Ed?* I figured out later I was saying that first one wrong, but Milo didn't notice. I don't know how we could've said it the way it was really spelled anyway. *How's your mom, Ed?* came from *MAD*'s version of *Dragnet*. After a while we just abbreviated it down to *HYME*. I found those old comics in a box out of the closet in what used to be my Uncle Tony's room back before I was born. There were *MAD* comics and *MAD* magazines in there. The magazines had stories about Khrushchev and Castro. We studied American History in the Fifth Grade but I never heard of those guys, so back issues of *MAD* were kind of educational. I learned all about the Cuban Missile Crisis and stuff like that. My grandma kept close watch while I went through the box because there were old nudie mags mixed in there too. I wasn't allowed to touch those. She took them away before I could even get a good look at the covers.

After about two hours of climbing, jumping, and swimming, we toweled off and changed and rode our bikes on the Trails. The Trails wound through a stretch of woods about a block wide and a bunch of blocks long. I never figured out how many there were. The Trails started a block behind Main Street and ended all the way over by Milo's street. I rode them all the time, sometimes with Danny and sometimes with Milo and sometimes all alone. Sometimes we passed other kids and sometimes we saw people in the woods, like random creepy old guys or high school kids making out.

We were back close to Milo's street when we heard the seven o'clock sign. Out of nowhere I said we should try to find it and Milo was right away all gung ho to do it. He was pretty much up for anything. That was one good thing about him.

We popped out of the Trails on Dutch Avenue and followed that to Baekeland Boulevard, which was like the main street on the south side of town. I never rode my bike this far before, but I figured it wouldn't matter if my parents didn't know where I was.

Baekeland Boulevard was mostly factories, but I knew the sign wasn't there 'cause I'd driven up and down it a bunch of times with my parents. Mainly to go to ShopRite. Milo led us to the light between Krauszer's and the Baekeland Tavern and we crossed real careful.

Dutch Avenue crossed the train tracks right in front of us. The other side of the boulevard was empty. We stopped on the far corner to talk about the sign. Milo thought it had to be someplace along the tracks, and that made sense to me. Maybe it was meant for the trains and not the town.

We pedaled up to the crossing. I knew for a fact lots of people died right there. Sometimes the crossing arms didn't come down in time. Also the Middlebrook Spooklights were supposed to be out here somewhere. I read in our local paper, the *Courier News*—which the grownups all called the *Curious News*—about a team of investigators who camped out along the tracks. They saw the Spooklights their very first night and all their sensors went wild. They had Geiger counters and energy detectors and all kinds of stuff and everything pegged out, but the Spooklights didn't show in any of their photos.

The older kids said the Spooklights were supposed to be the ghost of the Hookerman, an old time railroad worker who lost his hand under the train and got it replaced with a hook. I never understood why his ghost would haunt the tracks if he only lost his hand there and didn't die, but I heard the story from Mitch's brother Steve so I didn't ask questions 'cause I didn't want to get beat up.

A narrow path ran through the cinders right on our side of the railroad ties. I let Milo take the lead because it seemed like he'd been here before and knew where to go. Maybe he already knew where to find the sign.

Of course it only took about five minutes before we heard the whistle of a train coming and the *ding ding ding* of the crossing arms behind us. The path was so close to the ends of the ties that I knew we were gonna get hit if we stayed where we were. I wondered for a second if we would turn into spooklights ourselves if we got killed then Milo skidded off the track, slid into the ditch down below and went over, stopping short of the cattails and the water. When he hit he said "Ow!" not "HYME!" which would've been cooler. I fast-walked my bike his direction, hitching it left to right, and got about five feet away from him before the train went roaring by and I stumbled and fell and scraped my right hand's knuckles on the cinders. When I looked at Milo he was bent over, grunting and tugging at some kind of rusty lump stuck in the ground. After a major effort he held it up, and I recognized it right before he said out loud what it was. A cannonball. Revolutionary War, I supposed, since the Civil War never came this far north. I was pretty sure about that. At least they taught us that much in history class.

I envied Milo's find at once—and not for the first time. Several years back our parents took us walking along MacArthur Brook to the bridge, and Milo found this flat rock striped with bright green dried algae. It seemed to me the most perfect thing I'd ever seen. I tried everything I knew to convince Milo to hand it over to me. I told first him then his parents the algae would let out poisonous spores in the night but no one was buying my bullshit. When they finally did give me the rock on my birthday that fall I felt ashamed about my lie. I still kept the rock though.

I had to say Milo had an eye for finding things. And even a rusty and pitted cannonball was way cooler than any rock. "Is that what I think it is?" I asked.

"I think so. I hit it with my elbow when I fell. Crazy, huh?"

I nodded, almost in awe. Milo duckwalked his bike back to the track, the cannonball cradled in the crook of his left arm. "You think this might be the one that shot off the Hookerman's hand?"

"Wowzers. I dunno. Could be I guess. Are you sure you should take it then? What if it's haunted? I'll carry it for you if you want."

Milo didn't answer. He only rode on, wobbling along one-handed with his prize. I was envious and afraid all at the same time. I figured we had to be halfway to the back of ShopRite by now, and it was starting to get dark. If the sign was not the curfew, the streetlights coming on had to be, which meant my parents would be pissed if I didn't come home soon. We'd come all this way though, and finding the cannonball had to be some kind of sign itself. I figured if I told my folks I was at Cousin Milo's they might let me slide without a spanking.

I stopped and looked back the way we came. I could barely see the crossing far behind us. We couldn't take a shortcut because chain link fence ran alongside the tracks lower down, bordered by a marshy ditch choked with cattail reeds. On the other side was a junkyard, and the cars were stacked right up to the embankment. We were trapped along the right of way until the next crossing.

I turned back toward Milo. I meant to call him but I just froze with my mouth open. A great big ball of green light about four feet wide was floating in the air between him and me. Even though I couldn't see Milo through the glow I could tell he was facing away from it because I could see his feet and ankles and the bottoms of his bicycle tires underneath.

It was hazy around the edges and I thought I heard it crackle like static. Milo didn't move. The green light didn't move. I thought the Spooklights were supposed to go up and down the tracks. What else could this be if it wasn't a Spooklight? I counted by *Miss'ippis* and right at six *Miss'ippis* the light shot straight at Milo. When it hit he disappeared and his bike disappeared and the light spun toward me until I saw it was something like a giant eyeball, with the round part in the middle and the darker spot in the center. It just stared at me. It didn't do anything, but I couldn't move.

Right then a man's voice started yelling out of the junkyard across the tracks on my left, "Hey you kids, stop right there! You're trespassing! You're gonna get a whipping!" Then the light disappeared too. Poof, just like that. But the man kept on yelling, and why was he saying "kids" when I was the only kid there?

I pictured him running out from between two piles of wrecked cars, an old man in grimy blue coveralls, looking pissed off and carrying a cane that he swung in the air every few steps. His voice came again, this time from closer and on my right but I still couldn't see anyone, "Dammit you kids, stop right there!" Meanwhile Milo was already gone, gone, gone, so I turned my bike around and pedaled the hell out of there, listening to the unseen junkman yelling for me to stop and picturing him right on my tail. Once I got to the Dutch Avenue intersection I crossed Baekeland on the red without even looking and didn't once hit the brakes till I made it all the way home.

It was dark when I got back and my parents were all pissed off waiting for me. I told them I was with Milo all day so my mom called Aunt Marlo. Aunt Marlo was her sister. I heard my mom say, "Uh-huh, uh-huh," a few times then she hung up and I thought I was gonna have to explain what happened to Milo, but she looked at me all hard and said, "Milo's been in bed with hay fever since last Tuesday. Aunt Marlo says she hasn't seen you all summer and Milo hasn't been outside since he took sick."

I had nothing to say back so I got grounded for a week. I never saw Milo again. Turns out he didn't have hay fever. He had brain cancer. He died at the end of August. "Passed away," was how my mom said it. "Cousin Milo just passed away…" He was the first person I knew who died.

That following October was my twelfth birthday. Uncle Jacob didn't show up for my party but Aunt Marlo came. She brought me a square present wrapped all neat in metallic green and silver paper with a green bow. The box was so heavy I knew what it was before I opened it. I didn't wanna open it but everyone was watching so I made a big show of acting first surprised then happy when I looked inside even though I was freaking out. "He wanted you to have it," Aunt Marlo said. "He told us very specifically just a few days before he died."

Aunt Marlo said the word *died* like it was no problem. I looked at my mom and her face had that sucked lemon expression.

This happened almost two years ago but I've still got that cannonball sitting on top of a stack of *MAD* magazines in my closet. I haven't touched the magazines since I stuck it there. I'm trying to find a way to get rid of it without taking it back to the tracks. I think the best thing maybe is to throw it off the bridge at the end of Tommy Crocker Park, if I can only get someone to go all the way out there with me. Danny moved to Connecticut so I'm pretty much on my own now. I hang around with this one bunch of guys sometimes, but we're not really friends. Whatever I do I think I'm gonna have to do it alone.

A Note on the Above

This is the first time I have written any kind of "story note" to accompany my work. I really despise the whole "Notes on the Waste Land" syndrome, as I do most of Eliot, but this tale felt different to me somehow. I have never made it a secret that most of my stories employ real settings and often contain a significant amount of autobiographical material, and "The Green Eye" is no exception. Like several of my other stories, including "The Bad Outer Space," "The Croaker," "alligators," and "Do You Like to Look at Monsters," "The Green Eye" is set in Middlebrook, a fictional version of my New Jersey hometown, Middleton Township in Middleton County.

Both the Trails and the Tracks were real, and though the former were converted into condos in the '90s, my cousin Niles really did find a cannonball along the latter one day. He still has it. Niles was actually pretty cool though, and we hung out far more than the story implies. Pretty much all of the story is true except the protagonist's negative attitude toward his cousin, the part about the green ball of light, and the events of the denouement. He really did find a cannonball along the Tracks, but we never found the seven o'clock sign.

Jack Spicer's explanation of poetic alchemy in *After Lorca* has stuck with me since the '80s: "...every place and every time has a real object to *correspond* with your real object—that lemon may become this lemon, or it may become this piece of seaweed, or this particular color of gray in this ocean." The events of "The Green Eye" *correspond* with actual experiences, and it is those lemons, that particular color of gray, that I want to share here. I hope a comparison might offer readers some insight into my creative process, particularly in relationship to the role of place in Weird Fiction.

Consider how much Laird Barron has acknowledged the importance of the Pacific Northwest's ancient forests, Alaska, and upstate New York on his work, Jeff VanderMeer's open admission that Area X is largely based on the St. Mark's National Wildlife Refuge where he frequently hikes (or hiked), or the essential role of New England in the stories of Daniel Mills and Matthew M. Bartlett. Most important of all for me was T.E.D. Klein's novella

"The Events at Poroth Farm," which showed me how my home state could provide a perfect setting for The Weird. Klein's story is set less than half an hour from my childhood home, and it even mentions Pillar of Fire, which my friend Dennis/Daniel really did attend.

The events that inspired the more Fortean portion of "The Green Eye" actually happened in the winter—the winter after Niles found the cannonball if I remember rightly.

That part of the story had nothing to do with Niles, however. I chose him and his cannonball because I wanted to focus the narrative on just two characters. I originally envisioned "The Green Eye" as a flash piece. I suppose for me <3,000 words *is* flash. Even so it came out short enough I felt it could support this addition, and as the cannonball story also conveniently involved a junkyard, I concluded I could translate the events along that axis, from the south side of my hometown to the north, condensing a messy brace of histories into a single tale.

The events of that strange day center around a kid named Reggie Wombleton. Back in Sixth Grade, Reggie's role in my life oscillated between fair-weather friend and outright nemesis. We were both of us cutups, but somehow his humor always registered successfully with our classmates while mine fell mostly flat. That bucktoothed fucker was a fast talker, I have to give him that. I think his superior popularity had also to do with his moderate skill at some sport or other, most likely baseball, whereas I lacked any such proficiency. As a rival he always proved the victor, but if I accepted a slightly subservient social role I could fold myself into his entourage for a time.

Reggie and I shared a common interest in *MAD* magazine, which was my particular obsession from the Fifth Grade as far as my sophomore year at Middleton High. Whenever I managed to save a few dollars in those days I begged my parents to take me to Englishtown or Packard's Farmers' Market in Sourland Hills to search for more of the vintage issues with the tiny Grecian figures running through the letters of the masthead on their covers. I remember how agonizing it was for me when I had to choose one or two copies from the available smorgasbord because that was all I could afford, and the struggle to savor my new acquisitions slowly when I got home, let alone not to read them cover to cover on the ride back.

Reggie owned three whole stacks of vintage *MAD*s, going back as far as

1957, and he was always trying to sell them to me. Of course there was a catch. None of his copies had any covers. I don't remember why. I guess he just got them that way. He only wanted two dollars each, but I held back because I was thinking about the beautiful covers I'd seen on copies of old *MAD*s at the flea markets, most of all my holy grail, the December 1958 issue by Frank Kelly Freas depicting Alfred E. Neuman as a ridiculously in-effective scarecrow surrounded by birds and small mammals, even a gorilla and a giraffe and other more mysterious creatures shambling out of a yellow haze in the background. I never found a copy of that one priced within my reach.

What I can recall is the Friday after school let out for Christmas vacation our Sixth Grade year, Reggie's whole gang gathered in his basement and we decided to make a junkyard run. There was Reggie, Jim Sikorsky, Mike Hitchens, Jimmy Long, Carmella Guillermo the tomboy, and three guys from Starlit Drive, which was kind of the snazzier side of town. Of those last three I only remember Alex Lothrop. I was friends with Lothrop for a while way back in Second Grade, but he turned out to be kind of like Mitch, a bully with a bunch of mean older brothers. Carmella had short black hair and freckles and I kind of sort of almost had a crush on her a couple times, not that she ever said a word to me.

Middleton is sandwiched between the railroad on the south side of town and Route 22 and Dark Brook on the north. Reggie's house was right up next to the brook so you could look out his sliding glass doors in the back and see a neat little lawn with a few trees and step stones and the brook right beyond. I wondered if his parents had to lay out sandbags during the floods. Someday I need to write about the great Middleton floods of the '70s and all the freaky stuff I saw back then. Maybe I'll even write about the Door to the River...

The way I recall it, I went over to Reggie's after school that day to make an offer on some of his messed up *MAD*s, only to find the whole crowd hang-ing out downstairs. I don't remember for sure who suggested the junkyard run, but I think it was Mike Hitchens. I do know I was all gung ho on the idea myself. My other fixation from that time was vintage cars, and I had this idea I could score a DeSoto hood ornament, which if you got the right year and model was a naked lady with her boobs poking out. So okay, I had three obsessions then.

My only hesitation was that I would miss the *Hilarious House of Frightenstein*, this freaky haunted house show that used to come on at six o'clock every evening. I think the show came from Canada or something. Vincent Price did the intro, but a guy named Billy Van played almost every other part. He was always talking about this three-toed sloth that you never saw on the show, but it sounded scary so every episode I was hoping it would finally show up. I was really into both *Frightenstein* and *Land of the Lost* around that time. I'm counting those two shows as a single obsession. So *MAD*, old cars, and monster shows, one, two, three... And naked ladies. Four.

Once we backtracked from Reggie's to the bridge, crossed it and headed west, the gap between the brook and the highway got wider until we couldn't see either one or even hear the traffic on the highway. Most of this area was woods but we knew from older kids there were at least two junkyards out here somewhere. We'd all seen the plunder of classic car parts they brought back.

Reggie and Alex seemed to know where they were going so they led the way on our odd little odyssey. The dead winter woods made me think of a painting of the Jersey Devil I'd seen in a library book, but I was pretty sure from the same book the Jersey Devil never came this far north. The woods were creepy enough on their own though, and the sun was already so low we could barely see it through the trees.

After a while we came out on this big frozen pond, about a hundred feet across and all covered with grayish-greenish ice. The pond made me think even more of that Jersey Devil painting because in the painting the Jersey Devil is coming toward you over some kind of swamp or pond. All the guys ran right out across it and started sliding around. No one had ice skates but the ice was so slippery sneakers and shoes seemed to work just as well. Someone found a flat rock and they started playing a kind of soccer-hockey using the rock for a puck and hitting it with sticks and their feet. I stayed on the side because who knew how thick the ice was, and also because I didn't know how to play hockey. Even Carmella was playing.

I was kind of mad because I knew this delay meant I'd no way make it home in time for *Frightenstein*. Up until then I still had hopes. I noticed Hitchens wasn't playing either. Instead he was hunched right out on the center of the ice and hitting it with the hammer he brought along while everyone else laughed and slid around him. I walked around close as I could get to where he was and saw white cracks spreading out from his impacts. I called out "Hey Mike, what are you doing?" No one else seemed to hear me or notice what Mike was up to. It was like they were all having too much fun or couldn't see him or something.

At first he ignored me but after I said it again and added "Hey man, that looks dangerous," he turned and said, "Shut up you little *femme*, before I smash your head in." And he waved his hammer in my direction. I remember he had these bright green eyes. They were like the only thing alive in his entire face. He was the only kid I knew with eyes that color.

I shut up. I didn't really know Mike too well but I didn't like him. He was Reggie's friend, or maybe Jim's. He sure wasn't mine. I saw him in the hallways sometimes but we never talked. He always looked mean, not like a bully exactly but like he was angry about something. Knowing what happened with him later, that's easier to understand.

Mike kept on pounding on the ice, and I could see a web of fracture lines spreading through the happy sliding crew. I thought about what would happen if the ice shattered—would Mike be the first to go under? He was acting like he didn't care. Would the ice come apart in gigantic pie-slice shards, upending everyone toward where Mike went under? I knew I couldn't rescue everyone. Or anyone really. I was not a good swimmer and I did not like the cold.

Before that could happen Alex rounded everyone up, reminded them it was getting late and we had a ways to go. I was surprised when no one complained, not even Mike. We all followed Alex west through the woods. Somehow he was our leader now and no one questioned his decisions, not even Reggie.

Maybe Alex was a good guide or maybe he knew we were so close it didn't matter because the junkyard suddenly appeared right in front of us, its wrecked, flattened cars piled in towers nine to ten high. It looked dangerous and nothing like the fun junkyard in *Fat Albert*.

"Watch out for the junkyard dog and the junkman," Alex said. "They might be hiding out here anywhere."

No one said anything about a dog before. I hoped it wasn't a German Shepherd. The lady who moved in next to my best friend Dennis had like half a dozen of those and sometimes they got loose in the street. They scared the crap out of me. I had this *Time Life* book about the ocean with a two-page picture spread of sharks in a feeding frenzy, and I thought those German Shepherds might attack like that. I could picture the dogs running around with someone's guts in their mouths like the sharks, and I knew that someone was probably gonna be me.

Before I could ask about the dog everyone scattered. I got left with Jimmy Long, who was one guy I was at least kind of friendly with. And Jimmy had a crowbar, which was cool because I hadn't brought any tools.

"I really just came to break stuff," Jimmy said. "Headlights and windshields, you know? What about you?"

"I'm looking for a DeSoto hood ornament." I hesitated then added, "The kind with a lady on it."

"Hey, cool. Maybe I can help you then, okay?"

"Sure!" I realized I had gotten lucky, considering I had come emptyhanded and he had the crowbar. I wondered if he would try to keep the hood ornament if we found one. Maybe we would find two, one for each of us. Maybe the place was full of DeSotos.

"Let's go around inside. The cars aren't piled as high there."

"You've been here before?"

"Just once, with Alex. We were having fun till the dog came out and chased us away. Watch out for that dog."

I wanted to ask Jimmy more about the dog but he took off around the north end of the outer car wall and I followed. Inside, the cars were stacked in lower mounds, some only two-three wrecks high and easier to climb. But we didn't see any of the other kids. That seemed strange. I imagined them all attempting to climb the high outer walls, and I pictured Mike trying to knock one of those towers down while other guys were still climbing it. What was the deal with him? There was something majorly wrong with that guy.

This part of the junkyard was like being inside a small stadium of crushed-up cars. I looked over my shoulder and listened for the dog or its owner but I neither heard anything nor noticed any motion. Jimmy led on, deeper into the rusty arena, and I stuck close behind my only human connection.

Frozen puddles covered much of the ground, which made me glad we came here in the winter. In the summer it was probably a swampy mess. Clumps of dead weeds, some shoulder high, stood between the puddles. I looked for dog prints or human footprints but saw none.

Jimmy tapped with his crowbar at the hoods of cars we passed, which made me uncomfortable. I was scared the noise might draw one or both of the junkyard's guardians. The wrecks were big old cars like in black and white movies, the kind I hardly ever saw on the road anymore. I admitted to myself I didn't know those old makes and models half as well as I thought I did. Of course they were crumpled and rusted and wrecked, but they were also bulky enough I should've recognized their shapes.

By the time we got to the kind of U in the center I was trying to keep one eye on Jimmy and the other turned back toward where I figured that dog might come from which meant I was hardly looking at the cars. That's why Jimmy caught me by surprise when he stopped and said, "Isn't that a DeSoto right there?"

I looked up and saw a black DeSoto piled on top of a half-crushed blue Packard. The DeSoto's proud prow extended toward us intact, crowned by the very nude aerodynamic Valkyrie of my quest, arms bent backward, long hair streaming behind, proud metal bosom thrust out for all time.

"Heck yeah! Thanks man!"

"Sure, no problem. Let's go get it then!"

Jimmy was already scrabbling onto the Packard's hood and groping at the DeSoto. I followed from the other side, hoping not to show any hesitation in my commitment to my goal. In a moment we faced each other across the DeSoto's hood, my naked prize our midway point.

As soon as Jimmy started working to gain purchase with his crowbar's end beneath the bare angel's base I saw her close enough to recognize that unlike the immaculate examples I knew from vintage car pictures in library books and the few I'd seen at car shows, this goddess was scarred with metal leprosy, her chrome epidermis pocked with dozens of little scars as if she suffered from measles or chickenpox. I made some comment to Jimmy regarding her damaged state and he replied, "Do you want her or not? You ain't gonna find a better one out here, not today I don't think. Let's get this one."

I told myself I could repair the damage somehow, perhaps with a little sandpaper and a simple coat of chrome spray paint. I pictured myself running my thumb across her bust once I'd smoothed it out again. Somehow or other she would be all right. And she would be mine.

Chrome creaked and paint flaked as Jimmy pried the woman loose. Soon he had her back end free. The flying lady was part of a solid strip of metal extending at least two feet back down the center of the hood. "Help me now. Get hold of it and pull up with both hands." I complied, wincing at the roughness of the rusty pits that marred her perfection even as I ran my fingers across the swell of her breasts. Between his prying and my pulling she came loose in my hands. "Bammo!" said Jimmy, and I stood there, holding the unexpectedly heavy chromium bow with a naked pockmarked lady riding its forward end.

Right that moment I heard like the loudest barking I ever heard, coming from the open span of the U. Jimmy shouted, "Run!" and we both dropped to the ground, he holding his crowbar, me with my infected prize. I looked over my shoulder but as loud and angry as the barking sounded I couldn't see the dog. When I turned back I spotted Jimmy darting through a gap between the towering stacks I hadn't seen before. I followed without a second thought.

When I came out on the other side Jimmy was nowhere in sight. But Mike Hitchens was there, and he was not alone. An old man in blue coveralls and a greasy brown coat was standing about ten feet in front of him and not much farther from me. They were facing each other and the old man was reaching out toward Mike. I remember thinking the man looked wrong somehow, like his arms and fingers were way too long for a normal person. You can say I was just scared but I remember exactly what I saw. It was the second strangest thing I've ever seen. I'm still not ready to write about the first. Or the third.

I shouted "Run Mike, the dog is coming!" without thinking, and they both turned toward me. Mike looked right at me with this really dirty look and I remember seeing the last little low bit of sun spark off one of his creepy green eyes. The left one. The light was coming straight through the trees at eye-level by then. Then he jerked up his hammer like he was gonna hit me and yelled "Get outta here!" I backed up a step and he started running at me waving the hammer so I spun around and took off.

I ran between the trees the way we all came. At least the way I thought we came. Suddenly I wasn't so sure. Brittle brown sticker bushes blocked the path in some places and I had to dodge around them. Every time I took a detour I imagined Mike was getting closer with his hammer. I felt like they were all chasing me, not just Mike but the old man too with his wiggly weird Skeezicks arms—the old man and the dog I never saw and maybe even the Jersey Devil himself—but I couldn't hear anyone behind me which made it even scarier, like one of them might already be in front of me just waiting for me to run right into him—or *it*.

For a long time I was afraid to turn around and check because that would cost me time or even make me fall but when I finally looked I didn't see anyone and when I turned back around I almost ran into Reggie and Sikorsky. I didn't mention it before but Sikorsky was kind of like Reggie's sidekick. He asked me, "Did you get chased by the dog too?" It was probably the only thing he ever said to me where he wasn't obviously jerky and snide. Even when I was getting along okay with Reggie, Sikorsky always gave me attitude. In fact he gave me more at those times.

I took another look behind me, saw no Mike, no man, no dog, no Jersey Devil. I know I was panting by then and probably hunched with my hands on my knees. I used to get a bad stitch in my side whenever I ran back in those days. "Yeah," I answered. "You guys too?"

"That damn dog can really run, huh?" said Reggie.

I agreed, even though I had only heard it. Then Alex and his two friends found us, like they just popped up out of nowhere. The dialogue about the dog got repeated. Jimmy Long and Carmella came up before it was done. They both kept laughing and looking at each other. I couldn't tell why.

I was still holding the hood ornament, and I noticed no one else carried any car parts. I kept it hanging kind of low by my side 'cause I was embarrassed about its damaged condition, but no one asked about it. Alex said, "Let's get outta here, it's getting dark." Reggie agreed and everyone started following them back through the woods. We were all there except Mike. He was still missing. I was gonna say something but no one else seemed to care or notice so I just hurried up and tried to get in the middle of the line. No way I wanted to be at the back where something could get me. When we passed the pond again I could still see the milky cracks Mike's hammer made, even in the fading daylight.

It was totally dark by the time we made it back to Reggie's house where we all left our bikes. Right when I got home I heard the seven o'clock sign so I knew I was way late. My folks grounded me for a full week soon as I came in the door. My mom kept telling me how long the streetlights had been on, how worried they'd been about me, asking why didn't I call from Reggie's house to say I'd be late.

I don't remember ever hanging out with any of those guys again, but I must've because sometime I bought a bunch of Reggie's messed up *MAD*s. They're still in my mom's basement back at the old house in Jersey. I remember some had bits by Bob and Ray and Orson Bean inside. Bob and Ray were these old time radio guys who were back on WOR as part of the nostalgia craze in those days. WOR also ran *Mystery Theater* with E.G. Marshall. I outgrew *Frightenstein* and *Land of the Lost* soon after but I listened to *Mystery Theater* till it went off the air a couple years later.

One issue of *MAD* even had a Jean Shepherd story. He was another guy I listened to on WOR. I didn't really get his piece in *MAD*. From the title it sounded like a monster story but it wasn't at all. It was nothing like his shows on the radio either. I was kind of disappointed with that one.

I stashed the DeSoto ornament in my closet on top of my back issues of *MAD*, the stack without covers I got from Reggie I don't remember when. The corroded lady was such a letdown. I tried to think of ways to fix her but I was afraid I would only make her worse. I never wanted to look at her again.

I was worried about what Mike Hitchens might do to me when we went back to school, but he wasn't there. It took a while to get the whole story but I found out he murdered his dad. With a hammer. The way I heard it was they didn't try him as an adult because the story came out his father had molested him. Not just once but a whole bunch of times. Whether they stuck Mike in reform school or shipped him off to live with relatives I never heard. I just know I never saw him again after that. I felt glad he was gone but at the same time I felt bad for feeling that way, if that makes any sense. Even now I only admit this with hesitation.

That's pretty much it. I never went back to that junkyard. I don't think it's even there anymore. Reggie moved to Virginia at the end of Eighth Grade. Alex turned into a total dickhead and I kept away from him and his brothers the best I could. I'm not sure what happened to Carmella or Jimmy Long but I don't recall either one going to school at MHS. Carmella was way smart too, so I think I would remember her if I had classes with her in high school. Back in Fifth and Sixth Grade she always finished her timed math sheets ahead of me. Out of all of them I can only find Facebook profiles for Wombleton and Sikorsky. We have seventeen and thirteen mutual friends respectively, but I have never sent "friend" requests to either of them and have no plans to. The hell with Wombleton, and I never liked Sikorsky.

I hope my readers will find this digression but a brief one. Please forgive me if I've gone astray. I pledge by the sign of the three-toed sloth it's a one-time thing.

THE ALWAYS RISING
OF THE NIGHT

PROLOGUE

Thirty thousand feet over Detroit she thought of the abalone, cool in its slipcase on the watery rock, how she had gripped it but her grip had slipped as she sought to prise it from its muscular hold. She had wanted that beautiful big opalescent shell for herself, had an idea she could make jewelry from it, a craft at which she had long felt she'd excel but had yet to attempt. She envisioned an iridescent pendant on a necklace of shimmering discs, complementing her shoulders and the finely-formed hollow of her neck. A blade might have helped loosen the creature but she had declined both knife and weight-belt at the dive shop, even while Greg had accepted them, but where was Greg now? He had paddled on without her, without so much as a by-your-leave, to somewhere on the other side of some rock. He was always taking off without her. Once they were married she'd have to put a stop to that. Now Deidre found herself alone and so buoyant she had to keep kicking just to maintain her grip on the mollusk. Neither could she maneuver her legs low enough to leverage against the boulders or the bottom sand. Simply holding herself beneath the surface between snorkel-breaths required a tiring effort. Seaweeds waved all round her in the slow underwater flows while thirty years passed since she last saw the Pacific or any part of California. Four years since she last saw Greg alive. While the kelp rippled in her memory Deidre drifted into sleep, buoyed by the drone and vibration of the plane.

***

Brigit steered the boat between the dead treetops that rose above the surface of the lake, the *bbbzzzhhhhhh* of the motor varying faintly in pitch as she veered left, left, left, right, left to dodge dead standing trees above and below the surface. Despite the obstacles, she made every effort to stick to her search grid, constantly consulting her GPS and her laminated map with its division of annotated squares. Duncan and Braniff, the two undergrads she'd brought along—for balance and ballast more than anything else—sat quietly forward. To be sure, they represented the least annoying of their lot, and she suspected they were just as happy as her to escape from the increasingly chaotic scene at camp.

Duncan opened his mouth as if to speak…then pursed his lips. Both boys had received her withering looks more than once, and not just on this excursion. Brigit silently noted his reticence and thought, at least I've got that one trained. Maybe both of them. She could usually rely on her height and her red hair, both gifts from her late father, for a certain amount of effortless intimidation of the average male. She'd already heard some of the Brazilian program staff referring to her as *Valquíria*, which required no Portuguese to comprehend. Without making eye contact she casually ran her fingers up the sheathed machete hanging from her belt. Let that add a subtle reinforcement to their training.

Suddenly Duncan did speak, shouting, pointing, —Look, over there! Is that one?

He shouted so loud that even over the motor, Brigit feared he'd scare *it* off if *it* actually turned out to be anything. She shushed him as she followed the direction of his finger. What she saw vindicated him: fifty to sixty meters toward the nearest "island" sleek ripples of some swimming thing disturbed the surface, too large to be anything other than Pteronura brasiliensis. A giant river otter. Too large in fact to be anything other than a *group* of giant river otters swimming together, as giant river otters were wont to do. She eased off the throttle and set the choke to stop the engine, then raised her binoculars.

The little islands in Lake Balbina had been hilltops before the dam. Now each offered its own lush micro-habitat, almost normal though so tiny and isolate and with way too many trees growing right down to and past the waterline, where the dead drowned trees took over, their bare remaining canopy branches rising as much as twenty meters above the current surface.

The hills had become ecological as well as literal islands, surrounded by submerged trees. Lots of submerged trees. All dead. Islands of tropical life in a half-submerged cemetery of trees.

Not just dead trees though. The power plant killed all the wildlife. Beneath the reservoir of water a vast sunken second reservoir of decaying plant and animal matter gave off prodigious amounts of methane. The lake immediately became anoxic. Fish couldn't live in it. Without fish, larger animals could not thrive.

Lake Balbina was a shitshow. A trainwreck. An ecological abomination, a grossly under-generating hydroelectric project emitting enough methane to make its own measurable impact on global warming.

Yet recently Brigit's advisor had received reports from reliable colleagues of giant river otter sightings in Lake Balbina. She encouraged Brigit to make the trip, tapped connections, pulled strings, made arrangements. And so Brigit found herself out on this weird dead lake with its lonesome carbuncles of life. And here at last on this mad pursuit she had found her otters. And perhaps her dissertation topic. At last.

She steered the boat to glide silently on the last bit of its dwindling momentum toward the glistening dark backs as they approached the nearest islet. The dead treetops grew thicker around them. —Oars out and eyes out, she ordered the boys. Watch for underwater trees.

They'd gotten within about thirty meters from the little island when the first otter reached it and began to climb on shore with its distinctive side-to-side gait.

Except this otter was all wrong. For a moment Brigit could not process what she saw. The creature's back was *too* sleek, the creature itself far too long. With two meters on shore, the full length of the longest otter, it had barely exposed its body beyond its forelegs. This was not several large animals, but one huge one. She knew the boys saw at least some of what she did, the size alone an impossibility. They stared at her together, deferring to her expertise and desperate for her to share it all at once as their own comprehension shattered. Finally Braniff broke his silence. —Is that a crocodile?

—Quiet, Braniff. Calmly, but Brigit did not feel calm. She too had noted the elongated jaw, but with the binoculars she could also see the vertical yellow stripes on the glistening hairless and scaleless skin.

Since her preteen years wandering the Maine woods, her fascination had been with the largest animals in every order, every phylum, every clade, every class. Pleistocene megafauna became her academic focus because she could study their recent presence, even their limited survivals. But her knowledge ran deeper, including species long extinct. Now old learnings bubbled up all at once and images clicked. She *knew*. —That's no otter. And it's not a crocodile.

The boys stared at her, not daring to speak further but imploring her for answers with silent eyes. A name was in her mind. She did not speak it. Dared not speak it. Just thinking it felt dangerous. Prionosuchus.

—It looks like a salamander. A species that lived here two hundred million...

As she spoke, the creature hauled the full six meters of its impossible length on land, and now they were all close enough to see that for which even she had no answers: the iridescent sheen off the ridges of its ribs, its hindlegs, its tail, was no epidermal pattern, but the gleam of metal, seamlessly integrated into wet and leathery flesh. A line of embedded emerald green lights glowed along its tail, pulsing in some pattern either utterly random or indecipherably complex. The little lanterns put Brigit in mind of the running lights on a semitruck changing lanes at night on the interstate, or even some kind of aircraft.

Her improbable grail had diverged into the incomprehensible. She felt disappointment and elation simultaneously, both at levels beyond all her previous experience. She felt exhilarated and frightened and confused altogether but somehow she knew—*she knew*—she had found her moment. And she would rise to it.

—Okay boys, listen up. I don't know exactly *what* the hell that is, but we are damn sure going to get some photos of it. So show me how quietly you can paddle us in there. Carefully she extracted the camera from her pack, all the while without taking her eyes off the prize.

***

Columns and cordons all chlorophyll-green climb skyward, wide eyeless flyers spiraling round pylons too high for birds, though actual birds still flock at less vertiginous heights. The flyers with their many wings are green. The high floaters too are green. Everything at this height is green, even to some degree the sky itself and the strange cables that fade up into it, thinning to invisibility. The land below is green, and the high towers extend green in staggered arrays, the farthest hidden from any vantage by those in the middle distance. Verdant cables or vines connect some but not all. The steaming atmosphere and the vibrant particles that everywhere buzz, visible as wisps and clouds of varying density, fuzz the view from any angle.

Meanwhile each leaf and every stem, every single green surface, collaborates to detect signals only sensible to the ensemble entire. The great expanse of green pylons reads the messages of immensities, information cast across almost impossible voids and unfathomed interstellar depths, not necessarily intended for reception here. Or anywhere. Deep beneath the towers a decentered collective compiles, decrypts, studies, considers. Occasionally even acts. One such moment of action has arrived. A quantum circuit closes, a molecular relay clicks into place, miniscule mechanisms mobilize, dispatching and directing infinitesimal robots and ribosomes. A new sequence of code arises, mitosis accelerates. Particles neither strictly cellular nor entirely mechanical coalesce in a fresh and uncategorizable construction. A response commences. Not without urgency. Someone embarks on a journey. A stranger will soon arrive.

***

The Locatrice Implacable has been angling her schlepper northeast around the base of a dark jagged mesa for the last eleven kilosecs, always with an eye toward encroachments of the vast sulfuric acid lake on her left, its sickly surface glinting orange and carmine beneath distant flickers of lightning to the north. She hopes whatever storm those far off flashes herald will stay...far off. Here and there inlets of the lake's irregular shoreline jab at the shadowed rise of the cliff face to her right. The slope ascends such that she can come no closer to the mesa, despite the uncomfortable proximity of the lake. With its full complement of seven legs the schlepper would be reliable up to 67 degrees of inclination, but she'd had to deploy the explosive bolts to detach and jettison two legs damaged in her initial crash. Nor was the slope her only problem: even here she had to skirt talus blocks rising over twice the schlepper's height. If the rockfall grew too thick, some inlet ran too deeply toward the heights, or some arroyo cut too steep, she'd have to abandon her vehicle and walk. Or climb. Without the vehicle's reserve oxygen. Even with it she has already traveled too far from the wreck of her ship to return on the remaining charge. And the matter of her pursuers remains—if they too survived after forcing her down several hundred kilometers south of her original destination. Her countermeasures had spiraled off into the gray and scarlet clouds but she had no way of knowing whether they'd succeeded or how well. She can no longer go back. Either she will find the prize she has so long sought, or she will die in the endeavor. She has faced equally constrained options before, and if she hasn't always conquered them, she has at least survived.

For several kilosecs she's kept an eye on a faint red glow creeping over the mesa. Now that glow appears brighter. Its diffuse rouge hue stains the undersides of the dense toxic cloudbellies hanging low overhead.

Suddenly she rounds a point of the outcrop and sees *it* for certain. At last. After nearly half a gigasec dedicated to her quest, the unmistakable rippling scarlet arc of what has to be the Rhel rises ahead, wavering through the haze with its own peculiar indeterminacy, as if the complex meshwork comprising its edges conspires to present the appearance of a surface of intricate angularities within its overall curvature. Tiny figures swarming over it add to this uncertainty, giving it the appearance of endless activity, an ongoing construction. The figures must be vehicles or craft of some sort—at this distance individual beings would not be visible. At least not individual beings of human size and proportions.

But what is that distance? The entire vision defies any application of perspective or scale. As she progresses round the scarp, and the plain beneath the seething ruby oculus reveals more of itself, she sees other figures. Again she thinks them beings at first, even people like herself perhaps, standing reverent as if in worship. Then they clarify in her sight as rounded metallic cones, brassy structures or rockets, each glowing crimson with the reflected gleam of the mother orb. Is the Rhel a city? A ship? She simply cannot judge the size of its dimly burning disc. Hanging there so, hovering just above the horizon, it seems like a planet or even a sun. As the Locatrice begins to calculate whether she can reach it on her available fuel, a missile shatters a towering boulder a dozen meters to her left, spraying fire across the schlepper and sending chunks of rock clattering against its side. Seconds later the first droplets of sulfuric rain spatter her screens.

***

The Cadre of 17⚹π Vast Quasi-Optical Observational Structures in the Horologium Supercluster had long been conducting suprachronological scrutiny of their nearest neighboring supercluster, an activity from which its members derived an experience akin to pleasure—if an awareness that wove its way over many megaparsecs so slowly that dozens of local organic intelligences evolved and perished before all the Cadre's members could share in the sensation could be described as pleasure. The unpredictable cycle of activity originating in the mega-void dipole of that peculiar other supercluster provided the primary emphasis of these ongoing observations: activity that suggested some turbulence operating in or from that locus, yet outside that portion of the space-time fabric observable even to the Cadre, detectable only through the faintest spectral shifts and gravitational pulsations and manifest via incredibly complex fractal patterns over almost an entire gigaparsec while somehow occurring simultaneously, branching from galaxy-width to infinitesimal. Only the Cadre of 17⚹π's immense temporal scope gave them the ability to recognize the supraluminal correlations. Some members had advanced the proposition that these threads did not dissipate at the Planck length but disappeared somehow beneath or behind it. Still others hazarded the audacious suggestion that the observed activity marked the point of collision between their neighbor and an entire other universe. The rather haughty member from the Abell 3128 Cluster harbored an especially strong attachment to this speculation.

As a corollary to these ideas and observations, the conversation turned from time to time to the possibility that similar activities might even now be occurring, had occurred in the past, or would occur at some unknown point yet to come here in their own supercluster. No other topic became so divisive for the Cadre's members. Some held that such events happening in their midst could not have escaped their notice, while others asserted that it was precisely the proximity of these processes that defied the scale of their focus. A parallel but less vociferous discussion, in which the members fell out along somewhat different lines, related to the question of whether the nearby activity would remain contained or might spread to their own supercluster. Might have spread already. The dialogue ebbed and flowed along these lines, shifting in intensity, but rarely in alignment. The members guarded their philosophical investments rather dearly.

—Ahhh, intoned the member in the Abell 3047 Cluster, there goes another. Might it not be the loveliest yet? The others agreed, with the inevitable exception of the usual grumbling holdouts.

***

Though the high cool light of night was shining bright enough for the tiger salamander to pick her way east, the smell of water alone was enough to guide her. The smell of water and the faintest scent of males. Ahead were the permanent stock ponds and the vernal pools that the cows stomped out anew each year. Rain had fallen recently, and fallen again. And a third time yet. Fairy shrimp had hatched in the pools and already grown to adulthood. Peeper frogs called like birds but unlike birds presented no threat. The ground remained damp, the moisture trapped close to the surface by the water-swollen hardpan of montmorillonite clay just beneath. She trundled ever onward with the same stiff-kneed gait that had served her kind since her first ancestors clambered onto land, arriving alongside the earliest colonists, the scorpions and hairy spiders and enormous nightmare millipedes, well before the endothermic interlopers arrived. The land was so much more crowded now. Though this had been the way for a very long time, she felt it as wrong.

An earthworm crawled across the damp surface, probably in search of higher and unsaturated ground in one of the many mima mounds scattered throughout the Xebíco Vernal Pools Reserve. The water table in the mounds did not rise so close to the surface. Most any other time she would have pounced on the worm and gulped it down, but she had only one goal this night, and hours to go before she slept. Yet reflex stilled her in the presence of prey, and in that frozen moment she felt another presence, a threatening one. She felt it first in the faintest tremor of padded feet, the click of a claw on a rock, then a glimpse of motion, followed by the musty odor of fur, the worst of all the interlopers, worse even than the birds. Direct in her path stood a coyote, winter-lean and hungry, the mangy ridge of its back and the shape of its head clearly delineated in the cool light from on high. The worm wriggled on but the salamander remained locked in her stance, one forefoot fixed in midair.

Then she felt the greater wrongness, familiar from at least one previous journey though forgotten till she experienced it now again. She had no frame of reference for this, despite a quarter billion years of ancestral memory, though she knew it as a wrongness nonetheless. Something swept over her, a feeling like the brush of root hairs across her back in her borrowed ground-squirrel burrow, though nothing actually touched her here. The sensation continued for several minutes, varying in intensity, depriving her of valuable time. Yet she knew to stay still.

Suddenly she saw the high bright light in the sky, which was not right, not now, not at night, and it shone on an unfamiliar scene of trees much too tall and flying things that were not birds. She distrusted any flying things larger than insects, and these looked very large. Then the high cool light returned, but now all vegetation had disappeared leaving only dry cracked ground and a lifeless display of lingering death throughout the landscape. She heard the coyote whine in fright. More scenes opened to her sight. Some with the high bright light, some with only night, some with a wide red glow for which she felt a special dislike. Sometimes she smelled males along with these visions but all of the places smelled wrong. Eventually the sensation left and the high cold light returned to its rightful place. She smelled water and males again. Good smells. Yet she kept still.

Once the sensation of wrongness and the strange sights had passed, she noted the absence of the coyote, though she had not sensed any of the vibrations that should have marked its departure. The loathsome predator had not *left*, but it was *gone* nonetheless: gone with the wrongness, with the wrong places. Although the water and the males still called her strongly, she remained motionless as the high night light moved twice its own width west before she set off again. Meanwhile the worm crawled on, forgotten and fortunate. For tonight.

BOSTON TO FRESNO, VIA DETROIT

—Stroopwafel? Stroopwafel?

Deidre woke to a flat foil square in her face, the package hanging from a woman's hand, the question dangling from the word's ending lilt.

She tilted her head to meet the eyes of the sprightly blue-uniformed flight attendant. Just looking at the energetic woman made her feel tired. Why did some people have to be so relentlessly upbeat? Deidre accepted the crisp packet, its wrapper crackling in her hand. The stew pattered on as if to some unheard beat, repeating her Dutch dactyl twice for Deidre's neighbors in 27 E and F before passing them one square apiece. They accepted their snacks and tore the wrappers open as the flight attendant pivoted to peddle her pastries toward the tail.

Deidre unfolded the gray plastic tray from the forward seatback and set her prize down to examine its heraldry, a topic she'd once studied in a continuing education class. Argent, with a tan gridded disk. Images of Holland in delft's darkened azure and white respectant: A windmill. Kissing kids. Legends: *Daelmans. CARAMEL.*

What then was a stroopwafel? Some kind of cookie or wafer she guessed. Something Dutch. A biscuit to the Brits. Yet if it bore a crest, did it not belong to her by right? She couldn't get past the stew's blithe manner though. *—Stroopwafel? Stroopwafel?* As if the woman had said it all her life, as if the word had formed in her mouth at birth. Deidre pondered whether she'd heard her say anything else on this flight. She thought not. Maybe the stew spoke a one-word tongue. A *hapax legomenon* language. Perhaps while Deidre napped, a virus crept through the plane, depriving all aboard of their vocabulary. As they began their descent into Fresno would the pilot simply intone *Stroopwafel stroopwafel. Stroopwafel, stroopwafel, stroopwafel…*as he steered them on a steep descent directly into the control tower? Ugh. These thoughts didn't help. Her life needed fewer off-kilter thoughts, fewer weird cookies, fewer waffles. Less waffling. More reliability. More sense. More *sleep*. She deserved better than her lot so far. She needed some peace. Deserved a break. Had earned a rest. She hoped she might find that rest at Brigit's apartment, despite the tasks that likely awaited her there, the grief and the pressures of dealing with her daughter's disappearance. She pushed the unopened snack to the edge of the tray and let her head settle back against the seat.

Only to have her attempt at rest interrupted again almost at once.

—Ladies and gentlemen, we have a loose kitty on board.

The words came from the front of the plane. Not from the pilot's cabin but from yet another flight attendant holding a microphone curling out from the cabin wall via a dull black cord. Deidre could just see the woman's head and topaz-clad shoulders over the seatbacks of the two dozen rows ahead of her, beside the crewcut cranium of one of the three armed soldiers on the flight.

—If everyone would just take a look under their seats, we would surely appreciate it. I'm sure we'll find Mister Kitty in no time.

A small man in a gray sweater hurried up the aisle, hunched in self-efface-ment and repeating —He's mine, I'm so sorry. He's mine, I know, I know... as he passed each row, peering beneath the seats, his sweeping inspection alternating left to right. He walked with his back bent almost parallel to the floor, reminding Deidre of an engraving she'd seen long ago, two hunched sycophants encountering each other from opposite directions and unable to pass as neither knew the other's status. She could not recall the artist. But the man had the aisle to himself.

The silent man in 27 F slid his window shade up and sun flooded in: the new sun, the California sun, pure, severe: no longer the tired and tree-filtered Atlantic sun she'd left behind in Maine, that secondhand sun flown in each morning from Europe. Deidre winced and squinched her eyes shut, and in the hazy new red half-light behind her eyelids she hunched to slide her shoulder bag half out from under the forward seat, stuffing her uneaten stroopwafel in the front pocket by feel.

The pilot turned on the fasten seatbelts sign. She no longer saw the cat-man and no further announcements came on the subject. Didn't they, the passengers, deserve some explanation, some denouement to this episode? And if the cat-man had come first from the back of the plane, why hadn't he returned to his seat by now? He could not have gotten past without her seeing him again, but then how had the cat accomplished this same maneuver in the first place, presumably in the opposite direction? Everyone already seemed to have forgotten the incident. The plane began its descent. How could a cat disappear on a plane, let alone a man? Shouldn't the soldiers show some concern about this? Not her problem, in the end. Not her circus, not her monkeys. Not her cat. Not her man. Not her soldiers. Not her stew.

XEBÍCO

Once Deidre retrieved her luggage, cleared federal customs, and secured her rental, the drive up the valley from Fresno to Xebíco only took about ninety minutes. If she hadn't had to pass through a military checkpoint just south of a town called Madera, it probably would have taken less than an hour. Brigit's landlord had provided good directions for once she hit town though, and Deidre found the apartment without any problem. She also found the apartment manager in her office—Robin(!)—and Robin(!), as promised, had the key. Robin(!) seemed very cheerful, though for no apparent reason. Robin(!) was blonde, bubbly, bubble-shaped. Chipper. Like Barbie's friend Skipper...

—If you need anything else just let me know! Anything for Brigit's mom! Deidre took care to lock the door once she got inside. The brief key exchange was all the Robin(!) she could handle for one day. People like that wore on her, dominating the conversation through brute force the way they did.

Deidre gave her daughter's digs a quick inspection. The front room remained locked, but kitchen, living room, and bedroom all revealed a similar state of disorder. Of disaster. Assorted houseplants dead in random pots, some still green but brittle and faded, some brown, some gray or black with mold or rot. A few of the succulents looked to be hanging on all right. Glasses and dishes in the sink and on the counter, some dried and crusty, others furred with flourishing microbiological colonies. Books and papers and clothes scattered over every level surface, along with soiled silverware and more dirty plates. All this she'd expected. She knew Brigit's ways from many battles, both at home and at their store. Compelling her daughter to complete chores had always been a challenge.

Deidre decided to take a nap first. She could start cleaning after.

On the bedroom dresser stood a single framed photo of Brigit and Greg. Deidre remembered taking this photo—it showed her daughter wearing the medal she'd won in the state science fair her sophomore year for a project on Megatherium dentition. The award had come with a laptop and a modest scholarship. If there were any photos that included Deidre, heaps of junk probably buried them.

She set the photo of her lost family facedown on the dresser for now, and after pushing a pile of dirty clothes from bed to floor, flopped onto the former.

***

Deidre woke in the dark, fully-dressed on the ruffled covers of her daughter's bed. The time zone shift had gotten the best of her. Back in Maine it would be well after midnight. Not quite 10:00 p.m. here, but she'd had a long flight and she still felt tired. She decided that cleaning and straightening could wait another day. The plants that still survived would survive another night. The dishes couldn't get much more disgusting. She kicked off her shoes, unhooked her bra, and slipping each arm in turn out her sleeves, tugged it loose and dropped it to the floor beside the bed. She decided not to get under the sheets until she changed them. She didn't want to think about what sort of goings-on those sheets might have experienced since the last time anyone had changed them. Clean linens only, please.

She remembered how her mother always said never to go to bed with dirty dishes in the sink, but these weren't her dishes, were they? She tuned out her mother's voice just as she so often had in the past, closed her eyes, and went back to sleep.

***

The next morning, Deidre decided that housecleaning could hold off a little further. Until the evening anyway. She had appointments to meet

311

with both Cynthia Bowles, her daughter's advisor, and Calliope Duquesne, the Graduate Dean of the University of California, Xebíco. Though Deidre had never met either woman in person, they had all exchanged multiple emails and she had spoken to each several times on the phone. She did not expect to learn anything new, and she did not. The local authorities in Brazil had no leads, and neither did the university. Everyone had made every effort and every effort had been made. Because her daughter had disappeared during fieldwork, and because the ecotourism program Brigit had joined up with had been her discretionary selection, possessing neither university affiliation nor official accreditation, UCX held no liability. *Of course* all appropriate and available resources remained at Deidre's disposal. Brigit had been a brilliant scholar. Deidre noted the past tense creeping into their descriptions, though officially so far her daughter was only listed as missing, not dead. Yes, they were all upset too. At least two of Brigit's lab mates had requested counseling. No, their names could not be shared. Because FERPA.

Of course if Deidre was planning to travel to Brazil... but she was not. The State Department had already told her everything she could find out for herself. They remained in touch with local authorities. If they learned anything new, they would contact her immediately. Or so they claimed. She did not have the money. She spoke no Portuguese. She did not even possess a current passport, and a new one took a year or more these days. The State Department reps she had spoken with repeatedly emphasized all these points. What remained unsaid but clearly insinuated was the strength of the relationship between Washington and the current regime in Brazil, with both nations founding members of the Global Anti-Terrorism Alliance. Whereas the former state of California and the University of California were not so favored. Not these days. In fact, travel to California might have made her ineligible for a passport altogether. That and the lack of a permanent address.

Deidre feared if she flew to South America she too might disappear. When she was growing up the local kids used to play badminton. The birdie often got stuck in a tree. They would throw their rackets up to knock it down and the lightweight rackets always got stuck too. Then their sneakers. Their sneakers got stuck. Trees ate everything. Maybe Brazil did too. She did not want to end up like the long-lost Keds her mother had refused to replace.

Or like her daughter. At the very least she might not find reentry into the U.S. as easy as leaving.

Did Deidre have a place to stay in Xebíco? Oh. How long did she plan to stay? Oh. Obligatory offers to help in any way, but no specific *ways* suggested. Bowles and Duquesne offered only…offers, no real help. No one wanted to be liable. Their offers were symbolic, like keys to the city or honorary diplomas, not keys that opened anything real or revealed any mysteries. No missing daughter, no missing cat. Only metaphorical stroop-waffels. She hadn't come for waffling. She had come for her daughter. Or at least to clean up after her daughter. Not metaphorically: literally. To set Brigit's affairs at rest. These meetings were just additional steps in that process. Formalities. She didn't expect her daughter back. Like Greg, Brigit had left her for good.

***

By the time Deidre returned from campus the sun hung low in the west. She scanned for Robin(!) before she stepped out of the car. She had stopped for some fish tacos on the way back so she wasn't hungry, and she still had half her meal in a standard white takeout container. She did not yet dare open her daughter's refrigerator, which she feared might be worse than the sink, so for the time being she left the Styrofoam container on the counter, shoving aside a short stack of crusty plates. A fork coated with what looked like dried egg fell to the floor, and she left it. Housecleaning and house-straightening could wait a bit longer yet. She'd had a long day and had earned a nap.

She woke around the same time as the previous night, but this time feeling clearheaded and energized. After a visit to the bathroom she decided she owed it to herself to sample the local nightlife, if this town had any. She deserved a little fun before she dealt with the literal mess Brigit had bequeathed her. *Messes.* She consulted her phone and found an unexpectedly short list of clubs for a city the size of Xebíco. Especially for a college town. One looked promising. *Le Parti Pris.* Downtown, hardly a mile away. She saddled up the rental and delegated navigation to her phone.

***

Inside, she found the club wood-paneled, roomy, recently remodeled. Surprisingly empty. Back in the '80s, in *her* undergrad days at Old Queens, Thursday was *the* party night. For precisely this reason almost no one took Friday classes, something the townies all knew and resented, making for occasional unpleasant encounters, especially with local cops. All that was years ago though, and on the opposite side of the country. And the drinking age had still been nineteen in New Jersey then. Here she saw just three seats taken at the bar, and only two tables occupied, one by a group of soldiers in their pale camouflage-patterned uniforms. New Prigmore bars would have been packed on a Thursday night, and not with soldiers, but that was another time, another place. Alas.

Deidre claimed a barstool, as far as she could get from the soldiers, and the bartender arrived at once, her smile warm and appearing sincere. The young woman recited a litany of available microbrews, but Deidre ordered a whiskey sour. House whiskey, so as not to waste good whiskey in a mixed drink. Tonight was not the night to judge between a dozen different beers, or engage in some esoteric and expensive tasting scenario. Once the bartender brought Brigit's drink she delivered a refill to a scruffy older man three seats down the bar. Deidre noted how her smile was not as warm for him.

She struck up a conversation with the bartender. LaRue. Who it turned out knew Brigit. Why was Deidre not surprised? LaRue wore a choker of thick green beads and copper wire. Brigit had made it. Apparently LaRue had bartered for the choker, though she did not specify the nature of the exchange. Everything she said about Brigit was complimentary, though lacking in specificity. Brigit was so smart. So sweet. So talented at making jewelry. Everybody loved Brigit. *Of course they did.*

Otherwise Deidre enjoyed their conversation, punctuated by those moments when LaRue paused to wipe the counter or serve the few other customers. Not many more came in over the course of the night. LaRue was energetic and cheerful but not overwhelming. Before Deidre left she had acquired an invite to a gathering two nights hence, the address inscribed on a coaster. Sometimes a new place just opens up to you.

—Everyone will want to meet Brigit's mom!

Of course they would. *How could they not?*

The Always Rising of the Night

***

Deidre designated the next day for exploring Xebíco. As it turned out, the town did not offer much to explore. Generic shopping centers. A small mall with a derelict Sears at one end and a boarded-up Penney's at the other. Avocado Street, a long east-west boulevard bordered by discount supermarkets and big-box stores. That street, two sets of train tracks, and a creek bisected the little city along the same axis, all less than a few blocks apart. So did the 99, the highway on which she'd arrived from Fresno. She knew from one of her few phone conversations with Brigit over the last three years that people here referred to their highways by "the" and the number, not "Route" or "Highway" as folks might back east. A California thing. Well, she would blend in as best she could for the duration. Also, never call it Cali. She remembered that too—but not what to call it instead. Then again maybe she did not want to blend in too well. These days, being Californian came with its own dangers.

She stopped at the Walmart on the west side of town, bought half a dozen sturdy cardboard shipping boxes in their unassembled state. A roll of clear shipping tape. She had decisions to make about Brigit's stuff.

Yet she did not begin assembling any boxes when she got back, just set the flat stack on top of a relatively stable pile of books on the coffee table with the tape roll on top. Everything inevitable, but nothing a priority. She still had to think about what to pack, and where to ship it. Brigit had left her a lot to consider, a lot to sort out.

So far Deidre had seen every room in her daughter's apartment but one. She'd found the door to the front room locked when she first arrived, and thus far had left it that way. What would she find behind it? Mounds of dirty laundry? A dead pet? Right now she had a choice between cleaning the known rooms and the door of mystery. She chose Door #2, the devil she didn't know, hoping for something less dirty than the devil she did.

It took her almost half an hour to locate a screwdriver narrow enough to unlock the door. Inside she found what must have been her daughter's office space. Desktop computer on a tabletop desk, rows of books on plank and cinderblock shelves. Succulents and air plants almost entirely still alive. The entire room surprisingly neat. No dirty clothes, no crusty plates, no dead animals.

Deidre focused on the PC. It looked like the machine she had first bought for herself shortly after Greg's death then decided she disliked and had given to Brigit when she left for grad school. It had to be. She turned it on. What if Brigit had kept the original password? When the login screen appeared, she typed her special word. The home screen appeared. *Success.*

Deidre found herself facing an unexpected dilemma. Should she snoop on her daughter's computer? Unethical, yes, but technically, wasn't it still *her* computer? Especially if Brigit had never changed the password. After all, she might find some clues to her daughter's location and fate. In that case, she *owed* it to Brigit to search the machine. If Brigit was still alive. Perhaps even more so if she was not.

The internet browser appeared right away, with multiple tabs open, the upper one a page from a catalog of outdoor gear featuring various-sized spray bottles of permethrin, an insecticide for application on fabrics. That seemed obvious enough. She scanned the heads of the other tabs and saw "My Drive." Googledrive. If she was going to snoop, that seemed like a good place to start.

The paragraph she read proved less than helpful, unfortunately, and only left her confused.

Every day here I think it can't get any more incredible, and every day it does! Today all us newbies got fitted for our *odo-odos*, which are a kind of combination organic computer and atmosphere adjustor. For our fittings, Nisa took us up to the top of one of the green towers, the first time I had been that high. We worked out the conversion and it was something like five and a half kilometers. And it wasn't even the highest tower! Looking out the windows, we could see other towers disappearing into the clouds. Even the Locatrice seemed impressed!

She read a few more paragraphs but gave up when Brigit started going on about some kind of language class with lots of foreign words that didn't look at all like Portuguese. Deidre shut the computer back off. What was she supposed to make of nonsense like that? Maybe she'd read more later, but she'd had enough for one night.

2721 EL PORTAL DRIVE

Deidre arrived at the party half an hour late. Best to wait until everyone else had arrived, make a dramatic entrance. That usually got things off on the right foot, establishing her as a social focus, a V.I.P. The house lay at the end of a short *cul-de-sac* on the north side of town, within cycling distance of the university. Deidre had to drive back out after she found it and onto the next street over to find a parking space, which left her miffed. Someone should have reserved spaces in front of the house for important guests.

The front doormat read "GO AWAY." Very funny. She knocked, but no one came to greet her. She tried the door, found it unlocked, and entered. The home's interior was crowded, but not densely, the guests gathered in scattered groups, little human islands. She looked for LaRue, the only person she expected to know, but didn't see her. Navigating from the entryway through the living room (paintings of South American scenes, large flat-screen TV, larger bookcases, the latter packed with books on biology and ecology, evolution and revolution).

Still no LaRue, but when she reached the open area between dining room and kitchen, she spotted someone else she knew through a gap in the crowd: Dr. Cynthia Bowles. And somehow she knew immediately that was whose house she was in. The professor noticed her as well, and they shared a moment of unexpected eye contact. An awkward moment, but not for Deidre. She liked how this situation put Bowles off-balance and gave her the upper hand, considering that during their previous encounter Cynthia had kept her at a distance via the barrier of bureaucracy. Deidre made her way toward the other woman, and before she came within reach, Bowles said, —Ms. Llewelyn, I didn't…I mean, I'm surprised…

Deidre showed mercy. —LaRue invited me. Blank stare. —You know, the bartender from *Le Parti Pris*. Is she here?

Dr. Bowles's expression changed from alarmed confusion to partial comprehension. —Oh! LaRue. We call her Madame Mayor, because she's like the unofficial mayor of Xebíco. Because she seems to know everyone, right? In town, at the university. She's always at the center of any social scene.

—Yes, but is she here?

—No. I mean, I haven't seen her yet tonight, but she usually arrives a bit late. In the meantime, let's get you something to drink. What would you like? We've got beer and wine in the fridge. The bar is over there in the fishbowl room. It's pretty well-stocked. Alex is tending it, just let him know what you want. She pointed over her shoulder into a room that opened behind her. Deidre could see more guests inside it, and behind them tall windows that must open on the backyard, though darkness filled them now.

Deidre decided to offer more benevolence. —So this is *your* house? The other woman nodded, began to speak, but Deidre cut her off. —I didn't know that when LaRue invited me. She only told me that some of Brigit's friends might be here. I hope you don't mind that I'm here.

Just like that she knew she had put Dr. Bowles on the spot and firmly taken the upper hand.

—No, no, of course not. I'm glad you could make it.

—So *are* any of my daughter's friends here? Any of the lab mates you mentioned, perhaps? Can you introduce me to them?

—Ah, well, of course. I mean I don't know all of Brigit's friends, and I doubt everybody here knew her, but—Esperanza, come here a second, please.

Dr. Bowles gestured to a dark-haired young woman who appeared to be headed toward the bar.

—Esperanza, this is Deidre Llewelyn. Brigit's mother. She's here…visiting, and she'd like to meet some of Brigit's friends. You know her social circle as well as anyone—can you show Ms. Llewelyn around, introduce her to some of the people she might want to meet?

Esperanza acquiesced, her shoulders slumping slightly, and nodded to Deidre. —Let's go out to the bar. Most of the folks you're looking for will be there.

As they crossed the threshold into the outside room, Esperanza said, —Watch out for Sam.

—Sam?

—The cat. He likes to get underfoot.

Deidre looked down, forward, backward, all around, but saw no cat. Inside the room she saw at least a dozen happy, laughing people, some probably students, others, older, likely faculty. The bar, as such, was a repurposed lectern in front of a glass bookcase packed with liquor. Behind the lectern stood a lanky boy with unkempt hair, mixing drinks and holding court. Alex, presumably. Alex was kind of cute in a scruffy disheveled sort of way. Behind Alex, the windows opened onto night. Floor to ceiling—and a glass ceiling too. Deidre wondered whether this room had been a sunroom or even a greenhouse once. Its location on the south side of the house supported that conclusion.

Esperanza introduced Deidre to three of Brigit's lab mates: Keller, Lois, and Fatima, and to Alex, whose connection Esperanza implied but didn't specify—Deidre suspected Alex and her daughter had dated, perhaps been lovers. Her intuitions regarding such matters rarely ran astray. The introductions also included two faculty: a woman in her thirties and a man in his forties, both of whom had served on Brigit's committee. Dr. Seibold and Dr. Krantz.

Alex presented Deidre with the drink she'd requested: Redbreast 12 Year Old. Straight, no ice. She'd spotted the bottle on the glass shelf and decided tonight she deserved the good stuff. On Cynthia.

Keller, Fatima, and Dr. Seibold realigned themselves around Deidre. They expressed their sympathy and concern, asked obvious questions, focused on whether Deidre had any new information. Deidre gave the obvious answers. None of these people seemed to have any helpful information to offer. At one point Deidre asked if Brigit ever mentioned any green towers, something from the confusing passage she'd read in the online journal, but received only blank stares back from the grad students, a headshake from Dr. Seibold. Perhaps the towers were located near the lake where Brigit had been working? Wasn't it some kind of powerplant? Unfortunately, no one present had been to Brazil, let alone Lake Balbina. Their research interests lay elsewhere.

Before long the conversation shifted to other matters, including the massing of Chinese warships in the Pacific and the proposed division of California into multiple states. Apparently it now looked as if the pipe dream of secessionists in the northern part of the state, who had long sought to break off into their own state called Jefferson, might actually become a reality. Deidre was mildly shocked to hear her new acquaintances openly discussing politics, as if it were three years ago, before the last election and the military occupation of California, before the forced closure of UC Berkeley and UCLA, whose dormitories now served as troop garrisons. She hesitated to join in—she barely knew any of these people, therefore any of them could be federal informants. These days Brazil wasn't the only place people disappeared.

At this point in the conversation a helicopter flew low over the house. Deidre looked left, right, but nobody seemed to pay it any attention. Fatima leaned over to touch her left shoulder, as if to steady her, though she had not drunk near enough to become unsteady, in fact had so far only sipped her drink. —Watch out for the cat. He likes to get underfoot. Deidre looked around once more but still saw no cat. The wide black windows made her uncomfortable though. She found the empty darkness disconcerting. It made her feel as if she were in some fragile bubble on another world. Anything or anyone could be out there, looking in, and she wouldn't be able to see it. What might be outside in California? Bobcats, bears, Bigfoot even. Soldiers. Maybe Sam the cat. She thanked her unhelpful new acquaintances and returned to the kitchen.

She didn't see Cynthia anywhere, but LaRue now occupied the same spot in which the professor had recently stood. The position of honor. Shouldn't that go to Deidre as a visiting special guest? The bartender had already accumulated a little ring of admirers, and Deidre had to edge her way between them. Fortunately, LaRue acknowledged her almost immediately.

—Hey all, this is Brigit's mom. You know, the missing student. LaRue leaned toward Deidre and said more softly: —I hope that didn't sound insensitive. I always say it's best not to beat around the bush.

—You only told the truth, Deidre replied. Let's be blunt and maybe that will jog someone's memory in a useful way.

—That's the spirit. Don't give up. And you've come to the right place. Most of her friends are here.

—I know. I met some of them. None of them have been very helpful so far.

—Ah, OK then. Let me introduce you to someone you probably *haven't* met yet.

LaRue took Deidre by the left elbow. Deidre sighed, opened her mouth to explain that she had already met the gang around the bar, but then she realized that Madame Mayor was leading her in the opposite direction, toward a far corner of the living room, where a lean older woman with wavy gray hair listened to two younger women, probably more grad students. The older woman wore weathered khakis and a man's denim shirt, and she held court in front of an ornate tapestry depicting fanged creatures with big eyes holding knives and what looked like severed heads.

—Deidre, this is Candace. Candace, this is Deidre Llewelyn. Brigit's mother.

Candace immediately threw her arms around Deidre and gripped her in an intense hug. Clearly someone for whom personal space had little meaning. After several seconds, a long sigh, and several pats on the back, she released Deidre and stepped back, but without releasing her altogether, shifting her grip to her captive's forearms instead and staring into her face.

—You must be terribly worried. Don't be. I can't explain right now, but I believe there is more to your daughter's story than meets the eye. I expect you already have some sense of that. Brigit is a remarkable and resilient young woman. But then I don't need to tell you that, do I?

A peculiar detail struck Deidre. This moderately invasive woman was the first person she'd met in Xebíco who referred to Brigit in the present tense. What that meant, she did not know. Probably nothing. But it intrigued her. Most likely Candace was every bit the hippie flake this first impression suggested. But perhaps, just perhaps, she knew something. No one else did, that much was obvious. And LaRue had introduced her. Deidre felt a strange faith in LaRue. The Unofficial Mayor of Xebíco. At this point, she had Deidre's unofficial vote of confidence.

—Well, yes. She *is* my daughter, so I think I know her pretty well. But what are you saying? Do you know what happened to her? Where she is now?

—I don't know, not for sure. But perhaps… You know what the poets say, don't you? Show, don't tell. She leaned back several inches and let her grip slip to Deidre's wrists, then her fingers, which she held gently, almost caressing them, staring directly into Deidre's eyes. Deidre resisted the urge to pull away. —How long do you plan to stay in town? Will you be here through the end of the month?

Something about this woman made Deidre want to open up. —Well, I just got here, and to be honest, I haven't even booked a return flight. If you know Brigit well, you probably know her father committed suicide several years ago, and since she came here, I've been all alone in Maine. I broke my lease and put all my remaining things in storage before I left. She paused, pondered, continued. —Honestly, I don't really have very much to go back to.

—I understand, said Candace softly, nodding gently. —You're probably wondering how long you *should* stay here. So, do you think you can stay through the twenty-fourth?

—I suppose so. Brigit's lease is good through the end of August. It'll probably take me at least that long to sort everything out, all her affairs. Why the twenty-fourth? What happens then?

—Something else for show-not-tell. For now, why don't you go ahead and mark the date in your phone? She released her grip on Deidre's hands and gestured enthusiastically for her to take out her phone and type in the date. Deidre opened the calendar app, and went to June 24.

—What should I name the event?

—For now, just call it The Pool Party.

—And the times?

—Mark 5:00 p.m. for the start time. Don't worry about the end time for now.

At Candace's suggestion they also exchanged numbers. Deidre had no idea what kind of connection she was making or what she might be getting into, but she deserved to meet the best people in Xebíco. LaRue seemed like one of them. Could Candace be another? Everyone else had greeted her with bureaucratic formality. Even if this woman turned out to be wasting her time in regard to Brigit, somehow Deidre didn't think she would waste her time *altogether*.

Whatever the June 24 event turned out to be, she suspected it would be interesting. It would at least be a party—probably better than the current one! How it might relate to Brigit, she had no idea. She doubted there would be any legitimate connection—maybe a séance or some new age nonsense like that. But even table-thumping and Ouija boards would be better than the empty words she'd encountered so far. At least at a séance folks would be making an effort.

Deidre liked how quickly some of the genuinely important people in this scene had begun to recognize her importance and accept her. Even though everyone associated with the university had subtly blown her off, the unofficial leaders of the community had recognized her importance. The *choice hidden handful of the Divine Inert*, as Melville might have described them. Was she being offered initiation into a secret Xebíco? If such a place existed, she deserved that invitation. Whether or not she'd accept remained her decision.

LaRue spoke up again. —Did you know Candace is responsible for the location of the university?

—How so?

—Tell her, Can, or do you want me to?

Candace gave a half-smile and made an expansive gesture toward LaRue. —Go on. You do tell it so well.

—Okay, I will. So originally the university was supposed to be north of where it is now. But that area is full of vernal pools, which provide the habitat for endangered fairy shrimp. So Candace filed a lawsuit and forced them to change the location. The UC had to buy the golf course next to the road and move the university there. That's why there's a pond in the middle of campus. The whole campus is on the footprint of an old golf course.

Candace interrupted. —Just to be clear, I was not the only party filing that lawsuit. A whole group of us sued. Friends of the Fairy Shrimp. But we *were* victorious.

—They held up the groundbreaking for almost three years! Not only that, the university had to create the Xebíco Vernal Pools Reserve. Every University of California campus has some kind of nature preserve associated with it, but UC Xebíco is the only one where that preserve is located adjacent to the campus. There's literally a gate on the north end of campus that opens onto the reserve. How cool is that? Candace is kind of a local hero for that. They almost made the fairy shrimp the school mascot.

—I don't know about the whole hero thing. Certainly not to the UC administration, haha! Maybe to a few folks, but not that many even know the whole story. And of those who do, I think a lot of them wish I would just go away. But we saved the fairy shrimp, and the California tiger salamanders, and a whole bunch of other species, so that's something—even if hardly anybody knows about it. It matters to the salamanders. It matters to the shrimp. That's the important thing.

—I think I saw the gate for that reserve when I was on campus. How far back does it go?

Candace offered a wry half-smile. —Farther than you might imagine.

—I'd like to see it.

—And you will—on the twenty-fourth. That's where we hold The Pool Party!

MY DRIVE

Back at the apartment that Deidre had already begun to think of as her own, and feeling the effects of several whiskeys, she fought the compulsion to read more of her daughter's online journal. The struggle was brief and the compulsion won. What little she'd read so far, about green towers and language classes, had been confusing and hard to follow, even without the barrage of foreign words. She decided to scroll back to the beginning of the entries in the hope that things would be easier to follow if she picked up the thread at the start.

The initial entry began with the date of her daughter's departure from the United States: April 25. Brigit described her flights, the first one uneventful, the second from San Antonio to Manaus sounding awful: she had shared the plane with a middle school band from Provo, Utah, and the students had neither shut up nor kept still the whole time. On an overnight flight. Some had even taken their instruments down from the overhead compartment and played them in flight as they swapped seats and walked down the aisles. Sousaphones and clarinets. Deidre could only imagine. Brigit made no mention of stroopwaffels. Or errant cats.

From there everything seemed pretty predictable: clearing customs, getting picked up by the project coordinator in a rickety van, meeting other students, arriving at the residence hall. A whole paragraph about her ultra-light hammock with the built-in mosquito netting, how much she liked that hammock, how she strung it on the third-floor balcony and how great that was with the cool breezes at night while the undergrads sweltered inside without AC. Until 4:00 a.m., when strange birds began to scream in the jungle.

Deidre scrolled down, hoping for something juicier. A few entries further on Brigit visited a club, danced with various people. One cute guy who "spoke like only four words of English" but with whom she communicated "surprisingly well." But nothing more happened, and she eventually said goodnight to the cute guy and traveled back to the residence hall with the other students in the van. Deidre thought of herself at that age and sighed. She thought of all the times over the last ten years or so she'd told her daughter —You can tell me anything, and how Brigit never told her anything…and she sighed again.

Brigit got to know the other students just enough to judge them mostly vapid and immature—but she was the only grad student after all. Two of the boys and one of the girls tried to hit on her during the first week. One of the staff straight up propositioned her. She shot them all down. She had a "specific purpose" and that meant she had "no interest in distractions."

By the first week of May she began expressing concerns about João, the program lead. While acknowledging that she was more or less "tagging along" on this eco-tourism field school in order to search for giant river otters in Lake Balbina, she quickly began to find João dangerously incompetent, his decisions and behavior increasingly irrational. She and some of the other students suspected that he had contracted malaria and was obfuscating his medical status. He had boasted early on that he didn't need an antimalarial due to the natural strength of his immune system and had even encouraged others to discard their own medications.

Before they boarded the boat that would take them up Lake Balbina, Brigit described one experience in greater detail. Since it involved a tower, Deidre read it with care, as it seemed like this passage might connect to the section she'd skimmed previously.

This particular entry was dated May 2. Only twelve days before Brigit's disappearance. It began with a select group getting up at 6:00 a.m. and driving three hours out into the rainforest to the *Observatório de Torre Alta da Amazônia*. This 325-meter-tall structure was "one meter taller than the Eiffel Tower." It allowed researchers to take atmospheric samples high above the forest canopy. Only two students could ascend the tower at one time, together with their guide, whose name Brigit had neglected to record. He told them how he often slept atop the tower in order to obtain dusk and dawn readings. Brigit expressed her envy of his job, but most of the entry described her amazement at viewing the unbroken green expanse of the rainforest canopy from above: "I needed this incredible green-ness so bad, after so long in brown, dry Xebíco. It's even more intense than Maine!"

Deidre felt pride in her daughter for climbing all the way up the open metal framework of this tower, which was held in place only by a network of cables. Then she reached the part where Brigit described the entire structure swaying in the wind and she shuddered to think of her child up there. Brigit briefly mentioned that two members of the group had chickened out from climbing the tower. She had gone up with a boy named Duncan, and her entry implied that he had won some grudging respect from her for this accomplishment.

The last line of the entry was "While I was up there, I could finally forget about all the bullshit back home for a while. I wish I could have stayed forever, or at least all day. Easily the happiest I've been in years."

All the bullshit. Exactly what did that include? Grad school? The occupation of California? Their mother-daughter relationship? She remembered less than a year ago, when she had emailed Brigit a link to a particular Paul Simon song and copied the pertinent lyrics into the message. Brigit had never replied.

Suddenly Deidre didn't want to read anymore. Although this tower episode was the most interesting entry so far, it didn't seem connected to the towers in the incomprehensible section Deidre had read two nights before. And she'd been totally sober then. Tired, maybe jetlagged, but that was all. That passage had made no sense to her. She remembered only mention of multiple towers, which Brigit described as green, and of networks and flyers. One of the last bits she had read described a woman who had "come through the Rhel." Perhaps this was an acronym, but Brigit didn't write it in all caps like she did for IDESAM, the Brazilian agency that managed the tower. Brigit described the woman as a "serious badass" and wrote that she had a "new role model." Trying to read the entry had left Deidre frustrated. At least these earlier entries were more straightforward and comprehensible, if rather dull. But she'd had enough for one night. Maybe for a while. She had no eagerness to read about her daughter's "new role model" or a detailed discussion of what parts of her life Brigit thought of as "bullshit." Deidre set the computer to "Sleep" and prepared to do likewise herself. She had all day tomorrow to read more. If she chose to.

***

Deidre woke to the racket of another helicopter flyover. With nothing on her schedule she decided the time had come to address some of the mess her daughter had left behind. Beginning with the dishes. First she cleared one half of the sink, then she located some dish soap in the cabinet underneath. With the soap added and the hot water running, she gathered the worst of the dishes and silverware from around the apartment, all those with obvious caked on filth and crusted matter, everything that would have to soak before going in the dishwasher. What wouldn't yet fit in the sink she stacked on the counter.

After several rounds of soaking and scraping—including a couple instances of actual gagging over gray mucilaginous blobs she had to pry out of tumblers and into the trash with a butter knife—she managed to fill the dishwasher. Which contained only a single apparently clean wineglass when she first opened it. Deidre suspected it may have belonged to the previous tenant.

Emptying the trash seemed the logical next step, perhaps an imperative one. She found it only too easy to picture the things she had just jettisoned into it mating with whatever horrors already resided therein and producing some crawling nightmare offspring. Best to get the whole mess out of the apartment. Fortunately, she had spotted a partial box of trashcan liners under the sink while searching for the dish soap. Even more fortunately the smell was not overwhelming, probably because most of the contents were more than a month old and desiccated by now, except for what she had just added…and her uneaten leftovers, which she had left on the counter too long and had to discard. She quickly knotted the top of the bag as she lugged it out toward the dumpster she remembered seeing in the parking lot. This proved careless, as Robin(!) accosted her halfway there, appearing suddenly by her side as if she plummeted from one of the palm trees or popped out from behind a bushy bird-of-paradise plant.

—Hi! How's everything going? Good, I hope! You know to let me know if you need anything, right? Anything at all, *anything*! I'm here to help. Are you enjoying Xebíco? Have you had time for sightseeing yet? Have you seen the Parsons Parthenon House? The Fancher Obelisk? Have you been to Lake Tenaya?

This verbal barrage lacked any breaks even if Brigit wanted to reply. She mumbled a thank you when the younger woman finally took a breath, followed by —Just taking the garbage out. The obviousness of which made her feel foolish until she reminded herself that everything Robin(!) had said was equally obvious and banal.

—Have you met the men in black yet?

—The what? So much for the obvious.

—Oh, that's just what I call them. The government men who've been coming by to ask about Brigit. I call them that because of the movie. They don't really all wear black and one of them was even a woman, at least the first time. They've been here several times. I told them Brigit's mother would be here soon, and they said they would come talk to you.

—Did they say anything more? Anything about why they wanted to talk to me? Deidre's abdominal cavity suddenly felt both sick and empty. She twisted the neck of the trash bag in her hand.

—No, but I'm sure it's a routine thing they do, looking out for any American lost in a foreign country. They probably want to let you know about whatever progress they've made on the case. Nothing to worry about!

—Right. Okay. Well, thanks. I need to dump this trash now.

—Sure, sure, go ahead. Remember Tuesday is dumpster-emptying day, in case it gets full before then. It happens sometimes.

—Thanks. Well, have a good day.

Rid of Robin(!), but not of her disconcerting words, Deidre hurriedly tossed the trash bag into the dumpster and returned to the apartment, where she locked herself in before collapsing onto the only clear spot on the couch. Now she wondered just how much of a mistake she had made in coming to California. She tried to recall her conversations with the State Department reps. They had definitely discouraged her from traveling to Brazil, but had they given any hints she shouldn't visit California? Damnit. She should've stayed in Maine, whose governor regularly golfed with the president. No men in black ever visited anyone in Maine—at least not to her knowledge. And bigmouth Robin(!). Goddamn her. Idiot.

Suddenly she had serious doubts about hanging around this town until June 24. But where would she go? She literally had nowhere. Not back in Maine, not here in California. Nowhere in between. Nowhere and no one now that Brigit was gone.

Perhaps she could ask LaRue or Candace if they might let her stay with one of them for a while. But dropping off the radar like that would probably only reinforce whatever interest the men in black had taken in her. Oh god. A combined mother and daughter disappearance would probably get them both on some hot list. She would have to stay in Xebíco. And she would have to stay in this apartment, literally stay in it all day long because if the government agents showed up again while she was out somewhere they might get suspicious. Oh, she should have stayed in Maine. Goddamn Robin(!). And Brigit—why did she have to choose a grad program in California, a pariah state three thousand miles away from her mother?

She needed something to kill the jitters, but if she went out for coffee or a drink, the agents might visit while she was gone, and what might happen then? She could hear Robin(!) telling them, —Well, she was just here. I don't know where she could have run off to! Deidre would have to keep to the apartment until they returned. She didn't want to talk to them but she didn't dare avoid them. She felt her anxiety flare, but she had the perfect answer right at hand: a bout of intense cleaning, which was just what this abomination of a living space needed anyway.

Five hours later she had cleaned not only the kitchen but the bathroom as well. Considering the latter as she scrubbed her arms up to the elbows made her shudder. She had found bleach, rags, and a mop, but no rubber gloves. The bathroom had been bad. She couldn't believe a *woman* lived here, let alone her own flesh and blood. Fortunately the government people had not showed up while she was elbows deep in the worst of the filth.

She still had the living room to go, but now that she had removed all the dirty dishes from the coffee table, sofa, TV, and floor, she had made some inroads there. She would need to vacuum but she was concerned that she might not hear the door if someone knocked or rang with the vacuum cleaner running.

Deidre regarded the stacks of books and papers, the random junk, and suddenly felt tired again. Hadn't she completed enough Herculean labors for today? That last Augean stable could wait. According to her phone, it was 4:47 p.m. How late did men in black work? She doubted later than 5:00 if they were feds of some kind. And what else could they be? She had earned a nap.

***

She awoke over four hours later, showered, changed, and headed for *Le Parti Pris*. Time for that drink, and the reassuring presence of LaRue, who might even have some good advice.

En route, she considered the rental car. She couldn't afford to keep it much longer, so if she was going to stay, she would need to return it soon. Fortunately Xebíco was not very large, so afterward she could Uber most places she would need to go. She'd used Uber a couple times in Biddeford after she sold her car, and she felt like she understood the system well enough. But she would have to ask somebody to follow her back to the Fresno airport to drop the car off and bring her back. That meant going through the checkpoint again, probably in both directions.

Deidre was disappointed to discover LaRue not on duty this night. Instead, the same boy who'd been mixing drinks at Cynthia Bowles's party stood behind the bar. Alex. Her daughter's likely lover. He looked as surprised to see her as she was to see him. She asked for Bushmill's, on the rocks, regretting the order immediately. She would need to stretch her drink budget from now on. Her entire budget. Soon she would need to switch to beer. Or find someone else to pay for her drinks.

She felt like she should talk to Alex but she had no idea what to say. Fortunately the club was a bit more crowded tonight, and with no barmaids, the clientele kept him busy. Said clientele included four full tables of soldiers. Exactly how large was the garrison in this town?

After a few minutes, Alex reappeared across the bar from her, polishing half a steel cocktail shaker with a pristine white towel. He spoke in a slightly formal voice. —How is everything going so far? Have you learned anything new about Brigit?

Deidre stared back at him and replied in her own equally stilted tone. —To be honest, Alex, I haven't learned a goddamn thing. If anybody knows anything useful, they aren't telling me. What about you? What do you know about my daughter?

She almost asked —What was the nature of your relationship with my daughter? but she managed to restrain herself at the last moment.

Alex continued wiping the already-dry shaker. —I wish I knew more, anything that could help. I think everybody here feels that way. We're all really upset about—about what happened. But whatever happened, happened in Brazil, and none of us know what goes on there. We just want her back.

Just then one of the soldiers came up to lean over the bar on Deidre's right and order another round of beers for himself and his friends. While Alex was filling the glasses from a tap down the bar, the soldier turned to Deidre, smiled, and said —And how are you this evening, Mrs. Llewelyn?

Jesus fuck. Shaken, she retained her composure, and after only a moment's hesitation, replied —I'm fine, thank you. How are you?

—Doing great. We're all doing great. It's a great time to be here—out here having fun in the warm California sun. Don't you agree?

—I suppose it is. I'm glad you are enjoying it.

—We hope you enjoy it, too. But remember, the hot weather is coming. Temperatures are going to stay over 100 for most of the summer. Stay inside, be safe. Heat stroke is no joke. As Alex rounded the far end of the bar carrying the four beers to the table on a small round tray, the smiling soldier gave her a quick salute and turned to rejoin his group.

Before Alex could return, she slapped a tenner on the bar, gulped down what remained of her drink, and walked out, making every effort to appear casual and unhurried. She didn't look back at the soldiers, didn't look back at Alex, didn't look back at the establishment to which she no longer planned to return. What the hell had just happened? Exactly what had Brigit gotten her into?

***

The next day Deidre tackled the refrigerator and took stock of her daughter's liquor supply. Five bottles of Sierra Nevada Pale Ale in the surprisingly undisastrous fridge. The casualties therein had been limited to two fully blackened avocados, a head of lettuce that had deliquesced into dark brown mush in its plastic bag, and the tail end of a loaf of wheat bread covered in azure penicillin fuzz. Other than that, only long-term stable condiments. From a cabinet overhead she recovered a nearly full two-liter bottle of off-brand vodka. Some orange or tomato juice might've been nice but that was too much to ask and she didn't dare make a supermarket run. She didn't dare go out at all.

For the rest of the day she drank vodka and cleaned, trying to forget the soldier who had somehow known her name, the federal agents from some unknown bureau who were looking for her. Several low helicopter flyovers a day did not make forgetting any easier. At every moment she expected a knock on the door.

How had she gotten on the government's radar like this? She hadn't done anything suspicious. Granted, California might not be the best place to start a new life right now, but she had figured with everything else going on, she was not going to attract much attention, at least not this kind. True, she was accustomed to finding herself the center of attention, but not by the military and obscure government agencies. Brigit must have done something to set these wheels in motion. But what? Three weeks after the fact all she knew was that her daughter had taken a boat out to search for otters on a Brazilian lake and never returned. How had that brought the Eye of Sauron down upon her mother, who had been in Maine the whole time? So far Deidre's impression had been that both the government and the university were doing their best to shine her on. Had she been too insistent in her questioning? She didn't think so.

About 5:00 p.m. she started thinking about how she ought to eat something. Also how the rental car was eating into her extremely limited savings day by day, and she needed to return it ASAP. Although she could probably manage a trip to one of the nearer restaurants, she was in no condition to drive back to Fresno tonight, especially with the checkpoint in between. That trip would require someone to drive her back.

LaRue and Candace seemed like her only two options. She figured she'd gotten all she could out of Dr. Cynthia Bowles. Although she leaned toward LaRue, she no longer felt comfortable with anything pertaining to *Le Parti Pris*. She began composing a text to Candace. Remember me? We met at that party. You gave me your number. I don't know many people here and I really need a favor. Then she described the task. Send. Stare at phone. No response. Before long she passed out on the couch.

***

The next morning she saw that Candace's response had arrived during the wee hours. Did this woman sleep? It would be her pleasure to follow Deidre to Fresno, drive her back. It would need to be in the afternoon though— would that work out?

Deidre didn't feel up to going anywhere this morning, so the afternoon worked perfectly. Wouldn't Robin(!)'s men and woman in black be more likely to come in the morning anyway? If they didn't arrive by lunch, they probably wouldn't show up today. She pictured them as early risers, hoping to snare their victims unwary and unprepared. Deidre dreaded missing them almost more than she dreaded their visit. Just like shadowy government agents to deal in the catch-22. But she figured the chances of them showing up after lunch were less.

She made a breakfast of some initially unknown substance retrieved from the freezer that didn't look overly frostbitten or spoiled, frozen in a repurposed 32 oz. nondairy yogurt container. Food roulette. After several stints in the microwave it turned out to be a sort of curry. Chunks of eggplant and tofu. Her vegan daughter. Not bad though. If only she had some naan.

She sighed. A love of Indian food was one of the few things she and her daughter still shared. Time was they used to have dinner almost weekly at Jewel of India, the only Indian restaurant in Biddeford. They'd had some great times together there, some of their best. Real mother-daughter quality time. But Deidre remembered the last time they'd gone, a visit that had ended bitterly with Brigit almost shouting: —Just take me home, Mom. I've been talking to you for half an hour now, and you haven't listened to a word I've said!

This sort of line soon became Brigit's broken record. Until silence replaced it.

She cleaned some more, clearing surfaces and beginning to pack her daughter's books into the boxes she'd bought and finally taped together. That would do for now. Other items could wait. She located an upright vacuum cleaner in the small hall closet, emptied the overstuffed bag and began to clean the carpets. She remembered their store in Maine, how she had kept it clean until she just couldn't any longer. The first health code violation. Which wasn't her fault either. She knew the health inspector had it in for them because he was friends with their main competitor, the Tip Top Sandwich Shop. Had tried to explain this to her husband. If only Greg hadn't argued with the man when he gave them that first warning. Was that the moment when everything began to go sideways? Brigit had already left for college in Oregon by then, which left only the two of them to mind the store. It just wasn't fair. She had done so much to upgrade the store by then.

Soon it was lunchtime, and she finished the curry. She resisted the urge to wash it down with a beer. She had to keep it together today, at least until she returned from Fresno. She decided not to wait outside for Candace—she didn't want to risk another encounter with the ever-chipper Robin(!). Or the men in black. A meeting with them might delay her departure severely. Instead she watched her phone for the text from Candace indicating she had arrived, even while her ears strained to hear the sound of footsteps outside the door, the practiced federal knock. —Please don't show up now, please don't show up now. Whoever you are.

***

The trip to Fresno went smoothly—apparently the checkpoint was only on the northbound side of the 99—and the rental car company found no issues with her return, no scratches, no dings. No tracking devices, at least none they informed her of. Papers all in order. Mission accomplished, she hopped into Candace's faded blue Volvo for the trip back to Xebíco. To Brigit's apartment. To home, as much as she had one now.

As soon as they were back on the city streets, Candace asked —How are you holding up? None of this can be easy for you.

—Mostly I've kept busy cleaning. Brigit left a bit of a mess. She's always been messy. But, you know, the physical labor helps.

—Yes, I can see how that would be.

Deidre wondered how her new friend meant her last statement, as it could go several ways. She considered requesting clarification but refrained.

—That kind of loss is terrible, and the uncertainty of it all makes it so much worse. You don't deal with uncertainty well, do you?

Deidre responded hastily, regretting her words immediately. —Do you know what it's like to lose a child?

Right then Candace was driving up the on-ramp to the 99. Only once the car had found its place in the middle lane did she reply. —My son Jeremiah was in Seoul. He was twenty-eight.

Deidre felt like she'd been set up. How could she have known? How could she even respond to that? It took her half a minute, and all she could offer was a hesitant —When...?

—When the bomb dropped, yes. He'd gone there to work on a tech startup. They never found his remains, but that was par for the course. There's no way he survived.

—I'm so sorry.

—Thank you. So yes, I understand. And your case, Brigit's case, may be a little different. Like the song says, I don't want to share false hope. But I don't think you should entirely despair either.

Deidre felt confused, and she said as much.

Candace blindsided her again —Do you ever think about aliens, and why they have never contacted us?

There it was, the other shoe. Or sandal. This was more along the lines of what Deidre had expected from the other woman all along. In a way, this sudden twist came as a relief, as she no longer had to take the conversation seriously. She could simply roll with it as a distraction. —Go on.

—There are lots of theories about why we seem to be alone in the universe. The possibly small number of intelligent races in our particular spiral arm of the Milky Way. The limited time period during which any one of them might actually employ the electromagnetic spectrum for communication. And then there's the Great Filter.

—English please.

—The hypothesis of the Great Filter suggests that all intelligent species reach a point at which they are likely to bring about their own extinction. Nuclear war, global warming, the Singularity. At a certain point the odds of an extinction-level event increase exponentially. That's on top of the inevitable non-self-induced options: a comet or asteroid impact, supervulcanism, coronal mass ejection, a nearby supernova, the clathrate gun. Look where we are now. Probably most races never make it past their own orange tentacle guy. And perhaps those who did don't want to communicate with those like us who probably aren't going to make it.

—Are you saying aliens abducted my daughter?

—Oh, no. Nothing like that. Well, not exactly like that. But it's something that I can't explain. Like the cat. I can only show you. Share with you. Maybe. That's why I invited you to The Pool Party. So much easier to show you what I mean, let you experience it for yourself.

—Are you saying there are going to be aliens at this party? Deidre forced a smile.

Candace replied with her own genuine smile. —Probably not. She laughed softly. At least not the kind you might be thinking of. But you never know who will show up there, or where they'll come from.

Enough weirdness. Deidre attempted to shift conversational gears. —

Will I need a swimsuit? I didn't pack one.

Her companion laughed. —No, it's not that kind of a party. The full name is "The Sublime New Albion Pool Party." You can tell why I recommended you enter the short version in your phone. It's a reference to the poet William Blake, who believed you could immanentize the eschaton, find paradise on Earth. David, the guy who discovered The Event back and started The Pool Party back in the '70s, was really into Blake's work. Are you familiar with it?

Deidre nodded. —I've got a BA in English from Old Queens.

Candace returned the nod, smiling. —Then you understand. We're lucky David didn't call it something even weirder. Before he came out here, he was at Ohio State, where he hooked up with a professor named Eldridge Aethelred who built his own Church of William Blake in the woods and called it Golgonooza. You should have heard David carry on when he had a full head of steam going, talking about "the mallet of Los demiurgos" or "the hindrances of the vegetal polypus." It was really quite something, even if it was mostly a whole lot of nothing. He passed away back in the aughts, alas. He didn't take the best care of himself. Anyway, we hold the party in the Reserve, so there *are* pools, and a stock pond or two, but I don't think you would want to go swimming in any of them. They'll be drying up by now, muddy and surrounded by more mud, and cow flops, and full of slippery little creatures struggling to complete their life-cycles before the pools disappear altogether for the summer.

—What should I bring then?

—Just bring yourself. We'll have food and…entertainment. I think…I think you will find it a life-changing experience.

—I've heard that before.

—Ha-ha! Haven't we all? But The Pool Party really is something special. I'm genuinely excited to share it with you.

—Can you tell me more?

—It's difficult to explain. You really need to experience it for yourself. Seriously, if I tried to explain it, you'd think me even more of a whacked-out hippie chick than you probably do already. Who knows, you might try to jump out of the car. It's just one of those things you need to go through firsthand.

Candace paused. —Maybe *go through* is not the best way to phrase it.

Parts of the experience may be cathartic, but I believe it is what you need right now. What we all need really. What the world needs now, but there's not enough room for everyone, so for now it must remain a bit exclusive.

Exclusive made Deidre feel more comfortable about the mysterious event. She felt she belonged in *exclusive* places, at *exclusive* events. Though she was a few years too young to have visited Studio 54, she felt sure she would have been admitted beyond the famous velvet rope. Behind the green door. She wondered if Candace had ever visited the legendary club, and considered asking, but held back at the last moment. Candace turned to her again.

—The summer after Seoul, I almost didn't go. But some of the others convinced me to, and it made all the difference. I think it will be good for you too. Perhaps even more profoundly.

They'd reached the checkpoint and its vehicle queue. Candace withdrew her papers from a sleeve conveniently strapped to the overhead visor. — You'd better get your ID out too. Passport if you have one. And the receipt from that rental car.

The queue moved quickly, and soon an armed soldier waved them ahead toward one of his compatriots. The second soldier, like all those visible, wore camo and bore a holstered pistol at his side, an automatic rifle slung over his back. As soon as they had pulled to a stop, he stepped toward them and leaned down to peer into Candace's car, scanning the back seat for additional passengers. He shaded his eyes with one hand despite the awning overhead. For several seconds his gaze lingered on Deidre and her pulse leapt at the thought that he might be the same soldier who'd spoken to her in *Le Parti Pris.*

—Papers please, ladies.

Candace unfolded a single letter-sized sheet from the bundle in her lap, smoothed its creases with a stroke of her right hand, and passed it to the soldier with her left. He stood and scanned it for half a minute, then bent and returned it.

—Have a good day, ladies, he said, and then he took three steps back and waved them on. As the car ahead of them had not moved yet, Candace simply pulled forward a few feet until her open window no longer aligned with the spot where the soldier once again stood at attention, now pointedly ignoring them, his gaze fixed on a spot behind the Volvo. She refolded the sheet she'd shared and returned the papers to the visor sleeve.

—That's it? asked Deidre.

—Usually works, Candace replied. At least for now.

—What *was* that you showed him? It wasn't a bribe, I could tell that much.

—A sort of safe passage. It'll work until it doesn't.

—He didn't even ask to see my papers. I mean, I wasn't worried—I got through okay last time on my driver's license and birth certificate, although I had to show the rental car agreement and my plane ticket stub too. But it took a lot longer than…than this. How did you pull that off?

Just then the car ahead moved forward, pulling out of the checkpoint. It had been the first of the set of cars stopped for inspection, so they now had clear passage back onto the 99. The first soldier waved them forward, and Candace obliged.

On the highway again, their conversation veered into the quotidian, guided casually by Candace. Mostly restaurant recommendations. Mostly within walking distance of Deidre's/Brigit's apartment, though Candace did extend a somewhat noncommittal offer of future transportation.

Soon they were back in Xebíco, at the apartment once more, Deidre scanning the lot for tinted windows, pale government agents in sunglasses, or simply the over-ebullient Robin(!). The coast seemingly clear, she stepped out, thanking this woman she barely knew one more time for the ride. Then quickly inside.

One mundane chore completed, but so many left to go. Deidre flopped full-length onto the musty though now-bare sofa and soon descended into an uneasy afternoon nap.

***

Once again she awoke well into the evening. *Le Parti Pris* no longer felt like an option—the transportation issue alone largely took it off the table, and she didn't feel like cleaning any more. After all she'd accomplished, she deserved a break. Cooking and baking were also out for now—the informal inventory she'd taken of the kitchen made that clear. Given her currently sober state, it seemed an appropriate time to reexamine Brigit's online journal.

The computer responded to her touch like an old friend, and soon she returned to "My Drive." She skimmed through the journal looking for evidence of steamy romantic encounters or mention of conflicts that might reveal anyone who wished her daughter ill, but Brigit either hadn't recorded anything of this nature or she genuinely remained fixated on her otter search. And then Deidre came to the entry for May 11, the day before whatever happened had happened. This was the shortest entry so far:

Tomorrow I'm going to take one of the boats out to the island where we saw it. I'm going alone, but they're supposed to be taking João to the hospital in the morning, so I doubt anyone will notice me if I time it right. I'll take two fresh cameras (in case one malfunctions like the last time), and I hope to get some successful photos of it, or at least of its footprints. Just in case, I'll tell Duncan where I'm going, but no one else. Out of everyone here, I feel like I can trust him the most.

Deidre slumped back in the secondhand swivel chair. Now here was something new. No one had mentioned this, not what she'd read in this journal entry. Someone from State had mentioned a student in whom Brigit had confided her plans, but not the student's name, because FERPA, once again. Should she contact the feds and share this new information? But then the feds were looking for her, weren't they? Maybe not State, but some kind of feds anyway. When they finally came a-knockin' she could tell them all about it. They would probably confiscate the computer though, wouldn't they? Evidence. One of the only remaining connections Deidre had with her daughter. She should at least read through the rest of the entries she'd previously skipped while she still could. She clicked the scroll bar to move up. Accidentally scrolled down. And saw more entries.

The first entry bore the header May 14. Three days *after* the previous one. *Two days after* Brigit had supposedly vanished off the face of Lake Balbina. Obviously someone had found and accessed her laptop. If so, Deidre might find some useful information. She read:

How do I even describe the last few days? Obviously the most amazing days of my life.

My only regret is that I still haven't seen an Aepyornithid, and I probably won't anytime soon, since tomorrow I'm scheduled to begin training to ride one of the elevator-vines to the moon for a five-day visit. They have a job for me, managing some of the megafauna herds. Not a job in the sense I've known—no one here needs to work for a living, but a *position*, and one where I can make a real contribution. Things have happened so fast, but I guess that's because they were prepared for me. I certainly wasn't prepared for this! Or was I? No big deal, just a job that includes trips *to the fucking moon!* Somehow I feel more at home here than I ever did back on…back on Earth. The old Earth. They tell me this is Earth too, but in the local language they call it something that translates as *Green-Green*. It sounds like *Buhishbuhishtick*, although they've also got some numbers in there too, for the computers and cyborgs apparently, and since the numbers change at irregular intervals I haven't tried to memorize them. Fortunately Nisa and most of the folks I interact with speak English, so I can get by with that for now, although they say I'm doing well in my lessons.

Deidre tried to remember whether the State Department reps she'd spoken to had mentioned what happened to Brigit's laptop. Now she understood why they hadn't. Apparently someone had stolen it *and* hacked her password—and was attempting to create some kind of bizarre and elaborate smokescreen to cover her daughter's disappearance. And why would anyone do this unless they'd been involved in whatever happened to Brigit? Once again, she considered contacting the State Department with this information, and once again she decided to wait until the agents from whatever agency knocked on her door.

She read on, and came again to the passage she'd wrestled with several days before, about the green towers. She still didn't understand it—and if these entries were all nonsense, some kind of elaborate red herring, what was the point in even trying to decipher any of them? Then again, she might find some clue as to the identity of the perpetrator, even the current location of Brigit's laptop. Perhaps the person or persons behind this cruel pretense would inadvertently reveal themselves, and she might detect their misstep.

The next entry mentioned Gomphotheres and Diprotodon. Names she recognized from Brigit's childhood fascinations. According to the journal, these now wandered in herds across the Mare Nubium. On the *Moon*. What nonsense. She wanted to find this person just to yell at them that a red herring ought at least to be plausible. What a load of horse puckey. Although they seemed to have some knowledge of Brigit's interests, which just made the whole thing that much more creepy.

Enough of this. She scrolled to the bottom and came to an entry with yesterday's date. She barely skimmed it. A bunch of nonsense about the Lunar ecosystem. But...

Below this, an entry bore today's date. Shorter than previous installments, it had only a few lines:

I'm recommending that the Gompotheres should get more C3 plants in their diet. The best available options are sunflowers and wheat (the sunflowers here are HUGE). It's interesting what they have and haven't domesticated. Rice, for instance, but then rice-agriculture is so water intensive it wouldn't be a good idea up here anyway.

As Deidre watched, additional lines appeared, letter by letter, word by word:

If they accept my advice it becomes a question of how much wheat and/ or sunflowers they are willing to sacrifice. They haven't said exactly but I think they have surpluses. Of course, they're probably growing other C3 plants, but I don't know all of them yet. And some of them don't have English names.

Watching the spectral words appear, Deidre felt first shock and then rage. She inserted the cursor after "English names" and began typing:

Who the hell and why are you typing in Brigit's journal? Do you know who this is? This is her mother. How about I report you to the State Department? How would you like that?

The other cursor froze. Then, after a full minute, four characters appeared:

Mom?

WHO IS THIS? Deidre typed. What the kids called all caps rage.

341

Mom, where are you?

I am in my daughter's apartment in Xebico, California. On her OTHER computer. And whoever you are I'm not your mom. Who are you and where are you? Give yourself up before I contact the authorities. I am sure they can track you.

No more words appeared. No further reply. Deidre stared at the screen. Suddenly the document disappeared altogether. She threw the cursor into furious motion, consulting every possible menu, but it was gone—and she had neglected to save a copy to the desktop.

What had just happened? If someone had been attempting to create a false trail, why had they erased their efforts just when a potential victim took the bait. The most important potential victim, no less. None of this made sense. Should she tell the unknown agents about it when they finally arrived at her door? How would they respond without any evidence? They'd think she was crazy is what. Was shock therapy still a thing? Could the feds themselves be behind the ersatz journal entries? Perhaps they had disappeared her daughter, and now they wanted her, the mother, out of the way to cover their tracks. Could they be attempting to lure her to Brazil? Her hands began to shake. Oh no, not this again. She still had some of her daughter's vodka left, although she had relocated the bottle into the freezer. She retrieved it and poured several ounces into one of the glasses she had recently cleaned, finished half the glass in a single gulp.

Deidre decided the best thing for now would be to sleep if she could. She shut the computer down altogether and headed for the bedroom.

***

The next day, first thing, she turned on the computer and checked to see if the journal had reappeared. She found instead that she could no longer access Brigit's googledrive account at all. Yet the specter of the outrageous journal entries still weighed on her. She wanted to discuss the strange affair with someone, but who? Candace seemed an obvious choice. Clearly, she kept an open mind. To say the least. But then Deidre thought of the impending visit of the agents in black. If Candace knew about that entanglement, would she consider Deidre as a hot potato and rescind the invitation to The Pool Party? Deidre had begun to look forward to the mysterious social event. What else did she have on her calendar, after all? Literally nothing. LaRue would be the only other option, the only other non-bureaucratic local number she had. As much as she instinctively liked LaRue though, she now felt compelled to avoid her bar and everyone in it. Deidre began to wonder if everyone in this town knew more than her, whether she had become the central victim of some cruel prank.

Quickly she recognized this thought as paranoia and tamped it back down. Just because something weird was going on didn't mean that everybody she met was in on it. She could probably trust Candace and LaRue. Brazil appeared to be the epicenter of whatever vicious game she was caught up in, with ripples spreading out to branches of the current U.S. government. She had yet to encounter any evidence that anyone in Xebíco was involved. Other than that soldier at the club. True, pretty much no one associated with the university had helped her in any way, but that probably had more to do with concerns over liability than any potential foul play in South America. Just garden variety bureaucracy. Nonetheless she had good reasons for keeping this to herself.

With nothing else to do, she threw herself fully into cleaning once more, much like the way she would at the store when she and Greg quarreled. She didn't dare go out in case the agents returned. Without transportation she had nowhere to go anyway. At some point she'd have to go shopping, but first she had to make this place livable. Perhaps if she made enough progress by the evening, she would call an Uber.

Deidre began her labors with the dishes she'd already washed, stacking them and finding places where each stack fit in the kitchen cabinets. Render unto the kitchen what belongs to the kitchen.

Eventually it came time to put away the cleaned glasses, which meant finding the particular cabinets in which each category belonged. This took a minute, but when she did she spotted three familiar glasses right away in the dim recesses of a cabinet above the sink. Jars actually, specifically the tall twelve-ounce quilted Ball jars she used for canning her famous blueberry jam with hints of lavender and rosemary. Also her secret recipe cranberry sauce with orange rind and finely minced preserved ginger. All of which she'd sent her daughter periodically, with nary a thank you or reply of any sort. But Brigit must have eaten the preserves, and saved the jars as well. That was something to consider.

Deidre steadied herself on the counter and stood on tiptoes to peer deep into the cabinet, searching for more jars, perhaps the eight-ounce jars she used for her peach-apricot jam with a hint of nutmeg, or green tomato chowchow, but she saw no more than the original three. Still. Brigit had saved those. Had she kept them for sentimental reasons? Did she remember their blueberry picking trips? Deidre's attempts to teach her the basics of canning?

She remembered one day at the breakfast table, as her daughter scooped some blueberry jam from a jar just like these and spread it on half a toasted English muffin. Brigit had been around eight at that time

—Mom, she said, in the faux-adult voice she used back then for serious pronouncements, you should sell your jam in the store. I bet it'll be a hit, just like Lucy's salad dressing on *I Love Lucy*. You'll have your own brand. I bet you'll be famous!

Not that Deidre hadn't considered the first part of this before. She looked at her daughter, who had a smear of blueberry at the corner of her mouth, a detail she recalled all these years later.

—You know what honey? You might have a point. The next blueberry season she spent an extra week picking, sometimes accompanied by Brigit, two extra weeks canning. And the jam had been a success, even at eight bucks a jar. But not a tremendous one. The end of tourist season left her with three dozen unsold jars. She relabeled them with fresh dates the following year, but only made enough new jam for family and a few friends. Fortunately the health inspector had not caught on, but he hadn't started riding their asses until a few years later.

Next she packed more books, setting papers and unbound documents aside for the moment. Another round of vacuuming now that she'd disturbed the dust of surfaces. While she ran the vacuum she wondered how much money she could get for the books. Did Xebíco even have a second-hand bookstore that would buy them? Would an Uber driver let her load all those boxes in their car? She didn't want to make more than one trip.

Her tasks absorbed her attention enough that she soon forgot about the inevitable visit of the *Federales*. Not entirely but for ten, twenty, thirty minutes at a stretch. Once for almost an entire hour. They'd come when they came and she'd answer their interrogations as best she could. She almost wished they'd get it over with but mostly she didn't. She began to entertain some tiny hope they'd never show up, that they'd moved on to more important cases.

As the afternoon wore on into evening she no longer worried so much about the vaguely affiliated agents. She began sorting out the houseplants, the lost causes from the salvageable handful. All the deader than dead plants she set beside the door, while any that showed a glimmer of life she transferred to the counter by the sink. At last, after lifting a corner of the curtain to check for Robin(!), she opened the door and relocated the vessels with deceased flora outside, creating a sort of vegetable cemetery. Perhaps it would rain and the rain would revive a few, though Candace had told her it probably would not rain again until November.

With variations, Deidre's cleaning routine sustained her for the next several days. On the second day she worked up the nerve to ask Candace to take her to a grocery store, as she was nearly out of food. They waited until 6:30 p.m. to avoid missing the feds-in-black, though Deidre did not mention this reason to Candace. Deidre returned with milk, eggs, mayo, hamburger meat, cold cuts, a loaf of wholegrain bread, pasta, and a few basic vegetables—onions, tomatoes, celery, and a bell pepper stoplight. Soup mix and a few boxes of mac and cheese. She hesitated over the fancy organic kind she used to get for Brigit, the kind that looked like little rabbits, but settled for Kraft.

She also picked up two bottles of vodka. Smirnoff. She would have preferred Absolut or at least Stoli, which were more appropriate to her palate. She promised herself next time, when things were better.

She began to fall into a routine, assisted by carefully rationed Smirnoff, which helped her get through each day and then to sleep at night, despite the regular helicopter patrols that seemed to pass right over the apartment. Brigit had left her a lot of cleaning, and ultimately it provided an ideal distraction. By the fourth day she'd finally found a pair of elbow-length rubber gloves under boxes in the hall closet, so she gave the bathroom another go-round. At least her daughter had left the necessary cleaning supplies, mostly unused. Although the apartment bore no other signs of a cat—no litterbox, no frayed toys beneath the furniture, no scratches to upholstery,

Deidre had discovered an open but still full 40 pound bag of kitty litter in the closet. That was one thing she could get rid of. Maybe she could give it away, perhaps even to Cynthia Bowles. She dragged the sack toward the front door. Just as she reached the rectangular area of linoleum that defined the entryway, someone knocked.

Adrenaline flooded Deidre's bloodstream and her heart began to race. The feds were here at last. She stood the litter bag behind her, counted to three, and turned the knob.

Robin(!) stood there, her smile as painfully bright as the sun behind her.

—Howdy Brigit's mom, just stopping by to check how things are going. How's the apartment? Everything to your liking? Anything you need? Just holler if I can help, that's what I'm here for.

Deidre took a half step back and knocked over the sack of litter. She could tell just by the sound that it spilled over the linoleum and all the way onto the carpet. She watched as the eyes of her nemesis moved over the mess and registered its nature.

—Pets cost extra you know. How many do you have?

—None. Just that one bag of litter. I was going to give it away.

Robin(!) eyed her skeptically. —Brigit never registered any pets. What a model tenant. I used to tell the other tenants to be more like her. A model tenant. Something to aspire to.

Of course Brigit had been an inspiration. She seemed to have left a trail of admirers. Did they know how poorly their role model treated her own mother? What would they think of her then?

—I miss Brigit. We used to have these wonderful long talks, about everything and nothing. Have you found out anything more about her? Do they at least know what happened to her?

Deidre caught the edge of the door, and drew it halfway back in front of her like some pitiful shield.

—To be continued, please? She said. I've got a lot to do.

—Of course, of course! I don't want to hold you up. Just one more thing: since you're staying here, the rent is due July 1. Please have it on time. Unlike Brigit.

***

The July rent. She actually had enough left to cover it. But not August. Her options became fewer every day.

How things had changed. In Biddeford they'd had the general store, a wedding gift from Greg's parents. A gift to themselves really because it meant they could retire. Not that they got to enjoy their retirement much, as both of them died less than two years later.

The store had been in Greg's family for three generations with him, and potentially four with Brigit, though she showed little interest in helping out and preferred to spend as much of her time as possible outdoors. Unlike Greg, who spoke often about how much he had loved playing behind the counter and amidst the shelves as a child. Deidre politely described the original establishment as *quaint* and *rustic*, and immediately began changing things to reach a more upscale crowd instead of the usual bumpkins and local yokels. Greg objected to some of the changes as first, but in time, he gave way. She took this as his recognition of the rightness of her plans.

Greg's parents had relied heavily on the summer tourist crowd, and sometimes even shut down entirely during the winter months. Deidre found this unacceptable, as she mostly did the type of tourists the store had drawn. The first change she made was to get rid of the kitsch and tchotchkes. Out with the keychains and shot glasses and souvenir spoons, the snow globes featuring something supposed to depict the Wood Island Lighthouse but which looked nothing like the real thing. In with watercolors and woodcarvings by local artists. Deidre also redid the menu on the restaurant side, replacing second-rate deli sandwiches with a new lobster-themed menu. Whole lobster, lobster rolls, lobster salads. Blackened lobster. How Greg's parents never thought to make this obvious change, she could not understand. Fancier foods meant higher prices meant higher profits, she explained to him. Repeatedly. Of course, lobster meant a 100 gallon saltwater tank, but Deidre argued it would become an attraction in itself. At least the kids liked to look at it.

Business that first year under the new regime went surprisingly well. The country had just emerged from the Bush Recession, and the type of tourist trade they attracted showed interest in the products they now offered. Winters remained slow as death though. Greg manned both register and lunch-counter, but locals rarely even entered, let alone spent money there. He spent entire days in the store without seeing another human face. The few old-timers who came in only did so to chat. With Greg. Deidre had soon come to recognize the false friendliness in the eyes of these men and women who did not acknowledge anyone as a Mainer unless they'd been born within the state's borders, and she had little truck with these folks.

Greg urged Deidre to stock snow-shovels, windshield scrapers, de-icing spray, but she refused. They were not a hardware store.

Still, they got by, even prospered slightly. Until 9-11. Brigit had come along in January of 2001. Not the most auspicious time. Over the next couple summers business slowly picked up, though it never reached the levels of the later Clinton years. Then came 2008 and the Great Recession. The next three summers were the worst ever—according to Greg, worse than anything his family had experienced since the Depression, when they had extended credit to much of the town and accepted barter when they could get it. Fortunately they owned the property outright and saved on salaries by running the store themselves, which mostly meant Greg running the store himself. But they still had to pay utilities, and the winter heating bill was brutal. They had to keep the heat on full blast to keep the lobster tank from freezing.

Things began to pick up a bit during Obama's second term, but by then their meager savings had eroded. The health inspector's biased assault provided the final straw, with the notice of closure plastered on their door in July of 2015, after their best June in years. A weak trickle of tourists returned once they reopened, but the local clientele they had slowly built up over two decades never came back. They struggled on one more year before filing Chapter 11 in an attempt to save their home at least. That attempt proved futile. Greg's great grandfather had built the house, and each new generation had added a wing. Until Greg.

They found a cheap apartment in town, no ocean view. Deidre took a gig as a substitute teacher and Greg went to work at Walmart. Within a year he made Assistant Manager. Deidre at least had summers off to spend time with Brigit, though Brigit wanted to spend most of her time with friends or in the forest and never seemed to have any for her mother.

In 2018 Brigit left for college in Oregon. Why so far? In one of their now-regular arguments she shouted —So I can get as far away from you as I can. Deidre had let that comment slide, but the rift continued to widen, and after her first year in the Northwest, Brigit stopped coming home for summer, or even the holidays. Even before the police came to Deidre's door to explain they'd found Greg's car in the lot behind the still boarded-up store, a hose from the exhaust run through one window, and Greg, of course, inside.

Mother and daughter barely communicated at all after that. A brief email here, an even shorter text message there. Between her Bachelor's and grad school Brigit came home for three weeks, though when she did, she stayed with a high school friend instead of her mother. They did meet twice for lunch, and if their conversations were not warm, at least they never became heated. During this time Deidre offered her daughter the desktop computer, which she ended up shipping to California after Brigit moved to Xebíco.

Now Brigit had gone missing and some sick freak had stolen her laptop. Should she tell this to the mysterious feds when they finally paid their visit? Without any evidence, how would they respond?

Every day that passed without a knock on the door left Deidre feeling both anxiety and relief. From morning to evening she worked to distract herself. By 5:00 p.m. she felt safe in thinking she'd dodged the bullet another day. Yet they might have information for her. And she might have information of interest to them. Two possibilities existed and both caused her stress. Either she needed to have this conversation, or she would regret it dearly. She had no evidence to go on, no way to know. If only Robin(!) had told her more. At moments she regretted not asking the peppy manager during their last conversation whether the agents had returned, but mostly she did not want to know. Perhaps they had moved on to other cases, maybe even left town, and they would never come to bother her. So she stayed inside, avoiding the attention of bouncy Robin(!) and the unknown agents alike.

***

Then came the text from Candace, their first communication since the little shopping trip.

—Still up for The SNAPP? Tomorrow's the big day.

Deidre responded in the affirmative.

—Great! I'll pick you up around 5:00. I don't think I mentioned this before, but it's an overnight event. I've got a spare tent and sleeping bag for you if you need them, but you should bring a water bottle, toothbrush, toiletries, change of clothes. All right?

Deidre responded in the affirmative once more. She didn't mind camping and it pleased her that Candace had seen to her needs.

Wonderful. Pack everything in a backpack, just in case. Don't worry about dinner. We'll have plenty of food.

The food part was especially good news. Her supply of groceries had already grown scant.

THE SUBLIME NEW ALBION POOL PARTY

Deidre did everything she could to distract herself the rest of that day and the next. Cleaning. Re-cleaning. Dusting, straightening, organizing, sorting. Determining what to save and what to sell. And what to trash, though she dreaded another trip to the dumpster where she might encounter Robin(!) again. On the morning of the twenty-fourth she retrieved a dusty backpack she'd spotted in the hall closet and cleaned it out. A shriveled apple, over a dozen paperclips in several different sizes including one of the big triangular ones, crumpled papers that looked like old course notes, a dog-eared book called *The Ghosts of Evolution*. She peeked outside then quickly stepped onto the front porch where she held the pack upside down and beat as much dust off it as she could using a wooden spoon. Then she repacked it with her own items according to the list Candace had provided.

The overnight nature of the activity came as a complication—what if the agents came to her door before she returned the next morning? By now she had begun to hope they had chosen not to bother her. They'd certainly had their chances, and she'd done her best to make herself available. They couldn't expect her to stay inside waiting for them all the time. Still, she was not ready to put that hope to the test.

At 4:42 Candace sent a text saying she was on her way. Deidre shut off the lights and took up a position by the door with the backpack slung over her left shoulder. Her plan was to move quickly to Candace's car, head down, hoping to avoid any agents or rent-hungry Robin(!). She estimated her exposure as less than 30 seconds if everything went right. And if Candace parked close enough. Deidre had based that estimate on where Candace parked the last time.

At last Candace texted that she was outside. Deidre opened the door and locked it behind her, leaving the living room light on. The moment she stepped outside she began counting seconds in her head. She saw the now-familiar blue Volvo and scuttled toward it, opened the door and jumped inside without hearing anyone call her name. Twenty-three seconds.

—I'm ready, she said, and tossed her pack into the back seat. Let's go!

Candace went, with Deidre slumped in her seat, though not so low she didn't spot the shiny black SUV with government plates parked under some date palms three slots from the entrance to the apartment complex. Tinted windows kept her from telling whether anyone was inside. Oh hell, not now! This just wasn't fair! Hadn't they had their chance? She'd waited for them all this time and they never showed up. Then again, maybe this vehicle had come for someone else. Maybe it was just the IRS. Not that she had any desire to encounter the IRS either.

As the Volvo pulled out of the complex, Deidre watched in the side mirror to see if anyone followed, but as far as she could tell, no one did. At least not anyone in a black SUV. They pulled onto Avocado Street and headed east without any suspicious company that she could see.

—You're awfully quiet today. You aren't nervous, are you?

Perhaps she was, a little, but mainly she'd been pondering whether to warn Candace about the possibility of pursuit. Which she knew would sound crazy. Wouldn't it be ironic for *her* to say something far out and crazy-sounding to Candace? And so far she did not see any pursuers—unless they were in helicopters. She pressed her cheek against the glass and looked up, but saw nothing in the portion of sky visible between the trees.

***

They arrived on campus less than 15 minutes later, and Candace turned onto the access road that led behind the dorms on the western edge of the university. At the north end of the campus they came to a green-painted metal gate secured by a heavy chain. A few students crossed between nearby buildings but none paid any attention to the lone little car. Candace pulled up close to the gate and handed Deidre a solitary key on a braided lanyard.

—Will you do the honors, please? Don't forget to shut the gate and relock it after we're through.

As she stepped out of the car to follow these instructions, Deidre scanned the sky once more for aerial pursuit, but saw nothing. No vehicles behind them either.

Immediately past the gate they crossed a little one-lane bridge over the canal, then continued north on an orange dirt road, gravelly but well-graded. Ratty-looking ground squirrels darted across the road in front of them every few yards, for no apparent reason. Squirrels playing chicken. Far ahead Deidre could see a barn overshadowed by a large palm tree.

It took them longer to reach the barn than Deidre expected. As they slowly drew closer to it, she realized how much larger both structure and tree were than she'd originally thought. The tree was not a palm at all but something like a massive cottonwood with only a few surviving branches stretching out in greet arcs. Both tree and barn were huge. Her sense of perspective felt strangely distorted.

When they reached a second gate close to the barn, Candace got out and unlocked herself. —The lock on this one's tricky, she said. Let me get it.

One corner of the barn had completely caved in, and noticing how Deidre stared at it, Candace said, —Would you believe that barn is over 100 years old? It partially collapsed in a windstorm three years ago and the University announced they were going to demolish it. Yet it remains. Students still sneak out here for hanky-panky. Luckily none have been crushed. Yet.

Behind the barn a windmill turned slowly, though Deidre could not recall any breeze from when she'd stepped out at the first gate, and nothing stirred the grass or the leaves on the tree. A crumpled metal stock tank squatted beneath the windmill, and a small but picturesque herd of black and white cows grazed behind the barn. A few raised their heads to regard the Volvo as it passed, but none of them moved. They continued driving northward through vast fields of dry grass. Deidre looked one more time into the rear-view mirror, but saw only the barn, the tree, the windmill, and the cows.

—You may be wondering why we seem to be the only ones going to the party. I hope you don't think I'm abducting you.

Instantly Deidre considered that precise possibility, which had not occurred to her before. She looked around the car but saw no obvious weapons or implements of the kidnapper within Candace's reach. No guns, no knives, no rope. No zip ties or canvas hood. Candace continued.

—Most everyone else has already been camped out on site for a couple days now, some for a week or more. We try to stagger our entries—our relationship with the university remains somewhat…tenuous. And with the new puppet administration, it may be less than that. Best not to put it to the test. I came back into town to pick up a few things—and you of course. This way you'll get there just in time for dinner—and for The Event.

Their route had begun to curve to the east, following the edge of a gentle rise too low to call a ridge. Eventually, they reached a second fenceline and another cattle gate. Candace got out again to deal with this one, which bore no lock at all, only a complex knot of barbed wire, whose tangles she appeared to understand.

Beyond this gate, they began to follow a barely perceptible two-track that ran northward along the east side of the fence. Deidre could no longer see anything in any direction other than the fence, the faint trace of the road, the endless brown grass, and far to the east, the low gray line of the Sierra Nevadas, or their foothills at least. She hadn't even thought about visiting Yosemite. She ought to do that on this trip. Who knew when she'd be back in California a third time?

She began to feel a genuine anxiety. Wouldn't someone in the process of abducting you say they weren't abducting you? Wasn't that the most abductress thing *they could say*? What did she know about Candace anyway? And she had left without telling anyone where she was going, or with whom. Though whom could she have told? Robin(!)?

—How far out there is this party?

—It's pretty far out. We've got a ways to go yet. You're probably wondering why we hold it so far from town and everything else. You know what merchants say. Location, location, location. The party is all about the place. And the time. The phenomenon has a strong peak in January too, so we actually *could* hold it in the winter, but that's the rainy season, and the roads can get really muddy. The chances of rain here in June are next to nothing though, so June it is.

Their interminable progress continued, the fence always beside them on the left, the vast expanse of brown everywhere else. Suddenly the barely perceptible road veered to the east, leaving behind the fence, their only landmark. After perhaps fifteen more minutes, they reached another low rise.

—If you close your eyes now, said Candace, it'll make this part more fun. Deidre had her doubts, but she did as suggested. She did not lower her eyelids all the way however, instead peeking slightly beneath the scrim of her lashes to keep a watch on Candace, in case she suddenly pulled out a jeweled dagger or a dripping hypodermic from beneath her seat.

Candace made no such moves as the car crested the top of the meager slope, but Deidre's eyes quickly flew open at the burst of color she glimpsed from beneath her slitted lids.

For a moment she thought they had come upon a carnival or a medieval caravanserai in this endless desert of brown grass. Before and slightly below them in a sort of wide shallow bowl lay dozens of vehicles parked in a ring. Probably a hundred or more. Cars, trucks, vans, motorcycles, SUVs, RVs—even a few brightly painted school busses. She wondered how difficult those had been to get out here, although the roads had been relatively flat most of the way, with only limited stretches of washboard. Within the circle of vehicles lay a ring of tents, seemingly of every possible color and size, and an even more widely assorted array of flags and pennants flapped from hundreds of tall poles amidst the tents, giving the scene something of the feel of a Renaissance faire. More than a few poles flew the now-outlawed California state flag with its grizzly bear *en passant* upon a grass plat, or even the forbidden ensign of *Black Lives Matter* with its stark white letters.

Within the ring of tents and pennants she saw yet another ring, this one of people clustered around a wide circle of tables. Mostly folding tables but also a few for-real heavy wooden picnic tables. How had they gotten those all the way in here? Various plastic and canvas chairs lined the more portable tables. Even before they reached the outer circle of vehicles, Deidre could see that every table sported heaps of food and drink. Hunger rolled over her in a wave. For lunch she'd had only a ham and cheese on wheat with a glass of OJ. Technically a screwdriver with the last of the Smirnoff.

One more ring lay within that of people, tables, and chairs, not so much a ring as an irregular and amoebic ellipse composed of metal fenceposts. A silvery cable connected the poles, threaded through metal loops at their tops just above head-height. Colored ribbons hung from the cable every few feet. No one stood within or even very near this innermost ring of posts. Most of the people visible—perhaps 200 or more—appeared to be gathered around the food tables, talking, eating, and drinking.

Within that inner ring lay a small dwindling pond surrounded by a halo of green grass. More green stalks protruded from the water almost to the center of the pond. She realized this was the first actual vernal pool she had seen in the Vernal Pools Reserve. The fenceposts with their beribboned cable outlined the perimeter of the pool, or at least the band of green grass surrounding it, which perhaps marked its original extent.

Candace pulled into an open space next to one of the nearer schoolies and parked. She shut off the ignition and stepped out of the car, Deidre following. Candace pointed to two tents directly in front of them, one green, one red. —The red one is yours. I hope that's all right. I set it up yesterday.

Deidre actually would have liked some choice in the matter, red being her least favorite color, but she was hungry, and after all, she was only going to spend one night in it, and how much of it would she see in the dark anyhow?

—That's fine.

The pole beside her tent bore a black swallow-tailed pennon emblazoned with a red disc. Strips of the black background ran across the red, like clouds across the setting sun, although the actual sky held no clouds at all, and as before, she could not feel the breeze that kept it extended. The design meant nothing to her. She considered asking about it but Candace spoke first.

—C'mon, let's meet and greet, but most of all, let's eat. I can tell you're hungry. You can leave your stuff in the car for now. We've got a couple hours yet before The Event. She took Deidre by the hand and led her down to the ring of tables and food.

Everyone knew Candace, which came as no surprise. She led Deidre clockwise around the circle of tables, hugging and exchanging greetings, introducing Deidre mostly by name but sometimes identifying her as Brigit's mom, and in several cases leaning in to whisper some additional information into someone's ear. This bothered Deidre less than the possibility that Candace intended to make the full circuit of the tables before stopping to eat, but at the third table she paused and handed Deidre a plate. An actual wooden plate, not paper or plastic.

—Here you go, dig in!

Deidre noted with approval that this table had the best spread she'd seen so far, including a whole roast turkey and what appeared to be a plate of steaks, and the latter did not even look overdone. She realized then that none of the offerings on the first two tables had included any meat. She had no particular aversion to tofu, if done right, but as a guest, she deserved more. She began her plate with a steak, pleased to see translucent droplets of rosy blood ooze out around the twin tines of the serving fork, then added two slices of turkey breast, a golden-brown dinner roll, one scoop each of corn salad and coleslaw, and a thin wedge of watermelon that she balanced somewhat precariously on the plate's edge next to the salads. Normally she didn't like her different foods to touch much, but she was hungry. On the end of the table she found cloth napkins and metal serving ware, both of which she greeted with approval. She sat down next to a handsome man with wavy gray hair that still bore traces of black.

Candace introduced the man as her friend Roger, encouraged Deidre to go ahead and eat, and said she would be back shortly. Roger smiled, nodded, and held up his drink, a brown bottle with one of those resealable wire-and-porcelain tops. Deidre associated these with Holland for some reason, though she had no clear idea why. —Would you like a drink? We've got iced tea and bottled water around here somewhere, but may I offer you one of my own home-brewed productions? Tonight I'm featuring a peach-almond porter and a loquat IPA.

—Thank you. I'll try the IPA. She had no idea what a loquat was, though she suspected it involved some kind of exotic fruit. How appropriate for her exotic party night with her exotic new friends. She felt a bit adventurous. And a porter just seemed like too many calories.

Roger pulled another Dutch bottle from an old-school red and white metal cooler beside the table and held it out to her.

Deidre took the beer and as she did, she regarded Roger more closely. Not bad-looking at all. About her age, and with a full head of hair. Very fit. Although his clothes were simple—jeans and a faded blue polo shirt that almost matched his slate-gray eyes—something about him suggested a degree of affluence, of stability and success. Deidre guessed tech, or maybe a university administrator.

—And what do you do, Roger? For a living, I mean. I know you brew fancy beer.

—Nothing anymore—I'm retired! He laughed gently. I used to own a medium-sized trucking firm but I sold it about 10 years ago. Now I live off the interest from that and my investments. What about you?

—I'm a widow. This of course did not answer Roger's actual question, but she felt it addressed the unspoken one she hoped he was thinking.

—Ah, I see. And this is your first time at The SNAPP, am I right? I don't recall seeing you here before. How much has Candace told you?

—Not much, said Candace, who at that moment reappeared behind Roger, cradling a cardboard box with both arms. I'm going to let her discover it all for herself. Just like I did with you, how many years ago? She patted his left shoulder in a way that Deidre optimistically judged platonic.

—Now let the poor woman eat, Roger. You'll have time to chat later.

Deidre refocused on her plate while Roger chuckled an apology. She liked the way he laughed easily but not excessively. The food was good, and the IPA, after a brief struggle with the cap contraption, proved delicious. Whatever loquats were, she decided she liked them, at least in her beer. While Deidre ate, Candace spoke again, saying she had some business to take care of, and she tilted the cardboard box toward Roger to reveal its contents, then stepped toward Deidre and did the same.

—I need to put this little lady someplace safe before the real party starts. She's out rather late this year.

Inside the box a large black and yellow lizard scrambled amidst handfuls of freshly picked grass, struggling to get a hold on the side of the box and climb out. Not a lizard, Deidre realized, but a salamander. A big one. Its clawless toes gave it no purchase against the cardboard.

—Don't touch. They've got teeth and they can actually bite!

Deidre had no intention of touching the amphibian.

—I'll be right back. I'm going to put her in the back of my car for now then return her to the pond after The Event.

Candace had already turned toward the ring of vehicles as she asked Roger to take Deidre around and complete her introductions once she finished eating. He immediately agreed.

By the time she'd cleaned her plate down to a few streaks of salad dressing and a gnawed arc of watermelon rind, Deidre was on her second homebrew and knew a bit more about Roger, though nothing more about The SNAPP. Conveniently, her new friend turned out to be a widower. He'd tried online dating but it just wasn't for him. And he had his hobbies after all. Hiking, sailing, homebrewing. Did he have his own sailboat? Yes indeed, a

24-footer. Deidre mostly nodded with her mouth full, though she offered an appreciative wide-eyed *Ohhh* over the sailboat as she began to picture herself lounging on it. Before she knew it, he was escorting her around the rest of the ring of tables, and they each carried a fresh bottle of his loquat homebrew in hand.

Most of the other pool partiers belonged to Deidre and Roger's age group or Candace's slightly older crowd. She saw no children whatsoever, though about a quarter of the attendees seemed young enough to be in their late teens or earlier twenties. Some of the latter category introduced themselves as UCX students, and she suspected most of the rest of these were as well. She didn't recognize any of them from the party at Cynthia Bowles' house.

Bowles herself was there however. Once again Deidre allowed the awkwardness to play to her advantage. To his credit, Roger seemed to sense the tension and led her on quickly and without questions. Not until they'd come within several tables of their starting point did Deidre spot someone else she already knew.

—LaRue!

The bartender, not serving anyone tonight, immediately detached herself from a semicircle of admirers. —Deidre Llewelyn! Woman, where *have* you been? I haven't seen you since that party. And you never come in *Le PP* anymore! I was starting to think you were pissed off about something—I hope not!

Deidre apologized, mumbled an excuse about how hard it had become for her to get to the club without a car. LaRue smiled and waved it off.

—Now you're about to find out a big reason why so many of us stay around this town! Let's talk more, yes? Maybe after? And before Deidre could reply, she added —I'm so glad you made it! And you found such a great chaperone! Roger, I know you'll take good care of her. She winked—whether for Roger, for her, or both of them, Deidre could not tell—then returned to her entourage with a final 100-watt smile and a wave.

By now the sun had settled low in the west. The silver cord topping the fenceposts around the pool lit up, and Deidre realized it was actually a long string of the kind of Christmas lights that came in a tube, with segments of red, green, blue, and white alternating at random. She could now make out the hum of a generator, somewhere across the pool and hidden between the vehicles.

—Well you've met most everyone, said Roger. What'd you think?

—Everyone seems very nice. Indeed, except for Bowles, most had been outright friendly, many offering hugs. Almost too many. Each time someone embraced her, she felt herself stiffen a little less than with the last, an accomplishment for which she felt some small pride. She would not have minded a hug from Roger though, not at all, a point she had attempted to communicate with body language and telepathy. Neither seemed to be working.

Deidre opened her mouth to add one point, but clamped it shut again. Best she keep this observation to herself for now. She and Roger seemed to be hitting it off, and she did not want to offend him. The comment she bit back had to do with how strange some of the other guests were dressed— and how strange some of them *looked*.

True, many of them wore relatively normal clothes—Roger for example. After she'd seen all the pennants flying, she'd expected the participants to resemble those she'd seen in photos from Burning Man. Although plenty wore variations on the bright and multicolored attire of '60s hippies, none wore body paint. Nor did she encounter any nudity.

It was not so much the attire of her fellow pool partiers that put Deidre off a bit, but the physical appearance of some. Several sported full-face tattoos with peculiar designs. Or extensive scarification. Certain others had oddly shaped heads, notably a brace of broad-shouldered blonde couples with sloping foreheads and piercing blue eyes. True, one ran across equally odd-looking people occasionally, but here she'd met multiple examples at the same time, each with a different set of characteristics. One slender woman, completely bald and several inches taller than Roger—whom Deidre estimated at around 6'2"—wore a complicated arrangement of softly-glowing green tubes around her head. Deidre let her thoughts on all this ride. For now. Why risk insulting Roger? And after all, hadn't she come expecting some kind of weirdo festival? Really, The SNAPP didn't look all that different from the average Fourth of July gathering or tailgate party.

After the sun set completely, another series of lights came on, about a dozen bright rectangular spotlights mounted on tripods and evenly spaced around the circle pointing inward toward the pond, turning its surface to silver. As these lights stood between the vehicles, she hadn't noticed them before. The volume level of the conversation dropped. Around this time, several people she'd met earlier, including the green headgear woman, came back to her and said variations of —I didn't realize you were Brigit's mom! How wonderful that you can join us here tonight. You must be terribly excited!

Deidre had nearly finished her fourth IPA by this point and she just laughed and replied overly loud, almost shouting, —Yes, I'm so excited, though I have no idea why! And she laughed some more.

The night grew darker and the conversations more peculiar, though perhaps that was just the IPA. Deidre had begun to lean on Roger and he had swung an arm over her shoulders, which felt warm and right. Not a hug exactly, but more sustainable perhaps, as they could still walk this way. Candace returned and suggested Deidre retrieve her pack from the car, adding that she would find the back door unlocked and not to worry about relocking it. She removed herself from Roger reluctantly and walked back toward the Volvo.

She had to reach around the cardboard box to get her pack. Inside it the boldly-patterned salamander no longer struggled to escape. Instead it looked up at her, regarding her with an unreadable expression. —Hey, don't blame me, said Deidre, I would've left you alone, and she closed the door again as gently as she could.

When she returned, she noticed that most everyone else around the circle now wore packs as well, though not Roger or Candace. Most folks only wore small daypacks like hers, but more than a few bore full-sized frame packs, as if they were headed off on overnight hikes. Further down the circle she spotted someone wearing what looked like a World War I gas mask. She felt certain one person almost halfway across wore full SCUBA gear, but the glare of the multiple spotlights made it hard to be sure. No one had told her this was supposed to be a costume party! She would be upset if Candace had neglected that bit of information. She asked Roger.

—Oh no. Roger laughed softly in the way she'd begun to enjoy. She nonchalantly slid her arm back around his waist, and he returned his own to her shoulders.

Roger went on. —People are just…being prepared. You'll understand it all better soon, I promise. Then he extended his right hand and said, —It's nearly time. What say we stroll down to the pool and get in position for The Event?

Although she had very little idea what to make of this, Deidre gladly accepted, slipping her hand into Roger's, feeling his larger, rougher fingers enfold hers. She allowed him to lead her under the Christmas lights, for which he had to stoop slightly, and down to a spot where the ground felt slightly spongy beneath her feet. All around the water's edge she could see others joining them or already linked. She looked up questioningly at Roger but just then she felt someone else take her other hand. Candace.

—Well Deidre, are you ready? Has Roger told you anything?

Roger said, —I've been waiting for you to fill her in, Can. She's still your guest after all.

—Fair enough. So, Deidre, you're finally going to see what makes this place special, especially at this time of year. Most of all I think you're going to understand why I invited *you*, of all people.

Deidre still had no idea what was going on, but a hat trick of craft beers and Roger's company had gotten her comfortable. Her earlier concerns about pursuit and abduction had dissolved in alcohol and hospitality. At this point, she considered the evening a success regardless of what happened next. Human sacrifice, perhaps? Bring it on. Or just a fireworks show? A group sing—"Kumbaya" and "This Land is Your Land?" She could do that.

—So there's only one rule, and it's a simple one, OK? Don't break the circle, don't let go of our hands. You're going to see some places. Some… options. Some might look good. Some might look bad, and if they look bad it's a good bet they are. You'll see some things that look strange, even dangerous. But nothing can touch you, nothing can harm you so long as you don't break the circle. Just remember that, no matter who or what you might see. As long as we all stay connected, we remain only observers and no actual contact will occur. Got it?

Deidre nodded, though she didn't get "it" at all. In fact, she felt more confused than ever, if somewhat boozily confused now.

—Now here's the exception. A point might come when you—and I mean you in particular—might want to let go. To cross. And that's going to be entirely up to you. If you make that decision, just be one hundred percent certain it's what you want, because once you go you can't come back. And your window won't last long. Got it?

—I guess this isn't going to be a fireworks show after all, is it?

Candace laughed. —Oh, I think you will find The Event more spectacular than any fireworks show you've ever attended.

By this time everyone had joined them inside the fenceposts, and the entire group stood in one loose, sprawling loop, hand-in-hand. First the spotlights and then the Christmas lights went off, and only a faint purple twilight illuminated the scene. As Deidre's eyes adapted she saw LaRue several spots down from Candace, and the green tubes lady holding hands with Cynthia Bowles not too far down the circle on Roger's side.

She opened her mouth to ask Candace for more information, but realized almost everyone else had gone quiet. She no longer heard the generators either. She looked up at Roger. He smiled and squeezed her hand. Then he turned his head back toward the pond in a slow movement that seemed to suggest she should do the same.

Deidre's eyes widened. A three-quarters moon now hung in the sky which a second ago had been lit only by a handful of early stars. How had they managed this trick—a balloon? Impressive, but what—

The moon balloon seemed to vibrate, oscillate, and then it changed phases, becoming toenail slivers of various widths, blinking out and reappearing full but lower in the sky. Deidre said —Ohhh. The moon continued to bop around overhead, changing position, changing phases, several times shining green and blue like a miniature version of the astronaut earth. What a neat trick! How did they manage this? Had they drugged her? She didn't feel drugged, and she thought she would know. Predictably tipsy, but that was all, and that would not produce effects like these. Perhaps she was going to see something special after all.

Deidre looked down the line and realized that no matter how bright the moon became, it cast no shadows. They must be using some kind of lasers or video projectors, but she saw no beams of light stabbing into the sky. Did the ring of floodlights have something to do with this? She thought they'd gone off, but perhaps they'd switched to blacklights, or holograms.

Then the moon blinked out altogether and the sun lit up the scene. But this was not what caused Deidre to gasp. The pond had disappeared, along with all the grass. Now the ground was dry with deep cracks, no traces of water or vegetation. Nothing living at all. She realized she could no longer see the people on the opposite side of the circle. In fact, she could only see a few people to either side of her, with the rest lost as if in some kind of haze.

The sun began to bounce around the sky much the same as the moon had done, and the landscape altered radically in time with its movements. The pond and the grass reappeared and vanished again. Dense forests appeared and disappeared. Several times Deidre glimpsed tall gray buildings in the distance connected by weird trails of dark smoke. Long lines of armored vehicles drove over the fields. Gigantic zeppelins crossed the sky. The sun and the moon began to alternate. She felt dizzy. As if they sensed this, both Roger and Candace gripped her hands more tightly.

The scenes began changing more quickly, growing even wilder. Skies filled with purple clouds that shot giant forks of red lightning into glowing red ground. Oceans. Deserts. Skies of streaking comets. Suddenly she found herself staring into dark starry space, with no visible horizon, the Milky Way beneath her feet brighter than she'd ever seen it. Her body seemed to drift in this emptiness. She experienced a terrible wave of vertigo but her friends held her steady until a view with a landscape returned. Candace had been right. This was far more impressive than any fireworks show. Or any planetarium show. How the hell were they managing these illusions?

More moonlit scenes. Moon, sun. Grass, forests, scorched dead ground. A dark landscape of bronze cones and domes gleaming bloodily in a source-less red haze. Candace whispered something ever so softly, reverently even. Maybe a name. Terrell?

Not "Terrell." *The Rhel.* Deidre recognized the odd name from Brigit's journal.

Outer space again, this time crisscrossed by streaks of brilliant white light. Then the grass reappeared, though not the pool, and the sun shone on an array of impossibly high towers of varying heights. Deidre thought of Dorothy arriving at the Emerald City in *The Wizard of Oz*, although these towers were not the sleek green crystal of the matte painting in the classic film. They looked almost fuzzy somehow, and not one shade of green but many. Huge flying things with multiple wings swarmed the air between and even above the structures. She could not tell whether they were living creatures or aircraft.

She caught movement in her peripheral vision and turned to see the woman with the weird headgear step away from the circle and walk forward. The people who had held her hands—Cynthia Bowles and another woman she didn't recognize—immediately closed the gap behind her. The tall woman walked forward, diminishing rapidly as she advanced as if she'd stepped into a fast-motion film. In seconds she had shrunken to a distant dot.

The words of Brigit's journal returned to her. *The green towers!* Here they were, not a fiction but right in front of her. The sun flickered as if the scene were about to change again. And all at once Deidre understood.

She *understood*.

Brigit was *here*. In this world of towers. In this beautiful green world—or on its moon, which she could see overhead, all pastel jade and lapis, giant vines leading toward it from the tops of some of the structures.

Deidre tore her hands free from Candace and Roger and threw herself forward, shouting —Brigit! I'm here!

As soon as she disconnected from the circle she entered that green tower world. She felt the sun on her face and took a breath of air cleaner and sweeter than any she'd tasted in her life, even while hiking deep in the woods of northern Maine. She could no longer see the circle of people at all. She stumbled and fell to her knees, not in the marshy fringe of the pool, but onto a lush meadow dotted with orange flowers. Before her rose the incredible range of towers, green as treetops and far taller than any buildings she'd ever seen—and she had been to New York, to Chicago. As she scrambled to her feet she heard Brigit's actual voice. Not so much as a sound as the kind of impression one retains after waking up in the night remembering a voice one might have heard or which might be merely the relic of a dream.

—Mom! What are you doing here? The words lingered as an echo not in her ears but in her body and her mind.

—Brigit, where are you? Again, she spoke out loud, though she knew Brigit had not. As she spoke she stepped forward, toward the far-off vista of towers. She noticed animals the size of moving vans grazing nearby, horns on their noses in the shape of huge tuning forks. The name Megacerops popped into her head, a memory from another of her daughter's projects. And how often had Brigit complained that her mother didn't listen to her? The massive creatures covered in green fur ignored her.

—Hold on Brigit, I'm coming for you. Your mother is coming!

Her daughter's voice returned, still more a feeling than a sound, but stronger now, a wave of vibrations, as if Deidre stood too close to the stereo speaker in a club, and the wave gathered into a kind of shout.

— No, Mom! NO! You can't come here! This place is not for you! Just stay where you are! How far away do I need to go to get away from you?

A pressure like an enormous invisible hand shoved her. She stumbled backward and tripped over something soft and mobile that screeched, landing on her behind in cold shallow water, which instantly soaked her pants and sneakers. She tried to steady herself with her hands but they plunged between stiff grass stalks into a layer of mud several inches beneath the surface. She felt small animate things wriggle over her fingers and yanked her hands free. Other hands gripped hers almost immediately. Roger. Candace. As soon as they touched her she could see them again. They hauled her to her feet, or mainly Roger did, Candace providing balance.

The green towers had vanished. Instead, more dead Earths flashed before her, jagged spires of quartz and lava rock, dunes of ash, and yellow skies stained with wide spiral bands of red and black. She stared, dazed, for several more minutes, bizarre landscapes and views of outer space appearing and passing, until she saw the pond just as she had first seen it, though now lit only by the final twilight and a spray of stars. Several yards to her right someone in a turquoise-blue spacesuit advanced toward the circle, and the circle opened to take the person's hands. The moon flickered into view one more time then vanished. Tears blurred her view.

She knew whatever she had experienced had ended. A door had opened between her and her daughter then closed again, leaving them on opposite sides. Leaving them even more separated than before. The circle began to dissolve, people releasing each other's hands and hugging. She heard sighing, laughter, shouts of Hosanna! Someone blew a trumpet. Deidre began to sob uncontrollably. Her legs buckled, but Roger and Candace caught her, raised her back up.

Her friends held her close but not too tight, each gripping the upper half of one of her arms with both of their hands. Neither of them spoke. They just held her as if waiting for her crying to stop. Minutes passed and she felt others gather round and place gentle hands on her back. When she looked up she saw similar clusters forming, one around the person in the spacesuit, who had removed her helmet and appeared to be a woman with long dark hair. She saw Cynthia Bowles standing by herself, holding a scruffy Himalayan cat and crying softly. Few people in the other groups seemed to be crying though.

When Deidre's last great racking sobs had passed, she gasped out the words, —She shoved me away! My own daughter. Brigit. She's alive! I tried to go to her, in that green tower place, but she pushed me away. She rejected me! She didn't want me! My own daughter!

Roger said softly, —We know. We understand. It's okay.

But it wasn't okay! Brigit belonged with her—belonged *to* her! Deidre turned to Candace instead, who hugged her closer, her expression blank, and said —We always knew the possibilities. But this was for both of you, not you alone. Then she asked —But what about you? Did you find any kind of closure?

—Closure? What do you mean closure? What just happened? Where's my daughter? How do I get her back? *How do I get back to that place?*

As Deidre spoke she saw a fresh row of lights appear over the pool, bright and blue-white though cold like the moon. Low toward the horizon but rising. The Event wasn't over after all! Deidre's heart leapt at the thought she might get another chance and she attempted to straighten herself and pull free from Roger and Candace once more. She shouted her daughter's name again. —Brigit, I'm coming! Please, Brigit! I'm your *mother*!

Her reply came as the chop-chop of approaching helicopters.

ACKNOWLEDGMENTS

Linda Addison, Mike and Anita Allen, Patrick Shawn Bagley, Nathan Ballingrud, Shannon Barber, Laird Barron, Matthew Bartlett, Shannon Biggs, Christine Boccella Santangelo, Mark and Molly Bode, Greg Bossert, David Bowles, Daniel Braum, Tom Breen, J.S. Breukelaar, Michael Bukowski, Jesse Bullington, Chesya Burke, Gwen and Brian Callahan, Lisa Canavan, Selena Chambers, Gerald Coleman, Sam Cowan, Alex Cox, Melanie Crew, Jeanne D'Angelo, David Davis, Mike Davis, Milton Davis, Wyatt Dee, Arinn Dembo, Danaan DeNeve, Eli Dorsey, Seb Doubinsky, Scott Dwyer, Adam Dyer, Darlene Eberhart, Kirsten Eberhart, Inna Effress, Melissa Eisner, Kurt Fawver, Gemma Files, Lisa Flowers, KC Focht, Jeffrey Ford, John Foster, Christopher Gavaler, Richard Gavin, Craig Laurance Gidney, John Glover, Cody Goodfellow, Alicia Graves, Orrin Grey, Mike and Lena Griffin, Denise Brown and Nick Gucker, Alissa Haynes, Niels Hobbs, Stephanie Jeremiah, Kimberly Jones, Stephen Graham Jones, Michael Kazepis, Gwendolyn Kiste, Dean Kosko, Mark Kosko, Nick Kosko, Nicole Givens Kurtz, John Langan, Donald Levinski, Robert Levy, Livia Llewellyn, Des Lewis, Rebecca Lloyd, Ross Lockhart, Marc Lowenthal, Tanisha McClain, Anne MacNaughton, Anya Martin (who has read every word here as many times as I have, if not more), S.P. Miskowski, Mom (seriously, don't read it this time), Silvia Moreno-Garcia, Edward Morris, Holley Moyes, C.M. Muller, Josh Myers, Clayton Nelson, Dalena Ngo, David Nickel, Jesse

SCOTT NICOLAY

James Douthit-Nicolay, Adrianna Nicolay, Tyra Nicolay, Dwayne Olson, Patricia Frank-Ordasi, John and Kathy Pelan, Greg Powanda, Rick Powell, Katrin Pulver, Nivedita Ravishankar, Andrew Reichart, Matthew Revert, Greg Roemer-Baer, David Roth, Brian Salisbury, Jayaprakash Satyamurphy, Tiffany Scandal, Eric Schaller, Nisi Shawl, Christopher Slatsky, John Claude Smith, Justin Steele, Simon Strantzas, Sonya Taaffe, Anna Tambour, Molly Tanzer, Barbara Tapley, Yves Tourigny, Matthew Tso, Ann and Jeff VanderMeer, Neil Van Doren, David Verba, Damien Angelica Walters, Michaela Waltz, Dennis Weiler, Lesley Wheeler, Kimberly Williams, Candace Wiggins, Marian "Mug" Wilson, and Kim Bo Yung

ORIGINAL PUBLICATIONS

"Tenebrionidae" first published in *The Children of Old Leech*, Word Horde, Petaluma, CA, 2014.

Noctuidae first published in book form by King Shot Press, Portland, OR, 2015.

The Croaker first published as a limited edition chapbook by the Sidecar Preservation Society, Middlebrook, NJ, 2016.

after first published as a limited edition chapbook by Dim Shores Press, Carmichael, CA, 2015.

"The Green Eye" first published in *Black Static* #56, Jan-Feb. 2017.

All other works appear for their first time here.

ABOUT THE AUTHOR

Scott Nicolay is an archaeologist and caver specializing in prehistoric cave use and iconography in the North American Southwest/Northwest Mexico, Mesoamerica, and Island Oceania. His story "Do You Like to Look at Monsters" won the World Fantasy Award for Best Short Fiction in 2015. He is currently translating and editing the fiction of Belgian weird fiction author Jean Ray and editing the posthumous publication of works by American author John D. Keefauver.

www.ingramcontent.com/pod-product-compliance
Lightning Source LLC
Chambersburg PA
CBHW020418030726
47495CB00006B/1562